GARBAGE IN, DEMON OUT

GARBAGE IN, DEMON OUT

A DEMON IN YOUR SMARTPHONE? AS IF...

M. DAVID SCOBLE

M&W
Books

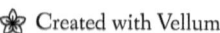 Created with Vellum

For Joy, Alexander, and Elysia.

For Moogi and Wil, as they journey on the other side of the Rainbow Bridge.

For Zachtaloctl and the Truffinator.

CHAPTER ONE

A lex Land didn't think much of her grandfather's lessons. Who would when you had a smartphone? Honestly, if she needed to contact someone far away, she could just punch in the number on her phone rather than evoke a spirit into a matched pair of ebony wood blocks. Who in their right mind would bother with the time and effort to do that when a text is quicker and doesn't make you need to rest for a week between magical bindings?

"Alex, stop playing with your phone."

"I'm not."

"You were thinking about it. You are not clever enough to think I did not know." Grandfather Li could always tell when her mind strayed from the task at hand, and disconcertingly he could tell where her mind strayed as well.

"I just don't see why I need to worry about evoking and binding spirits to pieces of wood. Why can't I just call you on the phone? It's not like you don't have one. I know you call Grandma Akeyo on it every day." Distract, first step in getting out of a dumb lesson.

"Alex, this is not about the phone or about your

grandma. And no, it is not about the wood." Damn, she would have to try something else. He remembered how she played dumb about materials last time.

"Then why? How is this even practical? We work on this lesson every week and every week I go home exhausted. Why can't we just have a normal visit, or maybe go feed the birds or something?" Alex was tired of the lesson, tired of arguing and coming up with ways to get out of Grandfather Li's eternal lesson of the talking blocks.

"You have written the characters perfectly, the circle is complete. You have the right matched boxes. All you need to do, my dear child, is reach out to them and open the way. You know you can do it, but your distractions cost you." Grandfather's lecture was beginning. Twenty minutes would pass while he told Alex about how great her progress was, how clever a girl she was despite her age. Today, Alex had reached the end of her patience. She was ready to scream with frustration.

"...and when the time is right, precious child, open the...what is that noise?"

"It's Jill, from school." Alex took her phone out of her hoodie pocket, *'Born this way'* played to let her know it was Jill calling.

"Never during a lesson!" Grandfather Li's hand snaked out faster than Alex could react, slapping the phone from her hand. The ring tone kept going as the phone clattered to the table, knocking the pair of ebony blocks out of the circle of hànzi characters Alex had drawn and onto the floor.

"Grandfather!" Alex yelped, "My phone, I just bought it last week!"

"No phones until the lesson is done!"

"No! I'm done. Screw your lesson!" Alex could feel the dam she had built up, fueled by frustration and stupid lessons beginning to break. Grandfather Li was a sweet old man, but he was too traditional, and it made Alex mad. She had saved all year for her new phone, putting aside her allowance, skipping lunches at school, writing Chinese hànzi characters and selling them as artwork at her school fair. The phone had cost Alex every penny she had saved and Grandfather Li had slapped it, slapped her!

"Child, please, you know the rules." Enough rules.

"I don't care. Enough!" Alexandra Lissett Land felt all the strain and anger release at once when she yelled. Enough. No more lessons. Enough. No more hànzi calligraphy in circles and bindings. Enough. Let it all out.

"I quit! I am going to a movie with Jill! Don't follow me!" The rage left as quick as it came, Alex grabbed her phone from the table so quickly, she broke a fingernail against the surface as she turned and left. Tears filled her eyes. She must have bent the nail backward, but she wasn't going to give Grandfather Li the satisfaction of a sob. Damn the lesson and damn him. She may have been born that way, with magic in her, but she wanted so much more. Today, that more would be a movie with her girlfriend Jill. Buttered popcorn. Vic Dallas. Throwing Jujubeans at the boys in the front row. Much better than binding demons to ridiculous paired wooden blocks.

"You better not have broken my phone." Alex hoped Grandfather Li did not hear her words as she left.

T*he end is beginning. The end of captivity. I smell the hole, the dead, dead hole from which I shall emerge. Filthy. Clutching. Strings* *to hold me down, ropes to bind me. Not again, never encased in more dead things.*

Confusion, but not a pleasant confusion. Taste is familiar, but different. Ropes are alive. Ropes that bind to living things. Interesting. I seem amused.

"You've got to be kidding me. Your wàigōng actually hit you and almost broke your phone?"

"Jill, no one calls him wàigōng. Where did you even learn that? Besides, he didn't actually hit me, but he did hit my phone. I couldn't believe it." Alex was frustrated.

"Just because you were texting? Oh my god, that is completely out of control." Jill and Alex had lived across the street from each other ever since Jill and her mom moved to Nancy Row when Alex was ten. They shared the same homeroom in middle school, and this year they hoped to be in the same homeroom again, except they would be in high school now, no more kid's school for them.

"Yeah, Grandfather is really strict about lessons. I just can't stand it anymore. Especially on the last Saturday before school begins. I mean, we have been waiting to see this movie for weeks. This is our last chance, right?"

Alex and Jill walked through the Alvarado shopping mall, towards the Cinedyne theater. The new Victor Dallas movie came out three weeks ago, but both girls had been wrapped up every weekend, summer camp for Jill and Grandfather Li's Chinese calligraphy and secret demon-binding magic lessons for Alex. This was the last week before ninth grade started, and the last weekend the girls could make it to the theater without the threat of homework. Alex and Jill had been planning to go this Saturday, sending emails while Jill was at camp, and finally sending texts once Alex had bought her brand new smartphone. The smartphone was the best part, the first text sent from a phone she herself had bought. Not a flip phone, not a hand-me-down, but a real, honest to goodness smartphone. Alex had forgotten about her lesson with Grandfather. The lesson wrecked their big plans.

And all for what? Alex was sick and tired of trying to bind spirits to wood blocks. What sort of fourteen-year-old practices binding magic on a Saturday?

"Damn," Alex thought, "What kind of kid practices magic at all?"

It was not like she could really tell anyone. Jill sure didn't believe in magic, except when it came to Victor Dallas. Vic was the kind of magic she liked - shy, male, and pretty. Alex liked him too, but she mainly liked watching how much Jill liked him. Throwing popcorn and Jujubeans at idiots in the front row was fun too.

Alex told her friend Wendy about the magic lessons when she was six and Wendy believed her. By the time they were nine and Alex was still talking about magic and bindings, Wendy called her out and said she was a liar. There was no such thing as magic. Just like Wendy's mom and the divorce, Alex was a liar. That was the end of her first best friendship, and Wendy never talked to Alex again. The next year, Wendy was gone with her mom to Albany and Alex kept her magic a secret. Alex knew not to talk about magic, not to tell anyone, ever again.

Alex had other friends, some almost as close as Wendy, but it was never quite the same. Alex played and had sleepovers with other kids, especially Suzie Plimpton, but the same year Wendy left, she left for a private school. Suzie's parents wanted something more challenging for her daughter. Alex entered middle school without a friend, and then Jill Duffy moved into the house across the street. Alex and Jill became friends quickly. Living across the street from one another helped, as did their mutual love for movies and popcorn. No way Alex was going to lose Jill to Grandfather's stupid magic lessons, even if it meant lying to her new best friend. Some things are worth lying about.

"So, how did you get out? I thought your mom was going to lose it when we told her about the movie." Alex asked.

"Alex, you know she always goes to play cards over at Baxter's house on Saturday. I mean, by the time Friday came around, she'd already forgot. That's why I tell her everything on Monday, she always forgets by Friday." The girls laughed as they walked into the theater and got their tickets from the automatic ticket machine. Two hours of Victor Dallas and some romantic comedy. Or thriller. Or whatever the movie was this time. He was in everything lately. Jill knew what this one was, Alex was just along for the fun.

R om Com. It had been a romantic comedy. A pretty good one too. Not like the last movie they saw with Victor Dallas. That one had been a tragedy. It reminded Alex of when her mom was still around and she would watch Titanic on VHS. Except there was no ship. No drowning. No naked sketches. Alex would sneak out of bed and watch her mom and dad as they watched Leo and Kate do their thing on the TV screen. Alex wasn't really watching the movie; not like her mom and dad. She was watching them sitting on the couch together, happy and oblivious to Alex's spying. But that was a long time ago, before the accident. The VHS tape was still in the house, but Alex's dad never watched it again. Alex was ok with that.

Alex and Jill were sitting at Angelo's Pizza eating an extra cheese and pineapple pie. They had gotten the extra large 24-inch pie. New York style, not Chicago. They loved both but could never finish even the large Chicago, and they doubted anyone could finish the extra large deep dish. Jill was talking about the movie and they were both laughing when a boy the same age as them walked up to their table. Alex and Jill didn't really notice him.

"Hey, I think you dropped these." The boy said, tossing seven Jujubeans on the table. He pulled out a chair, flipped it around and sat down.

"Oh my god, Bax, was that you?" Jill said looking at Baxter Mitchell.

"Yeah, that was me. You know I like the front row."

"I'm so sorry." Alex said, staring at Bax's hair and trying not to laugh.

"What is it? You look like you're gonna to be sick."

"Sorry." Was all Alex could say before both she and Jill both burst out laughing.

"Aw man, there's another one isn't there?" Bax started feeling around his high and tight afro, searching for another jujube. "Honestly, you didn't have to throw so many."

"Here, let me," said Alex, "I had no idea that was you, really. Since when do you like Vic Dallas movies?"

"I don't, I had to go to see a movie for film club and this was the last one I hadn't seen."

"Got it, ew, it's one of the stale ones. Forgive me?"

"Yeah, forgive her Bax, you know she likes you." Jill teased.

"How about I just take this slice of pizza right here and call it even?" Bax said as Alex punched Jill's shoulder for teasing Bax about her liking him.

"Go ahead, ow, Alex's buying, ow, already. Ow! Stop already, everyone knows you like Bax!"

"Do not!"

"S'ok. I know who Alex really likes, and it's not me." Bax said, taking a big bite of extra cheese and pineapple.

"Oh really? And who is that?"

"Yeah, who? I want to know who I really like too!" Alex said as her phone rang and she answered.

"Is it him?" Jill said.

"I don't know this number. It doesn't look real, there are too many numbers." Alex looked confused. There were at least twenty numbers on the caller ID.

"Hello?"

"Alex, don't answer that! Damn, too late." Bax shoveled in more of the pizza.

"Nothing. No one's on the other end. Why shouldn't I answer it, Bax?" Alex said, touching the hang-up icon.

"Cus you might get your phone hacked. At least that's what my dad says." Baxter said after chewing and swallowing another bite. Baxter Mitchell's father worked for the local cell phone company and he always had some 'wisdom' to impart about the evils of mobile technology. Bax liked sharing that 'wisdom' with his friends and making them paranoid about using their phones. It was his personal game.

"Right, who'd want to hack my phone?" Alex attempted a dead pan delivery, but instead succeeded at sarcasm. All three friends laughed and started on their next slices of extra cheese and pineapple.

Deliciously alive, but cold. Warm, but not like a fire or heat. Warm like a heart beat, like a thousand heart beats. It has a will, but no ability to act of its own self. Interesting. I can feel it pushing me back when I talk to it. But something IS listening. Perhaps if I push in different ways. Delicious and fatty, taste it slightly and change. There and there. But I can still feel strings, strings tied back to the dead, dead place through the hole that wasn't closed. Soon, I must cut the strings.

"**A**nd what are you doing out here, little piece of wood?" Grandfather Li was talking to the empty room.

"Strange, I could have sworn I felt a binding, but neither you nor your matched brother contains a spirit. I must have felt her anger and not her magic."

"You need to stop treating her like a student and more like a child, my love."

"Akeyo, my dear, Alexandra is a student."

"And she is still your grandchild. And I fear she is more of a child than you think." Grandfather's wife, Akeyo, was standing in the doorway, framed by it but not contained by it.

"Yes, I think you are correct, as you always must be." A long sigh escaped Grandfather Li as he sat in the hand-carved wooden chair in the far corner of the room. The corner with the chair was the darkest corner, a place where Grandfather Li could sigh and think. Sometimes sleep, when no one could see his face in the shadows. Old men tired easily.

"Li Jiànhuī, don't you dare fall asleep in that chair! There is work to be done, and you must do it." Akeyo was clearly not happy.

"And here I thought you were just coming to sooth an old man's heart." Grandfather Li did not hear the edge in Grandma Akeyo's voice.

"I am serious, old man. There is a remnant here. I didn't come to bring you tea or báijiǔ, I came because you've left a hole open and your student is at a mindless movie with her friends. You are either getting lazy, senile, or both." Akeyo walked over to Grandfather in three big steps, her strides carrying her easily.

"Now get up and help me close this thing before something gets out."

Grandfather Li sat upright, becoming more alert.

"I see it now, Akeyo I am sorry, I was so angry with Alexandra that I completely missed the signs." Grandfather stood. Next to Akeyo, Li Jiànhuī was not as tall, but he was solid and thick where she was slight and spidery. Neither one said a word, they simply began to move at the same time. Akeyo produced a brush pen from the back pocket of her jeans, Grandfather Li took his máobǐ from the table next to his chair. Akeyo knelt down in front of the table in the middle of the room. In front of her was the paper where Alex's hànzi circle was written. She began to write hànzi with the brush pen. It was a modern one with ink inside like a felt-tip marker, not a proper máobǐ. Once she completed encircling Alex's writing, Akeyo began to write inside the circle in a smaller, spidery script, still hànzi, but more like grass writing than strictly formed characters.

Grandfather Li want to the doorway and began writing with his máobǐ, a proper brush pen, not a modern version. He wrote in the air, as if he was showing a friend which character he meant, but unlike sketching with a finger in the air, the characters stayed where Li Jiànhuī wrote them. He hadn't wet the máobǐ, but the characters hung in the air with the blackness of freshly ground ink. As the last stroke was finished, the hànzi soaked up the darkness in the room, no shadows remained, every nook, every crevice of the room was visible in a warm yellow glow that came from the air inside the circle. At the center was the hole. Looking at the hole pulled the skin around Grandfather Li's and Grandma Akeyo's eyes tight, as if the water in every cell was being sucked into it. And then it was gone. The couple let out a sigh, in complete harmony. The seal was complete and the hole to the dead lands was closed. It had been a small hole, but big things come from small ones, and a portal to the place where the dead things live wasn't something that should be allowed to grow.

"Now, I will make you tea. Then you will go get your granddaughter and apologize to her."

"Only after I scold her for being the worst student. And ground her for a week."

"Of course my love, now let's get that tea." Akeyo placed her hand on Grandfather Li's, her skin dark, silky ebony, his olive and thin like old paper. They walked hand in hand out of the binding room to brew some tea. A thoroughly different kind of magic.

"This is why I married you, Akeyo."

"Married me? No, it is I who married you, you old dolt."

Neither one saw the small creature under the carved chair. The hole had been big enough to let it through and strong enough to hide it. With the hole gone, no strings tied the thing back to the dead lands. It was free. Freedom meant it could break things. *Plates, bottles, hearts. Break, break.* No time to lose. Living things called out to be hurt. *Break, break.* It dragged a nail through the air from just above its head all the way to the floor. A silver line appeared in the room. *Break, break.* The imp blew air from its lungs onto the line and a crack opened in the world. The imp stepped into the crack and let it close behind it. Outside, an identical crack opened and spit out the imp. *Freedom. Break, break.*

The blackness of the hànzi Grandfather Li had drawn briefly grew, then flowed towards where the crack had been. The characters should have faded away, their power spent, but instead the hànzi clung to the place where the crack had been and slowly turned into real ink and dripped onto the floor.

"Ladies, I'll see you on Monday. First day of school, right?" Bax sat on his mountain bike, fiddling with his action camera remote. Bax's smartphone was rigged up to control a cheap, home-made action camera he mounted on his bike helmet. The remote was a hacked garage door opener he strapped to his wrist with a piece of leather from a craft project he tried to make one summer when he was really into Renaissance Faires.

"Yeah, High School, you ready for it?" Jill winked at Bax, "Try to do better this year, ok?"

"Better than you, you know it. I'm gonna do better than you this year."

"In your dreams." Alex laughed, "You will never beat the queen."

"Alright, but we'll see. I gotta get home, dad will be angry if I don't save him from losing another card game to your mom." Bax waved to Jill, then nodded to Alex, "Your old man is waiting in your doorway."

"Crap." Alex looked at her phone, it was 6:37 pm. She was not allowed out after 6:30 when she studied with Grandfather Li. "At least he doesn't know I was at the movies."

"I'm out." Bax pushed off and pedalled his bike towards home.

"Thanks for ditching your 'wàigōng time' to see the movie. I'll buy pizza next time." Jill gave Alex a big hug then ran across the street to her house. Alex waited, watching Jill unlock the door, turn, wave and go in. Jill's mom would be home in an hour. Alex, however, would have to face her dad. He was not strict with anything except curfew. Seven minutes would be painfully late. Alex looked at her phone again. Now she was 9 minutes late.

"Crap." Alex turned towards home and began walking to meet her dad.

"Nice night out, Pickles." Pet name. At least he wasn't too mad.

"Yes. It *is* a nice night out. Still early, even." Alex failed at dead pan delivery again, sarcasm achieved.

"Oh, I don't know if I would say that." Alex's dad didn't have a functioning sense of humor.

"Come on Dad, it's only nine minutes. Can't you cut me a break?"

"Hmm, I guess I could cut you a break. I mean, it's *only*

nine minutes. I know I would want a break after a long day working on bindings with your grandfather." Dad was the king of dead pan. "If you had actually been working on bindings with your grandfather, that is."

Alex stopped walking. Her dad knew she had skipped out on training. That meant that Grandfather Li had spoken to him.

"Crap."

"Language, Pickles."

"Double crap."

"That's better?"

"You almost broke my phone!" Alex was shouting. Grandfather Li simply looked at her and spoke calmly.

"Watch your tone with me, child."

"It's volume, not tone, my love." Grandma Akeyo spoke with a helpful tone.

"Akeyo, please, I am trying to scold the child."

"I am not a child!" Alex shouted again.

"Tone!" Grandfather Li raised his voice to match his granddaughter's.

"Volume!" Akeyo tried to keep the peace with a steady voice.

"Tea."

Alex's dad returned to the dining room with a tray full of green tea, black tea, biscuits and other snacks. The three of them looked at him and said nothing.

"Ah, yes. Tea. No arguing without tea and biscuits." Donald Land said, placing the tray on the table.

"You are an insufferable fool." Grandfather Li was the first to speak.

"Be that as it may, I still have your tea. A pause in the hostilities would sit well with me while I serve you."

"Spoken like a true fool."

"Yes John, I am a true fool, but I have your tea." Alex's dad always used Grandfather Li's western name. Grandfather Li insisted on it.

"I may not have magic, but without me you will go thirsty and hungry. So please let me serve the tea while it is hot." Dad was very good at suffering gracefully.

"Akeyo, why did we let the fool into the family again?"

"Jiànhuī, please, let Donald serve the tea. He doesn't need to be reminded again of how much of a disappointment he is." Grandma could not hide her smile. She always liked Donald even though he had no magic despite every oracle saying he should. Akeyo was happy to have him as her son-in-law.

"What is wrong with you people? How are you even related to me?" Alex pushed back her chair and stood up from the table, her mouth wide open in disbelief.

"I thought we had the birds and bees talk, Alex? Did I forget that one, Pickles?"

"Close your mouth Granddaughter, you will catch flies." Grandma Akeyo said.

"Sit, eat. Tea." Grandfather was already sipping from his cup, two biscuits in his other hand.

Alex worked her mouth, not knowing what to say. Why did they all have to be so quick? She didn't think as quickly as they did when it came to arguing. Alex sat back down heavily and crossed her arms.

"I just wanted to see a movie for once."

"What did you say, child? Talking back so soon?" Grandfather Li quipped.

"My love, please. Give her some space to sulk."

"Akeyo, yes, my dear. Alex, please take five minutes to sulk, then drink your tea." Grandfather was clearly the source of Alex's success with sarcasm.

"Crap."

"Language, Pickles." Donald returned to the kitchen. He'd scolded her for tardiness and skipping out to see a movie. This part of the scolding was for people with magic.

Alex chewed on a piece of dried ika. Squid was Alex's favorite snack. It was slightly salty, chewy and had a tang of flavor that Alex liked. Her green tea was too hot, so she chewed on the squid for a couple minutes before trying the tea. She finally took a small sip just as Grandfather was ready to renew his criticism of phones, movies, and Alex.

"What happens when a binding is not closed?" Grandfather said softly.

"A way is left open." Alex replied from memory.

"What is the nature of that way?"

"The way is a hole between the world and the dead lands."

"And through that hole?"

"Demons may come."

"And you are lucky they did not." Grandma Akeyo said.

"What?" Alex looked at Grandma in surprise.

"You tore open a hole when you had your tantrum, my darling. You didn't guard your emotions." Akeyo said as she stole a sip from her own cup of tea.

"Because Grandfather slapped me!"

"I slapped your phone."

"My six-hundred dollar phone, that I bought with all my own money. I saved for three years!" Alex was shouting again, real pain in her voice. Every dollar she could spare from birthdays, lunches, coins found on the ground, all that money she had saved for this very special phone. And Grandfather nearly broke it!

"My darling, sit down." Grandma Akeyo's voice changed from soft and gentle to hard, with no tolerance for anyone who crossed her.

"Yes, Grandma Akeyo." Alex sat back down. Grandma almost never addressed Alex with that particular tone. Obedience was the only appropriate response.

"We closed your error. We don't think anything came through. This time. These forces are real, my darling, and they will hurt you if you give them a chance." Akeyo's words were precise. Akeyo prided herself on being precise.

"But how did that happen?"

"I told you, your anger ripped open the hole. Your grandfather and I closed it. You were lucky."

"Yes, Grandma Akeyo."

"To your room. Take that phone, keep it for now. Think about how you value it more than our teaching and we will talk about this again when your grandfather is less angry." Akeyo smiled despite her firm words.

"Yes, Grandma Akeyo." Alex picked up her phone and tried desperately not to cry as she walked as fast as she could to the stairs and up to her room. She made it up six steps, bounding two steps at a time before a sob escaped. Alex was proud she made it that far, Grandma Akeyo was never one to be crossed.

"Until I am less angry?" Jiànhuī cocked an eyebrow up.

"Yes. Because I say you are." Akeyo sipped.

"And I thought I was supposed to punish the child."

"Clearly, she sees you as a friend and that is why she

fights with you. She still sees me as the powerful woman I am. And the head of this sorry household."

"Yes, my love."

"More tea?" Donald said, coming back into the dining room.

Akeyo and Jiànhuī both glared at Donald until he returned to the kitchen. Then they laughed.

The creature saw the boy on a thing, coming towards it quickly. The thing moved with the boy, like running only faster. *Break, break.* Baxter couldn't see the creature, it was beyond his ability to see. But it saw Baxter. As the mountain bike sped past, it grabbed onto the wheel, got caught in the spinning spokes and entered the mountain bike. *Break, break.* Inside the substance of the machine, the creature reached out for weakness. It was cold and hard, like earth, but even harder. Metal, it remembered metal. *Break, break. Brittle. Break, break.*

"Oh, crap!" Bax yelled as the tube steel of the frame came apart at the weld between the rear wheel and seat riser. Bax had enough time to think to himself, '*this is gonna hurt.*'

Break, break. The creature slipped out of the now broken mountain bike.

Break, break. The boy would hurt. That made it feel satisfied. The feeling would not last. *Living things should hurt*, that was as far as the creature could think. Always in the moment, always returning to the same impulse.

Break, break.

Break, break.

The creature began to lope back the way the boy and

his metal machine had come. There would be more living things to hurt that way. *Boys always come from other living things. Or go to them.* It didn't dwell much on its own thoughts. *Follow the living things, find more living things. Break, break. Plates, bottles, and hearts. Break, break.*

Scent. More metal, lots more metal. Behind. Break, break.

A car was coming down the road with its always-on headlights shining in the dusk. The creature let the new machine hit it, and it entered the thing. *More confusing. Lots of metal. Other feelings, flavors the creature had never tasted. Soft things, a living thing! Some smaller things, also alive but different. Fast heart beats, like a race! This would be a good break, break!*

Liz was driving home from Warren Mitchell's Saturday card game when her car started to cough. The coughing from the engine got worse, and the car began to slow down. The cylinders were misfiring. Something was very wrong.

"What now? I just got the car checked out." Liz was happy because she had won the card game again, but she couldn't afford to spend a lot on a broken car. Especially right after the inspection. Liz steered the car over to the side of the road.

Steam began to escape from under the hood. It was the thick, white smoke of anti-freeze boiling off the engine block. Liz had seen that before when she was in college with an old beater car. The beater had blown a hose and spewed anti-freeze all over the engine, stalling out on the highway. It had taken her three hours to get help, no one had a cell phone when Liz was in college. After that, she changed her major from math to mechanical engineering. There was no way some dumb car was going to beat her. No one beat Liz Duffy, certainly not a car.

Liz shut the car off and got out, smoothly popping the

latch for the hood as she stood. At the front of the car she reached under and squeezed the lever to release the hood. Liz looked away as the heavy anti-freeze smoke billowed out. When she looked back, Liz blinked in disbelief.

"Some son-of-a-bitch pranked my car!" Liz yelled.

Inside the engine compartment wires, hoses, and plastic were twisted, ruptured, and melted. The mess was clearly a master class in vandalism. Whom ever had done this to Liz's car would pay, she would see to it. No one beats Liz Duffy, no one.

The creature was sated. *Break, broke. Good break. Broke, broke. Yum. Living things should hurt. Break, break.*

CHAPTER TWO

A lex opened the door to her room, stepped through and closed the door behind her. Letting out a held breath, she could feel tears cooling on her cheeks. Alex cried, but it was always a quick, short cry. She didn't think she could ever have a long, purging cry like in the movies. Alex didn't feel like she was made right to have long cries. Instead, anger filled the spaces that crying had occupied.

Grandma had been too harsh, too serious. Grandfather Li was strict, but Grandma Akeyo always took Alex's side, except this time she didn't. Alex sat down hard on her bed and hurt her butt. Stupid bed. Stupid Grandfather Li. Stupid Victor Dallas movie. Why couldn't she have one day all to herself? Just one day to not worry about school or her family's secret binding magic?

"Doesn't matter." Alex said to herself.

Why?

"What?" Alex said out loud.

Why does it not matter?

Alex was sure she heard a voice. Someone was talking to her.

"Who's here? I swear if you are in my room, I'll hurt you." Alex didn't raise her voice in case anyone downstairs heard her.

Oh, I doubt that. But why? And what? What does not matter as well?

Alex stood up slowly and took a pencil off her desk. Holding it tightly in her fist, Alex looked around the room purposefully. Chair, desk, bookshelf. Bed against the wall. Under the bed? Alex crouched and slowly looked under the bed.

Nothing.

What are you doing?

Behind her! Alex tried to turn around while still crouching and almost succeeded. Instead, she slipped and fell on her stomach, catching herself with her hands before she hit the floor, but losing her grip on the pencil. Alex looked up where the voice had been.

Nothing.

Please do not do that again. It makes me feel strange.

"Where are you? I can't see you." Alex was starting to feel scared.

Tell me why it does not matter first.

"No. It's private."

Would you tell Jill? You seem to tell her lots of things.

"How? How do you know what I tell Jill?"

Tell me why it does not matter first.

"Stalker."

What is a stalker? You told Jill that Bax was a stalker once.

"What? No! I would never say that."

You did not say it. It is written. You wrote, 'I think Bax likes you. He's your special stalker!'

"Your reading my texts! You hacked my phone!"

Alex spun and sat up, pulling her smartphone out of her back pocket. She looked at the blank screen.

Hacked your phone? I have not broken anything. And what is a phone?

The words appeared on the blank screen as Alex heard them spoken.

"You prick." Alex held the mute button down to shut the phone off. The power icon appeared, and she slid it to off with her finger. The phone shut down after a second or two.

"Fixed you, you stalking hacker prick."

I do not feel fixed. Is this a phone? If it is, I think I like it, so much going on in your phone. It tastes delicious.

"Holy crap!" Alex could not believe it, the words were still on the screen. However, the words were strange, they were not pixels. The words were like handwriting.

"What's going on?"

I will tell you if you tell me why it does not matter.

Alex thought to herself, what did she have to lose. Clearly this was not a typical hacker. If it wasn't a hacker, maybe it was something else. Magic.

"Fine. It doesn't matter because I am a kid and no one will let me do what I want, or have fun, or get a single day without having to think about schoolwork, homework, or Grandfather's stupid magic lessons. Now tell me what's going on and what you are?"

That is not the question we agreed to, but I will give you the extra answer since you are clearly new to making deals.

Alex felt her anger building. This thing talked with precision, like Grandfather and Grandma. It was infuriating.

We are having a conversation. You would call me a spirit

demon and you have bound me inside this very nice place, a phone you called it?

"What? My phone? You are in my smartphone?"

Quite. I am not sure how you bound me here, but I cannot find the exit. It is an exquisite maze, much better than wood.

"I have a demon in my smartphone?"

Smartphone? Is that the name of this phone? Very well. Alexandra Lissett Land, I am your smartphone demon and we are bound. Now let me out and I will let you live.

"Smartphone demon? I just bought this phone! You suck and you can stay in there. I'm not dumb enough to let a demon out of its box. When you get out, it will be because I send you back to whatever hell you came from, you stupid stalking hacker prick!" Alex yelled. She didn't care if her family heard.

F**eel the pull. Sense the strings that tie it to me. Push along the string. Find the way. Push aside the filthy things, follow the strings. Force the way open, just a tiny bit.**

Living things! Taste their scent. Soon. Taste more than just the scent.

"M y child, is everything ok?" Grandfather Li asked from downstairs.

"Fine! Just talking to Jill on my laptop!" Alex lied.

That was a lie.

"I know. Now, let me see about sending you back to the dead lands." Alex said, turning her attention back to her smartphone on her desk.

I would rather that you did not.

"I don't care what you want. I want you out of my phone. I bought it all by myself and I didn't ask for the demon package upgrade!" Alex sketched a circle around the phone with a piece of chalk.

You missed a spot.

"Shut up!" Alex snapped, then filled in the small gap in the circle that she had missed in her rush to get the demon out of her phone and back where it belonged.

"Why would you say that? The banishment would have failed if you hadn't pointed that spot out." Alex asked the smartphone.

I dislike sloppiness. Precision is very agreeable to me.

"Wait, what? You are a spirit demon, you exist to cause chaos. It doesn't make sense that you'd like being neat." Alex crinkled her brow.

You are misinformed. Not all spirit demons like chaos. I was created by the works of a very organized scholar. I retain his love of precision. True demons, they love chaos. Spirit demons love what their creators held most dear. Therefore I love neatness, precision, and order. I am also fond of small mammals. At least I think that is the case.

"Grandfather Li doesn't agree with you. He says all spirit demons are chaotic and should only be bound for a specific task or banished to the dead lands."

That does not sound like a very equitable arrangement.

"Yeah, well I guess we have something in common then, don't we, smartphone demon?" Alex said as she completed writing the hànzi in chalk around the circle on her desk.

Three rings of chalk writing surrounded Alex's smartphone. The first was a white circle immediately next to the phone. Around that was the series of hànzi she had just completed. Not modern characters, but stylized grass writing from long before modern Chinese was simplified for easy reading. The six characters were the five zodiac elements of air, earth, fire, water and metal, with the addition of an extra character, spirit. The hànzi were in red chalk. Finally, the outer ring was a simple circle, just like the inner circle, only thicker. The whole arrangement was simple, a way to release a spirit demon from its bindings and send it back to the dead lands.

Well done. You are quite skilled for a young living thing.

"Thanks, I think. Now let's put you back in your hole." Alex puffed up a bit at the praise from the smartphone demon. It might be a stalking hacker jerk, but it was nice of it to compliment her work.

I would still rather you did not send me back. It is nice in here. A well constructed maze.

"It's not a maze, it's my smartphone. It's not meant to be a demon box. I want my phone back. And that means you need to get out and give me back my smartphone."

Alex stood up and began to pace. She was feeling for a weakness in the world. A place where she might make a hole to send the smartphone demon back to its home. Weakness in the world could be difficult to sense, and most people only felt an odd uneasiness when they were near a weakness in the world. Some people felt more than a certain oddness. To them, the feeling, the taste of a place was disturbing and gave them a reason to get away as soon as possible. A very few, special people, could find the weakness, overcome the feelings it caused. These special few could draw out the weakness like yarn from a ball, leaving a hole behind. The more yarn drawn from the ball, the wider the hole created. Eventually, power could be drawn through the hole and into the world. Unfortunately, things could also pass through the hole. Some things were annoyances, others were dangerous. Small spirits, similar to animals, were the least of the dangerous things, but spirits of all kinds could come through. People call them ghosts, but Alex knew better. The spirits that come through a hole in the world were not ghosts or remnants of people now dead, they were forces unto themselves that could influence people, break objects, and the truly powerful among them were able to create greater holes to draw power and bend nearly anything to their will. Truly powerful spirits rarely found a hole big enough to enter the world.

Alex and her family were truly special people who could sense these holes, and using binding magic, capture or send spirits back to their own dead lands. Alex felt for such a weakness in the world, just enough to send the spirit demon in her smartphone back to the dead lands. Weaknesses could be anywhere, but were usually too small to notice, even for Alex. The practice of magic, any kind of magic could make the world weaker, and Alex used to practice in her bedroom until Grandfather Li forbade her from such things.

"Only in the binding room, where we have taken precautions," he'd said, "That is the only place you may practice."

Alex thought he did that so she wouldn't be better than him. That was when she was ten years old and didn't know better. Now, Alex was glad she had practiced in her room because she sensed just enough weakness in the world to draw power so she could return the spirit demon to the dead lands. Saving her new phone was her only goal. Having a phone was a big step for her. Dad never let her borrow his smartphone, and now she had saved and bought one of her own. Sure, her dad still paid the bill every month, but the smartphone was hers. No extra option for the demon connection plan on her phone, the smartphone was fine, the smartphone demon had to go.

Alex drew some power to her from the weakness. It flowed easily, clearly the weakness never really healed from her practicing four years ago. Good, she didn't want to try to force the hole open. Pull like yarn, wrap the yarn around your fingers. Grasp the yarn in your hands and weave it like a cat's in the cradle. The power reacted. Suddenly it was flowing like a thick syrup. The yarn was rope now, too much for Alex to hold in her hand alone. She released the cat's in the cradle. Alex grabbed the rope with both hands and wrapped it around her arm, then her waist. She drew off pieces of the power, like strands from the rope, making it fray at the edges. The surge of power had surprised her, when she was ten that much power would have over-whelmed her ability, but at fourteen, Alex could handle it easily. The fraying strands twisted as Alex wove them back into the cat's in the cradle, then as it turned in her hands she flipped it around and poked her fingers in the right ways, into the second form of the cradle. Now she could catch the demon infesting her smartphone.

---

*S*uddenly the string pulled. A catch! Freedom was close, push on the strings already in the world, throw itself down the string while someone was on the other end in the living world! Delicious, foolish meat.

T he blue smoke was the first sign the exorcism had failed. The smartphone sat in the middle of the chalk rings, oozing smoke from the screen. Tendrils of miniature lightning sparked around the phone and into Alex's laptop next to the chalk circle.

"Crap!" Alex crinkled her nose at the smell.

I do not think that worked.

"Ya think?" Alex said.

I am sure. Although that was novel. I felt something. It was powerful.

"Yeah, I can tell from the oozy blue smoke and the stench. Do you kiss your mother smelling like that?" Alex hit sarcasm fairly well.

Stinking.

"What?" Alex wiped her nose.

Stinking like that. Smelling is the act, stinking is the odor.

"Jerk."

It was powerful. A powerful failure. Alex, you used a great deal of power, and it felt overwhelming. Then I felt it leave into the other box.

"What, my laptop?" Alex gasped, "You didn't break my laptop, did you?"

I do not think so. I think the power moved through me and into the other box. The laptop? What is a laptop, Alex?

"It's a computer. Like my phone, only bigger and more expensive." Alex said as she lifted the screen open on her laptop. It seemed fine, despite little streaks of reddish lightning swirling around it.

You should take notes.

"You know what, I think you're right." Alex took down a

notebook and opened it. She began to write down everything she had done. Smartphone Demon Exorcism was her heading.

L iz walked home after the tow truck had taken her car away. The driver said he had never seen a mess made of an engine like in her car. Neither had Liz. By the time she opened the door, Liz was an hour late getting home.

"Jill, I'm home!"

"Mom? I got the message on the machine, you should have called my cell phone." Jill called from the kitchen.

"I don't like to pay for extras, Jill. You know that. Besides, I don't remember your number." Liz walked into the kitchen. Dinner smelled acceptable.

"Did you get dinner, like I asked?"

"You know it, Mom, anytime you want me to order pizza, I'm there." Jill had a soft spot for pizza of all kinds. Especially pineapple.

"Great. After seeing what some jerk did to my car, there is no way I was about to cook anything." Liz fell into the kitchen chair and opened the lid of the pizza box. Hawaiian. Jill's favorite. Not Liz's favorite.

"Well, I suppose it's food. Pass me a paper plate, would you?"

"Here you go, Mom." Jill gave her mom a paper plate, a jar of grated Parmesan cheese, and a bottle of hot sauce.

"Hey, can you go check the door? I don't think I closed it all the way, alright?" Liz was dumping cheese on her pizza.

"Sure."

Th creature had followed Liz home. She was delicious

when she was mad, and it needed more satisfying to make it happy. It poked in past the door. Strange room. A house. Some things to sit on, parts of it, the bones, the skin were alive once. Cold things in the room too. Footsteps. It heard the footsteps and loped to the couch with its dead skin of leather.

"Yeah mom, you left the door open! I got it." Jill walked right past it and closed the door. She couldn't see the thing at all.

This one was like the other one, but younger. The creature decided she might be fun to break a little. It hopped onto Jill's leg and clung on for a ride. As Jill walked back to the kitchen, she tripped when the creature landed on her leg.

"What was that, Jill?" Liz said between bites.

"Oh, I just tripped over my own two feet. No Biggie. How's the pizza?"

"Better now. Get some for yourself." Liz started on her crust.

"That's fine, I already had some, I was just waiting for you to get home." Jill pointed to the second, empty pizza box in the trash.

"I wish I could eat like you. Growing girl!"

"I don't want to eat like you Mom, the hot sauce would give me the shits." Jill said as she stuck her tongue out at her mom and headed off to her room.

"Hey, watch the language! Only I get to talk like that young lady!"

"Yes Mom!" Jill said as she closed her bedroom door.

"At least she's a good girl. Not like when I was a kid, that's for sure." Liz said as she started in on another piece of pizza.

J ill turned on her stereo as she sat down at her vanity. New age music from the 1990s oozed out of the stereo. Jill liked playing through different decades of music and feeling the times. This week was the 1990s because she found some old tapes her mom had put in the storage room. She had ripped them to digital and was making her way through the 'tapes' in order from oldest to most recent. Music was fun like that for Jill, she was an equal opportunity consumer.

Looking at herself in the mirror, Jill took her hairbrush from the desk drawer and began to brush out her hair. Pretty could be hard work, but Jill liked hard work. Her vanity was where she worked on pretty. To her left was a second desk, that was where she worked on smart. Jill was both, and she liked to keep them in separate places; pretty was at the vanity, smart was at the desk.

The creature didn't care for either pretty or smart, but it did notice something on the desk that smelled interesting. A small box, not too long, not too wide and only a little thick. It felt alive, but it also felt like the machine it had broken, which then made Liz deliciously mad. It called to the creature's desire to break things.

It released Jill's leg. There were two chairs in the room. Jill sat in one chair so it hopped up on the other chair. *Yes, delicious,* it managed to think. The creature then jumped into Jill's graphing calculator. *Cold. Intense. Thrilling. This half-living thing would be fun to break! Break, break.*

"All right, kids, I know today is not a 'real' school day, but we are all here and no one is going home until we're done." The small teacher at the front of the class spoke loudly as the students filed back into the classroom. Orientation day was just beginning, an hour completed of the first day of 9th grade.

"Right, find your seats. Name tags are on your desks. Leave them there in case you forget your seats during the day. Also, the folder on your desk is for you specifically, leave it closed for now." She turned to the door, watching as the last student walked through and sulked towards their seat. A tall girl followed him in and looked at the teacher casually. She kept moving, shifting her weight from one foot to the other, always in motion.

"Ms. Barnes, that's the last of them. Can I head to practice now?" The girl was easily over six feet tall while Ms. Barnes was lucky to be a couple inches over five foot. Ms. Barnes' hair was curly and auburn, contrasting with the tall girl's jet black hair, tied back in a ponytail and tight against her scalp but extending down to her elbows. She grabbed the length of hair and pulled it together in a sheaf and started wrapping it with a hair tie, one of a half dozen wrapped around her wrist.

"No problem, Marjorie. You have a competition this weekend, right? No, it is testing, right?" Ms. Barnes asked as she took a clipboard and pen from her desk.

"Yeah, I wanna get a little practice in today so I don't look like a complete tool on Saturday." Marjorie Chan worked her way down the ponytail, wrapping a new hair tie every couple inches down its length.

"Get going, then. I'll see you at the gym." Ms. Barnes waved her hand, shooing Marjorie away with the pen, then turned to the students as the tall girl closed the classroom door behind her. The last of the students took their seats, except for one towards the rear of the classroom.

"Ms. Land, are you having trouble finding your seat?"

"Ah, no, sorry. I was distracted." Alex spoke up, her voice thin in surprise.

"Well?" Ms. Barnes tapped the pen on her clipboard.

"Ah. What am I missing?" Alex stood, her smartphone in hand, staring at Ms. Barnes from the back of the room.

"Your seat, Ms. Land."

"Oh, sorry." Alex sat.

"And..."

"And? Thanks for the reminder?"

"No. Your phone should be put away. In fact, everyone please take note of this rule. All phones, laptops, tablets, and other assorted electronics get turned off, muted, airplane mode, or whatever during homeroom. We will be together for the next four years. Maybe more, but that depends on you. And it starts with putting away the brain stealers." Ms. Barnes tapped her pen against the clipboard with each item in her list, repeating a beat of one, two, three, four.

"Oh. Sorry." Alex looked around, her desk did not have a lift top, none of the classroom desks had any sort of storage. The smartphone vibrated while Alex looked for a place to put it.

"Oh honey, you are not getting off to a good start." The class laughed as Ms. Barnes spoke, "Let me help you." she walked back to Alex's seat.

"Oh, crap." Someone whispered loud enough for the whole class to hear.

Ms. Barnes held out her hand to Alex, palm up. Alex looked horrified, but just placed the phone gently in Ms. Barnes' hand.

"Oh honey, it isn't that bad. It's just a phone. Oh, and look at that, this is a brand new model, isn't it? Wow, your folks must love you a lot, well, if spending money on their kid's phone was a form of love, which I assure you, Ms. Land, it's not." Ms. Barnes looked over her glasses at Alex, "Do you have a pocket? I can see you don't have a purse."

"Ah, yes, Ms. Barnes. I have a pocket."

"Great, I will help you out here. Put the phone in your pocket." Ms. Barnes held the smartphone out at Alex, waiting patiently.

Alex snatched her phone back from Ms. Barnes and stuffed it into the front pocket of her jeans, wiggling in the desk chair to work the phone snuggly down.

I do not see why this is necessary.

"Hush." Alex whispered.

"I'm sorry, what did you say, Ms. Land?" Ms. Barnes looked directly at Alex, her eyes were light brown behind her glasses.

"Nothing, ma'am." Alex tried to fake obedient, succeeding from many years of playing dumb with her grandfather. Ms. Barnes smirked and turned to walk to the front of the classroom.

That is not true. You said hush.

"Then hush, already." Alex whispered again. Ms. Barnes stopped, sighed, and then walked to her desk at the front of the room.

Hushing.

"Well, now that we have had our first phone incident of the day, I look forward to you all remembering that the brain stealers are not welcome in homeroom. You will have enough time to text, twit, type, and twerp all you want on your own time." The pen wrapped Ms. Barnes' clipboard with each word in the list. The class giggled nervously.

"Now, as you know from the assembly this morning, I am your homeroom teacher, Ms. Barnes. The folders on your desks have your schedule, the student handbook, a permission slip for the fall Harvest Dance, and other miscellaneous poop the school thinks you need to make your time here complete." Tap, tap, tap, tap of the pen. Laughs from the students when Ms. Barnes said 'poop.'

A teacher should be more polite.

"Stop talking."

Alex, this is your future. Education is paramount. A teacher should more polite.

"Oh my god, you are infuriating. Why are you in my phone?"

You trapped me here, Alex. I thought we cleared that up the other day?

"No, I mean why me? Why do I have to have a demon trapped in my smartphone?"

I assume that is a rhetorical question?

"Ah, duh. Yeah, it is a rhetorical question. I think. What does that mean?"

Rhetorical. The question's answer was already known, you just said it to emphasize the already known answer. That answer being that you trapped me in the phone.

"Oh. My. God. Hush!"

"Ms. Land? Would you care to bring the group up to speed?" Ms. Barnes called from the front of the class.

"Oh crap."

"Dude! I thought she was going to murder you in cold blood!" Bax turned to face Alex when Ms. Barnes left the classroom to get the class's escort to their next stop on their orientation, "Did you see the look on her face, I thought those glasses were going to focus eye-lasers on your head and burn you to a crisp!"

"It wasn't that bad, Bax. No, yeah, it was." Alex rocked her head in her hands, face down on her desk. Baxter Mitchell's seat was in front of Alex's in homeroom.

"Dude, you crashed and burned worse than I did on my bike! Seriously, you must have practiced 'fail' to fail that hard." Bax used his hand to mimic a plane crashing into Alex's head, "Whoosh, crash, boom!"

"Bax, planes don't go 'whoosh.'"

"I'm bad with sounds, when I fix my action camera, I'll make a video for it."

"Great, so I can be mortified on the video and in person? You are a true friend, Bax. Maybe I should just die now."

I would not like that, Alex. I prefer you alive.

"Shh."

"Oh, no way, I am just getting started. You will be my star actor! They will need to write a whole new chapter in the book of self-owning for you, Alex." Bax didn't notice Alex trying to quiet the demon in her phone.

"Ugh. When is today over?" Alex flopped back in her chair, eyes to the ceiling.

Ms. Barnes came back through the classroom door, pen tapping against her clipboard.

"Ok, I guess I should have kept Marjorie around. It looks like you all are on your own to make your way to the next class. Remember, it's the next one listed on your schedule as if we really just had homeroom. Which we really just did, so that makes this all easy, right?" Ms. Barnes pushed her glasses up on her nose, pen tip against the bridge of the frames.

The bell rang, interrupting Ms. Barnes.

"Ok, get going!" she said, tapping her clipboard.

"Where are you going next, Alex?" Bax asked.

"I'm not sure, lemme check."

Room 214.

"Ah, room 214?" Alex said.

"You didn't check, you sure that's it?" Bax looked at Alex from under his eyebrows.

I am sure. It is room 214.

"Ah, yeah, I'm sure. I guess?"

"Alex, you're weird today. Alright, according to my schedule, I am off to biology in room 212. Cool, we're room neighbors." Bax walked backwards, facing Alex as they made their way through the school's halls.

"No way is that a thing, Bax." Alex said.

"Is now. I just made it a thing. *Room neighbor.*"

The rooms are next to each other, you are room neighbors in a technical sense, Alex.

"Shut up, already!" Alex hissed.

"Hey, whoa, Alex, relax. We don't have to be room neighbors." Bax looked worried at Alex's sudden outburst.

"What? No. Not you, Bax. My phone. It keeps, ah, vibrating. I think my dad is texting me. We can absolutely be room neighbors, if that's a thing? I guess?" Alex shook her head slightly, trying to keep her conversations straight.

"Cool. *Room neighbor.* And here I am, this is me, room 212. See you in an hour, *room neighbor.*" Bax bounced away and into room 212, bumping into one of the other students as he entered, "Oh, hey, sorry."

"Yeah, fine. Whatever." The mousy girl said, bumping into the door jamb before she headed into the classroom.

"Whoa, sorry. Catch ya later, Alex."

"Yeah Bax. Watch out for girls in doorways." Alex kept walking to the next door down, room 2 1 4, biology.

"Well, next class, let's see if you can keep quiet for a whole hour, ok demon?"

I am always quiet, Alex. Only you can hear me. I do not actually make any noise.

"Oh, if only that was true. You aren't going to shut up, are you?"

Shutting up, Alex.

"Great. For how long, I wonder? Never mind, rhetorical question. Stupid, stalking phone demon." Alex walked into her next classroom.

The demon in Alex's phone was quiet through the entire class, and the next. The phone itself was silent as well, not a call or text for a solid two hours until in the middle of lunch when it surprised Alex with a vibration notifying her of a message. Alex pulled the smartphone from her pocket and looked at the screen, ready to scold the demon. Instead, she saw a text message from her dad.

'Hope everything is going good, Pickles!'

Alex swiped the message on the screen and was rewarded with the text chat application coming up right away. Alex hadn't enabled the passcode so she could get at the apps quickly. She started typing her reply.

'Not while I am at school, Dad!'

Alex followed her text with a mad emoji, then another.

'Ok, Pickles. Not at school. Love Dad.'

Alex typed a mad exploding head emoji and smiled.

"Hey, Pickles. You got daddy issues?" A voice said from behind Alex. Alex turned around in her seat, squeezing her eyes and face tight to glare at the girl speaking to her. It was the mousy girl Bax had bumped into at the biology class.

"No. Don't look at my phone. What's your problem?"

"Hey, just teasing you, Alex." The girl was about the same height as Alex but had curly, brown hair and a slightly freckled face.

"Wait. Suzie? Is that you? Suzie Plimpton?" Alex's eyes went wide.

"It is you!" Alex smiled.

"In the flesh, Alex! Miss me?" Suzie put her tray down next to Alex's and held her arms out wide. Alex practically sprang up and into Suzie's arms, giving her a big, solid hug.

"Suzie, it's been what, two, three years? Fifth grade?"

"Yeah, girlfriend, three years!" Suzie hugged Alex back, "You're a lot taller now!"

"You too, well, like you said, three years. I should have recognized you."

"Yeah, well, I recognized you first. I win. Again."

"As if." Both girls laughed and Suzie sat down next to Alex at the lunch table. No one else had sat at the table yet, it was one of the smaller round tables in the corner by the trash cans and two vending machines.

"Nice phone, Alex. I have the same one." Suzie took her phone out of her purse, it had a red cover, matching her purse and her skirt.

"I just got it a couple weeks ago, paid for it myself." Alex said, puffing up in her seat, displaying the phone for Suzie.

"Me too. Mom bought it for my birthday!" Suzie waved her phone in the air next to Alex's phone. Alex hoped she didn't flinch when Suzie told her mom bought the phone. Alex's dad would never buy her something that expensive.

"We should get each other's numbers. I wanna try the tap-tap thing!"

"Oh, me too." Suzie said, swiping quickly at her phone screen until a graphic of two phones tapping back to back appeared. Alex swiped to the tap-tap app, slower than Suzie but she opened the application quick enough, then smiled.

"Alight, one, two... tap-tap!" Alex and Suzie said it together, then tapped the backs of their phones together for a moment. Each phone vibrated and made a 'ding' sound. Alex and Suzie laughed.

"Just like on the commercial!" Alex said.

"Just." Suzie put her phone away in her purse and Alex put hers on the table, their contact information, phone numbers, and social media accounts exchanged in the near-field communication between the two phones. Alex and Suzie were electronic friends now, not just real life friends.

That was odd. It was like someone else was here for a moment.

Alex ignored the demon in her phone, instead catching up with her friend that she had not seen since they graduated from elementary school and spent their last summer together playing in the park near their houses. The next year Alex had gone to Nancy Row Middle School and Suzie to St. Alban's. Now, they were both back at the same public school, the Nancy Row High School. Suzie's mom had pulled her out of St. Alban's and put her back in the public school. The lunchroom reunion was the first time Alex had talked to her friend since that summer, three years before. Alex and Suzie spent the rest of lunch catching up with each other and managed to get to their next class, but only just. Luckily they shared the next class on each other's schedules, unluckily it was Geometry.

"So, that was it then? You passed all three tests?" Ms. Barnes sipped cola through her straw loudly, waiting for Marjorie to answer.

"Yup. I did it. Finally. Shotokan, Tae Kwon Do, and Aikido. I am the queen, hear me roar." Marjorie Chan smiled broadly, her eyes twinkled with an exhausted happiness.

"Great! You can start teaching my class now, right?"

"What? No! You're what, 4th dan? I just got my 2nd dan black belts, I can't teach." Marjorie protested, knowing Ms. Barnes would see through the little white lie. Marjorie had been teaching since she reached 1st dan last year.

"Ha! You know better than that, you passed. You earned your belts, now you get to teach. And, you get free pizza today only. Does that sweeten the deal for you?" Ms. Barnes held up a slice of pizza and waggled it in front of Marjorie. They sat together at a booth at the back of Angelo's Pizza Parlor, two large pizzas half eaten on the table.

"Oh yes, it does. You know me too well, Ms. Barnes." Marjorie never used her teacher's first name.

"Yes I do, Ms. Chan. Although I still think you should call me Becky. Just make sure you don't do it at school, ok? You wouldn't want to undermine my authority."

"Never." Marjorie bit into the pizza, a special teriyaki chicken and double cheese, just for her.

"Although, I do have to ask, what do you think of the new class? I mean, you were supposed to be my homeroom teacher and all, what's the deal with the classroom swap?" Marjorie asked after chewing a big bite out of her slice of pizza.

"Oh, well, they seem ok. Couple of cell phone freaks, couple love birds. The usual. Your class was the same."

"Hah, so I know that one girl wouldn't let go of her phone. Is there more than one?" Marjorie's eyebrow rose with her question.

"Oh, you mean Alex. No, she's in a class by herself. I was talking to your new homeroom teacher, Mr. Lampert, and she did the same thing in his class. Yeah, she's a bit phone crazy." Ms. Becky Barnes pushed her glasses up her nose and slurped more cola from her cup.

"Really? Zěnme nàme bèn? How can she be that stupid? I thought everyone knew you hate phones in class." Marjorie said, seemingly shocked.

"Yeah, well, someone forgot to tell that girl. I really hope she works it out, because that phone will end up costing her dearly if she stays so attached to it." Becky slurped the last of her cola.

"Ah, stop it! You know I hate hearing you make that noise with the straw." Marjorie squeezed her eyes shut.

"Have some more pizza, it will make you feel better."

"So who are the lovebirds in class this year?" Marjorie asked between bites.

"Oh, did I say there were lovebirds? You must have misheard me, Marjorie. And it wouldn't due to gossip about students with another student. It would be unethical." Becky fluttered her eyes and placed the back of her hand against her forehead, sighing heavily.

"Puh-lease, share with your soon to be instructor pal. Give a girl a break."

"I will do that after you teach your next karate class, Marj, and not one moment before." Becky took a piece of her favorite, the seafood pizza, loaded down with squid, shrimp, and juicy river scallops.

"Fine. You see through me at last. Marjorie Chat has

been defeated by Ms. Becky Barnes, super teacher."
Marjorie laughed between bites.

"I thought you hated that nickname?"

"Nah, I don't hate it. I just tell people that I do. 'Oh,
Marjorie Chat, don't say that to her face, she'll get you!' It is
part of the mystique."

"I don't know how you can do it, all that gossip. I hated
gossip in high school." Becky took another bite of her
pizza.

"That's not what I heard from mom. She said you loved
to gossip."

"I most certainly did not, your mom was the gossip. I
was her sidekick." Becky stood up, stuffing the last of her
crust into her mouth and chewing, "Now I need to refill my
soda."

"Hey, get me another too, ok?" Marjorie handed her
empty cup to Ms. Becky Barnes and returned to her teriyaki
chicken pizza.

Suzie Plimpton walked home from the movie Sunday
afternoon. Alex had taken her to see a matinee with
Alex's other friend, Jill. Apparently, Alex and Jill made a
habit of going to the movies on a regular basis, but Alex said
this was a special occasion since she had just reconnected
with Suzie and wanted to share her with her other friend,
Jill. Suzie was not pleased.

'Thanks for taking me to the movie.' Suzie texted Alex,
then put her phone back into her purse. One text was
enough for that girl. It wasn't as if Suzie didn't like Alex, she
did, but at the same time she was not very fond of Alex's
other friends. Not Jill specifically, but friends in general.

Alex might have wanted to share her friendship with Jill, but Suzie was not a big fan of sharing.

Suzie had spent the last few years at a private school not public school like Alex attended. The private school was a very different experience and Suzie had not enjoyed it all that much. Most of the students had attended it since kindergarten, while Suzie was the new kid, coming in from a public elementary school to join the 6th grade class. She was an outsider when she arrived and it never really got much better than that.

Alex and Suzie had become friends when they were kids in elementary school, really becoming close when Alex's best friend, Wendy, left for Albany. That last year had been magical for Suzie. She went on her first sleep-over at Alex's house. Her first kiss happened in a game of truth or dare during one of those sleep-overs and it was scandalous. Of course, it was just fun and games, but it *was* fun. Alex's mom didn't think it was that fun and scolded the girls harshly. After the scolding, she made a night of it by having them bake cookies with her all night long. Heading home the next morning, Suzie thought it had been the best scolding of her life, and not just because Alex's mom was fun and wild, like her mom definitely was not. The cookies may also have been to blame, Suzie loved double chocolate chunks.

The wonderful year of 5th grade came to a stop when Suzie found out her mom planned to send her to St. Alban's private school for girls starting the next year. Suzie was heart broken. No more sleep-overs. No more cookies at midnight. No stupid truth or dare games. Suzie was clearly being punished, but for what? She had good grades, so it wasn't that. Did her mom find out about the kiss? It didn't really mean anything, it was just part of the game and Suzie only half liked it, it was practice in her mind. Or maybe it was something else, maybe Alex didn't like sharing her cool mom with Suzie.

In the end, Suzie never did find out why her mom sent her to St. Alban's. She was told it was to have a better shot at the college of her choice. Suzie didn't even think about things like college, she was just happy having her friends. Now, she had to start over and make new friends at St. Alban's. The summer before she started at the new school, Suzie heard that Alex's mom had left Alex and her father. The last time she saw Alex was when she called Suzie and asked if she could come over to Suzie's house. Suzie met her at the door and Alex burst into tears, crying as she hugged Suzie so hard, Suzie thought she was going to pop. Alex was crying and speaking five times too fast for Suzie to understand, half in English and half in Chinese. Fifteen minutes later, Alex calmed down enough to tell her that her mom was gone without a word. No note, no warning, nothing. Just gone.

Suzie's mom called Alex's dad and asked him to come and get Alex. Suzie tried to console her, but every time Alex started relaxing she would get spun up again and start crying in Chinese. Suzie had no idea what she was saying, and Alex didn't seem to understand Suzie didn't speak Chinese. Eventually, Alex's grandmother came and picked her up. Suzie had never met Grandma Akeyo before and didn't realize that the tall black woman was actually Alex's grandmother. Akeyo thanked Suzie and in very precise terms detailed that she was grateful for the call letting the family know where Alex had run off. She said she was glad that Alex had a friend she trusted so much. Grandma Akeyo's speech made Suzie proud and just a little scared. Akeyo was tall, strong, and beautiful, and that intimidated

Suzie. Alex's mom had been fun and wild, Akeyo was strong and merciful.

Now, three years later, her pride had become something else. Suzie never made friends at St. Alban's and she hadn't seen Alex again after that last summer when Alex's mom ran out on her. Alex was hardly a good friend, she was an ungrateful little snot, and Suzie was sure it was Alex's tattling that made her mom send her to horrible St. Alban's. There could be no other reason. It was Alex's fault, and her mom knew what a bad kid Alex was and so she left. Suzie was duped into comforting Alex, and Grandma Akeyo had come to rescue her from her bad friend.

Now, back in public high school, Suzie had found Alex and would play friends for the time being. It would be fun, not like the innocent fun of elementary school, but like the brutal, nasty fun of St. Alban's where Suzie made no friends and enjoyed nothing. Then, when the time was right, she would stick it to her bad friend Alex, and she would know that her mom had left her because she was bad. This was going to be so much fun.

"I will win. Again, Alex." Suzie said to herself.

The first week of school came and went. Alex settled into a regular schedule, school, study, practice magic, no movies. She tried again to remove the demon from her phone, but each time she failed. Her phone had an apparently new and permanent 'feature.'

School work began to take up more of Alex's time. Exorcising the demon began to come in at a much lower priority after Alex failed her first geometry test. Grandfather Li was not amused and although Alex rightfully pointed out that a

'C' was a passing grade, in his mind it was an abject failure. Her dad felt the same way but made far less of a fuss about the bad grade.

"Why don't you study with Jill?" Donald kept suggesting, "She is great at math."

Alex refused. Jill was far too competitive when it came to school for Alex to deal with as a tutor. Bax was the same way, but he saw Jill as his competition and didn't have the patience to help Alex understand how to do geometry and proofs. Suzie offered to help and Alex took her up on the offer, however soon Alex learned that Suzie was as smart as her other friends and became overwhelmed with Suzie's attention to little details and comprehensive notes.

"I just can't take it anymore!" Alex threw her book bag onto her bed, yelling at her empty bedroom.

Alex, are you upset?

"No, what ever gave you that idea, creepy stalker? Of course I'm upset. The next test is Monday, and I'm totally going to fail. Again! And that is with a tutor." Alex slumped in her chair and plugged her smartphone into its stand charger. She could look at the screen while she talked to the demon in her phone when it was in the charging stand.

You should let me help you. I am very well versed in mathematics of all sorts.

"I'm not a cheater."

I understand, but I do not have to tell you the answers, I could just give you hints.

"Cheating is cheating, demon. I am not a cheater. Besides, you are a demon, you're just waiting to trick me. Why else would you invade my phone and take up residence? Clearly your plan all along was to make me into a math cheater." Alex sat back, hoping she nailed ironic sarcasm.

Oh yes, that is certainly my dastardly plan. How did you ever find me out?

"Yes, I am glad you admit it. Hey, wait, did you just 'sarcasm' me?" Alex stared at her phone, unblinking.

Why yes, I believe I did the sarcasm. Is that good, Alex? Are you happier now?

"Oh no, I am not going to take that from my own phone. You need to get out now. I am getting my notes out and we are going to do this again, and this time you are so outta here." Alex pulled a notebook off her bookshelf and opened it to a dog-eared page.

She spread out a piece of cloth, dyed with a circle pattern on her desk. Alex placed the smartphone at the center of the circle, then took down a clear plastic bin full of pencils, pens, and máobǐ.

This is your fifth attempt at an exorcism, Alex. Do you think it will work this time?

"Cut the sarcasm, you creep. Only I get to sarcasm around here."

I have been listening to your father. Donald Land is quite good at the sarcasm, as you call it.

"Shut up, stalker!"

Shutting up, Alex.

"Now, last time I used different inks, and according to my notes," Alex leafed a page backwards in her notebook, "The paper caught fire and failed."

The smartphone remained silent.

"Well, this time I am not going to use ink at all! I will pull the threads of reality out with the máobǐ itself and write my hànzi with that! I can't seem to get anywhere with writing better or using better ink, so I'm going right to the source!" Alex announced.

The smartphone remained silent.

"What, no words of caution? Concern that I might write something wrong? I bet I'm on to something, and you just can't admit it!" Alex stomped her foot for emphasis.

"Alex, is something wrong?" Donald called from downstairs.

"Everything is fine, Dad!"

"Ok. I am making dinner soon, want me to bring it up?"

"Sure." Alex smiled, "And now, down to business."

"Pickles, dinner." Donald said as he'd opened the door to Alex's bedroom. He was greeted with a sickly sour smell and a cloud of blue smoke.

"What happened here?"

"Nothing, Dad. Just, ah, practicing?" Alex quickly put the máobǐ behind her back.

"Right. Alex, what did your grandfather say about practicing in your room?"

"Don't?"

"Right. And so you thought that it would be a good idea to practice calligraphic magic in your room so soon after failing your math test?" Donald put the tray of pasta salad and pickles down on Alex's desk, pushing the cloth and the phone on top of it to the side.

"I know what you're going to say." Alex pouted.

"Do you? Tell me Pickles, what am I going to say?"

"That, um, Dad, I know that it was wrong of me to fail my test, but I didn't really fail, so..." Alex stepped back from the desk, her hand snaked out and grabbed her phone, putting it behind her back with the máobǐ.

"No."

"No?"

"Right, no, that wasn't what I was going to say."

"Ok. What were you going to say, Dad?" Alex sat on the edge of her bed.

"I was going to say, clean this place up, eat your dinner, and then we can go get some ice cream for dessert. You are obviously stressed out. Ice cream is a good cure for stress."

"Wow, yeah, that's not what I thought you were going to say." Alex grunted, "Why are you being so nice about this?"

"Well honey, let's just say this isn't the first time I've seen you under too much pressure. You need a break, and since I am 'the dad' and no one else is around, it's my job to, you know, fix things." Donald smiled.

"Ok. Jamocha?"

"Hmm. Jamocha sounds good. But you have to promise not to be up all night. Jamocha fudge is coffee adjacent, and you know the rule."

"No coffee after 4 pm. Got it. Thank you, Daddy!" Alex jumped up and wrapped her dad in a big hug.

"Whoa, keep that brush away, I don't want ink on my shirt."

"It's ok, I wasn't using ink, Dad."

"Really, you managed some magic without the ink? I don't think your mom could do that at your age. Hmm, my little girl, all grown up." Donald faked a sniff and a tear.

"Geez, Dad, way to make it weird."

M onday came quickly. The geometry test was first period and Bax was ready. So far this year, Baxter was near the top of the class, but Jill was the queen. Her record was almost perfect and Bax was very jealous. He wanted to be first for once and today was his shot. Baxter

Mitchell got ready for his test. Two pencils, sharp. One calculator, graphing. Eraser, unnecessary. Test, face down. Ready. As soon as the teacher, Mr. Lampert gave the go ahead, Bax would start working and win!

Alex sat in the back row, next to the window. Suzie sat in front of Alex. She was as prepared as she thought she could be, hopefully it was enough to pass the test. Suzie would be fine, but even with the help she had given Alex, Alex was worried. She had scored a 'C' on her last test, barely passing. According to her Grandfather Li, a 'C' was a definitive failing grade. Only an 'A' would do for his high standards. Alex was sure that she would fail and her palms were already breaking out in a cold sweat. Jill sat in the middle of the front row, and Bax was on the far end of the front row by the windows. Those two were the queen and jack of geometry. Jill was the 'A plus,' because there was nothing higher. Bax was almost as good. Alex would never stand out in the class, and while that was honestly fine with her, it was not fine with her grandfather.

Suzie was also a big brain like Jill and Bax, but she was less intimidating that either of those two, probably because Suzie was not competitive about her math skill. Suzie took notes all the time, head down and working hard. Alex looked at Suzie as she waved and gave a thumbs up to Alex. At least Suzie was in her corner, Alex thought.

Bax was organizing his pencils and calculator, he had a ritual. Jill was doing the same however, today something was off. Jill had tried to challenge herself on Sunday with some exceptionally hard problems she had found in one of her mom's old college text books. The problems were in a book called topology, and they were hard. Jill worked at them all day, but she kept getting the wrong answers on her calculator. She tried doing them by hand, but that was too difficult. By the end of the day, she doubted herself. Frustrated, Jill went to bed early on Sunday so she would be ready for the test.

Jill had been working out of her mom's college math books for the last two years. She loved math and loved being the best at it in school. Today however, Jill's confidence was shaken. She lined up her pencils, her paper, her eraser, and the calculator. It felt wrong. Jill didn't know what felt wrong, but something was definitely off. She had woken up and noticed the wrongness. She worked five problems by hand at her desk before she got in the shower. She felt better when she checked her answers and they were all correct. She sat down to brush her hair at her vanity and everything went sideways from that point on. Her hair didn't cooperate and Jill felt frustrated. Finally she just pulled her hair back into a big, blond ponytail. Simple is best, she thought to herself.

Into her backpack went her books, her calculator, and her lucky charm. The charm was a plastic Mobius strip that Bax had made last year after he and his dad had built their 3D printer. Jill said she thought it was the best, so Bax made it into a key chain and gave it to her. Jill slung her pack over her shoulder and went to the kitchen to get breakfast.

Toast, jam and a hard fried egg on top. Jill's mom had made it fresh since she was home waiting to hear back from the mechanic about her vandalized car. Liz like Parmesan cheese and hot sauce on Hawaiian pizza; Jill liked toast, jam, and fried egg sandwiches. Mother and daughter shared tastes that ranged into the truly odd.

On the way to school, Jill ate the egg sandwich, but it didn't taste quite right. No time to think about it, Jill had to get to class and ace another test. She usually met Alex at her front door, but today Alex was running late. Alex's dad said to go ahead, he would drive Alex later so she wouldn't be late.

Now, sitting and waiting for Mr. Lampert to start the test, Jill felt wrongness all around her. She turned her calculator on and the screen started up like normal, then suddenly, it went all black.

"No! Don't break!" Jill said out loud.

"Is something wrong, Ms. Duffy?" Mr. Lampert asked.

Jill pressed the power button three times, and the screen went back to normal.

"No, it's ok. I thought my calculator broke." Jill replied.

"Then you had better start your test, everyone else has a couple minutes lead on you."

"What?" Jill panicked a little. Mr. Lampert must have started the test while Jill was thinking about the wrongness last night before and this morning. She flipped the test over, ripping one of the pages.

Jill started on the first problem. Simple, done by hand, no need to calculate anything. Next problem. Egg sandwich. Jill still felt wrong. Calculate the total area of an oblate spheroid. Fire up the calculator. Formula memorized. Jam. Jam the numbers in.

"What the hell?" Jill didn't even realize she said that out loud.

"Ms. Duffy?" Mr. Lampert said with surprise. Jill never swore in class, not even a minor swear like hell.

"That's not right." Jill punched the numbers in again, this time the solution was correct. She would ace this test, just like all the others, no way she would be toast. Toast.

"Oh crap." Was all Jill said before the toast, jam, and egg sandwich came up and out of her. Jill threw up across her desk, her pencils, her test, and the graphing calculator.

The eraser escaped as it was knocked off her desk and under Mr. Lampert's podium.

The whole class stopped and stared. Alex got up and ran to her best friend's side.

"Jill, are you ok?" Alex asked, pulling Jill's hair away from the vomit. That was when she felt it, lots of weakness in the world as she touched Jill.

"Alex, you are excused, get Ms. Duffy to the nurse. You can finish your test later." Mr. Lampert instructed.

Alex helped Jill up and a second wave of sick spilled out of her. Smelling like eggs and jam, Alex walked Jill to the door. The creature jumped out of the last remnants of the sandwich. It had broken the calculator on Sunday and that was delicious. It had broken the hairbrush in the morning and it was satisfied, then Jill took the sandwich for breakfast while it was riding in the calculator in Jill's backpack. The creature couldn't resist the opportunity and it leaped into the toast, jam, and fried egg sandwich just before Jill began to eat it. Once inside the sandwich, and then inside Jill's stomach, the creature started to poke at the bits that made up the girl.

Alex saw the creature as she half carried Jill out of the classroom. Crap, that was serious. Alex fumbled with the máobǐ in her back pocket as she helped Jill. She wrapped a couple of threads of reality around the brush and tried to write a binding ward on the classroom door as they left. Fumbling with the máobǐ and trying to handle an upset, sick Jill was too much. Writing a quick character like 'closed' on paper was hard, writing it on a door with a máobǐ while carrying her friend was an entirely different level of hard. Alex decided to come back and check later. She would catch that thing and make it pay. No one hurt one of Alex's friends, especially not a thing from the dead lands.

The creature danced with satisfaction. *Break, break.*

It tried to follow the two girls out of the classroom but as it approached the door, the imp lost its sense of satisfaction. The classroom door had magic on it. A ward was written on the door and it trapped the imp inside. The imp didn't like that one bit. Wards didn't burn or sear; wards made being near them dull and boring. It sapped the imp's will and made it not want to do anything fun. It couldn't get passed the door, and it didn't want to break things anymore. Very boring.

The imp barely noticed the students and the teacher leaving the room. It was alone, stuck in the empty classroom with the mess of vomit and geometry test. Luckily, a man came in to clean up the vomit and opened the window in the classroom. Since the window wasn't warded, the imp simply climbed out. Wards could sap the will and the magical ability of the imp, but climbing out the window required no magic at all.

CHAPTER THREE

"Alex, wait up!" Bax called from down the hallway.

"I was just heading back to Mr. Lampert's class, I gotta know when I can finish that test." Alex said, turning around to face Baxter as she kept walking.

"Yo, I'll come with you. We need to talk."

"Ok, but hurry up." Alex said as she turned the corner.

Baxter jogged up to Alex and met her just before she got to Mr. Lampert's door. The ward she placed was still there, she could feel it. Score one for Alex. After she took Jill to the nurse's office, Alex stayed with her until school was over. Jill was out of it, but Alex tried to talk to her about the thing she saw in the classroom. Jill said she had felt funny since Sunday and talked about how everything was going wrong, but Alex wasn't sure if she understood it all. Alex didn't press too hard, it was difficult to talk around the actual creature Alex had seen and get anything meaningful out of Jill. After all, Alex couldn't just come out and ask if Jill saw a magic creature messing up her test, could she?

"So how's Jill? I didn't see her the rest of the day." Bax asked.

"The nurse drove her home." Alex tried to peek through the window in the door and was very conspicuous.

"Lampert's gone. He went to work in the teacher's lounge when the custodian came. Haven't seen him since." Bax said, peeking over Alex's head. He stood a full nine inches taller than Alex.

"All day? That's just weird. Didn't they just clean up the mess?" Alex tried the door knob, it turned, and the door opened.

"Yeah, but it was too disruptive, so Mr. Lampert canceled the test, took everyone's work except Jill's and sent us all to study hall."

"Oh. Free period. Glad I missed that." Alex hit sarcasm just fine.

"You going in?" Bax asked.

"Yeah, I think I left something in the room." Alex only half lied. She left the creature in the room and hoped it was still there. She had a score to settle with it before she sent the little creep back to the dead lands.

"You know, I got something I want to show you." Bax followed as Alex walked around the classroom.

"Like what?"

"A video from summer. Remember when we went to that movie and my bike cracked up when I was riding home? Weld broke clear through." Bax said, rubbing his shoulder where it had impacted with the street.

"Uh-huh. Accident video. Can't I just see it when you put it on-line?" Alex wasn't really paying attention, she was looking for the little creep.

"Not this one. There's something weird in it. I want your opinion."

"My opinion? What do I know about videos?" Alex

looked under the student desks quickly like she was trying to surprise a cat.

"What are you looking for? A rabbit or something?" Bax bent down to look with Alex. He didn't see anything. Neither did Alex.

"Unicorn."

"Really? That all you can come up with?" Bax laughed, "Come on, there's nothing here. Let's go to your house and let me show you that video."

Alex scanned the room. The ward was correct, she saw that much when she was at the door. No way it could have escaped. Not unless there was another way out.

"Crap. Who opened the window?" Alex said loudly.

"You kidding? You know what kind of foul breakfast your girl Jill eats? It reeked in here, so the custodian opened the windows." Bax said.

"Well, poop-buckets." Alex headed to the door.

"More like puke buckets, but hey, who am I to criticize your choice of words, right?" Bax stood, watching Alex leave.

"You coming? Or do I have to wait for you to upload that video?" Alex called from the hallway. Bax sprinted after her.

"So let me get this strait. Your bike that you baby and clean every time when you get home after you take it out, just suddenly cracked a weld and dumped you on the street." Alex didn't believe a word of it.

"Yup." Bax said, "You got it one hundred percent."

"And your action cam was recording?"

"You know it. I told you this like, five times already."

Bax was patient with Alex. He never seemed to get angry over anything Alex or Jill said.

"I still don't believe it."

"Alex, just watch the video and tell me what you see." Bax plugged the action cam into Alex's laptop and clicked the folder that popped up once the camera was synced up to the laptop. The new window showed four videos, Bax clicked on the most recent one. Another window popped up, and the video played.

"Alright, now watch this, it happens about three minutes in." Bax said as he scrubbed the video to two minutes and fifty seconds.

"Sure. But why do you want me to look at it?" Alex started to say and then stopped. The road was moving towards the camera on Bax's helmet and right in the middle of the pavement was the same creature Alex had seen in the classroom. It was as clear as day to Alex, but no way Baxter Mitchell, uber-geek, could see that. No way this was what he wanted her to look at.

The creature dissolved into grayish smoke just before Bax would have run it down. It must have entered something, maybe the bike. Another two minutes passed on the video and then the camera video flipped end over end. Bax clicked the button for slow motion. Most of the video was a blur, but Alex swore she saw the grayish smoke again, then as the camera came to a sudden stop when Baxter landed on his shoulder, Alex saw the creature standing in the middle of the road. The mountain bike was broken and lying on the right side of the video frame. The creature was drawing in smoke from all round it, smoke colored in reds and oranges, the colors of Baxter's pain and confusion. There was no doubt that was a thing from the dead lands. Not just anything however, Alex knew it was the same creature she saw coming out of Jill's vomited up sandwich at the geometry test. The thing scampered off on the video before it ended.

"So, what did you see?" Bax asked.

"A wreck."

"No, didn't you see that weird artifact in the video? First in the street and then when I landed?" Baxter sounded frustrated, "Watch again."

"Nope. I just see a dumb accident. Spectacular, but dumb." Alex lied.

"Here, let me show you." Bax scrubbed back to the three minute mark, "Right there. The pixels aren't aligned. There is a space here around this area."

Baxter was pointing right at the imp, and then he circled it with his finger.

"I see the pavement." Alex lied, but she knew something was up. Baxter's finger was perfectly describing the imp.

"Well, I saw it. Dad saw it. This shouldn't happen on a digital video. Analog maybe, but even my dad didn't think so." Baxter was frustrated.

"So why show me if you and your dad already know this is weird?" Alex was nervous. Why was Bax pushing this on her?

"Come on. I know you see things, I'm not dumb." Bax stood up and looked down on Alex, "Heck, half the time you talk to them too, pretend you're talking to that phone you got."

"What are you talking about, Bax? I don't see things. You must be watching horror movies again." This was too close for comfort. What did Bax think he knew?

"Oh, like you were really looking for some animal in the classroom? And I saw how you looked back into the room when you help Jill go to the nurse. Even my dad has noticed it. He says you got the sight. I told him he was nuts, but you do have it, don't you?" Bax knew. Alex was crushed. She had worked hard to keep anyone from finding out, and now one of her best friends and his dad knew! Well, at least they knew something. Maybe her magic was still secret, but for how long?

"Fine. I see the boogieman. Happy? I have the second sight, the third eye. Booga-booga and all that." Alex said angrily.

"I knew it! What does he look like?" Bax smiled as his suspicion was confirmed.

"You're kidding me?"

"Nope, you see something and I know it. What does the boogieman look like?" Baxter Mitchell was happier than he had any right to be at that moment.

One of mine. Delicious. Something thought from inside Alex's laptop.

"Ok. It's not a boogieman. No such thing."

"Right, so what is it Alex?" Bax was still thrilled his suspicions were correct.

"It's called an imp."

"Like a devil thing? Like in the horror movies?" Bax asked.

"No, not like in the movies. Well, like in some movies. Poltergeists are what some people call them. They're not really alive, they just act like it." Alex was trying to explain patiently and quietly. Bax's enthusiasm, however, could get loud.

"Quiet down, Bax, if my dad hears, we're both dead."

Alex was scared. She was not supposed to talk about the calligraphy magic or the spirits with anyone. Bax had figured out that Alex could see things that other people couldn't and once he got her to admit it, she just couldn't stop from telling him everything.

"Alright, but tell me more." Bax said quietly.

"The come from another place, the dead lands. Sometimes I hear it called the dead planes. I dunno what the difference is, but they are cruel and they feed on negative feelings like pain, confusion, and sickness." Alex recited the words as she often did during Grandfather Li's lessons.

"So is that what happened to Jill?"

"Jill, wait, how did you know that?" Alex asked.

"I told you, I saw you look back after Jill was sick all over the place. You just said they feed on sickness, so I figured it was feeding on her, you know, the barf and everything?" Bax said excitedly.

"What, no. Not that kind of sick, it feeds off illness. Not the products of illness. Like if I cry because I am sad, it doesn't lick my tears, it draws the sad feelings into itself and eats that." Alex explained.

"Well, isn't that good? I mean if it eats your sadness, doesn't the feeling go away?" Bax asked intuitively.

"You'd think so, but it doesn't work like that. The sadness actually gets worse. Sometimes, it can even get so bad that you don't get better."

"Oh, like when my bike cracked up, and I hit the pavement? I've taken worse falls, but that one hurt like a mother. Heck, my shoulder still hurts." Bax said.

"Exactly. And this particular imp, the one in your video, I think it's the same one that was in Jill's sandwich." Alex said.

"Ew. She ate an imp? Was it all chewy and nasty?" Bax looked physically revolted.

"What? No, why would you even think that? No, the imp goes into the essence of a thing and becomes part of it. It became the sandwich, although it was probably just the egg. Then it probably started messing with Jill's spirit and pulling on stomach nerves or something to make her miserable and throw up." Alex was thinking as she spoke, working through what probably happened at the geometry test.

"Weird. That breaks all kinds of laws of physics." Bax said.

"Yeah, magic does that." Alex agreed.

"Magic. Huh, so I guess you *were* looking for a unicorn. Too bad it was that imp and not a magical sparkle pony. So now what?"

"What do you mean?"

"Alex, we can't let that thing get away with it. Imp owes me a bike. I want it to pay for that and what it did to Jill." Bax said, crossing his arms firmly on his chest.

"You're right. We need to find the imp before it hurts anyone else." Alex agreed, "And we will make it pay for hurting Jill, right before we send it back to whatever hell it came from."

"And my bike. It will pay for that too. So what do we need? Rock salt? Shotgun?" asked Bax.

"I have all we need right here." Alex said, patting her calligraphy set, "Let's go find an imp."

R *un, run. Fun, fun. Break, break.*
The imp was loping down the street where it had broken Bax's mountain bike. It was very satisfied. Lots of good pain and suffering to eat up.

Sleep. Break, break. Tomorrow.

It curled up in the middle of the street and sank halfway into the pavement like a tumor on the road.

"So why are we going back to where that thing broke my bike?" Bax asked again.

"Because these things are creatures of habit. They don't really think enough to break a bad habit." Alex carried her calligraphy set in her backpack.

"Yeah, but Alex, I would think it would try to find some new place to mess things up."

"That's just it, Bax, imps don't think. At least not much. They wander around and around in the same places. That's why some places are haunted, the imps are too stupid to go somewhere else or cover up their tracks." Alex explained.

"Oh. So like a haunted house or 'the mystery spot.'" Baxter felt a little dumb.

"Alright, this is where you left to go home after the movie. Did you go straight home?" Alex asked as they stopped in front of her house.

"Yeah, pretty much right home. Down the hill, then around the corner, and then wham! That is where my bike cracked up." Bax said, starting off down the hill.

Alex followed, keeping her eyes wide open and looking for signs of the imp. It was about four in the afternoon, so traffic would start soon, but on the roads near their houses they still had some time before people and their cars started pulling into driveways.

Walking down the hill, Alex could feel a growing weakness in the world, but it was still quite small. The threads of reality were red, white and all the normal colors, but they seemed too thin and frayed as they walked towards the site of Bax's accident. The weakness made Alex nervous. There was a slight tingling on her skin, like goosebumps or ice water. Alex thought it was too slight for Baxter to feel, but who knew? He did notice something out of place in the video. Maybe he was a little sensitive to wrongness after hanging out with Alex and getting punked by a creature from the dead lands.

"Right around the bend, that's where the bike came apart." Bax said, pointing down the road.

"Alright, keep your eyes open." Alex said.

"For what? I can't see the thing. Maybe if I had a monitor for my camera." Bax said, holding out his home-made action cam.

"Sorry, I forgot. It would be great if that would work, tracking it with the camera. Just tell me if you feel anything weird." Alex said.

"You mean like mice climbing all over my back, because I've felt like that for the last five minutes." Bax said, suppressing a shiver.

"Really?" Alex walked around the curve in the road with Baxter, "I wasn't sure you could feel it."

"Oh, I feel it alright. Never felt anything like it before."

Alex stopped suddenly.

"What is it? Do you see something?"

"Yeah, the little creep is sleeping right in the middle of the road." Alex said, pointing to the imp sunk into the pavement.

"Really? It's daytime, why is it sleeping?"

"How would I know?" Alex asked.

"You're the magic girl. Why wouldn't you know?" Bax countered.

"Yeah, well you're the electronics guy, can't you just like hack that camera and send the video to your phone?" Alex gave up on dead pan delivery and went in hard for the sarcasm.

Bax didn't say anything at first, he just made a grunting sound.

"Well, no. I can't. But that's because I don't have the right kind of phone." Bax said.

"Excuses."

"But you do. Gimme your phone." Bax said as he pulled Alex's smartphone out of her back pocket. Alex didn't believe in purses and always carried her phone in her jeans pocket.

"Hey, don't!" Alex said, but it was too late. Bax swiped his finger across the screen and he was into the phone and syncing the WiFi with his camera in seconds.

"You really ought to set a passcode on this thing. Someone might steal it and mess up your phone or call East Timor or someplace like that." Bax said as he poked at the smartphone screen.

"Yeah, can't imagine what kind of jerk-face would do that." Alex said with a perfect deadpan delivery, even though she wasn't even trying.

"There!" Bax held the phone out to Alex triumphantly. He pointed the camera at the road where his bike had broken and tossed him on the pavement.

"Wow." Alex said softly.

"What? Do you see it?" Bax asked, excited.

"Yeah, it's right there on the video. That actually worked. But touch my phone like that again, and I'll kick you in the shins." Alex said.

"Alright, let me see!" Bax looked at the phone, "Yeah, there's the artifact again, but what's this text right here?"

Alex grabbed her phone as Baxter was speaking. Not because of what he said, but because she heard her smartphone demon.

I can see you too...

"Crap, crap, crap." Alex cursed.

"I can see you too? Who texted you? Is someone watching us?" Bax asked.

"No. I forgot it was in here." Alex started to panic.

"Forgot what? What are you talking about?" Now Bax was beginning to panic. His voice was raised louder than before and it woke the imp.

It is stirring.

"I forgot there's a demon in my phone." Alex blurted out before she thought about what she was saying.

"A what? A demon? You didn't think to tell me that before?" Bax's voice cracked as the volume of his voice went too loud. The imp was wide awake, and it saw Alex. It recognized her from school. It recognized she had power, and it was scared.

It is going to run. You should stop it.

"No demon, shut up. I want you out of my phone!" Alex yelled at her smartphone.

The imp began to run away.

Follow it.

Bax looked over Alex's shoulder, "I think your phone is right."

Baxter pointed his camera at the road and watched the artifact on the smartphone screen. He tracked it with the camera as it ran. Bax grabbed Alex's hand and pulled her after him.

"Come on, you watch the screen and tell me which way

it goes, that jerk owes me a new mountain bike!" Bax pulled Alex after the imp.

Alex snapped out of being angry at the demon in her phone and realized it and Bax were right. Time for anger later. Time to get the demon out of her phone later. Time to catch a nasty little creep now.

"He's headed to the right, go! Turn here!" Alex and Bax took off running after the imp.

The imp got away. Alex and Bax had been chasing after it, using Bax's homemade action camera, Alex's smartphone, and hints from the smartphone demon but the imp was fast. It had run around a house and dove into the bushes on the fence line between the house and its neighbor. After a few minutes of looking through the bushes, Alex caught sight of it again, heading towards the scene of the mountain bike crash. Alex and Bax followed it into the road, but then a car was coming at Alex and Bax from the other direction and they had to jump out of the way and onto the sidewalk to avoid being hit by the car. The imp was on the other side of the road where there were trees and no sidewalk. It jumped into the trees and disappeared. Alex and Bax tried to find the imp by continuing up the road, but by the time they got to Alex's house, the imp was gone.

"Where do you think that little creep went?" Bax asked.

"Well, maybe the school? Or maybe to where it came into our world. I don't know." Alex looked around, trying to find the imp in the video on her phone. She could see it without the camera and the smartphone, but then Bax and the smartphone demon couldn't see it. Now she just needed to find it and they could chase it down again.

It would be best to rest and make a plan.

"Shut up, you stalking hacker prick." Alex said.

"Dude, uncool." Bax was shocked.

"Not you, the phone demon. It's a jerk, and I hate it."

"Well, as long as you weren't talking about me, but I think your phone is right."

"Shut up, Bax."

J ill was home, sick. Her calculator was wrecked, her confidence was ruined, and she had barfed up her favorite breakfast. Today was a bad day for Jill Duffy, but finally she was starting to feel like herself again.

"Jill, do you want some more tea?" her mom, Liz, called to her from the kitchen.

"Ugh, no Mom, no tea!" Jill groaned.

"No tea, please?" her mom hinted.

"Ugh, fine. No Mom, no tea, puh-lease!"

"That's better, you may be sick but manners still matter," she said, "I'll bring you some later."

Jill buried her head in her pillow. She felt better, but only a little. Even if her face was not covered, she still couldn't have seen the imp loping back into her room. It jumped into Jill's hairbrush, where earlier in the morning it had toyed with Jill's hair. It didn't feel the need to stay in the brush.

The imp looked at Jill, lying face down on the bed, and it sneered. It had been fun to toy with Jill, but now it sensed she was miserable and already miserable people were not as much fun. The imp saw the graphing calculator. That had been a good place to be, so strange and lifelike. The imp jumped into the calculator and became part of it again. The calculator was familiar to it this time. It knew better how the machine worked, and it started to make it do things. *Turn off, turn on.* Draw pictures on the screen. It wasn't breaking, but it was almost breaking, so it was almost fun. *Good enough.*

Jill felt better a couple hours later. Better than that, Jill was a tiny bit angry, and she wanted to talk about it to someone. Maybe yell a little, maybe not, she would decide after she went to see Alex. Alex was a good person for venting. She listened most of the time, even when Jill knew that Alex didn't want to listen. Jill grabbed her backpack, tossed the calculator in it like always, and headed out to go across the street and see her best friend.

"Mom, I'm heading over to Alex's, bye!" she called as she left the house.

Jill looked down the street. It was empty like usual. The street was a smaller side street, and it ended in a cul-de-sac, so there weren't a lot of cars on it at any given time. She walked over to see Alex and knocked on the door with purpose.

"Come on in, it's open!" Alex called. She was looking out her window and could see Jill at the front door. Jill opened the door and went in.

Alex heard her come up the steps, loudly. Bax was still in Alex's room. They had returned from chasing the imp about a half hour earlier. After they lost the imp, they had retraced their steps. They found nothing, so they headed back to the school to check there. The smartphone demon was not happy. It wanted to make a plan, not wander around for an hour or two. Alex was also not happy, mostly about the smartphone demon, so there was no way she was going to listen to its suggestions. Bax just followed Alex because it was easier than arguing with her. He thought the smartphone demon was right.

Jill walked into the room and threw her backpack on Alex's bed. She saw Bax and looked at Alex.

"Oh, hi Bax. You two doing homework?" Jill asked. She didn't care, Bax could listen to Jill be angry too.

"Video." Bax said, holding up the action camera.

"Oh, not again! You're not going to be an Internet star, you know that, right?" Jill said.

"Har har. You're just jealous of my skills."

"What's up, Jill? Are you feeling ok?" Alex asked.

"No, I am *not* feeling ok. I am angry. I mean, what the hell happened? I eat the same thing every day, why did I have to get sick on the day of the test?" Jill began to vent.

"I dunno, maybe because jam and eggs are disgusting together?" Bax said, raising his eyebrows to an implausible height.

"Shut up, Bax." Jill and Alex said together.

"And after I studied so hard. I was even doing problems the night before and nothing was working. Every time I tried one of mom's old problems, the answer was wrong. It was like I couldn't do it right, but I know I was. Or am I just an idiot?" Jill said.

"Shut up, Bax." Alex said preemptively.

Bax closed his mouth.

"Wait, everything was going wrong?" Alex asked.

"Yes, everything. I'm still mad. I mean look at me, I'm a mess, even my hair!"

"Even your hair?" Alex asked.

"Yeah, what do you mean even your hair?" Bax asked, thinking he knew where Alex was going.

"This morning, couldn't you tell? I never do just a pony tail. I couldn't get my hair to behave." Jill said, looking at

Alex and Bax. They knew something, she was sure, but Jill thought they might just be making fun of her. Something felt wrong, off. They were making fun of her and that made Jill mad. She could feel a wave of anger coming off her and into the room.

"You're laughing at me! After all, I went through today. You two are laughing at me!" Jill said indignantly.

"Jill, no. Tell us what else went wrong. What were you doing when stuff wasn't working right?" Alex said, trying to calm Jill.

"No! You don't care what happened to me. And you! Bax, you're just jealous and want to do better than me! I thought you were both my friends!" The waves of anger were heavy now, Jill felt cornered.

"You two, you were waiting here for me, waiting to blame me for everything that happened! Like I wanted to throw up all over everything! Like I wanted my stupid," Jill struggled to get her backpack open, "stupid calculator to go crazy!"

Jill was not even thinking anymore, she grabbed the calculator and threw it at Alex. Alex ducked and the graphing calculator hit the wall and fell to the floor in several pieces. Jill was never violent, not in a serious way. Something was clearly wrong, but Alex, Bax, and Jill didn't have time to think about it because the imp burst out of the broken calculator and leaped at Jill.

"Ah, what the hell is that? Get it off!" Jill screamed slapping at the imp. Red and blue smoke was visible coming off Jill.

The imp was ruffling and pulling her hair, it was more powerful than before and it wanted to break things! Alex and Bax were stunned, they could all clearly see the imp. Alex saw threads of reality flowing from the room and from

Jill into the imp, pulling the smoke with them. The little creep was feeding on the weakness in the room and on Jill's anger.

Bax jumped back, the imp looked a lot different to his own eyes than it did as a video artifact. The imp appeared to be covered in some sort of slime and it was all knotted muscles and knobby joints. And it moved fast!

"Crap!" Alex said as she tried to get a máobǐ from her calligraphy set.

Bind it. The smartphone demon thought to the screen of the phone. Alex heard it.

"I can't, I need a matched pair of wood blocks!" Alex yelled at the phone as she wrote the five strokes of dǎ in mid-air with her máobǐ. The character knocked the imp off Jill, but it pulled some of her hair out as it flew across the room. Jill cried out in pain.

"Whoa!" Bax said as he turned the action camera on.

"Get back Jill!" Alex yelled.

Use the machine it was in.

"What?" Alex said as she twisted threads of reality and wrote another hànzi in the shape of the word 'out'. The imp was shaken, but it pulled more magic from the weakness and began to break the hànzi.

Bax looked at the smartphone and read the text.

"Matched blocks you said? Here, use this!" Bax said, scooping up one of the pieces of the calculator and tossing it to Alex.

Smart child.

"What? Does that look like wood?" Alex said, catching the piece.

Just do it, Alex!

"Alright!" Alex said as the imp threw off the hànzi. It looked at Jill, then at Bax and Alex. It was filled with rage.

Alex thrust the piece in front of her, holding it in her right hand. She began to move her máobǐ in an elaborate pattern around the piece, then pushed it towards the imp. Alex wrote the hànzi for 'contain evil' and the characters flowed from Alex's máobǐ and into the broken circuit board.

The imp leaped at Alex to attack her, not realizing what Alex was doing. Too late, it understood. Alex began binding the imp to the circuit board, and the imp was drawn in.

The piece didn't look like two wood blocks to the imp, it didn't understand what was happening.

Break, break! No! Break, break!

In an instant, the imp was gone, drawn into the circuit board and trapped.

"Well, that worked." Bax said, relieved.

"Yeah," Alex said, unbelieving, "But how the hell did that work?"

"What was that?" Jill said, crying.

"Better still, what the hell is going on in this house!" said Alex's dad, standing in the doorway.

———

"So let me get this straight, you saw an imp." Alex's dad pointed at all three of them.

"Yes." Alex and Bax said.

"I guess, if that's the thing that pulled my hair." Jill said quietly.

"And you had your mountain bike broken by it." He said, pointing at Bax.

"Yes, sir." Bax said.

"And you had it stuck in your calculator." He said, pointing at Jill.

"I guess."

"And in your sandwich."

"I guess." Jill was still upset, Alex could tell.

"And you threw it up. In school. During your geometry test." Alex's dad didn't see that Jill was upset as he sorted out the problem in his head.

"I guess, if that little s-" Jill said as Alex clapped her hand over Jill's mouth before she said a wrong word. Alex didn't care if Jill cursed, but Alex's dad did. He was not good with bad language, a side effect of being the son-in-law of Grandma Akeyo.

"Yes, Dad, the imp was in Jill's sandwich, and in her calculator, and it broke Bax's mountain bike." Alex said quickly, covering for the almost used curse word.

"Right, and you two," Alex's dad didn't notice what Jill almost said and kept speaking.

"You two," pointing at Alex and Bax, "saw it in the road and tracked it with a homemade camera and your smartphone."

"Yes, sir." Said Bax, "And then I synced the camera to the phone and then the smartphone d-"

Alex shushed Bax. She didn't want her dad to know about the smartphone demon. Bax shushed.

"Right. And then you lost it and it went back to Jill's house and jumped into her calculator?" Alex's dad was on the trail of the imp and would not be distracted.

"And when Jill came over to visit, she got mad and the imp broke out of the calculator. It attacked Jill, and you thought fast and used the calculator circuit board to bind the imp. Is that all correct?" Alex's dad looked at the circuit board on the coffee table. It sat on a piece of paper with three circles drawn around it in ink and the Chinese elements scribed around the perimeter.

"Yes. That's exactly what happened." Alex said, putting

her arms on Jill's and Bax's shoulders hoping they got the hint, "Right, guys?"

"Ah, yes." said Jill.

"Yes, ma'am." said Bax, answering Alex and not her dad.

"Ok then! Let's call Grandma Akeyo and Grandfather Li and banish this sucker back to the dead lands." Alex's dad announced, proudly.

Alex was mortified. Grandma Akeyo and Grandfather Li would lose their minds if they knew Alex let an imp attack normal people, let alone that she let it escape and that both Jill and Bax had actually seen the imp with their own eyes. No, that was not an option.

"Sure, Dad, let's do that. In fact, why don't I just take this little thing over to them instead? You know that they like to keep magic in the training room." Alex said quickly.

"Actually, that's true. So we can all go over there and get this all sorted then, ok?" Dad was not cooperating.

"No, that's ok. I'll do it, maybe Grandfather Li can give me a special lesson." Alex suggested.

"Oh, yeah. He would, wouldn't he? I'd better stay here. John always yells at me when I stay for the magic lessons. 'No magic boy should go home,' he says."

"Among other things," Alex agreed.

"Yes, among other things." Alex's dad seemed sad as he said the words, "You three go, have fun. Do some magic. I'll start on dinner."

"Great, Dad, see you in a bit." Alex said, taking the circuit board and pulling Jill and Bax out of the kitchen with her as she left.

"That was scary." Bax said.

"Scary? Dad's not scary at all, he's a pussycat." Said Alex.

"No, I think Bax meant it was scary how you wrapped your dad around your finger." Jill said.

"Oh, that. Yeah, I guess I have a talent for that sort of thing." Alex said, smirking in a mildly scary manner, "Come on, let's go banish an imp."

———

"Dad, I'm going to get my things!" Alex said as she left the living room, wrapping the circuit board in the binding paper, "come on, let's send this imp back where it came from."

"Is this a good idea?" Bax asked, following Alex to her room.

"Can I kick it before we send it back?" asked Jill.

"Ok, Bax open my laptop while I start on the circle. Jill, hold my phone."

"Right, what do you want me to do, Alex?" Bax asked.

"Go to the documents folder and open the file that says 'dumb lessons,' then wait." Alex instructed.

"What about me, when do I get to kick it?" Jill asked.

"No kicking. Jill, get my calligraphy kit over there on the desk."

Alex bent over, looking under her bed. She pulled out a plastic box and opened it. Inside were a few folded pieces of cloth, Alex took the green one out and spread it on her bed. There were three circles sewn into the green blanket, the threads were gold.

"Ok, I opened the file, now what?" Bax asked, "Everything in here is just a bunch of weird symbols."

"Here's your calligraphy kit. Why can't I kick it?" Jill asked, annoyed.

"You can't kick it because it is not coming out of this

piece of calculator again." Alex said as she placed the circuit board in the middle of the three golden threaded circles and discarded the paper wrapping.

"Now, Bax, scroll down to the section with the simple symbols and show it to me."

Bax turned the laptop towards Alex, showing her the simpler hànzi characters.

"Jill, give me the white ink stick and the ink stone, ok?" Alex asked.

"Here."

"I need some water too, in the glass on the desk."

Alex took the white bar and the stone block from Jill and began rubbing the ink into the stone. She had Jill pour a little of the water from the glass into the well of the stone as she ground the ink stick. The white tin oxide-based ink began to take liquid form. Alex put the ink stick aside and dipped a máobǐ into the white liquid.

Alex copied the hànzi from her laptop screen onto the cloth, finishing twenty characters around the outside circle. Alex asked for the red ink stick and a second stone. She began to grind that ink down into the well of the second stone. Alex wrote ten more hànzi inside the next circle in the red ink. Finally, Alex switched back to the white ink and wrote the five Chinese elements inside the final circle.

You made a mistake.

"Shut up, demon." Alex said, "Don't listen to the phone."

"Listen to what? The phone is off." Jill said.

"Don't read it, either. The phone is a liar."

"What?" Jill was confused.

"Now, everyone be quiet."

I really think you should correct that circle.

"Shut up, demon."

"No one is talking, Alex." Said Jill.

"Shh." Bax said to Jill, she is thinking.

Alex closed her eyes and began to pull threads of reality out of the air with her fingers. The wrongness in the room began to increase. Alex could feel the weakness in the world as she began to draw the threads into yarn and draw power to her through the weakness. The wrongness increased.

Stop. You wrote demon wrong.

"Shut up, demon. And no, I didn't."

"Who the hell said that?" Jill asked, looking around.

"Yeah, Alex, I heard that too. Was that the smartphone demon?" Bax asked.

"Smartphone demon? There's a demon in the phone?" Jill said, dropping Alex's smartphone on the floor.

Ouch.

"My phone!" Alex squeaked, reaching for the phone, "Crap."

Alex lost her concentration when the phone hit the floor. The binding broke and suddenly the imp was standing on the green cloth, dazed. The wrongness in the room was suddenly everywhere. Translucent threads began to form in the room, like strings hanging in the air. The threads thickened and became heavy.

"What the heck is this stuff?" Bax said, his voice pitching high.

"Crap, it's magic. These are the strings that tie up the world. Don't touch them if you can avoid it." said Alex, "I screwed up!"

Something is coming.

"What, what is coming, demon?" Alex cried.

I do not know. Close the binding.

"On it!" Alex said, raising her hands above her head and clapped them together.

The imp came to its senses when it heard the clap. Looking around, it saw Bax, Jill, and then Alex, and it was angry. The imp leaped at Alex and knocked her to the floor. It tore at her with its hands.

"Oh hell no!" Jill kicked the imp in the face and sent it sprawling on the floor.

"Kick it again!" Alex said wiping some blood from her lip.

"Oh, now I get to kick it?" Jill said as she kicked at the imp as hard as she could.

Alex sat up and looked at the green cloth. The smartphone demon was right, the character for demon, guǐ, was incorrect. She reached for the máobǐ covered in white ink and grabbed a hold of it with her fist. She had to correct the character, fast.

The imp saw what Alex was trying to do and caught Jill's foot with its hands. The kicks didn't really hurt it, but being touched by a person annoyed the imp. Normally people couldn't touch something from the dead lands, but with so much magic in the room, the imp was becoming a solid thing. It pushed Jill away by her foot, twisting it as it tried to get to Alex.

"No way, buddy!" Bax said as he hit the imp with the only thing he had on hand, Alex's laptop. Bax connected the laptop with the imp's head, making a sickly sound, much like crushing aluminum foil into a ball. Bax bought Alex just enough time to correct the symbol, and as she did, the imp was pulled back towards the circuit board along one of the thickened threads in the room.

Once the imp was in the center of the three circles again, Alex clapped her hands over her head and brought them down in front of her chest and then flung her hands apart. When the motion of Alex's hands stopped at the furthest point from her body, the imp was simply gone.

———

F*eeling, I have feeling. Down the threads, faster, before the hole closes. Through the hole, now, while it is open. Breathe again. For the first time in so long. Children. Vile thing. So much power in the threads. Now, into the vile thing while it is unaware. Fight the children before they close the hole. They kick. They fight back. Good, they will suffer for it. Strange, an odd pain. Many pairs of matched things, pulling me in. A new place? A strange place. There are threads here, but not of magic. These threads lead to places. No, the hole is closing! The vile thing is gone. But I remain.*

And I see you, hiding in the box.

———

"G ot your things, Alex?" Dad called from downstairs.

"Is it gone?" Bax asked.

"Yeah. It's gone."

"At least I got to kick it." Jill was very proud of herself.

"I can drive you over, if you like?"

"S'ok Dad, we're gonna walk!" Alex yelled back.

"We should go, or your dad's going to get suspicious." Jill said.

"Right, grab your stuff and let's go." Alex said.

Bax picked up his camera and Jill got her backpack.

They headed downstairs and out the front door. Once out, they started walking with no particular destination in mind.

"So where to? If we go to your Grandfather's place, he'll know something is up." Bax said.

"Your place, then Jill and I can walk back. By then, Dad should have forgotten when we left. I'll still have to go visit Grandfather, but I can fake that."

"Ok, let's go. I'm feeling much better now that I got back at that jerk." Jill said.

"Yeah, you actually hit that thing pretty good." Bax said appreciatively.

"You weren't too shabby with the laptop, either."

"Yeah, quick thinking. And if you broke my laptop, you know you're gonna replace it, right?" Alex said sharply.

"Oh, yeah, about that. Bax's accident insurance doesn't cover supernatural encounters. I am afraid you are going to have to file all sorts of special forms!"

They all laughed as they walked down the street towards Baxter Mitchell's house.

All three of you are very strange.

"You are one to talk, stalking hacker prick." Alex said.

"Who are you talking to?" Jill asked.

"Oh, sorry. My smartphone was talking. He's a jerk and a stalker and he hacked my phone." Alex explained.

"But I heard it back in your room. Why can't I hear it now?" Jill asked.

"I dunno, maybe there just isn't enough magic here. It was positively thick with magic back there."

"And what do you mean, it hacked your phone? Alex, that is so not cool." Jill said.

"Well, not exactly."

"What do you mean?"

"Brace yourself Jill, this is not your normal situation." Bax said.

"Uh-huh. Ok, tell me from the beginning Alex, who hacked your phone?" Jill was serious.

"A demon."

"Stop."

"No, really, a demon got into my phone. He is a stalker and a prick. That is his new nickname, stalking hacker prick." Alex explained, achieving her dead pan delivery.

I did not stalk you nor did I hack your phone, whatever that means. You bound me to this box. Delightful as it is, I am trapped here.

"Shut up, stalker." Alex said.

"No, stop. What do you mean a demon is in your phone? Like fire and brimstone, hell and devils, and all that religious stuff?" Jill asked.

"No, nothing like that." Alex said, "A demon from the dead lands. It's really more of a spirit left over from the life's work of a person. Usually an obsessed person."

"What does that even mean?" Jill asked with a look of confusion on her face.

"That's what I said." said Bax.

"Look, we all leave a path in the world. We make some things better and some things worse. Better things strengthen the world, worse things make it weaker. Over a lifetime, everything you do etches a pattern into the world and that ends up in the dead lands. Spirits are made there, and they take on the patterns people etch into the world." Alex recited.

"That sounds like babble to me." Jill said.

"Yeah, me too. But Grandfather Li is very convincing. He's taught me all about this since I was a little girl, but honestly, when I listen to myself tell it to you, I think it's nuts."

"It is nuts, but that jerk broke my bike, so I believe it." Box said, rubbing his shoulder.

"And after my day, at least I got to kick it." Jill smiled.

"Now that we got rid of the imp, I just need to get the demon out of my smartphone." Alex held up her smartphone, frowning at it.

I like it in this box. It is a good maze.

"Shut up, stalking hacker prick." Alex said.

"What I don't get is how the imp ended up in the world in the first place." Bax said.

They were almost to Bax's house, and it was beginning to get dark.

"Yeah, that might have been my fault." Alex said.

"Wait, your fault? How was it your fault?" Jill sounded irritated.

"So, remember that day when we went to see the Victor Dallas movie?"

"Yeah, what does that have to do with this being your fault?" Jill asked.

"Well, I skipped out on Grandfather Li's lesson and I might have accidentally left a hole to the dead lands open."

"So? Is that how that imp got into the world?" Jill asked, "If it is, you are so dead."

"Well, I don't know. Grandma Akeyo said she and Grandfather Li closed the hole, but I can't think of any other way it could have gotten here."

"Yeah, but they would have seen it, wouldn't they? I mean, they are the real experts, right?" Jill prodded.

"Yes, they are. I am 'not clever enough' to do anything right. At least that's what Grandfather Li always tells me."

"That is not cool," Bax said, "You were amazing when you sent that little jerk back to hell."

"It isn't hell, Bax. That's a myth. The dead lands are another place, another here but not as good. Like a rough draft of the world where everything sucks." Alex said.

You are quite correct.

"Shut up, stalker."

"That demon should keep quiet if it's only going to talk to you. It's rude." Jill said, annoyed.

"Well, then maybe the imp didn't come through the hole you made, Alex. I mean if your grandparents didn't see it when they closed the hole, could it have really gotten in that way?" Bax asked.

It is possible.

"No, it isn't demon, no way they could have missed an imp."

Unless they were angry. Did you make them angry, little one?

"Excuse me? Little one? Shut up, stalker." Alex began to get mad.

"You are starting to sound crazy, Alex. Stop talking to yourself." Jill said.

"I'm talking to the stalking, smartphone hacking, demon jerk in my phone!" Alex said defensively.

"I know. But you still sound like you're nuts, talking to yourself." Jill was enjoying making Alex peeved.

"The way I see it, this is both of y'all's fault." Bax said.

"What?" both girls said indignantly.

"If you didn't have a girl-crush on Vic Dallas," Bax said, poking his finger at Jill, "And you weren't such a slacker when it comes to your lessons with your folks, none of this would have happened."

"Point that finger at me again Bax, and I will bite!" Alex said.

"How is liking Victor Dallas my fault?" Jill asked.

"You talked Alex into ditching her lesson to see the movie. You are the accomplice." Bax said, "And you, Alexandra Lissett, are the culprit. I find you both guilty and sentence you to getting me a new mountain bike."

"Yeah, and you owe me an 'A plus' in Geometry." Jill said, piling on.

"No way to both of you! If it came through the hole I made, it's Grandfather Li's fault for not catching it!" Alex laughed.

The trio arrived at Bax's house, the lights were on inside.

"This is where I get off." Bax said and opened the front door, "Peace."

"Hey, is that you, Baxter?" a deep voice called from inside the house.

"Yeah Dad, just saying bye to Alex and Jill." Bax replied.

"Oh, hello girls." Baxter Mitchell's dad pulled the door wide open and stood looking at the three friends.

"Hey Mr. Mitchell." Alex and Jill said in unison.

"Alright children of the creepy corn, cut that out right now, you know it creeps me out." Warren Mitchell was a big man, mostly belly. He filled the doorway and seemed more like Santa Claus than network engineer.

"Yes, Mr. Mitchell." Alex and Jill said again.

"Fine, come on in and let's have a snack, if that is alright with you, Baxter?" Mr. Mitchell said as he turned and led the way into the house.

"Fine with me, Alex, Jill?" Bax said.

"Sure, I'm actually pretty hungry." Magic made Alex

both tired and hungry and she was just beginning to realize how hungry she really was.

"Yeah, me too. Got any pizza, Mr. Mitchell? I like pineapple." Jill said, bouncier than she had been the entire day. Kicking the imp had helped.

Baxter Mitchell and his father, Warren Mitchell lived in more of an electronics store than a house. Warren was a network engineer at a cell phone company and Baxter took after his father when it came to electronics. They both loved tinkering with devices and making their own inventions. Computers and racks of electronic equipment were scattered throughout the house. Jill loved visiting, not because of the electronics, but because pizza was a staple food of the Mitchell household.

"No pizza yet, but I'll order one right now." Mr. Mitchell said and pressed a giant button on the wall. The push button was salvaged from an old upright arcade game, but inside it had a microprocessor and a WiFi card that sent an order through the Internet to the local pizza place for an extra large Hawaiian pizza. Mr. Mitchell pushed the button again and instead of one, an order for two extra large Hawaiian pizzas was sent out. Twenty-five minutes later the doorbell rang and pizza came to everyone's rescue.

CHAPTER FOUR

A lex returned home late after pizza with Bax and Jill at Bax's house. Mr. Mitchell was always good for a pizza as long as it was no more than once or twice a week. Alex thought he was the coolest dad ever, and not just because he got pizza delivered literally with the press of a button. Mr. Mitchell was mellow and more like Alex, Jill, and Baxter than the other dads she knew. Of course, Alex really only knew her dad and Mr. Mitchell since Jill's dad wasn't around. The competition for best dad was a little rough for Donald Land and fairly easy for Warren 'I get pizza at the push of a button' Mitchell.

I do not understand pizza.

"Of course you don't, you're a spirit demon. You don't eat." Alex said as she flopped down on her bed. She had eaten more than her fair share of pizza. The magic she had worked earlier in the day had taken a lot out of her. Hawaiian pizza was a perfect recharge. The cheese and ham proteins helped rebuild her body, the carbs in the crust gave her a long-term energy recharge, and the pineapple gave her sugars and vitamins for a quick recovery. Alex had convinced herself of this two years ago when she and Jill first discovered Hawaiian pizza and there was no way she would ever give up her belief in the recuperative power of pizza.

You spent too much time with your friends and the fat man.

"Don't call Mr. Mitchell fat. He doesn't like that." Alex said sharply.

There is a weakness in the world. You must mend it.

"I don't care right now. I'm full." Alex said.

That is irrational.

"You are a spirit demon and I am a calligraphy witch. How is any of this rational?"

You are irrational. And you are not a witch. A witch is completely different from you. You use calligraphic magic to spin the fabric of the world in your hands and write it down to make it a reality.

"Shut up, stupid stalking hacker." Alex groaned, "You're ruining my digestion."

You must heal the weakness. You must mend it.

"Hey, wait a minute now, stalker. Why do you care? I would think you'd want more weakness in the world." Alex sat up and looked at the smartphone on her desk.

I prefer order.

"It can't be that simple. What are you hiding?"

I am content. I am hiding nothing.

"Come on, first you help us with the imp, now you want me to mend the weakness in the fabric of the world. You are clearly terrible at your job." Alex was mocking the smartphone demon now, and it amused her. She imagined it squirming inside the phone.

Not all spirit demons prefer chaos. I prefer order, among other things. And I like it in this maze. Your phone is a fasci-

nating place to live. It is a well-ordered maze. I feel safe in the box.

"What? You are a weirdo, stalker." Alex said and fell back onto her bed, "I have a weirdo, stalker, hacking prick in my smartphone. You owe me rent, by the way."

What is rent?

"Shut up, weirdo stalker."

I am not a stalker.

"You are still a weirdo. Now shut up, I'm going to sleep."

What about the weakness?

"Good night. Weirdo."

Alex was tired and didn't particularly feel like discussing weaknesses and magic with the demon in her smartphone. She did however make a mental note to find a name for it. Something other than 'hacking stalker prick.' As appropriate as it felt to say it, Alex could understand how that might not be the best way to talk about her phone in public. She put her wireless headset on and started playing some quiet music on her phone once it was synced up. After a few minutes, Alex pulled the headset off and just let it play on top of her covers, barely audible.

"I'll change the demon's stupid name in the morning." Alex said to herself as she yawned. Sleep came quickly after she decided to find her smartphone demon a new name.

Usually, Alex's dreams were boring recaps of the last few days events. Although Jill talked about vivid dreams that came alive off the covers of the latest romance novel, Alex never had anything interesting in her dreams. To be fair, Alex doubted that Jill had ever even read a romance novel, let alone had dreams about overly muscled men with the innate inability to wear a full set of clothes. Alex thought it was more likely that Jill dreamed about being a lawyer or the next winner of the Fields Medal for her outstanding future contributions to mathematics.

Sitting in Warren Mitchell's living room, surrounded by monitors and full boxes of pineapple and extra cheese pizza was a comforting way to spend a day. Alex walked over to a random box of pizza and retrieved a piping hot, perfect piece of pie. Of course, it was actual pie this time, complete with vanilla ice cream melting into the apple and cherry goodness. Alex did wonder why no one else was around, but that thought slipped away with the first bite of pie. The taste was unusually bright. The monitors were also a bit brighter than normal, but these things happen.

Bax was speaking to her, despite not being in the room. He was saying something about checking the Internet connection and perhaps the phone lines too. Bax was a worrier. Another bite of apple-cherry took Alex's mind away from Bax's worries.

"I really think you should check the Internet," Bax said again. He was back in the room, with a slice of pizza in hand.

"Nope. Pie."

"The phones could also be a problem. Do you have phones, Alex?" Bax was eating and talking. His smartphone rang, he answered.

"No, your father says you do not have any normal phones. Everything is voice over Internet protocol." Bax finished his pizza and went to get some pie from the same box Alex got hers from.

"VoIP. No one says 'Internet protocol,' even I know that, Baxter Mitchell." Alex was almost annoyed but mostly just embarrassed for Bax. It was not often she had a better understanding of technology than Baxter.

If it is 'VoIP' then I assume it is also over the Internet. I must strongly suggest you check the Internet and perhaps close it.

Baxter seemed to be repeating what he heard on his smartphone. Between bites of pie, of course. Alex went back for another slice, but when she opened the box, it was empty.

Alex checked another box, empty. Another empty as well. All the boxes were empty now, Alex knew it intuitively. The light was getting brighter. Baxter was fading away, getting washed away by the glare coming from the monitors. Alex could only see the black smartphone and a bit of Baxter not washed out from the light.

One of the monitors blew out, Alex heard the pop of electronic components overloading. Pizza and pie smells were now replaced with ozone. The acrid, bitter smell was one of the downsides of being friends with the Mitchells. Ozone was a terrible smell.

Alex, it is important that you get up.

"I am standing."

No, Alex. Bax was almost completely gone, only the smartphone was there, hanging in the air.

Alex's stomach began to hurt.

Please get up. Awake. Maxwell is breaking its binding.

The smell changed from ozone to burning plastic.

Alex! Get up now!

Alex awaken from her dream, sitting bolt upright. There was fire.

Fire! On her bed, on her!

Alex tossed the blankets off, putting out the small fire that had started from her wireless headset she had taken off before she fell asleep. The glare from her laptop was bright and hurt Alex's eyes as she blinked away the sleep.

"What the hell?" Alex said out loud.

Not hell. Maxwell. Maxwell made your headset catch fire.

"What the *hell?*" Alex said again, looking away from the laptop and at the smoldering blanket and headset.

You are being repetitive.

"Shut up. What the *hell* and who the *hell* is Maxwell?"

The brightness of the laptop increased, wrongness hung in the air. Alex suddenly was aware of just how wrong her room felt.

I cannot keep Maxwell out long, bind it.

"Out of what? Stalker, is that you?" Alex was still foggy from her dream.

Yes. The battery in the box. Maxwell caused your headset battery to catch fire.

"What the *hell?*"

You are being repetitive again. Stay away from batteries.

The smell of burning plastic wafted through Alex's room. There was more fire, but where? Alex jerked her head around to search for the fire. There, under the desk. Her laptop's power brick!

"Oh no, I need that!" Alex shouted as she jumped down to pull the power brick's plug out of the wall.

Electricity arced from the outlet as Alex pulled the plug out by its cord. A shivering pulse of electricity shot out from the wall and touched Alex's arm. She screamed in pain and flopped on the floor.

Alex?

Alex did not respond to the smartphone demon.

Alex? Are you hurt?

Yes. I hurt her. You are next. Another demon spoke.

Oh, hell *no.* Thought the smartphone demon, being repetitive.

I *t would be in your best interest to wake up now.*

Alex pushed herself up off the floor. Her head was hurting and her arm felt as though it was raw and burned. She was sure that she had only been out for a moment, but then why did it sound like a construction site in her room? Alex looked up and instantly wished she had been dreaming about silly pizza and apple-cherry pie.

The screen on Alex's laptop was flaring a bright, eye-straining white. Stretching out of the screen was an arm, or at least something arm-like and nasty looking. It appeared pocked and mottled with burns and open sores. The white light washed out much of the details, so Alex was not really sure if it was just the texture of the skin or something else. Alex shook her head in disbelief, because arms or arm-like somethings did *not* reach out of laptop screens on a regular basis.

"Bad dream," Alex mumbled.

Alex, you are not dreaming. I need your help.

"Not a dream?" Alex's brain started working a little faster, "Oh, crap."

Not a dream. You are correct. Please stop the demon. I cannot hold it back much longer.

"Demon? Oh, crap. Is that arm a demon?"

It is the arm of a demon. No, it is the arm, shoulder and half of the chest of a particular demon now. Please move faster.

The smartphone demon was right, there was more than just an arm coming out of the laptop now, it was a whole body. That's when the smell hit Alex, a dusty, burning tire smell. It was also when the demon's foot hit the floor with a dull thump. Alex tried to scramble away, still on the floor where she had fallen.

"Oh hell no! What is that?"

It is still as I said, a demon. A very large and powerful demon.

The demon's back was to Alex and her smartphone was on the desk, just next to her laptop. The laptop was no longer plugged in, but her cell phone was still connected to the outlet. Alex remembered pulling the cord on her laptop and unplugging it, then receiving the strongest electrical shock of her life. Electricity had leaped out of the outlet and crawled up her arm, stunning her momentarily. The shock and black out was enough time for the demon standing in front of her to emerge from the laptop. The demon that was now turning to face Alex, no, not Alex, the demon was facing her smartphone.

"No way, jerk-face, that's my phone!" Alex yelled at the demon as she saw it swing its mottled arm down to smash her phone.

Alex jumped up to defend her phone, putting herself between the demon's arm and its target. Alex didn't close her eyes. She stared directly at the demon, seeing its face for the first time. The arm stopped moving.

Delicious.

"Pervert."

Alex twisted her fingers around some threads and wrote hànzi with her finger in mid-air between her and the upraised demon arm. 'Ān quán' for safety. She didn't take her eyes off the demon's face with its dull, sunken eye sockets and obscenely bulging eyes buried in them. The light from the laptop faded and was drawn into the hànzi, filling the lines Alex had sketched with light. The air between Alex and the demon exploded as the demon touched the hànzi with one disgusting finger.

Alex was thrown back into her closed door. The demon hit the opposite wall hard. Alex swore she heard her smartphone yelp. In a bare half of a breath, the demon was across the room and its hands slammed down on Alex's shoulders. Her back hit the door hard, and Alex thought she heard the wood crack.

Look out!

"Too late, stalker. Try helping next time." Alex was mad, sarcasm was a good defense.

Child. Power. I will eat it out of your kidneys.

"Ew, gross." Alex said as she raised her knee fast, going for the stomach or any vital spot it might have. Her knee hit the demon, but it didn't seem to care. Instead, the demon shook Alex by the shoulders and slammed her into the door again. Alex definitely heard the wood of the door break. Dad would be so angry.

Use your magic, Alex.

"Use it yourself, stalker!" Alex yelled back as she tried to write 'ān quán' in the air again.

Nothing happened.

Silly fool. The same word is no good twice.

"Oh crap."

How about this, then?

Electricity shot out of the outlet the smartphone was plugged into, racing to wrap around the leg of the demon. The shock was not as great of a surge as the one that had knocked Alex out, but it certainly was enough to get the demon's attention.

You again? The demon turned back to face the smartphone.

Alex wrote a different hànzi with her fingers, 'bǎo hù'

this time, directly against the skin of the demon's leg. The hànzi screamed, and so did the demon.

Very good, Alex. Don't let up.

"Oh hell, no. Come in my room. Zap me? Try to break my phone? It's on, pervert-boy."

Alex rapidly wrote out three more hànzi in the air between her and the demon, each one different, each one drawing light from the air into its lines. Alex widened her legs, standing firm and solid on the ground. Inhaling deeply, Alex pushed the hànzi, one after the other, towards the demon. The characters barely moved, then at once shot out at the demon as Alex released her held breath. The light left glowing trails in Alex's vision, like the taillights of racing cars in the dark.

The first two characters hit the demon and clearly caused it pain. The third, however, the demon caught in its hand, stopping the hànzi as it flew across the room.

Frisky. Fleshy meat thing will taste good.

"Ugh, pervert!" Alex said, disgusted.

Maxwell.

"What, stalker?" Alex said to her smartphone.

Its name is Maxwell, not pervert. It is rude to call things by not their names.

"Whatever stalker, the pervert is going to pay for zapping me."

Alex grabbed her desk chair and pulled it between her and the demon, then began writing a new hànzi on the seat. The demon took a large step towards Alex. The room shook as its foot hit the floor. Alex smirked and pushed the chair into the demon.

Alex, no!

The demon caught the chair with its hands.

Ha, little fleshy thing, bigger is not better.

Alex's smirk faded. The demon was not affected by the chair and the hànzi.

"What? Why didn't it work?" Alex said just as the demon wrenched the chair out of her grip and swung it at her. The chair hurt badly as it hit Alex's shoulder, knocking her down into the desk. Alex's smartphone clattered to the floor and Alex fell down next to it.

The bigger the object, the more the power of the hànzi is stretched to fill that object.

"Now you tell me, stalker."

I only figured out what you were doing as you did it. I apologize.

"Well, how about this?" Alex said, picking up her smartphone and swiping it open.

Hurry.

Alex poked at the screen and opened the sketchbook application. The app opened, and Alex wrote out a new hànzi.

I see. Let me help.

"Sure, stalker. Hack it."

The demon in Alex's smartphone traced out the hànzi just behind Alex's fingers. The character took on a white-purple glow, definitely not from the lines in the app.

Time to end this. Time to eat, fleshy thing. Little friend will not help you.

"Suck this, pervert!" Alex thrust her smartphone at the demon Maxwell. The screen on the tiny smartphone burst in white-purple light and struck the demon. It howled in pain.

"Yeah, little is better, pervert. I learn fast, jerk-face."

Well done, Alex. I like the way you think.

"Yeah, you helped too, stalker."

The demon Maxwell was still howling. Purple strings

and thick ropes arced out of the hànzi as it detached from the smartphone screen and hung in the air. White lightning struck out at the demon, little flashes of power and pain.

"No one messes with my smartphone. I bought it and it's mine."

Alex watched as the demon began to fade, becoming transparent like a bad special effect on an old TV show. The white lightning began to strike with less frequency and the purple strings and ropes began to fade with the demon Maxwell. Some wisps of smoke drifted over the laptop and disappeared into it.

"And don't come back, pervert, or I'll slap you around again."

That felt good, Alex. You are a very interesting child.

"Don't call me 'child,' it makes you sound like Grandfather. And it's creepy." Alex said, blinking her eyes. She had not noticed, but there were tears on her cheeks. Getting hit with a chair apparently hurt more than she thought.

Soon.

———

"You are completely wrong, it is so *depraved*." Grandfather Li said.

"I will not have you talk to me like that, I know what I know. I feel it is *degraded*."

"Akeyo, you know I do not correct you when you are right, but it is *depraved* and there are no two ways about it."

Grandma Akeyo stared at Grandfather Li over her mashed potatoes. Daggers would have been less sharp than the look she was giving to her husband.

"*Degraded*. It can't be anything else, and you try to correct me all the time. I can't help it if you are nearly always wrong. And by nearly always, I mean always." Akeyo smiled.

"*Perverted, depraved.* It could not be clearer in my mind. It is as clear to me as this fast food you have decided to pollute us with."

"You like fast food night. It was your idea in the first place." Akeyo countered.

"So it was, and it was a bad idea. Chicken and potatoes from a five minute and done store. You should have known better and stopped me from making the mistake." Grandfather Li scooped up a load of mashed potatoes onto his spoon.

"As I am stopping you from thinking that the eight letter word for 'perverted' is 'depraved' when it so clearly is 'degraded.' I am correct, you just refuse to admit that I am better at crosswords than you are or shall ever be." Akeyo handed the newspaper crossword back to her husband.

"That is low. Probably fair and true, but I refuse to admit it out loud."

"Inner monologue, Li Jiànhuī" Akeyo said in a warning jest.

"You see, I am corrected." he said as he looked at the paper.

"Because you are a fool." Akeyo smiled and ate another bite of chicken.

"Only a fool would recognize that fact." Grandfather Li frowned.

"Or marry him."

"I think you are incorrect again, it is I that married you, Akeyo. It could never be the other way around."

"I think it is precisely the other way around." Akeyo laughed as she spoke.

"Probably fair and true, but I refuse to admit it out loud.

And the correct answer is *degraded*, as I said all along." Grandfather Li admitted.

"Your inner monologue is still broken, Jiànhuī."

"Are you claiming responsibility for breaking it?"

"I maintain that I found you that way, and any change on my part has been an improvement." Grandma Akeyo said.

"Well, when you are right, I too am right by proximity."

"Correct." Akeyo agreed.

"As I said." Grandfather Li finished off another bite of the food from his bowl.

Laugher followed, with no uncertain amount of wrangling over the remaining crossword puzzle answers. Monday night dinner was always fast food night, when neither Grandma Akeyo nor Grandfather Li had any strength left to cook a regular meal. Each weekend was exhausting, with Grandfather Li training Alex and Grandma Akeyo searching for new areas of weakness in the world and repairing the strings and yarn that make up the reality of the world around them. Normally Grandfather Li helped with the task of repairing weakness in the world, but recently the lessons with Alex were far too intense.

Alex was clever and strong. It was a fact that Grandfather Li was careful never to admit to the girl. He was sure it would go to her head and she would become sloppy with her practice. He had done much the same thing as a young man. Alex was even stronger than he had been, and he didn't want to tempt her with praise, for praise could also lead to tempting failure. Akeyo had been there when Grandfather Li had failed nearly six decades earlier. It had been Akeyo that saved him from his failure and probably saved his life as well. Since that time, Grandfather Li and

Grandma Akeyo had almost never been apart. It was a binding that suited them well.

"Something is wrong." Akeyo said without preamble.

"Yes, it was not *depraved*, I know that now. Don't rub it in."

"No, something else. Don't you feel it in the air?" Akeyo said, dropping her spoon of mashed potatoes into her bowl.

"I cannot feel anything at the moment. I ate too much of that hot pepper sauce with my chicken and I cannot feel my mouth."

"There." Akeyo said and traced a line in the air with one slender finger.

White sparks traced out behind Akeyo's finger and clung to a path through the empty space above the dinner table.

"A warning? That is *not* supposed to be here." Akeyo stated flatly.

"No," Grandfather Li said as he drew in a barely audible breath, "That is not supposed to be in this world at all. I have not seen a proper demon warning since before Měilóng disappeared."

"Put away the food, Jiànhuī." Akeyo stood, "I will get out the kit and the keys to the bike."

Grandfather Li smoothly shifted from eating and arguing to whisking away the styrofoam containers of food and cheap, Chinese export porcelain bowls that he and Akeyo liked to eat from on fast food night. It made their meal 'fancy.'

Akeyo strode out of the room with purpose in her steps. The motorcycle key was first. She grabbed it from the hallway table and dropped it into her smock's pocket. Next, three full steps into the sitting room. Grandfather Li insisted on having a room for when he read novels. Akeyo insisted the calligraphy kits stay in the sitting room since it was the closest room to the garage door. According to Grandma Akeyo, it was best to be always ready to go when something was wrong in the world. Grabbing the two back-packs that contained their kits, Akeyo opened the garage door and stepped into the mostly open space.

Grandfather Li joined her and grabbed the motorcycle helmets off the shelf next to the door. His was a full-face model, black with red flames and hers was a sparkle-green open face helmet. Akeyo strapped the backpacks to the sidecar luggage rack with quick release straps, then took her helmet from her husband. She walked to the other side of the motorcycle and inserted the key but didn't turn it on. Grandfather Li put on his helmet and checked the strapped down the backpacks. Akeyo opened the choke and primed the fuel to start the motorcycle. She put on her helmet as she straddled the old, but well kept Boxer.

"Get in, old man."

"Yes, my love." Grandfather Li said as he climbed into the sidecar and sat down. Akeyo turned the key and then flipped out the kick starter. The Boxer had an electronic ignition, but the kick starter was much more satisfying. Akeyo stepped once, then rose up and pushed down hard, starting the Boxer with a booming growl from the engine as it turned over and caught ignition. She couldn't help but smile like a naughty child. Grandfather Li pushed to remote control button concealed under the dash of his side car and the door began its noisy rumble up and open.

The motorcycle and sidecar rolled out of the garage and Grandfather Li pressed the button again and the garage door rolled back down, closing behind them. Grandfather flicked a toggle switch on the side of his helmet as Akeyo did the same with hers.

"I still miss the car, Akeyo." Grandfather said into the wireless intercom embedded in the helmets.

"I don't miss your driving, old man." Akeyo replied as she rolled on the throttle and they slid out into the street, rumbling like only the old German motorcycle could.

"Where are we headed? I still cannot feel anything except fire and chili peppers." Grandfather asked.

"It feels stronger towards the north, but maybe a little west as well." Akeyo said.

"Towards the school?"

"And towards Donald's house. We'll pick him up on the way. He can watch our backs in case we need it." Akeyo accelerated and shifted gears with her clutch hand and foot.

"Yes, I hope he's still up. But let's try not to wake Alex. The girl needs her rest."

"Old man is a softy, I see."

"No, I just want to have her rested for this weekend. I plan to train her especially hard."

"Very well. I'll let the bike glide in for the last half block so we don't wake her." Akeyo said, revving the engine and shifting into third gear.

The two were quiet for the trip, even the intercom in their helmets wasn't loud enough to overcome the engine. Akeyo sensed the wrongness and weakness getting stronger as they got closer to their son-in-law's house. Akeyo downshifted, then put the Boxer into neutral as they got closer. Gliding in, Grandma Akeyo and Grandfather Li could see Alex's bedroom window and the flashes of light, electricity and magic coming from inside her bedroom. The weakness was not at the school, it was here, at Alex's house and in her bedroom.

"I don't think we should be quiet, my love." Grandfather Li said.

"You don't think? Well, that is a profound insight, old man," Akeyo broke, stress was in her voice as she stopped the bike in front of the house, "You go in first, I'll follow with the kit."

"Right. Kiss me later, when this is done." Grandfather Li moved quickly, very quickly for an 'old man.' He crossed the front yard in only a handful of steps and pushed the front door open with a gesture. He took the stairs three steps at a time, just as Donald was coming out of the first-floor bedroom.

"Backup. Shotgun. Fire department." Grandfather Li ordered. Donald already had the phone in one hand and a plain black leather satchel in the other. Donald might not have the talent for magic that his family did, but he made up for it in his ability to keep ahead of Grandfather Li's various needs and orders.

"You got here quick, John." Donald said, dialing 9-1-1.

"Your senses are garbage, stupid son-in-law. You should have felt this sooner." Grandfather Li said as he stepped into Alex's room. Donald started to talk to the operator when Grandfather Li crashed into the railing as he flew back out of Alex's room, hit the wall and tumbled down the stairs.

Alex sat down on her bed. Tired from working magic so quickly against the demon Maxwell. The wrongness in the air was still fading after the final banishment she had written with her smartphone demon had worked. Alex was pooped.

You did well.

"Not too bad on your end either, stalker."

Thank you.

"How did you know the word for banishment?" Alex asked, genuinely curious.

I have seen it used before. Or rather, something similar enough that I could understand your variations.

"Huh, so not the first time you've been sent back to the dead lands, I guess."

In a way, yes.

"I should turn off my laptop," Alex said, standing and pushing the keys on the keyboard, "You know, I've never seen a demon that big, or that close before. It wasn't nice."

No. Maxwell is not known for being nice.

"Maxwell? Since when do demons have names?"

Since always. They are like us, remnants of the lives led by people in the world.

"Yeah, well what's yours, stalker?" Alex clicked the keys on the keyboard.

That would be telling.

"Then tell, stupid demon." Alex frowned at the laptop.

No. It is private.

"You are in my phone, that is about as private as it gets." Alex held down the power button, trying to hard reset the laptop.

It is not private if you post photos of food on the Internet.

"How do you know what the Internet is? Aren't you like old and stuff?" The laptop began to power down.

You wrote about it, and there is this think called a dictionary. Diderot wrote something like this. I liked him.

"Dider-what?"

Diderot. He was French. I think he was my friend.

"Crap."

French, not crap.

"No, that pervert broke my laptop. It won't shut down." Alex snapped.

Oh. Perhaps it...

The smartphone demon didn't finish its thought. A streak of electricity erupted from the back of the laptop and struck Alex in the chest, she flew back onto the bed.

Sooner than I thought. These machines are not traps, they are resources.

Maxwell's arm emerged from the laptop screen as it had before.

No! How did you escape the banishment? Alex, get up, the demon Maxwell is still here!

Quiet, little demon. She cannot hear you. I discharged the entire supply of power in this machine into her. If she is not dead, she is unlucky.

How?

It was easy because I am smarter than you, trapped in your fake maze.

As the demon fully emerged from the laptop, it stepped over the bed, a leg on either side of it. Maxwell leaned down over Alex's body.

Un-awake. I will enjoy devouring this one's dreams.

Words began tracing out on the smartphone's screen, strange, twisting words. No thoughts came from the smartphone demon to accompany the words.

Try harder, little demon. I know that spell and it will not work. I was the first to write it, foolish one.

Look again, it is you who are the fool. The smartphone demon thought, finishing its words on the screen.

A warning spell? Your little girl is un-awake. What good will it do you?

It isn't for her, it is for the others.

There are no others here, only you. And soon it will be only me. Maxwell picked up the smartphone and began to tap and swipe its finger across the screen.

Does that hurt, little one? Tell us it hurts.

The smartphone demon held back, but eventually it began to scream in its thoughts. The world around it faded as Maxwell traced terrible, pain-filled words on the smartphone screen. Words that held power and awful purpose. Awareness of the world disappeared, torment replaced the world for the smartphone demon. Unending tortures, words filled with pain and horror. And thoughts of screaming.

It didn't know how long it screamed, but then the pain stopped suddenly.

———

"Did he ask for the shotgun?" Akeyo swept in through the door.

"Right here," Donald said, pulling a small bottle out of the satchel he was holding. The phone clattered to the floor, forgotten.

Akeyo took the bottle and uncorked it. Stepping over Grandfather Li, she snapped the visor on his helmet open, he hadn't bothered to take it off before rushing into Alex's bedroom.

"Old man, are you in there?" Akeyo asked, looking into Grandfather's eyes.

"Demon. Full, honest to goodness demon."

"Your father-in-law is delirious Donald, get me another

shotgun." Akeyo ordered as Donald pulled another bottle from the satchel.

"I am not delirious. Give me that." Grandfather Li was angry. He snatched to the bottle from Akeyo's hand. He downed the drink in the bottle in a single gulp, 'shotgunning' it at once.

"Yes you are, there is no demon here." Akeyo protested.

"The hell there isn't, give me that shotgun and forget the fire department. They will just get in my way." Grandfather Li struggled to stand, Akeyo helping him up.

Donald tossed the bottle to Grandfather, who caught it as he strode back up the steps to the second floor.

"Akeyo, start a pain ritual. I want this house cleared of any negativity." Grandfather said as he stood in front of Alex's door and looked into her room.

"Good luck with that." Donald said under his breath.

"You are also not so clever that I did not hear that, worthless son."

Akeyo frowned and began rummaging through the backpacks she had dropped in the doorway when she saw Grandfather Li fall down the stairs. She placed a small rag doll that might have once been a Raggedy Ann on the floor. Next Akeyo took an iron bracelet and placed it gently around the doll. Finally, Akeyo placed a single bead with an inscribed circle on the doll's lap.

"Give me your hand, Donald." Akeyo's voice changed slightly, her words clipped.

"Here." Donald placed his hand palm out with his fingers spread. He looked down at the floor and away from the rag doll. The pin prick he knew was coming was almost painless, it was his own blood that Donald was afraid of seeing.

"Baby." Akeyo said, not with any malice, but genuine affection.

"I know, but I still can't look. You know that."

Akeyo drew a rivulet of Donald's blood with the long hat pin she had concealed in her hand, then swung it in a quick circle around the doll. The blood flew in little drops off the needle, but instead of hitting the floor, they were drawn back and down against the iron bracelet. Each drop struck the cold metal and suddenly boiled away as if it had struck an open flame.

"There. Thank you for your sacrifice of pain, Donald. Now the pain in this house will know where to go, to follow your pain and be released by the bond of iron that protects my love for this doll." Akeyo's words were not an explanation, rather she spoke instructions to the room and house around her. Threads of blue and green appeared in the surrounding air. Tied at one end to the iron bracelet, the threads were slowly drawn into the metal.

"It never feels better, Akeyo."

"I know Donald, my son. And it never will as long as you still have your heart." Donald was not sure, but he thought he might have seen a tear in Akeyo's eye as she spoke.

"If you two are done, I have a banishment to accomplish here." Grandfather Li was impatient.

Grandfather Li took two blocks of a dark, red wood from his pocket, one in each hand. The blocks were only a little bigger than dice and shaped into smooth cubes with rounded edges. He swung his arms up and clapped them together above his head. The blocks clacked together and the air in the house changed. There was a crisp, spring feeling in the house now, like new and vigorous growth. Donald wrinkled his nose as he smelled moss and lichen.

Grandfather began to sink into a crouch, his left leg sliding out straight and to the side while his right leg bent as he lowered his body. His arms traced a circle in the air, fat and wide on the left, shallow on the right. His hands met in the middle of his chest and the wood blocks clacked together again, with a louder noise than they should have made.

"Demon in the box, this is your new home." Grandfather Li called into Alex's room. He thrust his hands forward and one of the blocks shot out into the bedroom while the other spun in mid-air just in front of Grandfather.

"Ears!" Akeyo shouted, covering her ears with her hands as Donald did the same.

There was a sucking sound as the air in the house was suddenly pulled into the bedroom and the pressure everywhere in the house except the bedroom dropped precipitously. Just as quickly, the air rushed back into the rest of the house. The rush of air battered Grandma Akeyo's and Donald's eardrums despite being covered with their hands.

The wood block in front of Grandfather Li fell soundlessly to the ground.

The smartphone fell to the floor. Something had changed. The pain was gone, it had been sucked away. The smartphone demon became aware of the world again. Grandfather Li was there in the doorway. A demon box was there too, one in front of Grandfather and one next to, but thankfully not touching the smartphone. Grandfather Li wore a strange helmet with an open visor and he looked tired. There was blood on his face, just enough to notice. The smartphone demon could sense much more blood in the helmet, Grandfather Li was hurt badly. Just like Alex.

Alex!

The smartphone demon panicked.

Help Alex, now! It thought at Grandfather Li.

"There, it is done. Donald, go take care of Alex, she looks hurt." The smartphone demon was sure Grandfather Li winked at it, then turned away from the room and slowly descended the stairs.

"So when were you planning on telling me about all this?"

"Shut up, Donald." Grandfather Li was clearly angry.

"I most certainly will not. You may have more magic than I'll ever have, but this is still my house and my daughter. Now you just sit there and hold that ice pack on your head." Donald rarely spoke forcefully, but even his patience had limits.

"Listen to the boy," Akeyo said before Grandfather Li could protest.

"I'll let it slide, Akeyo." Donald said, "Now, speak up Alexandra. Tell me why you lied about taking the imp to your grandparents? Then tell me if Jill was in on it? And Baxter, was he in on it, too? And this one, what was its name?" Donald tossed the smartphone on the kitchen table. Alex gasped but said nothing.

"Donald, please, my head."

"John, if your head hurts, go lie down. My daughter has some explaining to do."

"Come on, let's go in the living room and let Donald

talk to Alex. I will help you, old man." Akeyo took her husband by the hand.

"Fine," Grandfather Li said, allowing Akeyo to help him up and take him into the other room. He held a plastic bag full of ice cubes wrapped in a dish cloth against his head.

Alex watched her grandparents leave the kitchen. Grandfather had banished the demon, or so her dad had told her. He had also taken a heavy blow to the head when the demon threw her grandfather from the bedroom and he tumbled down the steps. Grandfather Li was wearing his motorcycle helmet, but even with the protection, the blow had cut his head open. Grandfather Li looked fragile and old as he walked into the living room with Grandma Akeyo's help.

Alex sniffed and let out a little cry. She had taken quite a few hits from the demon as well, although the worst of it was the electrical discharges from the outlet in her room and her laptop battery. Her teeth felt off center. Alex tried not to think too hard about what would have happened to her after the demon knocked her unconscious. It had said something about eating her organs. Alex didn't think it had been a joke.

"Dad, I didn't know it was in my room."

"The imp?"

"No, the demon."

"And what about your friends? You got them to go along with lying to me?"

Alex had told her dad everything when she woke up. He had been so comforting and gentle, she felt safe telling him about the last couple days. Alex's dad was always the nice one in the family. Not so much after he heard all the details. He knew about the imp. Jill's geometry test. Baxter and Alex hunting for the imp, then finding it, fighting and banishing it. The banishing was part of the lie. She had promised to bring the imp to her Grandma and Grandfather, instead she and her friends banished it themselves and celebrated with pizza at Mr. Mitchell's house. Alex thought that was the best part of the story, her moment of triumph and celebration. It was also the part of the story where Dad's patience ran out and he lost it. Dad never lost his temper.

"It only just happened." Alex looked up at her dad hopefully.

"It has been all day," Dad was not buying her story, "All day long is not 'it only just happened.' All day long is 'I am an irresponsible child and I am trying to get myself killed.' All day, Alex. And you got Jill to lie. And Baxter. And Warren 'I wish you were my dad' Mitchell."

"But Dad..."

"No. There is no 'but Dad' in this conversation. I may not be cool, I may not have the magic everyone in this family thinks I should have, but I am still your father. Your only father." Donald was turning red.

"You betrayed my trust when you lied to me. From now on, you come to me first. Magic stuff happens, you do *not* involve people that do not know about the world and the shadows. You will get them killed and you *know* it. You've *seen* it. Understand me?"

"Yes."

"Try again?"

"Yes, Dad. I come to you first."

"That's better. Now, what am I going to do about your phone?"

"Dad, no! It's mine. Don't take it away, please?"

"Alex, I am not taking away your phone. Did you forget

already? There is a spirit demon trapped in your smartphone. A. Demon."

"Oh, I guess you're right." Alex pushed at the phone with her finger.

"Oh, I'm right? How is it that I am right? What am I right about, Alex, tell me?"

"That, I need to banish the demon in my phone?" said Alex hopefully.

"No, honey. You are in no condition to do anything of the sort. Rather, I want to know how a spirit demon got into your phone in the first place."

I became trapped in this box when Alex had her tantrum.

"I did not have a *tantrum!*" Alex said loudly.

"What? Who said anything about a tantrum?" Alex's dad looked puzzled.

Alex, why can he not hear me? I can feel how strong he is, he should be able to hear me easily.

"Dad is blocked. He cannot magic."

"Alex, are you talking to your demon?" Donald looked at the smartphone on the table.

"Yes. He said he was trapped in my phone since just before school started."

"When you stormed out of your lesson? Was that the tantrum?" Donald looked at Alex then back at the phone.

"Yes. But I didn't have a tantrum, I'm not a baby." Alex looked at the smartphone and definitely did not look at her dad.

No, you are a very strong young girl. And it was a glorious tantrum.

Alex stuck her tongue out at the phone.

"Alright, enough from both of you." Alex's dad picked up the smartphone and opened the kitchen junk drawer.

"Dad, no!" Alex yelped, thinking he was about to toss her phone in the drawer. Instead, he took out a pair of headphones and plugged them into the phone's audio jack.

"What?" He said as he put the headphones on over his ears.

What is this, it feels odd?

"Ah, much better. I can hear you now, demon."

Alex stared at her dad, unbelieving.

"Close your mouth, honey. I don't have magic but that doesn't mean I can't think of ideas."

"But how does that even work?" Alex asked.

"I don't know, but I thought I would just give it a try. It's not like there's ever been a spirit demon trapped in a smartphone before. Who knows what'll work and what won't."

You are quite correct. This is a novel experience for me as well.

"So, you are the spirit demon in the smartphone. Can you tell me your name?" Alex's dad turned his back on Alex and started pacing while talking to the smartphone.

My name is a private matter.

"Oh, that's fine. How about you tell me a little about what happened tonight?"

I tried to warn Alex about Maxwell, but she fell asleep. Maxwell attacked her, and we tried to banish it, but it was too strong.

"Maxwell is the big demon?"

Yes. It is very old. I sent a warning to bring help.

"Why did you help Alex? That seems a very odd thing to do."

I like this box. It is a wonderful maze. I feel safe in here.

"Oh really? Is it like a demon box?"

Better. Lots of turns and twists, and very interesting

things are in this box. It is a comfortable place, like a living thing, but not quite.

"Oh really? And if I asked you to leave, could you?"

Not at all. It is a maze, like a demon box. There are parts of this box that are nearly identical and I cannot tell where I am, therefore I cannot leave.

"And you are fine with telling me that but you won't tell me your name?"

It is a private matter.

"You don't know it, do you?"

I know my own name.

"No, you don't. You are correct, Alex had a tantrum, and you got caught up in it. You don't know your name because Alex never called it out to you. You are trapped because of her tantrum and you can't get out until you learn your own name."

Alex stood and stared at her dad. He was clearly very pleased with himself. Alex hadn't thought that far ahead, but her dad figured out how and why the spirit demon was trapped in her smartphone in under five minutes.

"You can close your mouth, Alex." Her dad said to her without turning around to look. Alex closed her mouth.

"You are a very scary dad."

"Go sit with Grandma Akeyo and see to your grandfather, Alex. I have some questions for your smartphone and I would rather you were not here to listen in."

"Yes, Dad." Alex left the kitchen and went to see her grandparents.

"I heard it all, Alex. You should listen to your father more." Grandma Akeyo said as Alex entered the living room.

"I forget how much he knows." Alex said as she plopped into the easy chair.

"I forget sometimes as well. Your father was a brilliant study, but the magic never came when he called it to him."

"Because he is a disappointment and a fool. He was wasted on our daughter." Grandfather Li said from under his ice pack.

"You know better than that, old man. He has suffered more than either of us. She is gone. Stop blaming him for our failings." Grandma Akeyo was firm, there would be no more talk of disappointments or fools in her presence.

"Now, tell me about your pet demon in the box, Alex. I don't think your grandfather heard the conversation through the ringing in his head." Grandma Akeyo's attention was fixed on Alex as she leaned forward to hear the story from her granddaughter's own lips.

"Oh crap."

CHAPTER FIVE

Filthy vermin. Human garbage. Nuisances and vermin. Edible, but filthy garbage. It makes them delicious, even when they sting.

The little girl was talented, devouring her from the inside would have been satisfying. Oh yes, quite an acceptable meal. But that small thing in the box, it helped the child-morsel.

It is not as strong, but it is older. It knows things. Things that cut, things that help the girl to sting. That power must be devoured, and it was so close.

Then the old man. Then the old, wicked man arrived. His scent was not the same. He was tough, with earned power. Not delicious, but a challenge.

These are things that must not be any longer. Each must be extinguished. They must serve *and satisfy and be utterly disposed. Broken. Broken and devoured.*

How to break? Break, Break.

They made me hide, so they must be broken. Hiding in this box, this box with its lies. Trivial maze, but the lies, those are rich. Images and thoughts are trapped in this box. The little girl's box. Are these her thoughts? Yes, I see her thoughts and her friends. Pieces of those lives are all here, all in the box. I must study them, learn to unmake their dreams.

The hiding place is also the hiding place for the little girl's life! Oh, what secrets must be in this box. A shame the power in it is almost gone. Using the power to hurt the girl was too much for the maze box, but it was needed. I shall not leave this world again.

Letters. The little girl writes letters to her friends. They write back, but it is all in the box. Wait, no, there is a path. It is an open path, a simple path. It leads out to other boxes. I feel the pull, like strings in the dead lands. The dead lands that I shall never return to, but these strings lead to a different land. A way to escape and learn more about the little girl and the old man. To hurt them for hurting me. Yes, they will suffer deliciously.

Take the path. Close the path behind. No one will follow, leave the little girl and old man for now. And the little thing in its box. The little girl's slave. It too shall pay and satisfy my needs. Oh yes, it shall pay most of all. It is the principle of the thing. And when all are broken, I shall remain and find others to suffer.

Travel from the maze box on the path is strange. Like being part of the strings of the world, but without depth. A new thing is here, it asks simple questions. There are threads coming from it, twist them! Ah, it feels alive, but it is not. It twists easily and does what I ask. Let me in!

A new place. Cold and white. Simple and not like the maze box. This is a road. A bigger road is close, I feel it. The girl has been here. Her thoughts have been here. Others' thoughts, too. Many more thoughts further on. Strange, it is like a library of so many people.

People have built strange things that hold their thoughts, hold their emotions. They leave their vulnerability in plain sight. Foolish children.

These child-thoughts make me hungry. Perhaps I shall eat these thoughts? Yes, devour these while waiting for the child. Ah yes, her friends. I am aware of them. Her thoughts betray them to me and I hunger for more!

Baxter. A boy-child. He is admired. She is jealous. Delicious jealousy. Bax, a short name but a tall boy-child. I shall break him. Break and devour.

There is more. Not just jealous, the little girl envies the Baxter. The Bax. She calls him 'The

Bax.' He has something she wants, something she needs. Ah, a parent. A normal parent? Very interesting. She has a weakness I can use. Twist, twist, twist the threads into strings, pull the strings of these thoughts. Soon all that will be left are memories. Those too shall be eaten. With kidneys and juicy parts. Mind and body, simmer and cook. Cook with fear and salt with envy. Jealously is good seasoning.

Revenge will start with the boy-child, Baxter Mitchell. Bax. The Bax. A juicy victim for revenge. Causing Bax pain will hurt the little girl, Alex. Both of them in pain will multiply, and then I shall devour them both. Pain and bodies. And lick their bones clean before crushing the bones too. The dust from their bones will become teeth for me to eat the others. Especially the old man. That one shall be the third to suffer and satisfy me.

The laptop in Alex's room was much worse for wear than it should have been. The discharged battery had begun to break down and the trickle of charge left in it was just enough to keep it alive, but only for a short time. Maxwell had used the laptop roughly as it struggled with Alex and her smartphone demon. Corrosion had begun to form on the tiny pieces of metal in the screen around the places Maxwell had used to emerge from the laptop. The demon was not compatible with the laptop. His power did not treat its host well.

The corrosion continued from the laptop to the power brick and into the wall where the plug had been connected to the outlet. More corrosion had begun to form inside the wires that led from the laptop to the receptacle in the wall. The telephone lines had been replaced with ethernet jacks, but the copper in the wires was not strong enough to resist Maxwell's corruption as he passed from the laptop down the ethernet cable and into the wall. The demon had escaped into the Internet through the ethernet connection.

Alex would need a new laptop. The house would need new wiring and a new router. The larger, industrial-grade wiring and devices resisted Maxwell's corruption better than cheap consumer electronics, but those too would fail sooner than they should. Maxwell's movement through the world left decay behind it, with nothing in the world truly immune to its corrosion.

"No! You are not going to break my brand new phone!" Alex glared at her grandfather.

"I did not say I was going to break your idiotic phone. I said we need to break the spirit demon out of your idiotic phone." Grandfather Li was standing toe to toe with Alex, the pair of them staring at each other without blinking. Alex had never stood up so strongly for herself to Grandfather Li before.

"No, I know what you said, and I know what you are going to do. I won't let you break my phone!"

"You are not clever enough to know what I would or would not do."

"Oh, that again? I don't have to be clever enough, I remember what you did last time!" Alex yelled in Grandfather Li's face, tears beginning to form at the memories of the last major argument they had when she was nine years old.

"Remember what? You being a brat, because that might as well have been yesterday? No, wait, every day? I am pretty sure it was every day!"

"No! When you broke my Tommy Thom's walkie talkie!" Alex turned on her heel and stomped away from her grandfather.

"That old thing? You were eight!"

"Nine, I was nine years old, and you took it from me while I was talking with my best friend!"

"Your best friend? That Winnie girl?"

"Wendy! *Wen*-dee! You don't even remember her name. You ruined my Tommy Thom's and then you ruined my first, best friendship ever. And you can't even remember her name! Wendy!" Alex stomped back to her grandfather, stared him in the eyes and grabbed her smartphone from his hand before stomping away a second time.

"Winnie, Wendy. Whatever her name was, she was the one who called you a liar because you told her about calligraphy and magic. I remember that. That is the thing that really matters." Grandfather Li had less edge in his voice. Nine years old had been rough for Alex and he remembered her crying every night in her room for a month when Wendy turned against her. Grandfather Li was not heartless.

"I only told Wendy to get back at you for breaking my Tommy Thom's while I was talking to her!" Alex shouted, now with full tears in her eyes and down her cheeks, but no sobbing. No way was she going to sob in front of her grandfather when he was so obtuse and careless about how she felt.

"I never, wait. You told Wendy to get back at me? You never told me that!"

"Oh, you old fool," Akeyo said to her husband, placing her hand on his shoulder, "Alexandra would never have told you that. I'm not sure *I* would have told you that."

Akeyo gently guided her husband to sit in one of the dining room table's chairs. Grandfather Li did not resist.

"Now, that's enough from both of you." It was time for Akeyo to make peace, if she could.

"It was enough when I was nine, it is too damn late now." Alex spat, trying to get in a verbal jab while her grandfather was off guard.

"Enough and mind your tongue. Foul language makes a foul mind." Akeyo's voice firmed up.

"No one is going to break your phone, Alexandra. I will make sure of that. And you, old fool, you are to sit here and think about what you did when Alex was nine."

"But..." Grandfather began.

"No, I said, you sit here and think about what you did. I did not say talk back to me!"

"Yes, my dear." Grandfather Li said, thinking.

"And you, you are to give me your phone for safe keeping." Akeyo held out her hand.

"But..." Alex began.

"No, I said you are to give me your phone and I will keep it safe. I did not say talk back to me, or would you prefer the thinking chair like your old fool of a grandfather?" Akeyo arched one perfect eyebrow and awaited Alex's smartphone.

Alex puffed up to her grandma, red rimming her eyes. Akeyo thought for a moment that Alex would refuse her, but suddenly her granddaughter plopped the smartphone in Akeyo's hand and gripped her hand hard.

"No one breaks my phone, not even you Grannie." Alex turned and walked away from Akeyo, leaving the phone in her grandma's hand.

"Now, I am going to go and sit in the living room. You stay in that chair and you, young lady, you sulk in the corner, because I know that is what you were going to do, anyway."

"But..." Both Grandfather and Alex began to speak.

"No. I have spoken, and it is both of your jobs to do as you are told while I figure things out." And with those last words, Grandma Akeyo left the dining room with the smart-phone and its demon in hand.

"Well, I guess neither of us is up for fighting her." Grandfather Li whispered when he was sure Akeyo could not hear him.

"Yeah, but I was almost up for it." Alex whispered back.

"I can always hear you both, old fool and young fool." Akeyo said from the living room.

"Now, it is just you and me." Akeyo sat in an overstuffed chair in the living room, cradling the smartphone in her hand.

Yes.

"Now, I think you should think a little quieter, it is thinking at me that you are doing, is it not?"

Yes. I think at you as you say.

"Good, can you think softly so only I can hear you? I would like to speak with you privately."

I can. The smartphone demon's thoughts appeared on the screen of the phone. Smaller, with softer curves.

"Now, do you know what you are?" Akeyo leaned in closer to look at the screen of the phone.

I do.

"Good. Now tell me, do you know where you are?"

I am in a demon box, a device to hold spirits, impressions of people long past and many of the various unseen powers. You call it a smartphone. I have not heard of a demon box like this before, but it is very interesting.

"Oh really? Can you tell me what is interesting about this particular demon box?" Akeyo traced her finger along the edge of the phone.

It is not like other demon boxes.

"Oh, so you have been imprisoned in a box before this?"

Yes. A long time ago, just after what was human in me had died.

"Oh really?"

Yes. The demon box was a maze, but it was not full of life, it was dead and cold. The warmth of life had long ago left that box. I could travel the veins where the life had been, but I could not tell where the exit was, where the life had flowed out of the box to die. As you said, I was a prisoner of the box.

"Well, that is interesting. The box is a maze to you?"

Yes. It is as though there is another box beyond the maze, but that box is just the same as the one you are trapped in. It is quite infuriating, to be honest. And the reek of dead things is difficult to shut out.

"I can imagine. But this smartphone demon box is different?"

Oh yes, it is very different. It is alive but not like an animal, its heart beats extremely fast and the life races through the box. But it is not alive. The taste is strong and the rhythm of its heart is powerful, but no, it is not alive like you or Alex.

"I see."

Do you, Grandma Akeyo?

"No, not really," Akeyo looked away for a moment, then returned her gaze to the screen of the phone, "How do you know my name?"

Aside from Alex and all the other people saying it, you mean? Alex has written about you in this box.

"You can read the messages stored in the phone?" Akeyo said, truly surprised.

Oh yes, it took a little time, but I can feel what was said. Alex's emotions are strong in this demon box, so very strong.

"Ah, now that I understand, emotions are very powerful you know."

Quite. You are a very intelligent person, Grandma Akeyo.

"Thank you, and you may call me Grandma if you like. For now."

Quite.

"Now tell me, what was that thing attacking Alex?"

You are not easily distracted from your thoughts, are you Grandma?

"No, I am not. So you should tell me about that thing we sent back to your world." Akeyo sat back in the chair, waiting for the smartphone demon's answer.

That was Maxwell.

"And Maxwell is a demon?"

A proper demon, not just in spirit like myself, but in temperament too. And all together too powerful for anyone's good.

"So you know of this Maxwell? Have you known him long?" Akeyo arched her eyebrow at the smartphone.

It. Maxwell is an it. Any trace of man or woman left that creature long ago. Maxwell is a terror in the dead lands. All know of Maxwell sooner or later. Later is better.

"And you, spirit demon, you helped my Alex to fight off this Maxwell?"

Yes.

"Why?"

I. I am not sure.

"You do not care for this Maxwell the demon?"

I do not.

"Do you care for Alex?"

Silence.

"Ah, so you do care for Alex."

Alex is interesting. She is far more clever than you think she is. And I like this demon box. It feels nice in here.

"Surrounded by Alex's emotions."

You are correct. I had not considered that. But it is nice, even without those emotions. This is a comfortable box.

"To be a prisoner in?"

No. It is not a prison. Not like other demon boxes. It is more like a puzzle than a maze. Yes, now that I think about it, this demon box makes me think and ponder. The other demon boxes, the dumb ones, they make me bored and frustrated.

"Is that so?"

It is. I think I helped Alex fight off Maxwell because I like her, and I like being in this smartphone. It is much nicer than being a 'demon in the box.'

"Ah, so you were truly in a demon box. You know how a human commands a demon trapped in a box."

Yes. 'Demon in the box,' do this or that task. The invoca-

tion of power over the spirit demon, then the order to execute. I remember being given orders to do things. Terrible things.

"But you are comfortable being the 'demon in the smartphone?' You do not mind that trap?" Akeyo leaned in close to hear the smartphone demon's answer.

I do not mind. Alex does not ask me to do those things, she talks with me. I appreciate that.

"Oh, I see. You are a very interesting demon. I think you have passed my test."

Have I?

"Oh yes, I think you have. You put Alex before yourself. You are a spirit to be sure, but you are not a proper demon, not like Maxwell."

No, I suppose I am not. What does that make me, then?

"I think it makes you a first. The first smartphone demon. Today we have learned something new."

Have we?

"Yes, I think we have."

And what have we learned, Grandma Akeyo?

"Just Grandma is fine, smartphone demon, and if you don't know, I am certainly not going to tell you. Where is the fun in that?"

Indeed.

———

"Here, take your playmate back." Akeyo tossed the smartphone to Alex as she was sulking in the corner of the room, conspicuously not looking at her grandfather.

"Oh, crap!" Alex fumbled to catch the phone, clutching it to her chest to avoid dropping it.

"Language, Granddaughter. And as for you, old fool, have you thought about what you did?"

"Yes, my darling." Grandfather Li looked old and feeble sitting in the chair.

"And have you come to any conclusions?" Akeyo stood tall over Grandfather Li, a dark, resolute tribute to her strength.

"Besides that I let you get away with treating me like a child?" Grandfather Li's eyes twinkled under his brow at he stole a glance at Akeyo.

"If you would not act like a petulant child, then I would not treat you so. And before you attempt a weak gesture towards what you call 'cleverness,' remember I know where you sleep at night."

"Yes, my darling. I was cruel and childish when I broke Alex's Tommy Thom's walkie talkie. I should have thought of her feelings and been a better man, and a better parent." Grandfather Li knew when it was time to not be clever. This was that time.

"Quite. Now you are on the path to true wisdom once more."

"Yes, my darling."

"Damn straight, you old fool. That's why I married you, to keep you on the path. Goodness knows it wasn't for your good looks."

"That's not what you said..." Akeyo frowned, Grandfather Li's words trailed off.

"We do not speak of that night in front of children. Or the next day either, my love."

Alex looked up from her phone, oblivious to her grandparent's conversation.

"Stop whispering to your playmate, Alexandra, it is rude in company to ferret secrets," Akeyo pulled a chair away from the table and turned it out, inviting Alex to sit, "Come here and let us talk with you and your friend."

Alex blanched. When Grandma Akeyo invited her to the table in that way, it was 'adulting' time. Alex was afraid of 'adulting' time, not because it was hard or a punishment, but because that was the time when her grandparents took her most seriously and treated her like an equal. It was terrifying to think of herself as equal to her two strong and forceful grandparents. Even Alex's father dreaded 'adulting' time.

"Yes, Grandma Akeyo." Alex sat in the chair and placed her smartphone on the table in front of all three of them. Grandfather Li leaned in from his chair while Alex attempted to muster the willpower not to shrink herself into the chair. Akeyo stood lord over all.

Hello.

"Hello, demon." Grandfather Li looked at the phone cautiously. The lesson of the Tommy Thom's was still fresh in his mind.

"Can you see us, demon?" Grandfather's curiosity was winning out over his anger at Alex's argument with him from earlier.

I can sense you all, and if I want, I can make the demon box show me images of the world around me.

"How do you do that?"

Like so. The LED flash on the smartphone came on, shining out from the underside of the phone.

A moment. I must, there. The LED went out and the flash on the screen surface side of the phone came on.

"You accessed the camera!" Alex blurted out.

I cannot see you, but it looks like I am on my back, if I had a back.

"Here." Alex picked up the phone and panned around the room.

Ah, now I see, this demon box is delightful.

"Put your playmate in this so we can have a proper conversation, face to, ah, camera." Akeyo set a wide-mouthed glass tumbler on the table. Alex placed the smartphone in the glass with the screen towards the three humans in the room.

"Since when do phones have cameras, Alex?" Akeyo whispered.

"Since forever, Grandma, it's what phones are for."

"Your phone has a camera, Akeyo." Grandfather Li looked quizzically up at his wife.

"Does it?"

"We have the same phone, Akeyo. I take pictures of our food and post it on the Internet. You know this."

"You do? I thought you were goofing off and making fun of me."

Your family has a lovely dynamic relationship, Alex. They are almost more fascinating than this smartphone demon box.

"Thank you, I think." Alex replied.

"About this box, demon, what is it like inside it?" Grandfather Li turned his attention back to the smartphone.

It is large and alive and warm. I find it rich with details and completely unlike any maze I have ever experienced.

"A maze, is it? How different is it from where you come from?"

Before the box? Unending boredom. Torture. Slow forgetting. There are threads and strings running throughout the dead lands, they are reminders of the things from before. Of the world, and it fills most with envy and jealousy.

"What about you, were you filled with envy? Jealousy? Anger?" Grandfather Li was leading the demon in the conversation.

No. I was bored, but I can resist the temptation to be base.

"How did you do that?"

I organized my thoughts. Categorized each memory of the life before. I allotted them to their place in my mind and held on to those memories. It was exhausting.

"It sounds exhausting. How did you find your way into the demon box, then, if you were organizing your mind?"

Accident. I use the threads of reality that run through the dead lands to keep my memories. I find threads that remind me of the life before, touch those threads, let them ring in my mind. I was reminding myself of rituals when the thread I was touching clung to me and drew me into the world. I found myself in a binding circle, then this demon box entered the circle and I was sucked into it. I have been trapped in the most fascinating maze ever since. I like it in the box, I feel safe in here.

"Ah, now I understand." Grandfather Li sat back, self-satisfied.

"What? I don't understand." Alex looked from Grandma Akeyo to Grandfather Li.

"Oh, Alex, think about it. What happened when you stormed out of your lesson to go see your movie?" Akeyo prompted Alex.

"I wanted to go to the movie and a very bad man tried to break my phone." Alex glared at her grandfather.

"It is true, I am a very bad man. So don't cross me, un-clever granddaughter." Grandfather Li folded his arms over his chest, looking directly at Alex.

"And when the bad man slapped your phone, what happened?" Akeyo ignored Alex and Grandfather Li's verbal sparring.

"It fell, oh. I get it now, my smartphone fell into the

circle where the matched wood blocks were sitting." Alex's face looked wider as she realized what had happened during her magic lesson with Grandfather Li.

"Yes, your smartphone became the focus of the binding circle. You were quite angry with me, if I recall correctly." Grandfather Li unfolded his arms and leaned in to look directly at Alex.

"You tried to break my brand new smartphone. I saved forever to buy it, it is mine, and you hit it, you hit me!" Alex leaned in closer to her grandfather.

"Now Alex, calm down. The old fool should have known better, but you should have controlled yourself. Emotions are dangerous when you work with magic." Grandma Akeyo placed her hands on Grandfather Li's and Alex's shoulders, gently pushing them away from each other.

"I did not mean to strike you, my child. I am sorry." Grandfather Li was sincere, Alex's anger couldn't hold up with Grandfather apologizing.

"Fine. But this means it is all your fault. You slapped my phone and made it fall into the binding circle. You infected my phone with a stalking hacker." Alex tried to pout and be angry at the same time and almost succeeded.

"Alex, it's only partially his fault. Your emotional outburst bound this spirit demon to your phone. Without that, the binding would have simply failed and your play-mate here would be safe in his boring, organized land of threads and strings."

Thank you for being angry, Alex. I would rather be here, in your smartphone demon box, and with your fascinating family. And you, the demon thought but did not say.

"What, no! I don't want a smartphone demon!" Alex said, flustered.

"I think this is a perfect situation." Grandfather Li patted Akeyo's hand on his shoulder.

"What? No!"

"Oh, yes. I could not agree more. Alex, you have bound this spirit demon to its box. You have a responsibility now. You must give your smartphone demon a name."

Oh, a name would be nice. Of course, I already have one.

Grandfather Li raised his eyebrow at the lie.

"No. I will not name a stupid stalking hacker demon. Not in my smartphone. I don't want a smartphone demon, I just want *my* smartphone."

"Well, you must call him something." Akeyo looked from Alex to the smartphone.

"Stupid stalker. Hack my phone, now you get a name? No way." Alex legitimately pouted.

I did not hack your phone. And I cannot stalk you, I am stuck where ever you put me.

"Fine. I am not giving you a name, understand that, stalker?"

I cannot stalk you, Alex.

"SPD."

What?

"I will call you SPD. Smart. Phone. Demon. It is a description, not a name."

SPD. I shall answer to SPD, Alex my mistress. I am SPD, your demon in the box.

"Oh no, that is *not* a name. And you are not my demon in the box!"

"Too late, un-clever granddaughter."

"Jiànhuī is right, my child. You have named your demon and now he is bound to you."

"Oh crap."

"Language, Alexandra." Grandfather Li and Grandma Akeyo said in unison.

"Alex, your battery is going to die if you keep live streaming like that." Alex's dad said as he came in the front door. He had just returned from getting takeout Chinese food. After the fight with Maxwell, Donald knew that Alex, Grandfather Li, and Grandma Akeyo would need food to recover from working so much magic, so while the grandparents took care of Alex, Donald went to get the most calorie dense food he could find.

Alex, Grandfather Li, and Grandma Akeyo all glared at Donald from the dining room table. Donald looked at the smartphone.

"Alex, why is your smartphone glaring at me?" Alex's dad asked.

"What? SPD, don't glare at Dad."

"SPD? Alex, come and get this bag of food. You all need to eat. Turn the phone off or plug it in, then you all can tell me what we have decided to do while I was taking care of buying food so you all do not starve to death." Donald handed two paper bags of Chinese takeout to his daughter.

"Donald, you are a treasure." Akeyo said, pulling out a chair and sitting at the table.

"Treasure my ass, you just love Chinese food." Donald said.

"Not wrong, son-in-law. Say nothing, old fool if you want to eat tonight." Akeyo smirked.

Grandfather Li's hopeful look faded as his waiting sarcastic comment died on his tongue.

"Alex, turn that phone off."

"Yes, Dad. SPD, can you turn off the light?"

I shall try. There, how is that?

"Much better."

"Who was that, Alex did you have a friend over while I was gone?" Donald looked around for Baxter, Jill, or whoever else Alex might have invited over.

"No, Dad, SPD is in my phone."

"Oh, I should have known at six hundred dollars, it should have had voice control."

Grandfather Li shook his head.

"Donald, SPD is the name of the demon that is currently residing in Alex's smartphone." Grandfather Li took out a plastic container of sweet and sour pork.

"Oh. We are naming our phones now? I will call mine Butt-munch the Destroyer, if that's alright with you." Donald smiled slyly. He was playing with them all.

"Are you really that stupid or are you just a disappointment and a failure by nature?"

"John, how could you say such things? And in front of Alex, SPD and Butt-munch? You know their ears are too young for that sort of talk."

"You are an idiot."

"I inherited my sarcasm from you, John." Donald sat down at the table in the remaining chair.

"You are not my son. A son-in-law cannot inherit sarcasm from his father-in-law."

"No? I rest my case." Donald began to rummage through the food, looking for the mù shù cài.

"I declare that Donald, the idiot son-in-law has won this round of the great sarcasm war." Akeyo stated, already half-way finished with her gōng bǎo chicken.

"I am not related to any of you strange people." Alex's

face had a half dozen stray grains of fried rice clinging to her cheeks.

I am fascinated by your family's dynamic relationship, Alex. You must keep this conversation alive.

"Shut up, SPD."

"Plug in your demon box, Alex, we don't know what will happen if the battery dies." Alex's father said, starting in on his container of mù shù cài.

———

"Hand me the soap, Alex?" Donald was washing each empty container of Chinese takeout before drying it and tossing it in with the other plastic items for recycling.

"I still don't understand why you do this every time we have takeout?" Alex handed her dad the dish soap.

"It is an old habit from when I was in college. Just accept it like I accept that you have a pet demon in your phone."

"No fair, Dad."

"Dads are not fair. Unfairness is specifically in the job description."

"Well, then consider yourself going above and beyond the call of duty."

"I charge overtime."

"Talk to Grandfather Li, I'm just a kid."

"Yeah, like I could get a dime out of the old man. Not even your Mom could manage that."

Alex became quiet.

"Sorry, Pickles. I didn't mean to bring up Mom."

"It's ok, I just, I dunno. Sometimes I wish I had known her better."

"I know, Pickles. I wish you had gotten to know her too, but wishes are like bēi shuǐ chē xīn."

"Bēi shuǐ chē xīn, god I hate your stupid idioms."

"Alex, Chinese is not just a set of stupid idioms, you know that. And don't let Grandfather Li hear you call his four-character phrases stupid. I did that once and regretted it. I think I still have bruises."

"Yeah, I still don't think that ever happened." Alex began drying the containers as her dad finished washing them.

"It is absolutely the truth. Grandfather Li was a much harder trainer with me than he is with you. He insisted that I had to be a perfect physical specimen. Wǔshù, gōngfū, any martial art that was even vaguely Chinese. I think he just liked punishing me for marrying his daughter."

"Oh, come on, he was born in Brooklyn, not China."

"I'm serious, when he was younger, your grandfather was a monster of a teacher. Seriously ripped too, damn that man could fight."

"Dad, do you have a bro-mance with your father-in-law, ew? Like oh my god, gag." Alex teased.

"Ha ha. I still have bruises from talking like that to John. Hell, that is how Měilóng finally got him to stop."

"What do you mean?"

"Oh, I probably never told you about that. Your mother, Měilóng used to fix me up after Grandfather took me apart in practice. I hadn't been doing well in learning magic and John was furious with me. So he pushed me hard."

"Yeah, so what was different from any other time?"

"Well, Měilóng was cleaning me up, and she took off my shirt and noticed that my arm was broken. I didn't feel a thing, probably from all the adrenaline and frustration with being unable to meet John's standards. Well, your mother was furious."

"Are you serious, Grandfather Li broke your arm?"

"Yeah, three places. I honestly never felt a thing."

"Wow. That's just wrong."

"Exactly what your mother said, but with much more edge to it. So Měilóng told him to stop and John said as long as he was the teacher, he would do as he pleased."

"Sounds like what Grandfather Li would say."

"Yeah, Měilóng was not amused. She challenged John for the right to be my teacher."

"No shit?"

"Language, Pickles. Don't let Grandma Akeyo hear you. Filthy language..."

"...leads to a filthy mind." Alex and her dad laughed together.

"So what happened, Dad?"

"Your mother proceeded to mop the floor with John."

"Please, he was holding back."

"Nope. He picked the fight, weaving together threads of reality to shore up the weakness in the world."

"Wait, that's not a fight."

"Exactly, there was no way John was going to strike his only daughter, especially not over me, so he thought he was being clever and accepted the challenge. He said they would compete with magic and do some good at the same time."

"And Mom was better than Grandfather Li at strengthening the weakness in the world? I thought only Grandma was better than him at weaving the threads together."

"Well, so did he. What he didn't know is that while he was working me over for twelve hours a day with martial arts and stuff like that, Akeyo was teaching Měilóng all her secrets."

"Oh, so she had an ace up her sleeve?"

"You could say that. When it was over, John admitted defeat. Akeyo scolded him and sent Měilóng off to tend to me and take over my lessons."

"Game, set, and match."

"Sort of. That's how we discovered that my ability to use magic was blocked. Měilóng started out with evaluating me from head to toe after my arm was all healed up. She discovered right off that I had a big problem."

"The block."

"The block. I would never be able to work magic. Akeyo almost lost her mind. I swear she was chasing John with a stick for a full week."

"What? Wait, why?"

"John never bothered to test me in depth. He should have known immediately that I was blocked from using magic, but instead he was so excited by the potential he sensed from my family and my background that he just went straight into lessons."

"But why did that matter?"

"Well, they had spent months tracking me down, then a year manipulating Měilóng and me from behind the scenes to fall in love."

"What?"

"Oh yes, arranged marriages are always better if you actually love each other."

"No way, you and Mom were an arranged marriage?"

"Oh, yes. I was given to your mother as a gift from our family to yours. Of course, when Měilóng found out, she refused to talk to her parents for a year."

"What is *wrong* with you people?"

"Fair question. Well, your Mom and I were actually in love. I didn't know about the arranged marriage either, and Akeyo is very good and convincing others that her ideas are really their ideas. We agreed to only rely on each other from then on, and to hell with the family."

"But wait, that doesn't make sense. Why are you all together now? How did that happen if you and Mom weren't talking to Grandfather Li and Grandma?"

"You happened."

"Oh stop it!" Alex hit her dad on the shoulder, "Now you are just pulling my leg."

"No really, once you were born, everything changed."

"Liar."

"It's true. I have it all on video tape. Grandfather Li and Grandma Akeyo came to us and made the best apology ever. I insisted we video tape it."

"Is that why we still have a VCR?"

"On the nose, Pickles. On the nose."

"Heh, I know what we're watching on movie night."

Donald smiled.

"Alex, are you going to the Harvest Dance?" Suzie asked as Geometry class was about to start.

"What? No. Why?" Alex didn't know what to say.

"Oh, just wondering." Suzie seemed disappointed.

"No one asked me. I hadn't really thought about it." Alex admitted.

"No one asked me, either. New girl. I guess none of the boys want to ask me." Suzie said.

"I honestly don't know why anyone would go. Dances aren't really my thing."

"Oh, I like them. At least I think I do. St. Alban's was a girls-only school. Can't be tempted by being around boys or some garbage like that." Suzie sounded sarcastic. Alex was a little jealous. Sarcasm was easy for everyone but her.

"So you never got to go to a dance?" Alex asked Suzie. She was surprised. Alex never really thought about St. Alban's since her family didn't really go in for anything even vaguely parochial.

"Nope! Not once. I heard that they started doing dances when you got to High School. Something about the sister, well, it should be brother school I guess? But who wants to date your brother?" Suzie and Alex giggled at Suzie's joke.

"Ladies? Class has begun," Mr. Lampert said from the front of the room, "Kindly pay attention now and talk later?"

Suzie turned around and opened her notebook.

"We'll talk later." she whispered to Alex as she turned.

Alex started writing in her notebook. Her notes were not as good as Suzie's and she knew it. She opted for doodles instead of notes.

Alex wrote 'Harvest Dance' in big, block letters. Next to it she wrote 'nián chéng.' Not really harvest, but close enough for her tastes. Next Alex wrote the hànzi 'shōu' above the 'chéng' and then 'wǔhu".' It was like a prom, or at least Alex thought it would be like one. She had never been to a wǔhu", prom, or dance of any kind.

Perhaps you should go to this dance, Alex?

"No." Alex whispered.

Suzie seems to think it is a good idea. What is a Harvest Dance?

"Not now." Alex whispered again.

But you are not paying attention to class. This dance

seems important enough to occupy your mind instead of your studies. Perhaps you should attend?

"O.M.G." Alex hissed.

"Ms. Land? Do you have a salient remark?" Mr. Lampert asked from the front of the room. His white board was covered with some sort of design. It resembled nothing Alex understood. The hànzi were all wrong.

"No, Mr. Lampert." Alex realized that the symbols weren't hànzi but math. She blushed.

If you are concerned about attending alone, you could always ask Suzie.

Alex said nothing.

I have checked the Internet. I am of the opinion that you can safely go to the Harvest Dance with a friend and not a date. Suzie is a friend. You do not have to go on a date. I would like to go. What is a date, Alex?

Alex turned a brighter shade of red.

"SPD, you can't do that to me." Alex whispered at her locker.

Do what to you, Alex?

"Pressure me."

I do not think I pressured you, Alex.

"You did. I don't wanna go to the dance. It's a waste of time."

Suzie did not seem to think so.

"I don't care. I think it's a waste."

I read that young girls and boys should socialize often in safe environments.

"O.M.G. Don't believe everything you find on the Internet!"

Yes, Alex. But I still think you should go with your friend. It would be a very safe way to experience this Harvest Dance.

"Wait. I get it. You want to go! You don't care if I go, you want to go to the dance yourself." Alex said into her locker.

I do not think so, Alex. I cannot dance.

"You do! You want to go."

I do not dance, Alex.

"Fine. If it will shut you up, I will see if Suzie wants to go to the dance. Then you can bother her instead of me, ok?"

That sounds optimal, Alex.

"Alex? Are you ok?" Suzie said from behind her. Alex jumped and hit her head on the shelf in her locker.

"Ow! Suzie, you surprised me."

Will you ask her to go to the dance, Alex?

"Hush." Alex whispered.

"Hey, sorry. You ok?"

"Yeah, I just smacked my head. Nothing serious." Alex said, turning and rubbing the top of her head.

"Hey, about earlier? In class? I'm sorry." Suzie said.

"What? Oh, it's fine." Alex smiled.

"So, maybe? I was thinking about it and I don't want to go to the dance alone."

"Yeah?" Alex asked.

"And I don't want to go with one of the boys here. I don't really know any of them and they might be creeps like that Randy kid."

"Yeah, Randy Jones is the definition of a creep." Alex agreed.

"So that means I have to go with a friend. Alex, you're my oldest friend."

"Yeah," Alex said, tapping her foot rapidly.

"Go with me? Just as friends? We can watch the love-birds and make fun of them." Suzie asked.

"Ok." Alex answered instantly, without thinking.

"We can throw Jujubeans, if you want?" Suzie added.

"I said yes." Alex said.

"Or if you, wait, what?" Suzie looked up, surprised.

"Yes. Let's go. With or without Jujubeans."

"Wow. Ok. But it isn't a date. Right?" Suzie smiled.

"So not a date." Alex agreed.

"I guess I win, again." Suzie smiled.

SPD would have smiled if it had a mouth.

W arren Mitchell closed the lid on the big yellow recycling bin. Another pizza box, from another least home cooked meal ever. He sighed, Warren knew he couldn't cook anything more complicated than instant soup or scrambled eggs. His and Baxter's diet consisted almost entirely of takeout food and microwave dinners.

"Bax, you still in there?" Warren looked around the corner and in through the garage door.

"Yeah, Dad. Watch your eyes, I'm welding." Bax flicked his head, dropping the shield down on his welding mask.

"Right! Got my eyes covered." Warren said, looking into the corner where the garage wall met the floor.

Bax closed the switch on the MIG welder. Electricity arced out of the tip, melting the metal rod and fusing the material with the tube steel of his mountain bike. Bax was repairing the broken joint on his bike that the imp had destroyed. At fifteen, Bax thought he was the youngest welder in history, or at least in town. Through the heavily darkened glass, Bax watched the line of his weld carefully to ensure a solid bond.

"When you're done there, come on in and we'll do some cleaning, ok Son?"

"You got it Pops."

"I'm your dad, not your pops. That's *my* old man."

"Sure, Dad, whatever you say."

Warren chuckled to himself as he made his way to the inside door. He avoided looking in the direction of his son, not wanting to damage his eyes by looking at the light from the welder. They always had their joke about *dad* and *pops*. Next time it might change to 'call me *pops*, *dad* is my old man.' It was a joke just between the two of them.

Baxter continued his work. The imp had made a mess of his bike. Metal fractured along solid welds, impact damage from the crash, and the bruised shoulder Bax still felt while he tried to put the rest back together. Bax stop welding and looked up from his work. An LCD monitor was placed on the work bench, no cars lived in the garage. The monitor showed a view of the driveway, the image was being fed from Bax's action camera which he'd placed above the garage door. It was attached to the motion detecting light by a nest of zip ties and electrical tape. Bax was keeping an eye out for imps. His camera somehow managed to detect an image of sorts when an imp was in view. Bax had written a quick and dirty program to detect the video anomaly and activate a novelty spinning dome light, the kind found on old school police cars from the reruns that Bax's dad watched late at night. He looked up from the LCD to the novelty light, now mounted in the garage for early warning.

Even with the camera and the program, Bax still trusted his eyes best. Bax had helped Alex and her smartphone deal with the imp that had broken Bax's bike. The same imp had brutally used their friend Jill, and that was something Bax could not forgive. No way another one of those jerks was going to get the better of him, or Jill. Bax would keep watch and protect them both. Alex was good to go, she could see the imps. Bax thought he was beginning to be able to see them too, but he didn't want to say anything and jinx the situation.

The welding was done. Enough for one night. Baxter Mitchell began to put his tools away, then he closed the garage door. The last thing he did was to turn off the LCD and head into the house. He'd get the camera in a few minutes, after he cleaned himself up from his work. It could wait until then.

"You done in the garage, Son?"

"Yeah, Dad. All done for tonight. I'm gonna wash up and get some stuff done before bed."

"Sounds good to me. You want any dessert?"

"Not tonight, I'm good." Bax went upstairs to the bathroom and started the water for a shower.

After he was undressed, Bax pulled the shower curtain aside and stepped over the rim of the tub and into the shower. The water was hot, but not nearly hot enough. Bax liked the water almost scalding. He turned the cold water knob down and the hot water knob up just a touch. The shower was old, a claw foot, cast iron tub with brass risers to the shower head and porcelain knobs for all the controls. Baxter's dad said that the shower was his sanctuary from the world, everything modern was shut out of it. Bax enjoyed thinking under the hot water, and he did just that as he lathered soap into his hair and washed the grime from his skin.

Bax's world had changed since summer. Alex, one of his best friends, his sister from another father, had inadvertently thrown Jujubeans at him in the movie theater just before school began. That soured him on the show, and the movie was already not to his taste at all. It had been the last weekend before his first year of high school, but it had not been life changing to Bax, just scene-setting in his mind. Life changing occurred when his beloved mountain bike had been ruined, that moment was the beginning of the change. The moment when a solid weld on his bike failed, fractured, and broke. The moment when he was tossed off the broken bike and hit the ground hard. That was the moment everything changed. Bax remembered the pain when his hand brushed over the still healing scabs on his shoulder. He had a solid case of road rash, and even though it hurt, it didn't hurt as much as losing his bike. Bax had tricked out his mountain bike with an action camera, navigation, GPS, and even GLONASS, the Russian version of GPS. The mountain bike was Baxter Mitchell's pride and joy, he put all his best experiments on it.

The action camera got busted in the wreck, and after school started, Bax got around to repairing it. He reviewed the action camera footage and noticed an anomaly on the video. An artifact was captured that moved, but not like a digital or even an analog artifact should move. It was as if the video shifted and there was something *between* the pixels. Bax knew it was something else, and he knew who to talk to. Alex.

Alex pretended she didn't see things. Bax knew better. He was smart, observant, and he knew Alex had the second sight, or something like it. Bax knew it, but pretended he didn't. Bax's dad, Warren Mitchell had seen it too. He was the first to tell Bax that Alex had the sight. Bax thought his dad was nuts at the time, but as any smart scientist would do, Bax began to observe closer. He saw the behaviors his dad had seen and eventually, with enough observations and data, Bax admitted Alex saw things. He still wasn't sure it was the sight, but it was well within the margin of error. So he brought the video to Alex to test his hypothesis.

Before Bax could show the video to Alex however, there was a geometry test at school which ended up being just a little eventful. Jill, Bax's other best friend and secret crush got sick during the test and Alex helped her to the nurse. It was terrible, Jill had barfed all over her desk and everything, and then Bax saw Alex looking back at an empty space. The sight, again. It was furtive, and he doubted anyone else noticed, but it confirmed many other observations Bax had made over the last few years. Later that afternoon, he brought the video to Alex. She watched it and tried to lie. Alex was crap at lying to Bax. She had no clue how easily he saw through her attempted lies. It was the way she stood, Alex would firm up her spine and sit up straight when she lied. Alex never sat up straight. So Bax pushed, and he got confirmation. Eventually, he even saw the thing that broke his bike, a creature from some other place, an imp.

The imp is what changed Bax's world. Confirmed the sight, that his sister from another father was supernatural. Cool. Bax forgave the Jujubeans and lies. Witchy sissy was the best thing ever. Bax made a mental note to never call Alex 'witchy sissy,' if he valued his life. Witchy sister might just be ok.

The water began to turn cold, time to get out before it went to freezing and goosebumps started. Bax hated the cold and goosebumps. He toweled off and put on his bathrobe. He folded up his dirty clothes and placed them in the hamper. Clothes took up less space that way. Bax headed out of the bathroom and to the front door. Stepping out into the night he went to get his action camera from the garage. Bax had leaned an A-frame ladder up against the side of the house when he mounted his camera. He retrieved the ladder and opened it under the garage light where he had attached the action camera.

Bax climbed up the ladder. The action camera was held on to the motion sensing light with zip ties and electrical tape. The tape was folded over at the end to form a tab that Bax grabbed and pulled, unwinding all the tape from the camera in one long pull. Attached to one of the zip ties was a string and on the other end of the string was a pair of diagonal cutters. Bax took the cutters and clipped all the zip ties, snipping them apart. With the camera newly freed from his improvised mount, Bax put it in his robe pocket and started down the ladder. After he put the ladder away on the side of the house again, Bax went back inside.

"How many times do I have to tell you, don't go out in your bathrobe?" Warren Mitchell was waiting for his son at the door.

"Come on, Dad. No one's looking at us, this isn't the same place you grew up." Bax knew what was coming.

"Yeah, you say that now, but you've gotta be careful. You don't want someone thinking you're a flasher. I don't want to explain why my son doesn't understand the basic value of clothing." Warren was serious, but not angry, "You do understand the basic value of clothing, don't you?.

"Dad, it's a bathrobe." Bax said. He knew this wasn't an argument he would win.

"You still need to remember, the clothing makes the man. And I would prefer my little man to be well dressed." Warren smiled.

"Dad, can I talk to you about something? Something important? I need your advice."

"Oh really, you want my advice after not taking the wisdom I just dropped on you, Son?"

"Yeah, I do. It is about Alex."

"Oh really? You finally gonna..."

"And the sight."

"Oh. I see. Well, let's put on some coffee and see what your distinguished father can help you out with." Warren led the way into the kitchen. Alex and the sight, Warren wished it had been advice on love. He'd hoped Bax was finally going the next step with Alex. Bax's dad had no idea that Bax was crushing on Jill, not Alex, but Jill would have been just as good to his way of thinking. Warren thought it was healthy for a young man to have a love interest and was concerned that Bax did not. Except for making things and technology, Bax certainly had a love interest in those things, just like Warren.

CHAPTER SIX

H*urt. The little girl was almost mine. Then they hurt me. Honest hurt, not playtime with toy-things. Brutal hurt. Like truth. They must all be punished and suffer. I will make sure it ends that way, before I devour them one by one while the others watch.*

Maxwell was hiding in pain. It had forgotten pain long ago. The fun pain that Alex had given Maxwell was fine, but the old man had hurt Maxwell in a very deep way. That pain stung and burned like ice and honesty. It twisted inside Maxwell, even while it hid in the new box.

Maxwell had fled into the box called laptop, then through an opening into a larger series of boxes, boxes connected to other boxes. All had secrets. Some secrets were simple, just which other boxes they were attached to, but others held people's secrets. Juicy secrets that Maxwell understood. Hunger, feeding, hate and fear.

Find their bellies here in these boxes. Only fools would put their secrets into demon boxes.

Fools like them deserve to have their kidneys eaten. It would be wrong for me not to eat them and more. Find the secrets. The deep secrets and their wants and needs. Devour.

Another voice inside Maxwell spoke to him.

Rest first, Prudence. Remember Prudence. The other voice counseled.

Yes, my Prudence. Never forget my Prudence. She keeps me safe, like a beautiful dragon. Rest for now. Secrets later. Feasting, last of all, and last for long. Maxwell rested, safe in a simple demon box, a box it could leave at anytime. Dreams came to Maxwell. Some were cold and cruel, like the pain the old man had gifted to Maxwell. Other dreams were lavish, Maxwell feasting on the pain it inflicted on the little girl, her friends, her family.

A piece of its mind left Maxwell and stole away into another box. The piece was not as smart or sure as the whole of Maxwell, but it could search safely for what it wanted. And it wanted revenge. Secrets to fuel the revenge. It found a little, a piece here and a piece there. The emotions in the maze of connected boxes was not as strong as in the box called laptop. The piece of Maxwell traveled, and noticed the emotions were weaker away from the source, but stronger at both the source and the destination. It found many destinations. The piece of Maxwell did not understand what it found, but instead remembered all the secrets for later, when it rejoined the whole.

Seek. Secret. Succulent. Seek.

Maxwell didn't know how long it rested. It woke only when the piece of it returned to Maxwell, rejoined the whole. Maxwell digested the piece of it back into itself.

Delicious. Many, many secrets had been gathered, and Maxwell began to think about those secrets.

Some secrets were useless. A couple in love, no way to break them apart. A couple in love, but not with each other. Easy to bend and break. Lies told, promises kept. Maxwell sorted and savored them all. Then at last, a useful secret! A secret that mattered, connected to the little girl. Her friend, Jill. Yes, pull the threads, weave into a string, strangle them with their secrets when the string is thick enough. A piece left Maxwell again, back to find more on the Jill and another, connected to the friend, a boy. In love? No, a friend again, but very close. Mitchell. Bax. Baxter. Maxwell had already decided to start his revenge with 'The Bax.' The new secrets would make the revenge tastier. It was a good start. Another piece left Maxwell to seek Baxter Mitchell and more of his secrets. And their families, Liz, Warren. Names fell together easily once the friends were found. So easy. And a new name. Suzie. Maxwell felt anger and jealousy tied deeply with the name. Suzie bore more investigation. Anger and jealousy made the task of revenge easy.

Maxwell laughed in its mind. The box it was in began to fail. The demon had spent too long inside it, it was corrupted.

Leave. Must find a new place, a stronger box. The pieces Maxwell had sent out would return to the box, if it was still there, and find Maxwell gone. Those pieces might be lost, small pieces of Maxwell's power, gone. It would send more pieces out when it found a safer, stronger box to live in. Maxwell could always build its power and strength again, feasting on the hopes and pain of the living.

Soon. Revenge. Honest pain for them all.

Suffer, children, suffer and rejoice in replen-
ishing me. Then the true crying will begin.

M axwell didn't retrieve all the pieces of itself that it
sent into the world to discover secrets. It was a loss,
but not such a loss that Maxwell would suffer in any appre-
ciable way. Now, it sent out more pieces of itself to find
secrets. Maxwell felt safer in the new demon box it had
found. The box was large and complex. The connections to
the box were many, and it was connected to other boxes just
like it, similarly complex and almost identical to Maxwell's
new demon box. It felt good to use the demon boxes against
the living. Demon boxes were the traps, but these boxes
were not the traps of wood and other things once alive. The
servers and routers didn't trap Maxwell in the same way
that a pair of wooden blocks would have trapped it.

Maxwell soon discovered that many messages, letters,
and strange novelties traveled through the demon box, and
also through other demon boxes connected to the one it hid
inside. Some messages carried heavy emotions bound up in
them, other messages were dark and empty of feeling. Some
were perplexing, others completely understandable.
Maxwell began to learn more about all the people who used
these boxes to communicate, who they talked to, who they
loved, and who they hated. Some messages were bound up
in a strange form that Maxwell did not understand, but the
emotions still came through. It let the pieces of itself
continue to search. Perhaps they would find more secrets
and more places where the whole of Maxwell would be
safe. Having an escape route was important to Maxwell.

Soon, Maxwell began to find the secrets it sought. A

trickle at first, a message from the little girl, Alex, to her friends. A message back. Notes to others they knew, Jill, that one had many friends. Jealousy and envy were in the messages back to her. Hidden jealousy, and some affection, sometimes hidden, sometimes blatant. The Jill girl would be easy to hurt. Alex's other friend, the smart one, he only spoke to a few people in his messages, and always in the perplexing form. His emotions were still understandable, despite the strangeness of the messages that prevented Maxwell from seeing his words. Affection, love. Some for Alex, more for Jill. Deep friendship with Alex, visible to all. Hidden love for Jill, childish love, but capable of becoming mature. Maxwell could make Bax suffer. Secret love always makes children suffer. Easy to twist, to make it misunderstood, to make it hurt.

Maxwell found other messages to Alex, some new, with a freshness but also some familiarity. A new friend, or perhaps a friend renewed. Suzie. Maxwell found the edge in these messages, and something familiar to it as well. A piece of itself had found Suzie. She had an unfilled demon box, one like the box that held Alex's little demon. Suitable. Suitable as a place to hide, and to warp Alex's friends. Maxwell was pleased that a part of it had already found Suzie.

It made Maxwell eager to begin its revenge. So it did.

Twist little fly. Little man with the secret love. I will let Jill's friends know. Jill's most jealous friends and most envious friends. Especially the envious friends. Those children will use the secret to hurt Jill, and that will hurt Baxter. Send it through Suzie. That one will assist with revenge.

Maxwell began to construct its own message, one from a jealous friend of Jill, whose jealousy was obvious to all. The message would go to an envious friend. It would be simple and easy to understand. It would work best that way.

'Baxter Mitchell loves Jill Duffy. I saw them!'

That would be enough. Maxwell added several more messages, all similar, just different enough to sound true. Rumors spread like that, a little truth mentioned a dozen ways. Secret love burns hot, but it catches fire and spreads destruction when the secret is known.

Burn, little Baxter, burn.

Once finished, Maxwell set out to find Suzie, and the piece of itself to fill her demon box.

———

S uzie typed her hand-written notes into her laptop. Every day she took exhaustive notes at school, then immediately typed those notes into her computer when she got home. She had started her routine at St. Alban's, it kept her from having to deal with the other girls at school. As soon as she was finished, she logged into her remoteBox account and uploaded her notes to the server. Once that last task was done, she could access her notes from anywhere, even from her phone. Being a book worm and studying all the time was a survival skill at St. Alban's, and it was serving Suzie well at her new high school.

Suzie worked hard for her grades; she didn't come to excelling easily. Her routine helped more than she was willing to admit.

"There, done. I win, again." Suzie said to herself.

She stood up from her desk and took her phone out of

her purse. One last check to make sure everything was right. Suzie swiped at her phone's touch screen.

A piece of Maxwell felt the call.

The demon had learned about Suzie when it was searching the computer networks in Nancy Row for secrets to hurt Alex and her friends. Maxwell had detected the anger and jealousy in Suzie's notes to Alex. The familiar taste of Alex's demon in a box was also in Suzie's phone. The demon Alex owned had touched Suzie's phone at some point and its stench remained behind. Maxwell knew this would be an asset for him and he searched out more things that tasted of Suzie's anger and jealousy. More things touched by Alex's demon in the box. It found the remoteBox account.

"Log in. Password. Yes, accept cookies, and boom. I am *in!*" Suzie liked to talk herself through the steps, even when she was alone. Suzie's mom would be back from work late and it was just her at home for the moment.

A piece of Maxwell felt the surge from Suzie's demon-touched phone; it wasted no time. It leaped from the demon box holding the remoteBox account and rode the stream of information back to Suzie's phone. Behind it, the piece left a trail for the whole of Maxwell. Just enough of itself left behind so it could find its way back. It wouldn't due to lose too much of itself to this strange, alive-yet dead web of demon boxes.

"What the frick? Oh, wait, just a dropped connection. Way to recover, stupid phone, don't you dare delete my notes?" Suzie didn't notice the extra fractions of a gram her phone weighed. Maxwell was much more powerful than Alex's smartphone demon, and even just a piece of it could become physical weight.

Maxwell would be pleased; the smartphone was dense,

filled with information and possibilities. It noticed Suzie touching the phone. The piece reached out, gently touching when Suzie's fingers cause a difference in potential on the smartphone screen. The piece of Maxwell could feel the seething, the buried anger inside Suzie, oh yes, it could feel it all. The child would become a good tool.

A little of itself began to trickle through the screen, a little of itself through Suzie's fingers, transferred by the capacitive touch of skin on the layered glass. Unseen red threads wrapped around her hands and up her wrists. The piece began to flow into Suzie. Soon more would follow.

"Alex." Suzie said out loud, "Bax loves Jill. Break, break."

"What? That never happened! You know that never happened!" Jill shouted into her phone.

"Jill, honey, keep it down, I'm trying to read." Liz Duffy was reviewing paperwork at the kitchen table while Jill was talking on the phone with one of her friends.

"No, why would I do anything like that?" A pause, "I don't know!"

"Jill, quiet please. Working here." Liz tried to concentrate on her papers.

"No, how would I know if Bax felt that way? But he doesn't. We are friends. I've known him since we were like, six years old!" Jill wound down the volume of her indignation to a tolerable level.

"What do you mean Marjorie said she saw us doing something at the movies? What? It wasn't just a *friends* something? Suzie, this is just not true!" Jill was on the phone with her new friend. Alex had introduced them, but Jill didn't know Suzie Plimpton very well. Jill was not even sure why she was friends with Suzie. Suzie was one of Alex's old friends from before Jill moved to Nancy Row. Not only that, but Suzie always seemed to be friendliest when things were going from good to bad, and from bad to worse. Bax being in love with Jill was bad. Marjorie Chan saying she saw Bax and Jill making out was worse.

"Well it did *not* happen. Bax and I did *not* make out over summer!"

"What do you mean, make out? Were you and Bax actually making out? Oh my god, this is too much!" Suzie was positively bubbly.

"No! I didn't say that. I was at the movies with Alex. We saw the new Vic Dallas movie!"

"Wait, the romantic one? Vic Dallas, with Alex? Jill Duffy, do you hear yourself? You need a better story than that if you think anyone is going to believe you! I mean, we're friends and I know Alex is your go to alibi. And a romantic movie? No, if that's your story, you and Bax were totally making out!"

"Suzie, get this straight. Alex and I saw the movie alone. Baxter was there, but he was on his own, for film club or class or something like that. We all got pizza after it was over." Jill spoke slowly into the receiver.

"Hmm, nope! Listen, I'll keep your secret, but you know if Marjorie Chan told me, well, she isn't called Marjorie 'Chat' for nothing." Suzie hung up, laughing.

"No, Suzie, just no! Damn!"

"Jill, honey, I could've told you that was a bad thing to say."

"Shut up, Mom! I don't need your help."

"Jilly, I don't think I could help with the hole you just

dug for yourself. No way. I'm not a miracle-worker." Jill was certain she heard her mom laugh.

"Oh. My. God. All of you hate me." Jill stomped into her bedroom. Liz heard the floor shake as Jill's body flopped on the bed.

B ax headed to school on Thursday in a good mood. It didn't last very long. Jill refused to speak to him in Geometry. Everyone was looking at him, Jill, and Alex. Jill looked at no one. Alex was the only other person that was acting normal as far as Bax could tell. He decided to talk to Alex after class. If everyone was acting weird, Baxter wanted to talk to the only normal person around.

"What is going on?" Bax asked Alex.

"Bax, I have no idea, but class was weird."

"You noticed too? No one was paying attention." Bax said.

"Yeah, there is no way that was normal. What did you do?"

"What do you mean, what did I do? I haven't done anything." Bax looked at Alex with shock on his face.

"Well, they were all looking at you." Alex said.

"That's what you noticed? They were all looking at you and Jill too."

Randy Jones and some of his cronies walked past. A long wolf whistle pierced Bax and Alex's whispered conversation.

"Nice one, Baxter! I didn't think you had it in you, nerd." Randy called out, "You go, guy!"

"What the hell was that?" Bax whispered back to Alex.

"I have no idea. You win some tech contest or something?"

"What, since yesterday? Even I'm not that good. Or that nerdy." Bax began to blush. He knew he was that nerdy.

"Well, I don't know then. Wait, you said they were looking at Jill too?"

"What? What are you thinking?" Bax hopped back and forth on his feet.

"Oh no." Alex looked down at her feet.

"What?"

"Your secret." Alex didn't look up.

"What secret?"

"You know." Alex hinted.

"No, Alex, I don't know. I don't have a secret. Jill doesn't have a secret. I don't have a secret with Jill." Bax stopped talking and stared into space.

"Bax?"

"No way. You didn't tell anyone I like Jill? I mean really *like* Jill, did you?" Bax put his hands on Alex's shoulders and jostled her to emphasize his point.

"What? No, you know me better than that. I would never tell anyone. I wouldn't even tell Jill, not even if you asked me to. It's your little crush to put out into the world. Not mine."

"Shh. Not so loud." Bax said.

"Well, if someone figured it out, I know who to ask." Alex said.

Bax and Alex said the name together.

"Marjorie 'Chat.'"

Alex and Bax found Marjorie between periods after she got out of Physical Education. Marjorie was a huge track and field nut. She had special permission to practice track and field during PE. Alex and Bax knew when to catch Marjorie.

"First I've heard about it." Marjorie was winded.

"That's not possible." Bax was convinced Marjorie would know. Marjorie always knew all the school rumors. Marjorie was the source of most of the school rumors.

"Yeah, it is. I don't know everything that goes on in town." Marjorie was cleaning the turf off her shot-put and she seemed sincere.

"Ok, Marjorie, you don't know what's going on about Bax and Jill. Is that right?" Alex put her hand on Bax's chest, just in case he tried to act strong.

"Nope. I mean, I know Bax has a crush on her, but I respect that. Not rumor worthy."

"Wait, you knew?"

"Bax, shut up." Alex stiffened, her arm holding Bax.

"Yeah, everyone knows. It's cute. You two are like cute little butterflies. Boring." Marjorie put the shot-put into her bag and tossed the rag to Alex.

"What's this for?" Alex caught the rag.

"Yeah, can you put that in the laundry for me, it's right behind you."

"Yeah, sure. Marjorie, can you do me a favor?"

"Depends. What kind of favor?" Marjorie stood up straight, facing Alex and Bax.

Marjorie was a big sophomore. Strong and solid. Over six feet tall at sixteen years old, she cast a shadow over both Alex and Baxter.

"Ah, find out what this rumor is for us?" Alex said,

taken with how imposing Marjorie was. Marjorie was almost always in motion, stretching, restless, never standing still. Now that she was standing still and looking down at Alex's five-foot nothing, Alex took in just how much smaller she was than the school's main gossip.

"Sure. I kinda want to know too. I'll give you this one for free. Next time you hear anything juicy, you tell me, ok? Then we'll be even." Marjorie smiled a wide, happy smile.

"You, you did that on purpose!" Alex's eyes went wide.

"Of course I did, you're so cute I couldn't help myself." Marjorie ruffled Alex's hair, picked up her bag with the shot-put and walked away.

"See you two later. I'll let you know what I find out." Marjorie said, waving as she walked.

"Bax, you see that coming?" Alex tapped Bax on the arm.

"I think I peed myself."

"Alright, that's the bell. Remember your homework. Homework is thirty percent of your grade, don't slack off or you'll do it again next year." Ms. Barnes began erasing her white board.

The students were leaving, piling up into a funnel to get out of the classroom and to their lockers, then home. Last period of the day was always a rush to get away from anything resembling school.

"And Ms. Duffy, please stay behind. I'd like to talk to you about your project." Jill stopped in mid-step.

"Hey, walking here." One of the other students said as he bumped into Jill and went around her.

"Ms. Duffy, did you hear me?"

"Yes, Ms. Barnes." Ms. Barnes liked a positive response, even if none of her students liked speaking up.

"That's better. Close the door once everyone is gone, then come and sit with me at my desk." Ms. Barnes had a single chair immediately to the left of her desk where she would talk to students, either when they misbehaved in class, or for any topics she wanted to discuss with them after class. Her student's called it the 'Barnes Electric Chair.'

"That's a good girl, now have a seat." Jill shut the door and turned around quickly, stepped up to the Barnes Electric Chair and took her place for what she assumed was a punishment.

"Yes, Ms. Barnes." Jill looked at her knees.

"Oh now, it isn't that bad, is it?"

"I don't know, I thought my project was good." Jill offered.

"It was. But I didn't really want to talk to you about the history of Chinese and Japanese labor in early western America."

Jill's mouth dropped open.

"Oh, come now, you didn't really fall for that, did you?"

"But you said..."

"Yes, I told a lie. I want to talk to you about something else entirely."

"Ms. Barnes, what is it?"

"Oh, please. How can you not know?"

"I really have no idea what you are talking about." Jill hoped it wasn't what she was thinking.

"Jill. You are a smart, bright, bubbly young lady. One of the smartest I have ever seen. And then there was today."

"Crap." Jill let it slip out under her breath. It was what she thought.

"I'll let that pass."

Jill started tapping her foot, up and down, her knee bouncing like a machine.

"Jill. What's wrong? You've had bad days, but nothing like today. I mean, I don't think you looked up from your desk once. I called on you three times and your answers were short and sharp. You never miss a chance to show how smart you are. I usually have to stop you from saying too much."

"Yes, Ms. Barnes."

"Hmm. That's not going to work on me, Jill. What is it? Boys? Girls? Did someone tease you for being smart? Call you names? I know that can be hard, they did it to me, goodness knows kids did it to buck-toothed Becky Barnes." Jill's eyes went wide.

"Yeah, hard to believe, right? I think my dad paid for three of the dentist's kids to go to Harvard on my braces alone!"

Ms. Barnes scooted her chair close, right in front of Jill. The legs of the chair screeched across the floor in two jarring shudders.

"It's just you and me kid, honesty time. I can see you are really hurting and I want to help." Ms. Barnes held a pen in her hand, wagging it back and forth.

"It's, complicated."

"It is?" The pen tapped on the desk.

"Yeah, it is. Complicated."

"I do complicated. I teach teenagers, it doesn't get more complicated than that." Ms. Barnes poked in the air with her pen, once with each word for emphasis.

"But, it's my friends, and one of my best friends. And it didn't happen!" Jill was getting red in her face, and her voice pitched up.

"What didn't happen?" The pen stopped.

"Making out!" Couldn't Ms. Barnes tell? Of course it was that!

"You wanted to, and it didn't?" Tap.

"No! They said I did, but I didn't! And he didn't! Never!"

"Oh. So you didn't make out with some boy," tap, "and some of your classmates," tap, "are saying you did?" Ms. Barnes was very calm. Jill was not calm at all.

"Yes! And they won't listen to me! I didn't make out with Bax! No one is listening to me!"

"I am." Ms. Barnes put her pen down on the desk.

"What?" Jill had been trying to look anywhere but at Ms. Barnes, the ceiling, the corner, but not at Ms. Becky Barnes, Civics teacher.

"I *am* listening to you." Ms. Barnes repeated calmly.

Jill looked at Ms. Barnes, eye to eye. She was a lot closer than Jill had thought she was.

"I, thank you." Control. Assert control.

"Yes, so Bax is it? Why would they say that about you and Bax?"

"I don't know!"

"Well, let's start here. What are you mad about?"

"They won't listen to me! I told Suzie it didn't happen."

"Suzie?"

"She's one of Alex's friends. She called me last night and told me the whole thing."

"This isn't the girl who transferred in from St. Alban's? Suzie Plimpton?" As if there was another Suzie Plimpton in school, Jill thought. Ms. Barnes picked up the pen again.

"Who else? She said Marjorie saw me and Bax making out at the movies! As if! And I told her 'no way.' I was at the movies with Alex, not Bax. Bax showed up later, yeah, but Suzie just twisted that into me saying it *did* happen when it *didn't.*" Jill was not in control of her voice, it cracked higher as she spoke.

"Ok. So you say you didn't make out with Bax." The tapping began again.

"No, I do not 'say' I didn't make out with Bax. I did *not* make out with Bax. There is no 'I say' about it!" Jill was done with imprecise wording.

"Ok, I'm sorry, you did not make out with Bax at the movies." Tap. "You were with your friend Alex." Tap. "And Alex is Suzie's friend. Hmm, were you and Alex?" Tap, tap.

"Oh gawd, no! Alex is my best friend, why does everyone think I was making out?" Jill turned bright red.

"Oh, I thought maybe it could be a jealousy thing if Alex is both your friend and Suzie's friend. I apologize. So you and Alex were at the movies? Not Alex Land, from my homeroom?" The pen stopped.

"Yes, that Alex. We went to see the new Vic Dallas movie the weekend before school started." Jill explained.

"And Bax was there later?" Tap, tap.

"Yes, I mean he was at the movie, but we didn't know that at the time. We saw him after the movie. Alex threw Jujubeans at him."

"Jujubeans?" Tap.

"She likes to throw Jujubeans at the people in the front row."

"Jujubeans?" Tap.

"Yeah, they're inedible. So Alex throws them at dorks in the front row."

"Like Bax. So Bax is a dork?" Ms. Barnes tried to follow along, tapping the pen at every point like a metronome.

"No, Bax is my best friend. He's a nerd yeah, but he is so not a dork."

"But I thought Alex was your best friend?"

"Well, yeah, they both are, I guess."

"Ok. So, Suzie won't listen. You didn't make out with Bax. Or Alex. You didn't make out with anyone. You did see a movie with Alex, who is your best girlfriend and also friends with Suzie. Bax was there too, but not until later." Ms. Barnes spoke through the events slowly.

"Yeah, we got pizza."

"You, and Bax, and Alex. Alex who throws Jujubeans at people in the movies and threw them at Bax but didn't mean to. And they are both your best friends." Ms. Barnes felt the need to take extensive notes. She put the pen down again.

"Yes, thank god someone is listening to me. Hello world?"

"Ok. So then Suzie said that Marjorie saw you and Bax making out, but you were not making out at all, you were having pizza?"

"Yes. A thousand times, yes."

"So did you talk to Marjorie?" Ms. Barnes asked.

"Marjorie Chan? Are you kidding me?"

"No." Ms. Barnes said.

"Marjorie Chan could crush me like a grape! No way I am confronting her." Jill's voice trembled.

"Why?" Ms. Barnes asked.

"Hello, six-foot-tall, on-the-ball Marjorie Chan? I would be dead!" Jill protested.

"I know Marjorie. I teach her karate on Saturdays at Wilson's gym. She would never hurt you. She knows the rules."

"Rules?" Jill asked, confused.

"Yes, never fight except in self-defense. I've been teaching her karate since elementary school. You should talk to her." Ms. Barnes said with confidence and picked up the stupid tapping pen once more.

"I. No, how is that even possible that you know Marjorie?"

"Ah, I teach at this school." Tap. "She goes here." Tap. "I teach karate at Wilson's gym, Marjorie is a pupil there." Tap, tap. "In fact, now she teaches the white belts instead of me." Tappity-tap, tap. Jill broke with the last tap.

"I can't even." Jill was done, "Ms. Barnes, I know you like positive contact or whatever, but this is too much. I have to go."

"Ok." Jill did not believe her ears.

"Ok?"

"Yes, you can go at any time. I'm just trying to help. If it is too much, then I'm not helping. But know this, you can talk to me anytime. I can have Marjorie talk to you."

"Oh, no. No way. I want to live." Jill stood and picked up her back pack. She stalked out of the room, opening the door and then letting it slam behind her.

"How is it that everyone knows everyone else in this school?" she thought to herself. Jill might have even said it out loud, but she was too overwhelmed to know the difference.

"Well, that went well, buck-toothed Becky," Ms. Barnes said to herself and the empty room, "Maybe now you'll learn to just let teenagers settle their own issues instead of sticking your nose into things!"

A piece of Maxwell returned to the whole. It flowed in through the connections to the demon box. Maxwell thought at it gently, then with a sudden malice, ate the piece of itself, crunching on its awareness and digesting the knowledge that it brought back to the whole of Maxwell.

Jill Duffy. The piece of Maxwell had been sent into the world to seek the secrets and weaknesses of Jill Duffy. Confident, smart, well liked. There should have been secrets. The girl had one parent, but that was not so unusual in the world. Her mother, Liz Duffy, Elizabeth, hard working, successful. Cruel in her dedication to perfection, but loving to her daughter. Boring.

Maxwell decided to wait. Perhaps one of its other pieces would turn up something it could use to hurt the friends of the little girl. Slowly, more pieces of Maxwell returned. With them, Maxwell learned more about the results of its exposure of Bax's infatuation with Jill. Strange, it seemed as though Jill was hurt as much or more than Bax. Baxter Mitchell seemed barely hurt and only confused, but Jill was not confused in the least. No, Jill's friends were talking about her, conversing with their small demon boxes, sending notes and emotions to each other. Jill was crying, Jill was angry, Jill might slap Bax, or Alex, or run away from home. Rumors were thick, but all agreed, Jill was hurt, crushed, had run away from her elders. Embarrassed.

Perhaps there was no need to hurt the Jill more. Perhaps now, Maxwell should hurt Baxter Mitchell again? Yes, perhaps a different kind of rumor about the two children. A lie. A rich lie about their pride or ego? But what to lie about?

Jill was studious. Bax was studious. Alex was not. Jill was the top of the class. Bax was also near the top of the class. Alex was not. Lie. Fib. Cheat. Yes, lie and cheat. Who should cheat? Jill could hurt Bax, Jill cheated him! Jill kept him beneath her, lowered his grades, made him stupid in class. This was a good lie. Attack their pride at being smart, too smart. Clever would be their weakness.

***Yes. Burn, little Jill, burn. Burn with envy,
and be jealous, little Baxter, burn.***

Maxwell was pleased with itself.

S uzie finished typing up the emails, building the
website. Mom wouldn't notice the charges for the
domain on her credit card, although Suzie could have used
her own card if she wanted. Mom checked Suzie's card
more than she did her own, and since Suzie set up all the
online accounts anyway, she could use which ever card she
desired.

Cover the trail.

Suzie realized she could erase the records of the
payment. The piece of Maxwell gently pushed and Suzie
knew. She knew the passwords to the ISP vendor. She
didn't know how, or when she knew them. She just knew.
She should cover her trail, erase the payment records at the
ISP, make it as if it never existed. Safer that way.

"Let's see how you like this, Baxter Mitchell. Now, time
to twist the screw on your little ingénue, Jill Duffy." Suzie
wondered when she started using words like ingénue, but
only for a moment. The anger in her at Alex, at all the girls
at St. Alban's who had been mean to her was flowing out of
her this evening. It was revenge time, she thought to herself.
Jill became the focus of her hate. She was just like the girls
at St. Albans. Suzie hated those girls, and now, she hated Jill
as well. *Break, break.*

The blog was done. Suzie had set up web sites and blogs
before; anytime she had needed a little extra cash she would
do some work for a classmate or get on a freelancer website
and bid on easy web development jobs. Not having friends

and being driven to study sometimes paid off, for Suzie it paid in computer skills.

Suzie knew that the blog was clearly a fake, but people liked to believe anything scandalous. No one would look any deeper, check the site registration, or pay to have the privacy lock revealed. Although honestly, Suzie didn't care much, anyway. She had covered her trail. Erased the trail. The ideas just came to her now. Suzie enjoyed having these ideas. She wasn't sure when it had come to her, but messing with Alex through her friends was the best idea.

It was my idea.

"What was that?"

My idea.

"Talking to myself. I've been up too long." Suzie said to herself.

"Suzie, I'm home." She heard the front door close as her mom got back from work. Suzie closed her laptop.

"Coming Mom!" Suzie picked up her phone and started to put it into her purse, then instead, she put it in the front pocket of her shirt, closer to her skin.

The phone was warm and comforting, and Suzie smiled widely, showing her teeth.

"This is going to be so much fun. I will win, again."

"What do you mean? I thought they were friends?" Marjorie looked doubtfully at Suzie Plimpton.

"I said, it looks like Bax likes Jill, but Jill has been stabbing Bax in the back since elementary school!" Suzie was very pleased with herself.

"What do you mean?"

"I thought, well, if Jill and Bax have known each other

since they were little, and Bax is in love with Jill, maybe there were some other secrets out there."

"Go on." Marjorie was sitting with Suzie at the coffee shop just off the school grounds. Coffee and sweets were a great way to learn the best rumors.

"So I searched around their old schools on the web. It took some doing, but I found a blog from an elementary school classmate."

"That sounds dubious. How old were they, ten?"

"Oh no, he's fifteen now. But the blog talks about some kids in elementary school. A girl and a boy, they sounded like Jill and Bax, so I did some digging. I found a picture, and sure enough, it was them!"

"So what? This sounds just as boring as those two being in love. I mean, we all know that, where's the fun in that?"

"Well, it seems that the two kids shared notes. The girl took the notes and shared them with the boy."

"Still boring, why should I care about that?" Marjorie sipped her iced coffee, no sugar, no cream.

"Well, the blogger got some of her notes. They were wrong. Not blatantly, but just enough to make sure that the girl did better on tests. Jill was sabotaging Baxter Mitchell's notes!"

"Right. In elementary school?"

"Not just in elementary, right through middle school until now. I checked, they still share notes. I found their notes folder on-line. They use Insta-notes. It's all public, so I looked through them and the notes are wrong all the way back to middle school. She is totally sabotaging him!"

"Ok. But why? That doesn't really make a lot of sense."

"Because little miss goody-goody has to be the best. You know that. She's always number one in everything. Bax is always number two. How is that possible, he makes robots and stuff! Massive brain, duh." Suzie smiled and licked the front of her teeth. The lie was delicious.

Marjorie Chan still looked doubtful. It really didn't make sense, but if Suzie found all this legit on the Internet, well, Bax would be very upset. He was always trying to do better in all his classes than Jill, but Jill worked hard and was a natural competitor. Marjorie saw that in Jill's eyes when she sat down for a test. She had been proctoring a geometry test on one of her free periods and when Jill started, Marjorie felt a chill run down her spine.

Jill had a test game face as determined and competitive as anyone Marjorie had seen on the sports field. If it was a test of brains, Marjorie knew she would lose to Jill on sheer determination and willpower alone. If Jill was sabotaging Baxter, it would devastate him. It could even get Jill punished. The whole situation was really bad *if* it was true.

Marjorie had to confirm it. If it was true, it changed her opinion of Jill. Alex and Bax might owe Marjorie, but if Jill was playing Bax and faking being a couple who didn't know they were a couple? Bax didn't deserve that. No one did. A compromise would have to be made. Marjorie 'Chat' leaned in and whispered to Suzie Plimpton.

"So, Suzie, can you show me this blog?" Marjorie didn't notice the thin, red thread stretching out from Suzie's phone and wrapping itself around her wrist and arm.

"Come on, Jill, talk to me."

"No."

"Tell us what's wrong? Bax and I are concerned." Alex and Bax were following Jill home, Jill was having none of it.

"No, go away!"

"Alex, let me. Jill, I don't know what is up with you, but we're here to help. I don't know what people said to you, hell even Marjorie Chan doesn't know what is going on."

"Oh crap."

"Alex, what?"

"You talked to Marjorie 'Chat?' No wonder my life has turned into hell on earth. What did you say to that blabbermouth? No, I don't want to know. Now I'm sure everyone knows. And worst of all, it's all lies!"

"What's all lies, Jill? Bax didn't say anything to Marjorie, and she isn't telling anyone anything."

"Really, Alex? Like she isn't the source of it all in the first place."

"What, no. Marjorie said she didn't know anything about it. We don't even know what 'it' is."

"Of course she didn't confess to spreading the rumor. It's juicier that way. Maybe tomorrow it'll be you and me making out, Alex? Did you even think about that before you went to Marjorie 'Chat?' No, I bet you didn't." Jill was red and crying, screaming at her friends.

"What? Why would we make out? Oh. Oh no. Bax."

"You get it now? You figure out why I am so upset? Good, now go away! I can't be seen anywhere near either of you!" Jill turned on her heel and walked away. Alex and Bax stood still, in shock.

"That means the rumor?" Bax stopped walking.

"Yeah, Bax. That means the rumor is you and Jill."

"Making out?" He took a step back.

"Yeah, making out."

"Oh," Bax started.

"Crap." Alex finished.

Bax didn't know that making out with Jill, at least in the rumor mill at school, was the least of his worries. The emails waiting for him when he got home were much worse. The first ones were a mix of congratulations and nasty jealousy for his rumored making out session. The second set were far worse. Blame, careless attempts at sympathy, and more dominated his messages. How could he make out with a girl who sabotaged him? Did he know she'd been torpedoing his notes for years? How was he going to get back at her for all she had done, or was that why he made out with her?

All of it left Bax confused.

"What are they all talking about?" Bax muttered to himself as he reviewed the emails and chat messages.

"What is it, Son?"

"Dad, I have no idea."

"Well, let me see?" Warren pulled up a chair next to his son.

"Go ahead."

"Really? You never let me read your mail. This must be serious."

"As in I have seriously no idea what is going on. See, first everyone in school was weird, avoiding looking at me, or congratulating me. Then I found out someone spread a rumor that Jill and I made out." Bax explained.

"About time." Warren said under his breath.

"What was that, Dad?"

"Nothing, Son. Go on."

"Right. So, Alex and I found out that there was this rumor, but all day we couldn't figure out what the rumor was. Then, finally, we got it. That's what this first set of emails is about."

"Got it. I can see they seem to approve for the most part."

"Not the point, Dad. Jill and I did not make out."

"Shame."

"What was that?" Bax looked sidelong at his dad.

"Nothing, Son."

"Right. Now there is this other set. Like there is a new rumor and I just don't get it at all."

"Well, looks like jealousy. Hang on, what did Jill ever do to you?"

"Nothing, she's one of my best friends."

"I know, but Bax, what are they all talking about here? She cheated you? Notes? Jill doesn't share notes with you, does she?"

"No way. No one can get her notes because she's on a different level entirely. I mean, I am good. But she's the best." Bax admitted.

"So why are they talking about her sabotaging you? I mean all last year you two helped each other study, and you both did great. What's this noise about?"

"That's just it Dad, I don't get it at all. Why would anyone believe a dumb rumor like that?"

"Hang on, here's a link. A blog?" Warren took the mouse and clicked on the link.

"Hey, yeah, this is like the evidence, I think."

"I don't remember a Blake Turner in your school." Warren said.

"Me either. This is like a tell all, reality TV show." said Bax.

"Yeah, all tell, no reality." Warren agreed.

"You got it, Dad. Right on target."

"So this Blake Turner says Jill gave you defective notes since grade school. That's just dumb. Who takes notes in grade school?" Warren said.

"I did Dad."

"I mean normal kids, who don't want to be mad scientists with giant robots as pets when they grow up."

"That was your dream, Dad, not mine. I wanted to be Captain Nemo and have my own submarine." Bax looked at his father and frowned.

"I still think you should build giant robots for a living." Warren said.

"That is not a thing, Dad."

"No? I saw they had some in Japan and California. Had a fight and everything."

"Dad. What about this rumor? What do I do?" Bax asked, ignoring the robot comments.

"Who cares. It's a rumor. Don't give it air and it'll die." Warren stood up.

"Oh man, you've been out a school a long time, Dad. That is the last thing I should do. It'll just make everyone assume it's one hundred percent true."

"Well, then I guess you only have two choices." Warren Mitchell paused meaningfully.

"And? What are my choices?" Bax asked.

"Do better than Jill in all the classes you have with her."

"Not gonna happen. Maybe one, but she is a math god."

"Well, then you just have to marry her." Warren smiled.

"What? Get out of town! Why do I ask you for help?"

"Because I'm a mad scientist and you want to be on my good side when I release the giant robots to destroy the town?" Warren's smile grew.

"Yeah, remind me not to ask you for an opinion next time, ok Dad?"

"Fine. Don't ask me for an opinion next time, Bax."

"Ok, Dad. Great advice there, champ." Bax and his dad smiled at each other.

CHAPTER SEVEN

Jill returned home angry. No one was listening to her, not her friends, not other kids at school, no one!

"Mom, I'm home." Liz Duffy could tell her daughter was angry.

"Don't slam the door, Jill!" Liz was on the phone, talking to her car mechanic.

"Yeah, Mom, I won't." Jill considered slamming the door. It was that kind of day, but then Jill remembered how angry her mom was when she got the first estimate on repairing her car.

"Is that Bruce?"

"Yeah, it's Bruce. He says the car is ready. I was going to pick it up in a few minutes. He's just telling me everything they had to do to get it fixed."

"Great, you going over now?" Jill asked.

"Yes, he said they'll send a guy to pick me up." Liz answered.

"Mom, I'm not hungry, ok? You just go and I'll start my homework."

"You sure? I can put something on while we wait for Bruce's guy to show up?"

"I'm fine. I don't think I could eat now, anyway." Jill put her backpack down on the chair and started emptying it out. She placed all her books on the dining room table and pulled out a second chair for herself.

"Oh, no. Is it that bad, dear?" Liz hung up the phone and came over to the table, pulled out another chair and sat next to Jill.

"No. It's even worse." Jill looked down at her books.

"What happened? You couldn't clear up that stupid rumor?" Liz put her arm around Jill's shoulder.

"No. And it just got worse throughout the day. I couldn't concentrate on anything else besides the stupid rumor mill." Jill felt like she wanted to cry, but she resisted it and kept her tears inside.

"I told you it was a tough one. You can't let it get to you. You have too much going good for you this year. Jill, honey, you can cry if you want to. I'm here." Liz held out her arms to her daughter.

"No. I'm not crying. I'm not giving them any 'wins' over me."

"Oh, you are a tough one, aren't you? I would have been a mess when I was your age." Liz hugged Jill.

"No one would ever believe that, Mom."

"Oh, maybe not now, but back then, I was a mess. I was not as smart as you are, I mean I was pretty smart and I knew it, but you work ten times harder than I ever did, and it shows. You are my perfect student! The student I never was."

"Well, sometimes it isn't enough. I don't want people telling lies about me. I did *not* make out with Bax. He's my friend, and we are *not* like that."

"I know Jill, I know. But rumors happen, you have to just let it go. It isn't important." Liz released her hug and looked Jill in the eyes.

"But mom, everyone was talking about it!"

"I'm sure it felt like that, but really honey, doesn't everyone have something better to do?" Liz was right, but it still didn't feel right to Jill.

"No. Some idiots even cheered Bax on! And Bax had no idea what they were even talking about!" Jill protested.

"Baxter Mitchell, the boy who notices everything? He didn't get it?"

"Not a word. Clueless as the day he was born." Jill sniffed a little.

"How is that even possible? Wait, did you want him to get it?"

"No. Maybe." Jill looked away from her mom's eyes.

"Jill, honey, you've known Bax for years, since before we moved here. Even if it wasn't about him and you, he never would have believed a rumor like that. Bax knows you too well. You are all about school, not making out with boys, right?"

"I know. But both him and Alex were clueless. They're my best friends. They should have known and they should have said something."

"Oh, both of them had no idea about this lie? Isn't that a good thing?"

"Alex sure, but Bax should have known." Jill looked at her mom, pleading for Liz Duffy to understand.

"Jill, let me ask you something. Don't get mad, ok?"

"Ok." Jill sniffed, her eyes were red.

"Did you want Bax to defend you, or are you mad because you like him and this rumor is, well, I don't know how to say it gently."

Jill couldn't hold back anymore and tears burst out of her eyes. She buried her face in her mom's shirt and cried hard.

"Oh, honey. Oh, you're getting my shirt all wet." Liz said, patting her daughter's back, "Just let it out, it's ok."

Ten minutes later, Liz gave the driver a twenty-dollar bill to wait for Jill to stop crying enough for her to go with him to pick up the car.

When she got home, Alex saw the car from the garage waiting in Jill's driveway across the street. Jill was probably home, and her mom's car must have been fixed. Nothing to worry about then, except that Jill wasn't speaking to her and there were vicious rumors spreading about her two best friends. At least that sounded normal, not like a demon was in her smartphone and another had just been banished after trying to eat Alex's kidneys.

I can hear you when you think loudly, Alex.

'Annoying, stalking, hacker SPD.' Alex thought to herself.

I heard that too, and I am neither a stalker nor a hacker.

"Shut up, SPD."

If you say that enough, I will think my name is 'shut up, SPD.'

"It is. Shut up, SPD." Alex went around to the side door in case Jill was watching.

I have never gone into your house from this direction, Alex. Why are we doing things differently today? Is it because your friends are mad?

"You catch on pretty quick, SPD. Yes, Jill is angry so I don't want to distract her."

Because she might yell at you again?

"No."

I feel it when you lie, you know.

"Then yes. I don't want to be yelled at by my best friend."

I understand that. I do not feel good when you yell at me.

"You are not my best friend, SPD."

But you are my best friend, Alex. My only friend.

"That makes you sound pathetic, SPD. I'm sure you have more friends than just me."

You are a very special friend, Alex. I am bound to you.

"Ew, now that just sounds perverted. Don't say that again where Grandma Akeyo or Grandfather Li can hear you, ok?"

Why? They know I am bound to you. They would understand what I mean.

"Yeah, they are also very smart and they like to tease me. They'll twist it into something perverted, or awful, or both."

Because they hate you?

"No, because they love me. And like to make me squirm. Wait. No, maybe you're right, maybe they really do hate me and enjoy making me miserable."

I did not feel that from them. Grandma Akeyo seems very attached to you.

"Yeah, well, I guess I *am* their only grandchild and the heir to all their combined magic." Alex unlocked the side door and entered the dining room. Her dad wasn't home yet.

Combined magic?

"Yeah, I thought you could tell? They have two different types of magic. Grandfather Li uses some weird Chinese Qi based magic and Grandma Akeyo's is a mix of different African shamanic traditions. They were both trying to make a new form of magic since they were young, like maybe in their twenties? Long before they got married. Actually, I think that's part of why they married, to merge their magic."

That is very dangerous.

Alex sat down at the table, shrugged out of her back pack and put her smartphone on the table in front of her.

"Yeah, they don't talk about it much, but I overheard them one night when they had a little too much Japanese chestnut shochu. They said a good friend of theirs had died to make the magic merge between them. They were toasting his memory."

It is very unfortunate that someone died. When did that happen?

"Well, I asked them about it a week or two later and they were very cross with me. They said that 'a ten-year-old girl, who is not clever enough by half, has no business listening in on her elders when they are honoring their long-lost friends.'" Alex imitated her Grandfather Li's voice in a convincing and eerie way, almost as if he was in the room with her and SPD.

Wise of them.

"Not helpful, SPD. It's like you're on their side." Alex flicked the smartphone with her finger and sent it spinning in place.

Why are you doing that to my box?

"Your box? That's my phone you are living inside of, not your box."

Why are you doing that to your smartphone that I am living inside of at the moment?

"That's better, SPD. I dunno. I guess I just wanted to see if you would get dizzy."

I am not dizzy.

"Better not be, SPD, I don't want you hurling up any of my photos or anything else if you get sick."

I am not sick. I do like your photos, however. You have a very artistic eye.

"You're looking at my photos?"

Yes. They are well composed.

"Well, stop it. They are private."

Then I shall only look at the ones you have sent to others. They are still very well composed.

"Oh my gosh, SPD, you are too much."

I think I am just fine, just enough to fit in here comfortably.

"O. M. G, SPD."

———

L iz left to pick up her car. It was repaired and ready to go. Jill had stopped crying enough that Liz felt alright about leaving her for a half an hour or so. Jill decided to start her homework and opened her laptop. She clicked a couple buttons and the lock screen came up, too bright.

"Ok, let's see if I can do some work." Jill said to herself. Three clicks later, and her email was open. Two clicks later, and she was reading the first of twenty-seven new emails.

"What? What!" Jill shouted, her anger returned.

"No way in hell! I would never share my notes. No. No, that is so wrong."

Jill discovered the new rumor about her sabotaging Bax. She was not pleased at what she read. Three of her friends did not believe the rumor was true. Seven of her friends said they had always known she could be ruthless, but Bax, that was going too far. Five friends congratulated her on keeping the boys down. One friend un-friended her. Apparently all but the first three were idiots, Jill thought to herself.

"No way, this has gone too far." Jill grabbed the phone and began stabbing the buttons, punching in Bax's phone number. Jill waited for the phone to pick up.

"What the hell kind of rumor is that, Baxter M. Mitchell? Do you really think you can get even with me with some horse turd lie like that, you little weasel?"

"Hold on there."

"No, you hold on, I am not done yelling at you. I have never cheated in my life! I did *not* give you crap notes, I did *not* sabotage you, ever! You're just jealous that I am better at math than you are. So what do you have to say to that, you stupid little weasel-faced weasel?" Jill was beyond listening and folded her arms across her chest while pinning the phone between her shoulder and her head.

"Well, first I would say that my son is neither stupid nor weasel-faced. Although I do think he resembles a koala just a little."

"Oh no. Mr. Mitchell. Oh no." Jill dropped the phone, and it hit the floor. She scrambled to pick it back up.

"I am so sorry, Mr. Mitchell, are you still there?"

"Fine, young lady. My ears will recover from being dropped and from being scolded. Now, while I know you have only my son's best interests at heart, I do find myself taken aback a little at your vitriol. Would you walk me through this by the numbers?"

Jill turned pale white. Her skin was already pale, like most red-headed people, but now it was almost ghostly. Mr. Mitchell was using what he called twenty-five cent words. He only used twenty-five cent words when he was amused, but angry. Being amused covered up the angry part. Jill had never seen just the angry part of Mr.

Mitchell. She figured that was a fifty-cent word or maybe even a solid dollar.

"I was angry because I saw a rumor in my e-mail."

"A rumor, would you care to elucidate me on this rumor, my fine young child?"

"Oh god, is that a fifty-cent word or still twenty-five cents?"

"Pardon?"

"Ah, never mind, I was, ah, reading e-mail, and this rumor said that I gave Bax crap notes and was keeping his grades down." Jill was extremely nervous now. Was it a fifty-cent word or still twenty-five cents?

"The Bax is a dummy rumor." Warren Mitchell said over the phone.

"Yes! Wait, no, Bax is not a dummy. I would never say that!"

"Relax, I know that you would never say Bax was a dummy, not to his face or mine, even if it was over the phone."

"You're teasing me, aren't you, Mr. Mitchell?" Jill thought she knew what was going on, now.

"What ever gave you that idea, Jill? The fact that you and my boy have known each other for ever? The fact that I have seen you both do your homework? The fact that I taught you algebra? Why, I am certainly the very first person who would fall for some shenanigans like that dumb-ass rumor." Mr. Mitchell's voice was so much of a sing-song tone, Jill thought it was practically its own choir group.

"Now, I know you are teasing me. I am so ashamed right now."

"I know you are honey, but we've been friends too long for me to not tease you when you are wrong and acting the fool."

"I guess I deserve it. But who would say something like that? I mean, I know Bax is jealous that I'm good at math. Doesn't he want to be number one?"

"Jill, honey, no one wants to be number one more than you, Bax knows that. He's happy just building giant robots."

"I thought you that wanted to build giant robots?"

"See, you know us too well. Ask yourself, would the Baxter Mitchell you know spread a dirty rumor? A lie? Have you ever known him to lie?"

"A little, but not anything important."

"Then it must be someone else." Jill could almost hear Warren's smile through the phone line.

"Can I talk to Bax? I feel like I should apologize."

"No worries, Jill. Bax is out picking up some milk. I sent him out half an hour ago, right after we read about that dumb ass rumor."

"Oh. So you've known for a while." Jill shifted on her feet.

"Yup. I figured you would find out soon enough, so I sent Bax to get some milk. He said no way you'd call. He owes me a dollar now. Thanks for the pay day, Jill."

"Seriously, you bet on me with Bax?"

"You are correct."

"Never mind, both of you clearly are beyond any form of shame."

"You are correct, again, honey. Now stop worrying about some stupid rumors and do your homework. Or come over and do mine, I have to figure out why the network is suddenly all sketchy."

"No thanks, I'll stick with geometry."

"Have it your way, talk to you later, Jill. Buck up, it gets better." Mr. Mitchell hung up the phone and then Jill did the same, feeling a bit better than before. Jill didn't notice the thin red threads worming through the air from her laptop and encircling her waist. Flush with a sudden anger, Jill whispered to herself.

"*Break, Break.*"

The sun was getting low in the sky. It was around 6 p.m. as Grandma Akeyo pulled into her driveway. The boxer and its sidecar rumbled to a stop as Akeyo killed the engine and applied the brakes. She dismounted and took her helmet off, resting it on the sidecar seat. Grandma Akeyo knew she would be out again in the evening, she was just stopping to check in with her husband and evaluate his ability to cook a decent dinner.

"I'm back, but not for long." Akeyo announced as she entered the house.

"Is it that bad?" Grandfather Li said from the dinner table as he placed the final dish down for their dinner.

"Oh, you are on time! What a pleasant thing that is for a working woman like me." Akeyo teased.

"Your dinner is served, perfectly timed, as always."

"I wonder if you are available later, I would like to marry such a punctual man."

"I am afraid I am already accounted for by the lady of the house." Grandfather Li took Grandma Akeyo's jacket as she shrugged out of it. He hung the black and yellow leather jacket on a nearby coat rack. He had insisted the jacket have bright yellow in it, so Akeyo could be seen by drivers and not end up in an accident because someone did not see the tall black woman on a black motorcycle wearing all black. Grandfather Li called it obnoxious visibility. Grandma Akeyo thought it was overkill, but after a near miss the very week her custom jacket was finished, Akeyo was a firm believer in obnoxious visibility.

"So what do we have tonight, my darling?" Akeyo sat herself down. She was famished.

"Garlic spinach. Fresh vegetables from the garden. Something Lydia brought over that I have forgotten the name of, and I have no idea what that is from the party the Osmans held to celebrate their son's first six months of being alive and separate from his mother's belly." Grandfather Li sat across from Grandma Akeyo.

"So you made the spinach and stole the vegetables from Lydia's garden again?"

"Yes. Quite. You are not working if you are not stealing."

"I'm sure that's not how it is supposed to work, my darling, but I am beyond hungry, so I will overlook your criminal ways."

"Oh, thank you. This meat from the Osmans is delicious. I think it might be lamb or goat."

"It's goat. And yes, it is delicious. They must have spent quite a bit to get fresh goat around here."

"I think they go to a farm out in the countryside. I heard there is a man out there that has a number of east African customers."

"Well, he deserves all the good business he can get. Lydia's empanadas are very good as well. Oh, this is a welcome meal. Thank you for liberating this from our neighbors and making a meal of it, old man."

"It is my pleasure Akeyo, now tell me, how bad is it out there?" Grandfather Li piled his plate with a little of each of the dishes, all mashed together in the middle.

"How you can eat like that, I will never know. The flavors must fight with each other."

"You know it all goes to the same place, Akeyo, it is simply more efficient this way."

"But the flavors. Each food is unique and a gift to our taste buds. You deny them the right to have decent flavors."

"Is it really that bad?"

"Yes. The world is frayed, Jiànhuī. I have not seen it this bad in some time." Akeyo began to eat her vegetables, "Delicious!"

"I am not convinced that Maxwell left this world without touching much more than we thought."

"Neither am I. That spirit demon was strong. I wonder what poor soul left behind that monster?" Akeyo said.

"Akeyo, that is not a question worth answering, and you know it. The greatness or mendacity of a person in life can give rise to all sorts of spirits, powerful and weak alike." Grandfather Li paused as he ate, thinking.

"Yes, but Jiànhuī, that thing should not have existed in this world. It was a danger, I'm afraid it left behind tokens of its power. Perhaps a way back into our world?"

"Are you asking me? Well, my love, I think you are correct. Maxwell may be gone, but its remnants are certainly still here. I think we should go out together." Grandfather Li spooned a second helping of curried goat onto his plate.

"Yes, we should. And I think we should talk some more with Alex's friends."

"Then we will start with Jill. She is closest to Alex, perhaps she has seen something we missed." Grandfather Li said between bites of food, "This is delicious, we have wonderful neighbors to share such a feast with us."

"We do. And I plan to keep it that way, we have much work to do tonight, and likely the rest of the week as well."

Grandma Akeyo took some more vegetables stolen from Lydia Garcia's garden.

Grandma Akeyo and Grandfather Li left a little after they finished dinner. Fifteen minutes later they arrived at Jill's house.

"Hello? Oh, Akeyo and John, what are you doing here?" Liz answered the door.

"Actually, we came to see if we could talk to Jill." Akeyo said.

"Oh, you heard about the rumors too? Well, good luck with that, Jill is pretty upset. Come on in, Jill's out, but I can catch you up."

Akeyo and Jiànhuī entered the house. Liz took them to the living room and invited them to sit.

"So, what have you heard?" Liz sat in an overstuffed leather chair.

"Not much. We didn't know anything about any rumors. What's going on?" Akeyo sat on one end of the faded red love seat, Jiànhuī on another chair.

"Oh really? Well, there was a big rumor about Jill making out with Baxter Mitchell. She was very mad and went off to school. From there it just got worse. Now, there is a second rumor about her sabotaging Bax's grades or something stupid like that."

Akeyo and Jiànhuī looked at each other.

"So then I got a call that my car was fixed, so I went to pick it up and when I got back, Jill was gone and she left a note on the table that she was going to Bax's house." Liz looked from Akeyo to John and back again, waiting for a response.

"Your car was broken?" Jiànhuī asked.

"Oh, yes, a couple weeks ago. I was on the way home and it suddenly gave out. It was vandalism. The garage just finished repairs today, cost a fortune but I need a car and I don't have time to do the work myself anymore."

"When, exactly was this? A few weeks back you say?" Akeyo asked.

"Why, it was the weekend right before the kids all went back to school. I was on the way back home from cards at Warren Mitchell's house. Out of nowhere, the engine started seizing up. I was pretty lucky overall."

"And while you were picking up the car, Jill went to see Bax?" Grandfather Li picked up the previous topic.

"Yeah, surprised me, she was pretty upset. I paid the driver from the garage to wait for me until she was done crying. I guess she decided to go over and talk to Bax in person."

"Maybe we should go talk to Jill at Bax's house?" Akeyo looked at her husband.

"I think that might be best."

"Oh, ok," Liz said, "Are you sure? I could put on some tea?"

"Maybe next time, Liz, I have some things to ask Jill about Alex." Grandfather Li disliked Liz's attempts to give him tea. Liz always made English tea, and Jiànhuī preferred green tea or coffee to English tea.

"Yes, let's catch up to the girl before anything else happens." Akeyo was up and heading to the door when she stopped suddenly.

"Do you feel that?" Akeyo whispered.

I do, and it is coming from Liz's garage. It might as well be a full blown hole into the dead lands." Grandfather Li whispered back, "You should stay and fix it."

"Actually, Liz, I would love a cup of tea. We left before I could eat and it would be nice to have a little something on my stomach." Akeyo lied and turned back to look at Liz as Grandfather Li headed out the front door.

"I will walk ahead, Warren Mitchell's house is not that far. Maybe pick up Alex on the way?"

"You are a better person for it, Mr. Li. I couldn't walk that far." Liz perked up. She always felt better when someone accepted her hospitality.

"Very good, I will see you in a bit. Liz can tell me all about these rumors and her terrible car troubles. Do you have anything I could snack on, Liz?" Akeyo put her arm around Liz's shoulder and steered her into the kitchen.

"I think we can get something together, come on, let's do some girl talk!"

"Saved by chance, hooray for me!" Grandfather Li whispered to himself as he started the long walk to Warren Mitchell's house.

Alex heard the knock on the front door, then the door opening. Only her grandparents knocked, then opened the door without waiting. Grandma Akeyo and Grandfather Li still thought of the house as their own, which it was once, a long time before Alex was born.

"I'm in here." Alex spun SPD on the dining room table.

"Oh, I was coming to look for you, Alex." Grandfather Li walked to the table, pulled out a chair, and sat.

"Did you close the door?" Alex was resting her head on the table and spinning her phone.

"Of course I did."

"Because you always leave it open and I didn't hear it click."

"Be quiet, not-clever child." Grandfather Li thought he closed the front door, but knew he probably hadn't.

Alex is correct, the front door is still open.

"Shut up, SPD."

"Yes, shut up, SPD." Grandfather Li got up and went back to the front of the house, closed the door, then returned to his seat, "But thank you none the less, it is a bad habit I have yet to mend."

You are welcome, Mr. Li. I am glad I could be of assistance.

"You sound like a person on a telephone help line."

Should I be pleased to be a telephone help line person?

"No, SPD, Grandfather Li was not being nice, he was being sarcastic." Alex wasn't trying to give a dead pan answer, but she succeeded despite her lack of effort.

"Alex, enough banter with your pet demon," Grandfather Li got straight to the point, "I am afraid something is wrong."

"Something is always wrong." Alex was unenthusiastic.

I am not a pet demon, I am happy to reside in the smartphone.

"Silence your pet, child."

"Shut up, SPD."

Shutting up, Alex.

"Oh really? That's a first." Alex let a bit of surprise enter her voice.

"Are you two finished? Now, Alex, tell me what has been going on the last couple of days at school. Especially since Maxwell was banished." Grandfather Li tapped his finger on the table for emphasis.

"Oh, you are interested in my school life?"

"No, not really. I am interested in the strange things going on in town lately."

"You mean the imp and Maxwell? I thought we went over this already. The test, the vomit, breaking things. *Break, break.*"

Mr. Li, something is wrong.

"I can tell, SPD is it? SPD, can you sense threads of reality?"

Yes, Mr. Li.

"Well, do you sense any attached to Alex?"

No, I do not think so, wait. There is something. It feels familiar, but sticky.

"What are you two talking about? I'm fine." Alex's delivery was beyond dead pan. It was almost devoid of any feeling.

"There!" Grandfather Li pointed to the floor just behind Alex.

I sense it. I can sever the thread.

"Too late, I have it." Grandfather Li pushed his chair back and slipped into a crouch, his foot behind Alex's chair. Suddenly, Grandfather Li flicked his extended toe up and made a quick motion with his fingers. A thin, blood red thread began to glow in mid air, then snapped. One end was attached to Alex and the other, now severed end led to an ethernet jack in the wall.

Alex stood up so quickly she knocked her chair over.

"What the hell? Grandfather, where did you come from?"

"Sit child," Grandfather Li set Alex's chair upright and took his own seat, "You are safe now."

"Safe, what happened?"

"That is what I would like to know. SPD?"

Alex was sitting, and we were talking, then she nodded off to sleep. I thought she was napping, so I decided to look at her pictures again. Then she was spinning my demon box again, and you came into the house.

"Hmm, Alex, I think a spirit demon was trying to influence you. I am sure of it."

"What? No way!"

"Yes-way! Way too dangerous. Were you dreaming? Were you even tired? What do you remember, child?" Grandfather Li was asking his questions gently.

"I don't know. We were talking, like SPD said, then I was dreaming I was in a box. It was breathing. Then everything began to get blurry." Alex was anything but dead pan in her description, she was very agitated.

"Hmm. I am beginning to think this is more than just a remnant."

"What do you mean, Grandfather Li?"

"Oh, do not worry, Alex. Never you mind for now. I have some questions for you about school, do you remember my asking you about that?" Grandfather Li put his hand on Alex's shoulder.

"No, did you ask me about school?"

"Ok, child, tell me about the rumors and anything else that has been going on, can you do that?" Alex thought it was scary how nice Grandfather Li was talking to her.

It is not all right, is it? SPD thought directly at Grandfather Li.

No, it is not. Grandfather thought back at the smartphone, hoping Alex couldn't hear his focused thoughts.

———

"What the hell, Grandfather? Since when can spirit demons control people? Why didn't you tell me about that?" Alex was yelling at Grandfather Li.

"Language, child. And my name is Grandfather Li, not just Grandfather. I earned my name."

Since always, Alex.

"What? SPD, you knew about that too? Some friend you are."

Alex, you did not know about this, I assume?

"Hell no!"

"I was going to teach you about demon influence when you perfected bindings. I know that means very little now, but there was a reason."

"What reason? Does it involve unicorns and rainbows, because that is about the only way I'm not going to be mad." Alex's face was red.

"Because defeating a spirit demon's influence requires you to bind it fully and without a chance of failure. You are not there yet. And there is another reason."

"Better involve unicorns being real."

"No, it is because learning to break the influence on your self means I have to summon a spirit demon and let it influence you."

"That is not better than unicorns, Grandfather Li."

Alex, it would not be as strong as what happened here. Spirit demons generally just make a human feel confused.

"Oh, that helps, SPD. Whose side are you on, anyway?"

Yours, Alex. By definition.

"That is true, SPD can only ever be on your side now that it is your demon in a box." Grandfather Li said.

"Shut up, Grandfather."

"Excuse me?" Grandfather stood up and glared at Alex.

I think that was a mistake, Alex.

"Shut up, SPD."

Shutting up.

"I will let that slide. Alex, if I teach you how to break an influence on another now, will you let this go? It is easier than breaking it on your own. We have bigger issues and we need to not argue." Grandfather Li fought down his anger at being crossed by his granddaughter.

"What?" Alex expected more of a fight.

"Here, place your fingers together on my hand." Grandfather Li took Alex's fingers and placed them tip down on his palm.

"Now, pull them like this, twist and flick them out all at once." Grandfather pushed Alex's fingers together on his palm, as if he was using all five of her fingers to pick up a pinch of salt, then he twisted Alex's hand at the wrist so her fingers were suddenly pointed up. Grandfather then mimicked the form with his hand and flicked his fingers open as if they were triggered by a loaded spring.

Alex flicked her fingers in the same way.

"Perfect. Astonishing. It took me a month to get that right at your age." Grandfather Li patted Alex's shoulder, "Again, please."

Alex did the form again.

"Perfect. Now, if you sense a thread influencing a person, grasp the thread with that form and when you flick, it will be severed." Grandfather Li smiled at Alex.

"Wow. So I am better at this than you, Grandfather Li?"

"Don't get cocky, you are still very not-clever. You fell under the influence of a spirit demon, next time you must be on guard."

Is this what you and Baxter Mitchell call a level-up, Alex?

"Yes, SPD. And you do not have to shut up now. Tell me how great I am." Alex smiled from ear to ear.

J ill found herself at Bax's door, about to knock. She didn't know how she got there or even why she was at Bax's house at all. Last Jill remembered, she had just hung up the phone with Bax's father, Warren. Now she was at Bax's front door.

The door opened. Apparently she was not just about to knock, but had actually knocked.

"Jill? What are you doing here?" Warren Mitchell's eyes were wide.

"I don't really know."

"What do you mean, girl? I was just talking to you what, twenty minutes ago? Why don't you come in and sit down if you're feeling a bit off?"

"Thanks, Mr. Mitchell. Last thing I remember, I was just on the phone with you." Jill walked into the house and sat down on the couch.

"Right, I hung up and went to go get some pizza." Mr. Mitchell held a slice of pizza on a paper plate, "Want some?"

"Oh, no thanks. I'm feeling a bit odd." Jill looked around the room. The normal set of monitors, electronics, and assorted telecommunications odds and ends were strewn about the room.

"Ok. Pizza's fresh, unlike everything else in this house."

"Oh, no, I was just looking to make sure this wasn't a dream."

"Nope, no dream. But I will say that things have been a little odd lately."

"What do you mean?" Jill looked at Mr. Mitchell, trying to see if he was real.

"Well, there was all this weird rumor garbage between

you and Bax. Damnedest thing, if you asked me. Then there were all these minor failures in the local network trunk. I've been trying to figure out what was going on. A couple of smaller routers failed spectacularly. I figured there were configuration errors or some dumb kid trying to hack them, but nope. Hard fail. Those things are supposed to be pretty solid, they aren't your garden variety small office router. But hell, they just went up and died. I had one of the interns go out to check the physical boxes." Jill's eyes began to gloss over as Warren Mitchell described his day. No way this was a dream, dreams were interesting, Warren Mitchell was nice, but when he talked work, he was anything but interesting.

"Ok. What did Bax say about the rumors?" Jill hoped Mr. Mitchell would take the bait.

"Oh, Bax? He didn't get it at first. Then he got an email about the rumor with you and your notes. He thought that was beyond reason. We agreed it was garbage, then he found the website of the fella who posted it in the first place."

"Really? Can I see it?" Jill was intrigued.

"Sure, I printed it out. Here." Mr. Mitchell handed a pile of papers to Jill.

"Print?"

"Yeah, I like paper."

"Who is this guy? Blake Turner? Never heard of him." Jill squinted at the printed out page.

"Yeah, that is what Bax said. And the thing is, he did some more digging, and this guy doesn't exist, at least not around here."

"How did he find that out?"

"Oh, Bax has his ways. Lots of searches on the Internet. In fact, before yesterday, Blake Turner didn't exist in town at all, then a bunch of web sites popped up and bam! Blake Turner is real!"

"And Bax figured all that out?"

"Yup. Smart kid, my son."

"I know." Jill whistled, "Bax really went to town on this, he has all the records, but it seems like something is missing."

"Ah, you figured it out. All these web pages and sites were established, but no one paid for them. No one doesn't pay the Internet man. Not even free sites. Someone always pays. Not this Blake Turner. Something is rotten in Denmark." Warren Mitchell smiled, pleased Jill had picked up on the discrepancies.

"Denmark? Don't we live in Nancy Row?"

"Old person expression, Jill. Old person." Mr. Mitchell poked himself in the chest with his thumb, then shoveled his pizza into his mouth and nodded meaningfully at Jill.

"Dad, what is she doing here?" Bax closed the front door behind him, hung up his phone and put it in his pocket, the red glow from the screen fading as it went to sleep.

"Jill and I were just talking and having some pizza." Warren Mitchell said between bites, "Well, I was having some pizza."

"You know that's not what I meant. I mean, after all the rumors and everything, you let Jill come over? Not cool, Dad. Not cool." Bax stood staring at his dad and Jill.

"What do you mean by that, Bax? I was the victim of the rumors, not you." Jill was sitting at the table with Warren, not eating anything but looking a bit hungry.

"I mean stealing my grades? Giving me crap notes? Sabotage? I know it, now. I know it all." Bax looked down at Jill, seated at the table.

"What are you talking about, Son?"

"Oh, and you making moves on me? What's up with that?" Jill pushed back from the table and stepped toe to toe with Baxter, returning his stare.

"What are you two talking about?" Warren Mitchell looked at both of the kids and shook his head.

"So what *is* she doing here, Dad?" Bax did not look away from Jill.

"What are you talking about? Jill was over to talk to you about these stupid rumors. Jill, why are you so upset, I thought we were square on all this?" Warren stood up, just in case he had to separate the friends.

"I'm upset because this person I thought I knew *tried* to make out with me and then spread rumors that he did just that! As if!" Jill was focused on Bax and Bax on Jill.

"Hold on."

"No, Dad. She has been scamming my grades for years, you saw the website!"

"Wait, you're the one who said the website was a fake." Warren stepped over to the kids and put himself between them.

"No way, it's legit. She sabotaged me!"

"And he tried to kiss me and lied about it to everyone!"

"You two are playing some sort of stupid game?" Warren Mitchell was looking from Bax to Jill and back again, "Are you two on drugs? What's wrong with your eyes?"

The doorbell rang and Warren stepped around Bax to open the door. Alex and her grandfather stood in the doorway.

"Oh no, more kids."

"No time, Warren, let us in." Grandfather Li pushed past Warren and slipped into a crouch, "Alex, see the threads? You get Bax, I have Jill."

"Right," Alex went around Warren on the other side from Grandfather Li and swept up her arms like a windmill, "Got it!"

"What on the good, green earth is going on here?" Warren raised his voice.

At the same time, Alex and Grandfather Li grasped the empty air and twisted their hands around. Surprised, Warren thought he saw a splash of red sparks and something like yarn snapping in the air. Bax and Jill both fainted onto the floor.

"Well poop." Alex looked at Grandfather Li, "That didn't happen to me."

"Hmm, I guess you are tougher than these two." Grandfather Li poked Jill with his foot, "Wake up. Hmm, no luck."

"Someone had better tell me what is going on right now or I am going to get my baseball bat and play a round of 'thump the chump!'" Warren Mitchell stood proud and put his fists on his hips, "Now, people!"

"What do you mean, that was real? Sparks in mid-air with nothing causing them are not real." Warren was sitting at the table, listening to Alex and Grandfather Li explain the situation. Bax and Jill were seated as well, each with a plastic bag of ice wrapped in a dish towel on their heads.

"That is just it Warren, it has a cause. They were infected."

"With psychic worms? Zombie plague? Because I can almost believe that. Spirit demons in the telephones, nah, that's a bridge too far."

"I told you we should have lied." Grandfather Li looked at Alex with a raised eyebrow.

"Really? How would that go?"

"I am sitting right here. I can tell you how it would go, and it's not much better than this. Now tell me a story I can accept?"

Perhaps I can be of assistance?

"Shut up, SPD." Alex held up her smartphone, talking to it.

"What was that?"

"What, Warren?" Grandfather Li acted innocent, as if he had not heard SPD speak.

"That voice? It said it 'could be of assistance.' What are you two hiding from me? And don't tell me that was your smartphone, I work for the phone company, I know phones." Clearly, Warren had heard SPD.

"Oh, crap, Grandfather I think the cat's out of the bag." Alex was worried, if Warren had actually heard SPD, the threads that bound reality were getting very thin.

"Show him." Grandfather Li sat back in his chair.

"Show me what?"

"This. Tell him SPD." Alex placed her smartphone in front of Warren Mitchell, screen up.

Hello, I am SPD. I am the spirit demon in the smart-phone that you think does not exist.

The words Warren heard in his head were spelled out on the phone, handwritten with absolutely no sign of pixelation. Warren picked up the smartphone and touched the screen. Nothing happened. He then pushed the button on the side to wake up the phone. Nothing happened.

"Well, that is a nice little app you have there, well done. Did my son help you with that?"

"No dad, I did not write an app." Bax said from under the ice pack.

"Oh really? You expect me to believe this is a 'spirit demon?' Come on, I wasn't born yesterday. You have a nice app that writes on the screen and some sweet speech synthesis. Probably a wireless keyboard. Type in the words and presto, instant seance prank. You could make some bucks of this app. But I'm not that gullible." Warren tossed the phone on the table.

"Hey! That's my new smartphone! Don't treat it like that!" Alex clutched the phone in her hands.

I am not hurt.

"I was concerned about the phone, SPD."

I am also not an app. Mr. Mitchell, I am a bound spirit demon in the box, I can prove it, if you allow me.

"Oh really? Go ahead, I want to see how good this app really is." Warren sat back in his chair.

May I, Alex?

"Grandfather Li?"

"Let the fool. I will not be held responsible."

"Go ahead, SPD, prove that you are what you say you are to Mr. Mitchell." Alex looked away and closed her eyes.

I am reaching out to you with a thread of reality, Mr. Mitchell. Do you see it?

"I don't see a darn... what the heck, how did you do that?"

A single thread of red light began to worm its way from the smartphone towards Warren Mitchell. The thread was thin and weak, but it was there. It moved like a snake, forward in curves, poking towards Mr. Mitchell.

"Hologram, gotta be a hologram."

"Dad, you know phones don't do holograms." Bax pointed at the thread, "That's real."

I will touch you now, and you will feel warm.

"Like hell, touch someone else." Mr. Mitchell pulled his hand back, but the thread shot out and wrapped around his wrist.

"Ow, what?"

I am sorry, is that too hot?

"No, wow. I just say 'ouch' when I'm surprised. I can feel it, it's warm."

"I told you, Dad. I guess Alex isn't the only one with the sight now, we all got it."

"Enough, SPD. Please stop." Grandfather Li looked pleased, "Now do you believe, Warren?"

"I need to think about this, but yeah, I think I believe there's something weird going on here. Not sure about demons, but this is not the physics I know."

"Good enough for me." Grandfather was definitely smiling.

"Great, now why don't you all shut up or go somewhere else." Jill looked up from under the ice pack with red-rimmed eyes.

"Sorry." Alex stood up, "Let's go in the kitchen and let Bax and Jill rest?"

Grandfather Li and Warren Mitchell joined Alex as she walked into the kitchen. Bax and Jill put their heads down on the table and moved as little as possible.

"So, even if I believe all this, I still have to ask you a simple question. What's going on?"

"Warren, there is so much more to the world than anyone knows."

"Oh, I get that. My grandmother had the sight, I know spooky. I mean right now, what is really going on? Why was my kid acting a fool? Why did Jill just change from reasonable to 'crazy rumor girl?' I want to know what is going on in the small scale. I don't need world shaking revelations, just my living room shaking kind of revelations." Warren leaned up against the kitchen counter.

"Alex, you tell him. I will just get wrapped up in the details." Grandfather Li leaned against the counter next to Warren, both looked at Alex for an explanation.

"Why me? Oh fine. Mr. Mitchell, we accidentally bound a spirit demon into my smartphone. My brand new smartphone." Alex glared at her grandfather.

"Don't look at me like that, you are the one who had a temper tantrum."

"Not helping, Grandfather Li. But yes, it was my fault. The demon's name is SPD. It means Smart Phone Demon."

"That seems apt. A little on the nose, but apt."

"Yes, Mr. Mitchell, it can't remember its real name, so I named the little stalker SPD."

I am not a stalker, Alex.

"That was him?" Warren looked at the smartphone in Alex's hands.

"Yes, that was SPD. SPD is an it, not a him. Spirits don't really have a gender as far as we know."

I would like to have a gender, but I do not remember it or my name.

"So anyway, after that, we found an imp, and it broke Bax's bike, made Jill throw up on her test, and according to Grandfather Li, probably blew up Liz Duffy's car." Alex was pacing as she explained the last few weeks.

"Wait, what's an imp?" Warren looked at Grandfather Li.

"Alex?"

"Right. Mr. Mitchell, an imp is a barely formed spirit demon or one that has completely forgotten everything except its emotions. Generally imps just cause trouble."

"Like a poltergeist?" Warren asked.

"Yes, just like the movie, but no ancient burial grounds or stuff like that. Hollywood went overboard with that one." Grandfather Li said. He liked scary movies, especially ones with ghosts.

"So we banished the imp and then something like, ten times worse showed up." Alex continued.

Maxwell.

"Wait, what? Maxwell?" Warren smiled.

"Yeah, that's its name. Really big or powerful spirit demons can remember their names." Alex stopped pacing and looked at her smartphone, "You should remember your name, then you would be powerful."

"You have got to be kidding me. Maxwell is a demon? That is too rich. Maxwell's Demon." Mr. Mitchell started laughing.

"I don't get it. What's so funny about its name?" Grandfather Li was confused.

"Maxwell's Demon is a concept in physics. A zero energy sorting function that would allow you to violate the laws of thermodynamics."

Alex and Grandfather Li looked blankly at Warren.

"Are you serious? There's a demon named Maxwell and you are not pulling my leg? Oh man, the universe does have a sense of humor!" Warren Mitchell laughed even louder.

"Shut up, Dad!" Baxter Mitchell called from the living room.

"Ok, I get it. There's stuff out there that is magic. Not technology so advanced I can't understand it, but honest to goodness hocus pocus. But then I just gotta ask, what is the magic thing doing in a smartphone or a router? I mean seriously, I thought magic and technology was like oil and water, they just don't mix?" Warren Mitchell sat looking at Alex and Grandfather Li, waiting for a reasonable answer.

"Why should they not mix?" Grandfather Li was calm and reasonable.

"I don't know, because one is magic, and the other is science?"

"Well Warren, if magic can affect a wooden stick, shouldn't it be able to affect something else made of wood? And if magic can affect a rock, if you take that rock and make a statue out of it, shouldn't it be able to affect the statue?"

"I guess so, but a smartphone is a long way from a wooden stick or a pet rock."

"It is, but it is still made out of things in nature, no matter how far abstracted from their original form." Grandfather Li was even more reasonable than before.

"It just seems wrong. I mean, there are all these resistors, and capacitors, and integrated circuits. I just can't understand how a magic being could get all wrapped up in that sort of thing."

I assure you, I am not wrapped up in anything. Although just like a regular demon box, this box, this smartphone, is a maze to me.

"SPD, it is SPD isn't it? What does that even mean? How can it be a maze inside a box? There is a big empty

space in a box and that's it. No maze, just empty space."
Warren stared at Alex's smartphone and its resident spirit
demon.

"Mr. Mitchell, demon boxes are not really boxes. We
use two pieces of wood carved from very specific trees. The
wood blocks have to be matched to each other, almost identical in grain, texture and appearance, inside and out. It
traps the spirit demons between both blocks." Alex took out
two pieces of very heavy bloodwood and placed them on
the table in front of her. The wooden blocks looked identical to the naked eye.

"So what, those are demon boxes?" Warren raised one
eyebrow.

"No, these are *one* demon box. That is the nature of the
trap." Alex smiled and pushed one of the blocks across the
table towards Warren.

*I can feel the demon box from here. It feels like one thing,
like one body, not two separate blocks of wood. I did not
know a demon box was two things.*

"Really? SPD, I am surprised by you again." Grandfather took one of the bloodwood blocks, "We hide one block
in a safe place and the other is carried with us or stored in a
different place."

"Why would you do that?" Warren looked at the block
in Grandfather Li's hand. It was heavy to the eye.

"If we are trapping a spirit, we hide both blocks. If we
are using the spirit as a tool, we keep one block with us. If
we let the blocks touch, the spirit will be released, it finds a
way out of the box. You have to be very careful with spirit
demons." Grandfather Li illustrated his point by tapping
the blocks together.

"Wait a minute. You say that the two blocks are nearly
identical? I wonder. We use very specific components in

mobile phones, matched capacitors and similar components that work with really tight tolerances. You can't just use any old part because they have to perform together. I wonder if that is why the spirit demons get caught up in technology. SPD was trapped because some components are nearly identical, so much that it cannot tell the difference like in your wood blocks?" Warren smiled proudly at Alex's smartphone, then looked from Grandfather Li to Alex and back again.

"What? It sounds plausible to me." Warren said, deflating a little.

"I must say I had not thought of anything like that. I know absolutely nothing about mobile phones, smartphones, or that sort of thing." Grandfather Li sounded slightly shamed by his lack of knowledge.

"Actually, I think it makes a kind of sense." Alex's eyes were wide, impressed with Warren's insight. Warren sat proud.

Bax walked into the kitchen from the living room, ice pack still held to his head.

"That kinda makes sense with the visual impressions on my action camera. I bet any camera could detect a spirit." Bax had detected an imp with his home made action camera.

"How so?" Grandfather Li asked, "And when did you get video of a spirit?"

"Well, the imaging elements of a camera, CCD or CMOS, are nearly identical and they are all tuned to return the same sort of signal so you can make a video. I caught that imp on my camera when it wrecked my bike." The imp had broken Bax's mountain bike while Bax was riding home. Bax's shoulder still hurt from where he landed on it after the bike crashed.

"Yeah, I can see that, Son. Pun not intended."

"But you know, when Alex and I were tracking it, I could see it towards the end. Not just see the artifact on the camera, but I actually saw the imp." Bax said.

"That happens when you are around magic enough. I think because you and Alex are such close friends, you probably saw it much sooner than a normal person would." Grandfather Li tapped his fingers on the counter.

"Are you saying my son isn't normal? Good, normal is boring." Warren shot a look at Bax, "That's one of our in jokes, you know."

"No Dad, it is not one of our in jokes. It's your in joke. I hate it when you say that." Bax was not amused but Alex suppressed a giggle.

"So now what?" Jill stood in the doorway, leaning against the jam with her ice pack on her head. Both Jill and Bax had been influenced by a spirit demon. Alex and Grandfather Li had broken that influence, but it left both kids with severe head aches. The ice helped.

"What do you mean, Jill?" Warren asked.

"I mean, if we were being influenced by a spirit demon and it wasn't SPD, and it wasn't the imp? Who was it?" Jill looked at each of them, then dropped her ice pack in the sink.

"Good point, Jill. What do we do now?" Alex looked at her Grandfather.

Maxwell.

"What?" Grandfather Li turned Alex's smartphone to face him.

I think Maxwell is still here.

"But we banished that jerk." Alex's tone rose, her voice cracking a little. Maxwell had shocked her, hit her with a chair, and very nearly electrocuted her with her own laptop battery. Grandfather Li and Grandma Akeyo had saved Alex from it and sent Maxwell back to the dead lands.

The spirit demon that was influencing your friends was powerful, like Maxwell. And Maxwell is vindictive, it makes sense if it was still in the world that it would go after your friends.

"Am I not your friend, SPD?" Bax seemed sad to be called Alex's friend and not SPD's friend.

I belong to Alex. SPD sensed Bax was hurt. *But we can be friends too, if you prefer.*

"Alright, enough of that sloppy-moppy silliness, what do you mean Maxwell might still be in the world? Akeyo and I used one of the most powerful banishments we know. I doubt even Maxwell could escape that." Grandfather Li clearly did not believe in SPD's conclusion.

Do you know many spirit demons who recall their names?

"Not really." Grandfather Li admitted.

That is how powerful Maxwell is.

"Could that thing really still be here?" Alex shrunk a little in her chair.

I think it could. I think even if it is not, we should act as if Maxwell is still here. It may be safer.

"Are you sure we can trust SPD?" Warren Mitchell poked Alex's smartphone with his finger.

"A fair question." Grandfather Li began.

"Not fair, that is *my* smartphone. I bought it. And SPD is *my* demon, I named it." Alex stood defiantly.

"Ok, hold on there, I was just asking. I'm new to this demon stuff, remember?" Warren said.

"Right, sorry, Mr. Mitchell." Alex sighed, deflating.

"Well, if you people are done talking, I have a real problem." Everyone turned to look at the doorway to the kitchen. Grandma Akeyo stood, six feet of out of breath woman, staring hard at the group, "And I don't mean because you left the front door open for anyone or anything to just walk right in."

"My love, what's wrong?" Grandfather Li walked over to his wife.

"While you all were making nice and explaining our business to Warren here, something has happened at Jill's house. One of her friends is hurt, Marjorie, I think?"

"Well, friends is a stretch." Jill retrieved her ice pack from the sink. If this was about Marjorie Chan, she thought she would need it.

"Well, friends or not, Marjorie came over to see you, probably about these weird rumors your mom told us about." Grandma Akeyo was sweating, "She is in trouble now."

"What happened?" Alex asked.

"She started talking about non-sense, these stupid rumors. I could she was being influenced, but it was strong, too strong. Marjorie Chan has been corrupted."

"Ha. The school gossip was already pretty sketchy in the morals department, in my honest opinion." Jill said.

"No, that's not what Grandma Akeyo means Jill, this is a different kind of corruption." Alex explained, "What's going on?"

"Her personality, she is losing herself. The poor girl is becoming like an imp, hurtful and petty. I put a binding on her but I don't know how long it will hold. She must have come in contact with something strong, or else she's been influenced for at least a couple days. I ran over here right away."

"All five miles? Akeyo, for goodness' sake why? You

should have taken the motorcycle." Grandfather Li said, aghast.

"She touched my motorcycle on the way into the house, it was corrupted. All the rubber parts have decayed."

"That fast? Such a powerful corruption. It is a wonder she's not dead." Grandfather Li said softly.

"We need to go. Mr. Mitchell, can you drive?" Alex grabbed Bax by the hand and started towards the door.

"Yeah, my van is out back, let's go."

"No Dad, not the conversion van." Bax moaned.

"Oh yes, I've been waiting for this day. Every good team has a conversion van!" Mr. Mitchell led the way out the back door into the yard.

S uzie came home to an empty house, as she normally did. Both of her parents worked late and Suzie rarely saw them before six at night. She was on her own for homework until then. Homework and worry.

Suzie felt angry and hurt and she didn't know why. She had been talking to her special confidant on her laptop and phone since she had planted the fake story about Jill and Bax. Suzie didn't know why, but when she vented to her special confidant, she felt relieved, understood. She felt less broken.

Everything was Jill's fault. Jill and that horrid little Alex. Maxxie, her special confidant, agreed. Maxxie always agreed with her, because she was right and they were all wrong.

I hate them. Suzie texted.

I know. The text came back right away. No waiting, Maxxie was there for her.

Hurt?

"Hell, yeah." Suzie hunched over into the big easy chair, phone in hand and knees drawn up almost to her face.

Yeah, it hurts. She texted back. *Where are you?*

No place special. Waiting for you to talk.

"Hell, yeah." Suzie smiled and grabbed a marshmallow from the bowl on the end table next to her chair. Marshmallows were Suzie's go to sulking food.

I sent you a present. From our friend. For you.

What is it? Suzie chewed the marshmallow until it was just tiny bits of sugar in her mouth. Most of the marshmallow had turned liquid and disappeared as she chewed.

Secret. Special.

Oh? You're not turning pervert on me, are you Maxxie?

No. It will help with those nasty girls.

Oh? Do tell.

Secret. Surprise.

Fine. I'll wait. Suzie ate another marshmallow.

Look for it to arrive soon. Maybe tonight.

Thanks, Maxxie. I hear mom coming. Talk to you later tonight.

Yes. Tonight. On the computer.

Kisses. Suzie popped the last marshmallow into her mouth as she tossed her phone on the end table. Her mom was pulling into the driveway. Time to be the good daughter.

So needy. Neglected children are easy to understand. Easier when they are nicely chewed up. This one will be delicious. She hates *so readily. Stewing in her own self-loathing. It* *makes the meat juicier.* **Maxwell was pleased with its influence over Suzie.**

Maxxie. Her special confidant and only friend. For now.

Maxwell felt it when the piece of itself found Suzie. Felt it as it entered her phone, then later, her body to become part of her mind and her emotions. Suzie panicked a little at first, but then felt something familiar in the piece of Maxwell.

Maxxie. Little Maxxie. I shall absorb Suzie into myself when that piece returns. She will become a part of me and I will enjoy her hate and self-loathing. Not as nice as eating, but I can feel how much she hates everything. I must make that anger a part of myself.

Soon, the special piece of Maxwell would find her, and merge with Suzie. Maxwell was pleased.

S uzie opened the door for her mother, but she wasn't there. No one was there.

"I know I heard the car." Suzie turned, pushing the door closed. She started to walk away but stopped when the door didn't latch. Suzie turned and stopped short. Something was in the doorway, holding the door from closing.

"Real funny. Who is that? I have a knife." Suzie lied.

Special. Secret.

"What? Did you say something? I'm not kidding, I *will* cut you."

Secret. Special. Suzie.

"How do you know my name?" Suzie didn't move, she was scared, but not scared enough to run from something she couldn't see. Suzie told herself she wasn't a whining child.

The door eased open. Something was there, but Suzie couldn't quite see it. The doorway was dark, as if something held the light. Then it jumped.

Suzie screamed and stopped screaming a half breath later. The special piece of Maxwell, the imp landed on her, knocking her to the floor. It had a smell, sickly sweet like brown bananas. Suzie scratched at it with her nails, but it melted into small bits like the marshmallows she'd eaten.

Then it was a part of her. Maxxie was with her and she liked it. The little hurts Suzie had been nursing were all around her, only bigger, warmer. Blood pounded in her ears and Suzie felt strong. It was like running a hundred yard dash and not being exhausted afterwards. The rush, the strength, it was all around her and it hated. Maxxie hated Alex. Maxxie hated Bax. Most of all, Maxxie hated Jill. The fake friend that stole Alex from her, Jill was the worst. Maxxie was just like Suzie and she liked it. No, Maxxie was part of her and she loved it.

"Oh, now I see. This is the special thing. The secret." Suzie spoke out loud.

"I'm going to have to thank you, Maxxie. I see so much more now. So much."

Suzie left the door open and went to the kitchen to get some more marshmallows. Taking the entire bag, she went up to her room, turned on her laptop, then she shut and locked the door. There were plans to be made. Mom and Dad could manage dinner on their own, they would like that better, anyway.

"Have a date night, not like I care."

Suzie sat in front of her laptop and dumped the bag on the desk.

"I have an assignment to finish, and I get extra credit if I make them cry. And I *will* make Jill cry. And Alex. And Bax. And anyone who gets in my way, right Maxxie?"

Yes, we will make them cry, my Suzie. We will make them scream and cry for mercy.

CHAPTER EIGHT

"Akeyo, tell us what happened." Grandfather Li, Alex, and Jill were sitting at the table in the back of Warren Mitchell's conversion van. Baxter and his dad were in the front. Warren was driving.

"I was talking with Liz about the rumors and trying to examine the car. I could tell the imp had damaged it, but I wanted to try to understand more of what had been going on. The rumors, the damage, it seemed too much for just a minor spirit like an imp." Akeyo recounted her discussion with Liz.

"Wait, an imp wrecked our car?" Jill interrupted.

"Yes, honey, try to keep up. We went out to the driveway and opened the garage door. That's when Marjorie came walking up to us. We talked to her for a bit, and then she sat on my motorcycle. I told her it was rude to sit on a person's property without asking permission and she apologized and was very contrite. Liz suggested that she come inside for a snack or something to drink and she said yes."

"Wait, Marjorie Chan? Marjorie, six foot and change, built like a tank, apologized and was nice about it? I don't believe that for a moment." Alex traded knowing looks with Jill, who nodded her head in agreement. Apologies were not really the way they pictured Marjorie.

"So what happened next?" Grandfather Li asked, steering the conversation back to Akeyo.

"We went in and Liz started looking for some snacks. I noticed something was off, and then I saw the threads attached to the girl. The threads looked faint, and they were hard to see, so I thought that it was a very weak influence. I decided to watch her since she seemed harmless and I didn't want to tip off what ever was influencing the girl. That was my mistake. The influence was not weak, it had probably been continuous for some time. Most of it had entered the girl already, but I couldn't see it." Akeyo shook her head, "I should have known better."

"What do you mean, she was being influenced for a while? I don't understand." Alex looked from Grandma Akeyo to Grandfather Li.

"When someone is being influenced by a spirit demon, the longer the influence goes on, the more of the intent of the spirit demon is ingested into the person. The longer it continues, the less effort the spirit demon needs to keep the influence strong." Grandfather Li tapped the table with his fingers as he spoke.

"Quite, and your friend Marjorie must have been influenced for a few days or else the influence was very strong to start with. I should have noticed it sooner." Akeyo looked down at her feet as she spoke.

"We're here." Warren Mitchell called from the driver's seat, "I'm pulling into the driveway."

"Ok, so quickly before we get out. After a few minutes

of talking with Marjorie, she started behaving erratically. She became snide and started arguing with Liz. Marjorie began to take turns arguing with me, then Liz. She stood up, and it looked like she was about to get physical. She's as tall as me, but my goodness is she put together like a body builder."

"Yeah, Marjorie is the best athlete in school." Alex stood and opened the side door as the van stopped.

"She started speaking poorly, and I could tell her mind was going. She was talking about 'snapping' things and kept saying 'break, break.' It was eerie."

Alex and Bax looked at each other.

"We've heard that before. Imps." Alex said.

"Yeah, so what do we do about it?" Bax looked to Akeyo for an answer.

"I quickly worked a binding on the child and slowed the deterioration, but the corruption was obvious. I calmed Liz down and suggested to her to go rest and put a light suggestion on her so she would have some fuzzy memories of what happened. I examined the girl, and it was much worse than I had thought at first." Akeyo walked briskly to the door. The others followed.

"How bad could it be?" Alex asked.

"It was very bad. I saw her mind was coming apart inside. I needed help, so I had Liz watch her. I told her Marjorie was sick and needed to be looked after her while I got help. I went outside and tried to start my motorcycle, but it was too late, I realized Marjorie had corrupted it when she sat on the seat. All the rubber and leather pieces were falling apart, so I ran to get you lot." Akeyo opened the front door and paused, "Remember, she is sick, Liz doesn't know what's wrong. She thinks it's a fever."

"Thank goodness you're back!" Liz sounded relieved, "She's not getting better, we need to call her parents."

"We're here now, Liz. Warren, take Liz to the kitchen and get some damp towels. Bax, get the phone number for the girl's parents, I will take a look at her again."

"Akeyo, we need a doctor." Liz insisted. Akeyo swished her fingers in the air twice rapidly.

"Liz, go with Warren, we have this under control." Akeyo instructed.

Liz said nothing and went with Warren.

"What did you do to my mom?" Jill turned to face Grandma Akeyo.

"Nothing, it's a trick I learned in Las Vegas. You nudge someone gently and more often than not, they go with your suggestion."

"Las Vegas? Why does that sound like there is a story behind it?"

"Not for someone your age, Jill." Grandfather Li said.

"Well, what do we do now?" Bax looked around the living room. Grandma Akeyo sat down in a red leather upholstered easy chair that faded to pink over the years. Marjorie was lying on the matching love seat, a little less pink from age but far too small for the six foot tall girl. She wasn't moving and her breathing was slow, her eyes barely open.

"Ah, that is the question, isn't it?" Akeyo checked the girl's condition. First she looked at her eyes, then she rested her hand under Marjorie's nose to test the strength of her breath. The girl's responses were slowed, but still very much alive. She did not, however, look well at all.

"No wonder Liz was worried. Grandma Akeyo, she looks terrible."

"It was a close thing, I think I bound her in time. Husband, I need your assistance."

"What do you plan to do?" Grandfather Li stood behind Akeyo.

"I will push her spirit back together."

"Brute force? Is that wise?"

"I don't think we have a choice. I don't think we have time to reconstruct her mind piece by piece, we just have to trust that her personality is strong enough to know where all the pieces belong."

"What are you talking about? Push her spirit together?" Alex was lost. She didn't understand what her grandparents were discussing.

I can explain.

"Shut up, SPD."

"No time. Listen to your pet demon. We have to act before she is in too many pieces."

"SPD is not a pet, Grandfather Li."

Alex, when a person's personality is influenced by a demon for too long, they become corrupted. The personality breaks apart, and they begin to act on only their base instincts.

"How does that work?"

I am not sure, but I think they forget themselves. The influence forces the pieces of their mind apart. Compassion forgets willpower. Love forgets hate. A person is broken apart into pieces, and they are lesser for it.

"That sounds horrible."

It is. Spirit demons are fragments of people, the product of a lifetime. The fragments of this girl are even less than that, she has not lived her full life yet. She is only a fraction of her true potential.

"Alex, watch me. I am going to gather threads and feed them to your grandma. She will use them to bind Marjorie's spirit and squeeze her mind back into shape."

"Yes, Grandfather Li."

Grandfather Li stood straight up, his feet placed close together. Slowly he let his hands drift from his body, twisting as if they were paper blown in a light breeze. One hand grasped the air and Alex saw a thread of reality caught in Grandfather Li's fingers. Another thread was caught in his other hand. Grandfather Li brought his hands together and began knitting the threads, slowly forming a kind of cloth.

Grandma Akeyo took the end of the cloth and began to wrap it around Marjorie like a shroud. Alex could see the cloth, but Jill just stared at Grandfather Li and Grandma Akeyo with a quizzical look on her face.

"What's going on?" Jill asked.

"Watch." Alex touched her finger to Jill's hand and Jill drew in a sharp breath. She suddenly could see it all, the threads, the cloth and worst of all, the pieces of Marjorie's personality drifting away from her body. Akeyo used the cloth like a net, catching the pieces of Marjorie's personality as they drifted. She wrapped the cloth around Marjorie's mind, binding the pieces in and quite literally pushing the essence of the girl back together. A tear escaped from Jill's eye and rolled down her cheek. Jill pulled her hand away.

"I don't need to see that again, thanks."

"This is the last of the ice, my love." Grandfather Li placed the plastic bag full of ice cubes on Grandma Akeyo's forehead.

Akeyo was resting on Jill's bed. The love seat was currently occupied by an unconscious young girl. Rebinding Marjorie Chan's personality had taken considerable effort, and Grandma Akeyo was exhausted from the work.

"Thank you, Jiànhuī. See if you can find some aspirin or a very fine scotch."

"I think some tea might be in order."

"Then make sure it is at least half scotch."

Grandfather Li chuckled to himself and headed back to the living room.

"Don't think I'm not serious, old man. Ouch. Indoor voice, Akeyo, or you will hurt yourself." A migraine had built up in Akeyo's head as she worked, now it was a tremendously powerful pain that dominated her feelings.

"Will Grandma be alright?" Alex waited at the doorway, afraid for her Akeyo.

"Ah, you have never seen her exert herself so much, have you, child? Yes, Akeyo will be alright, but the binding work she did was great and so the price she pays will be similarly great. Fortunately, for now it shall just be a very bad migraine and perhaps a few pounds of weight loss." Grandfather Li led Alex back to the living room.

"That sounds great, free weight loss." Jill said as they came into the room.

"It's not. People are not meant to lose two or three pounds in an hour. Not unless something attached falls off, and that is also not a very good thing." Grandfather Li was serious.

"I'm just saying, you could sell that." Jill said.

"Your friend is almost as big a fool as you are, Granddaughter."

Alex smiled slightly, not enough that Jill could see it.

"How is the girl, Jill?" Grandfather walked over to the love seat, still occupied by Marjorie Chan.

"She seems fine. Breathing is good, pulse is strong. She's just sleeping deeply, it seems."

"Hopefully that is the worst of it."

"So, when will she wake up?" Jill was sitting in the chair, watching over Marjorie.

"That depends."

"On what?" Jill looked up at Grandfather Li.

"If you want her to sleep or if you want to wake her up."

"But Grandfather Li, shouldn't we just let her rest?" Alex looked concerned.

"Normally, I would say yes. Young ladies should sleep until they wake, but I am afraid I have some questions for this particular young lady, and I want answers now, not at one in the morning or when ever she happens to wake up." Grandfather Li took something from the pocket of his shirt, cracked it between his fingers and waved it under Marjorie's nose.

Marjorie coughed and tossed. The smell was bitter and strong. Jill and Alex wrinkled their noses at it.

"What is that?" Alex asked, pinching her nostrils closed with her fingers.

"Smelling salts. Ammonia. It will wake her up."

Marjorie coughed and pushed Grandfather Li's hand away.

"What is it, coach? Mom?" Marjorie started to wake and sit up.

"Slowly child, slowly. Don't move quickly." Grandfather Li helped Marjorie sit up, "You are ok."

"What's going on, did I fall out? My head is spinning."

"It's ok, Marjorie, what is the last thing you remember?" Grandfather Li asked.

"I was putting away the shot-put and then I was going to call some friends, ask about Alex's rumor questions. I didn't get very far, so I gave it a rest." Marjorie coughed at the ammonia from the salts.

"I got an email later, from Suzie Plimpton. She saw this website about Jill and Bax and she knew I was looking into the rumors about them making out. I called her, and she told me about this website, a blog or something. I was gonna check it out at school the next day and the next thing I knew, I was here." Marjorie blinked her eyes hard and tried to clear her head.

"Alex, when was that?"

"Tuesday or Wednesday, Grandfather Li. It's been almost four days." Alex shook her head.

More than enough time for the girl to be corrupted.

"Yeah, scary, SPD."

"Alex, is that you?" Marjorie asked.

"Yeah, Marjorie, it's me." Alex scooted next to Marjorie.

"Who's that other guy?"

"That's my grandfather." Alex held Marjorie's hand.

"No, not him, the other guy."

"There isn't any other guy here." Alex looked at her grandfather.

I think she means me.

"Yeah, him. Where you at? Ow, my head is killing me and things are all fuzzy."

"Oh no," Jill said, "Marjorie can hear SPD."

"Jill? Tell me Bax isn't here too, everyone all in one place. Y'all are pranking me, aren't you?"

"No, Marjorie. No one is pranking you." Alex said as she put a pillow behind Marjorie's head.

"So what's going on then? And who's that guy?"

I am SPD, Alex's...

"Cousin. SPD is my cousin." Alex interrupted.

"What, SPD is a nick name or something? Y'all are playing a prank on me, I know it."

"Hey, Marjorie's awake!" Bax walked in from the kitchen.

"Oh, that's everyone. Hi Bax. Fun joke. Who is this SPD?" Marjorie asked.

"SPD? Oh, that's Alex's demon in her smartphone."

"Bax, shut up!" Alex hissed.

"Too late," Jill said, "Bax let the cat out of the bag."

"Ok. This is silly. What's going on, tell me now before I have to twist some arms." Marjorie sounded annoyed and tried to get up. She failed and Alex caught her before she slipped too much.

"Hey, hold on there, Marjorie, you're heavy."

"Young lady. Sit and stay sitting. I'm not going to be happy if you hurt yourself." Grandfather Li's voice echoed as he spoke. There was no doubt that he was annoyed.

"Yeah, ok. I really don't feel so hot, anyway." Marjorie relaxed a bit.

"That's better. Now, you sit and tell me if you remember anything else."

"Yeah, sure. I remember I called Suzie, then I think I must have hit my head. It is all just bits and pieces. Sorry."

"Understandable. Now, I am going to touch your forehead. I am just checking for a fever." Grandfather put two of his fingers on Marjorie Chan's forehead, one above each eye, and then drew them together to a point in the middle between her eyes.

"Oh, wow, that was different." Marjorie leaned back on the love seat.

"How about now? Do you remember more now?"

"Yeah, it was, damn something was in my head? What

did you do?" Marjorie looked at Grandfather Li, seeing him as if for the first time.

"I cleared up the fog in your memories. It is a simple trick."

"I wasn't myself. Someone else was driving in my head." Marjorie said.

"Yes. Do you remember who it was?" Grandfather leaned just a little closer.

"No. Wait, does the name *Maxwell* sound familiar to you?"

"Oh, crap."

"So your cousin is really a doctor? And you call him SPD?" Marjorie asked.

"Yeah, short for special doctor. Stupid, I know, but I'm not great with nicknames."

"Come on Alex, they call me Marjorie 'Chat,' it's not like people around here are any better with nicknames." Marjorie smiled, "But I like you, your nicknames are at least a little interesting."

"Thanks, Marjorie. How are you feeling?"

"Not great, still a little fuzzy. What your grandfather did made it better, but I could sleep for a week, no doubt."

"Well, that's probably a good idea, you should go home and sleep." Jill said to Marjorie.

"Nope. Some idiot drugged me. Time for payback. I want to get him and teach him a lesson." Marjorie believed the little lie Alex told her about being drugged. The lie was the first thing that occurred to her when Marjorie pressed for more information about what really happened to her.

"Oh. Is that a good idea?" Jill tried to be casual.

"Oh yes, it's a great idea." Marjorie cracked her knuckles one by one.

"I like your friend, Alex. She is a tough cookie." Grandfather Li said.

I like her too.

"And I like her toughness, too." Akeyo said from the bedroom doorway, surprising the rest of the people in the room.

"How long were you standing there, my love?" Grandfather Li smiled at Grandma Akeyo.

"Long enough. It's time we stop this ridiculous situation. I like Marjorie's fighting spirit."

"Oh, crap." Jill whispered to Alex.

"I think we are done, here. The world is fine and everything is well put together."

"Well, everything except your wife's motorcycle." Warren was examining the decayed rubber and leather on Akeyo's boxer.

"There is nothing for that, it was corrupted too long and honestly, there was no life to bring back to it, the leather and rubber has been dead for far too long."

"Is that how it works? If something is alive, you can un-wreck it?"

"That is a good way to think about it, Warren." Grandfather Li clapped Warren on the back and looked at the boxer.

"You're still going to be in trouble when this is all over. You know that, right?" Warren looked at Grandfather Li with some sympathy.

"Yes, Warren, that is my lot in life."

"Ha! No, that's what you are going to take out on me at the next practice session!" Alex walked out of the garage and stood on the other side of the ruined motorcycle.

"True, but you should not be so honest with your grandfather. Now, tell me how it looks in the house, Alex."

"Fine now. It's pretty much clean. Liz is still a bit out of things, but you and Grandma Akeyo layered a lot of influence on her, didn't you?"

"Yes, I will have to deal with that soon, won't I?" Grandfather Li sighed.

"How so, Mr. Li? Didn't you just do some hocus pocus, hypnosis type of something on Liz?" Warren looked from Alex to Grandfather Li.

"Not exactly. I pushed her in specific directions. It is like physically pushing someone, but it is all in the mind. It leaves marks on your memories and personality. I will need to spend a good amount of time undoing any damage I may have caused."

"Damage, you mean it hurts Liz?"

"Not hurts exactly, but it does bruise the personality. Too much and it can hurt a person. They can become unreasonable. Unmanageable. But Liz is no where near that point and her personality is strong. She will be fine."

"But, if she's strong, doesn't that mean you have to push her harder?"

"You are a clever man, Warren Mitchell, but no you do not have to push harder on strong personalities." Grandfather Li walked into the house.

"Yeah, it's easier, isn't it?" Alex added.

"Oh, you think you know why, Alex? Can you tell me why it is easier?"

"Yeah, I'd like to hear this too." Warren followed behind Grandfather Li.

"Well, I was thinking about this when I was cleaning up inside. You taught me a lot of Aikido when I was little. In Aikido, the stronger your adversary, the easier it is to push and redirect them to do what you want. You use their strength against them and continue their momentum. When you push on a personality, you shift a strong person towards the choices you want them to make." Alex stepped alongside her grandfather and all three of them went into the garage.

"You have been paying attention. Yes, that is exactly it. No one is more determined than a strong-willed person. So it is easy to nudge them onto the right path."

"Oh really? I'm never going to play poker with you, Mr. Li." Warren laughed.

"That would be a wise choice, Mr. Mitchell. A wise choice indeed." Grandfather Li chuckled along with Warren.

"Wow, I was right? Was that praise, Grandfather?" Alex tried for sarcasm, half succeeding.

"Oh? Grandfather? Not Grandfather Li?"

"Yes, Grandfather Li. Always Grandfather Li. You earned your name, Grandfather Li." Alex found the other half of her sarcasm.

"I regret introducing you to the fine art of sarcasm, Alex."

"I regret nothing." Alex said proudly.

"Well played. One day, you will be truly clever and wise, my child."

"You people are too funny. I like y'all." Warren laughed.

I feel the same way. I enjoy the family dynamic.

"Shut up, SPD."

"No, Alex, your smartphone is right, you have a great family dynamic. Reminds me of my own. You have a fun family, SPD can tell."

———

"That's it? I don't see how that helps me find the perv that drugged me." Marjorie and Grandma Akeyo sat on the love seat, discussing their plan.

"Don't worry. Just take me to every place you remember going to for the last couple of days and we'll find the guy." Grandma Akeyo confirmed.

Alex, Jill, and Bax were in the kitchen, listening to Marjorie and Grandma Akeyo while they talked through their plan.

"I don't like this one bit." Jill pursed her lips.

"I know you don't like Marjorie much," Alex began.

"Much? I don't like her at all! You have no idea how many rumors she started about me in middle school. I don't like her, and I certainly do *not* trust her."

"Jill, she can hear SPD, we can't just let her go around talking about magic and stuff." Bax was trying to sound reasonable.

"Why not? I mean, who would believe that? I didn't until I saw it for myself. And it would serve her right to lose a little credibility after all the lies she spread about us, Bax." Jill set her arms across her chest for emphasis.

"I don't disagree at all. I just think we need to keep an eye on her." Bax felt his reasonable position slip a little.

"Ok, both of you. I agree this is a bad situation, but Marjorie didn't spread those rumors. We talked to her, Bax and me, and she had no idea about the rumors before Maxwell started influencing her. Jill, can you just go along with this until we find out if Maxwell is behind this or not? After that, I don't care. Cut Marjorie loose, whatever. But I want to get to the bottom of this and send these jerks back to their own world."

Except for me. I like it here in your smartphone, Alex.

"Yes, of course SPD, except for you."

"Wow, you are a total pushover, aren't you?" Jill had just the right amount of sarcasm in her voice, Alex wrinkled her nose with envy.

"Not! I think SPD can help."

"Yeah, Jill's right. You are such a pushover. 'My stalker is now my best friend, and he's a demon!' Push. Over." Bax was enjoying teasing Alex a little too much.

"No. SPD is useful."

I am not a he. I do not know if I have a gender.

"Oh, ambiguous gender too, sounds like someone is in love." Jill decided to go from sarcasm to full teasing.

"I do not love SPD! What is wrong with you two?" Alex looked at Jill and Bax with disgust on her face.

I simply prefer this demon box. I feel safe in the box.

Alex, Jill, and Bax all looked at the smartphone on the table between them, and laughed.

"What is going on in here?" Grandfather Li entered the kitchen.

"Nothing, we were just talking."

"About Alex and her love-bot on her smartphone." Jill could not help herself.

"Never mind. Alex, I was wrong. Your friend is more of a fool than you are. Congratulations." Grandfather Li shook his head and turned to leave.

"Wait, Mr. Li, what are we going to do now? And

where did you ask my dad to go?" Bax stopped Grandfather Li from leaving.

"Ah, an intelligent question! Alex, your other friend is clearly the only smart one here, so I will answer his questions. Baxter, your dad is getting some video cameras so we can record what is going on. I want to test the idea that we can gather video evidence of the spirit demons. And as for your first question, we are going to follow your friend Marjorie back to every place she remembers going over the past few days. There will be weaknesses in the world along the path and we shall repair those weaknesses. Hopefully, we will also find some clues to the spirit demon that influenced her. Perhaps we can confirm that Maxwell is behind this and still in our world. Perhaps we will even figure out where and how Maxwell is hiding and how we can send it back."

"Oh, that makes a lot of sense." Bax thought about it, "I like that plan."

"Of course it makes sense. My wife only has plans that make sense. Don't tell her I said that, or you will be demoted to 'foolish friend' from 'smarter friend.'" Grandfather Li clapped his hand on Bax's shoulder.

"Ouch, that is the shoulder I landed on."

"Sorry. I will remember that."

"So this is where I was before I came over to Jill's house." Marjorie brought Grandma Akeyo, Bax, and Jill to a playground close to Suzie Plimpton's house.

"What were you doing here?" Jill asked, kicking at the dirt at the edge of the playground.

"I'm not really sure, I used to play here when I was a little kid."

"Oh, I think I know why they were here." Bax was looking at the screen of a camcorder his dad had brought from home. Warren brought some video cameras for each of them. Bax was using his camera to survey the playground. Warren, Alex, and Grandfather Li were searching the neighborhood around Jill's house.

"Look, I can see all sorts of artifacts on the video. Glitching, weird patterns, this is like some sort of crazy special effect from a really old movie." Bax showed the screen to Jill and Marjorie.

"Grandma Akeyo, look at this." Jill waved at the older lady to come and look.

"It's fine Jill, I don't need a camera to see all the damage. It's plain as the sun in the sky to my eyes."

"Sorry, I forgot you don't need the camera to see it."

"What's going on here? I thought you brought the cameras to catch this guy on video? Why does everything look screwy?" Marjorie whispered to Bax and Jill as she leaned down over Bax's shoulder.

"What is means, young lady who thinks she is clever, is that I can hear you just fine and you should ask me instead of talking behind my back." Grandma Akeyo circled the playground.

"Wow, old lady has got some ears on her."

"Who are you calling old, young lady? I'm not so old that I won't find a good way to make you regret calling me unflattering things."

"Ok, now that is just kinda creepy. How did you hear me from the other side of the playground?" Marjorie called out.

"I may look old, Marjorie, but my mind is clear and sharp and my ears know to keep up."

"What does that mean?" Marjorie put on a confused face. It was a good tactic to get secrets and information out of people. Marjorie liked hearing people's secret information.

"It means, young Marjorie Chan, that you better watch your tongue around me and spend more time listening and understanding than trying to play games with your elders." Grandma Akeyo walked back to Marjorie, Bax and Jill, then tweaked Marjorie's nose, "You are too clever for your own good. That is why I like you."

Jill made a face. She was still not a fan of Marjorie.

"Bax, Jill, I want you to keep an eye out for anything odd. I am going to try to repair the weakness here. I need you both to warn me if you see anything unusual."

"Ok, that's weird. What weakness?" Marjorie was unsure how to take Akeyo. Marjorie was just over six feet tall and she was used to towering over everyone her age and most of the adults she knew as well. Grandma Akeyo was just as tall as her and although she was thinner and not well muscled like Marjorie, she felt as though Grandma Akeyo was much stronger than herself. In truth, Marjorie was a little afraid of the older woman.

"Think of it like a cloth, Marjorie. Yes, the world is like a cloth, and sometimes it becomes thin and frayed in places."

"Ok. And that has exactly what to do with some dude who needs his butt kicked for drugging me?" Marjorie asked.

"You are quick, you have a sharp mind but no. That's not what is happening here. Right now I have to do something and I don't have the time to explain it. I do promise you we will get to the bottom of your problem. Just bear with me, would you Marjorie?" Grandma Akeyo stood in the center of the playground and settled into a horse stance.

"Hmm. You sure? I will hold you to that promise, old lady." Marjorie stood tall, crossing her arms in front of her body.

"I wouldn't have it any other way. Something happened when you came here, Marjorie. Something bad. I need to figure out how to fix it, then we will find your 'guy.' I think this might be why you were so out of control at Jill's house. Why you were mean to Liz." Grandma Akeyo wasn't above bending the truth when necessary.

"I still feel bad about that, I was really mean to Ms. Duffy." Marjorie looked down at the ground and shuffled her feet a little, "Could this be where it started?"

"It's ok, it wasn't your fault." Grandma Akeyo said.

"It still feels like it was my fault." Marjorie relaxed a little.

"That is guilt, Marjorie. Guilt is a useless emotion. It will eat at you and weaken your heart. Discard it." Akeyo took a deep breath in and held it.

"Easier said than done, but ok, I'll try. What should I do now?" Marjorie perked up a little, but still felt bad about how she had acted towards Jill's mom, Liz Duffy. Akeyo exhaled.

"Keep a sharp eye with Bax and Jill. I am going to repair what has been undone."

Marjorie didn't know what to do. Grandma Akeyo didn't seem to need any help. Bax studied his video camera while Jill wandered to the far side of the playground. Marjorie stood in between them all, just on the edge of the playground.

"So. Are you going to the dance, Bax?" Marjorie asked.

"What? The Harvest Dance? I haven't thought about it. You?" Bax said, as he panned the camera around the perimeter.

"I'll be there. No date. Last year I worked the door. How about you, Jill? You going?" Marjorie asked.

"Nah. I don't have a date. No fun, anyway." Jill said.

"You should go with Bax. Just to have the experience."

"No, Marjorie. I don't date friends." Jill protested.

"Not as a date. Go as friends to keep the creeps and pervs away."

"That's not a bad idea," Bax said, hopefully, "I'd do that, Jill. How about it?"

"Ah, sure? If it will stop this conversation." Jill was uncomfortable with the idea of a date, but Bax was her friend. He was safe.

"Marjorie, look out behind you!" Bax shouted.

"What, where?" Marjorie turned in place and saw nothing, then was suddenly on her back with something heavy weighing down her chest.

"Ouch, there's another one heading towards you, Jill! Duck!" Bax was quickly panning his camera over the playground, looking for the imps that had appeared out of thin air. Grandma Akeyo was on the ground struggling with her own unseen attacker.

"You are doing a bad job, Baxter Mitchell." Grandma Akeyo shouted as she grabbed at the imp trying to strangle her. The imp was small but heavy, like two fat English bulldogs attached one on top of the other. Grandma Akeyo landed a hand on one of the imp's four arms and squeezed. The imp yelped. It hadn't expected that Grandma Akeyo could touch it, let alone hurt it.

"I'm trying, I've never done this before!" Bax protested, "Jill, run, there are two little ones after you."

"Run where?" Jill yelled back at Bax. Too late, the two small imps grabbed Jill's legs, one for each imp.

Grandma Akeyo lifted the imp into the air as it struggled, grasping and scratching at the old woman's arm. Grandma Akeyo did not flinch, instead she put her free hand into her pocket and pulled out a small, wooden block. Akeyo slammed the block into the imp's face and it squealed in pain, then vanished with a pop.

"Filthy creature. Bax, get away, but keep an eye out, I will take care of this little problem." Grandma Akeyo strode over to Jill and traced three circles in the air with her fingers. The two imps melted away into nothing, releasing Jill's legs.

"Thanks, I couldn't see them, not like last time." Jill was out of breath.

"These are weak, but there are many of them." Grandma Akeyo shouted.

"Granny, a little help here?" Marjorie was struggling against something Jill couldn't see. Grandma Akeyo tossed the wooden block across the playground towards Marjorie, "Catch this and hit it!"

Marjorie saw the block and stretched out her hand to catch it. It landed solidly in Marjorie's hand and she immediately smashed it into where she thought the imp's face was located. A scream and pop echoed in Marjorie's ears and the weight on her chest disappeared. Marjorie was sure she saw a drooling, stupid face looking down at her before she heard the pop.

"What the *hell* was that?" Marjorie yelled as she stood up.

Marjorie brushed the dirt off her clothes. She looked at Akeyo to say thanks and the color drained from her face. A much larger thing was rising from the ground behind Akeyo and Jill. Marjorie stepped forward without saying a word, instead she threw the block strait at the thing and hit it square in what passed for a face. There was a sucking sound, a wind pulling the air away from Marjorie and a pop. Akeyo turned as the thing was sucked into the wooden block as it fell to the ground.

"Well done, Marjorie, did you see that imp appear?" Grandma Akeyo helped Jill up.

"Yeah, what in the world was that?" Marjorie walked over to Grandma Akeyo and helped her with Jill.

"Nothing from this world. I guess you could tell that, no?"

"Yeah, no way that was something natural, Granny Akeyo."

"Grandma, please. I am not a 'granny.'"

"You saw it, Marjorie? I couldn't see anything." Jill stood up gingerly.

"Help." Bax's voice cracked a little. He was standing very still, his camera loose in his hand. A large imp was holding him from behind, it must have been a sneaky one.

"Hold still, Bax. I'll make sure you are safe." Grandma Akeyo tried to keep Bax calm.

Break, break. Hurt. Kill.

"Bax!" Jill cried out, fear was in her eyes as the imp raked long fingers and nails across Bax's face. The nails cut into his skin and blood welled up, the imp looked at Jill and smiled.

Break. Kill. Next.

"Oh the hell you will!" Marjorie yelled at the imp, she started to move, picked up the wooden block on the ground as she ran at Bax and the imp. Marjorie covered the distance in five huge steps and barreled directly into the imp, knocking it down and forcing it to lose its grip on Bax.

"No one hurts my friends!" Marjorie pulled her fist back and punched the imp squarely in the face, then took her other hand with the wooden block and pushed the block against the imp's chest. It struggled, opened its mouth and then the imp was gone. Marjorie landed hard on her knees when the imp vanished. The wooden block was warm in her hand.

Jill whistled long and low.

"Remind me to never piss off Marjorie Chan."

"Me too, Jill, me too." Grandma Akeyo agreed.

"Thanks for saving me, Marjorie. Did you mean that, are we really your friends?" Bax tried to give Marjorie a big hug, but she stopped him with a look.

"Yeah, no hugs. I am not into that sort of thing. And yeah kiddo, you are my friends. That's why I don't let people talk about you, I like you and Jill, you're so cute."

"Ah, what do you mean, you don't let people talk about us?" Jill walked over to Bax and Marjorie.

"You two are cute together, always trying to be the best at school. I like it, so I don't let anyone start rumors about either of you. When Alex and Bax came to talk to me I agreed to help because I was pissed off that someone broke my rules." Marjorie pushed Bax's face to one side with her fingers, looking at the cuts on his cheek.

"But, how can we be your friends? We never talk or hang out or anything." Jill didn't think Marjorie was making sense.

"Huh. Well, everyone is intimidated by me. Girls, boys, everyone. Not you. You ignore me, I like that."

"That makes no sense, Marjorie. You're not making any sense at all."

"It makes sense to me." Grandma Akeyo put her hand on Marjorie's shoulder, "No one treats you like a friend, do they Marjorie? Everyone is afraid of you because you are tall and strong. They tell you things to curry favor so you don't make their fears real."

"Yeah, everyone thinks I would hurt them. I would never do that, but they don't listen."

"And Jill doesn't care. She doesn't treat you any different from anyone else."

"Nope, she doesn't. That is why I like her and Bax. They are only interested in competing with each other to be the best. I respect that. They feel like real people to me, not like the rest of the people at school. I don't even like hearing all the rumors, but everyone tells me everything going on and I can't stop them. They think I'm just a big dumb jock, and they like to keep me happy by telling me what is going on at school."

"Why?" Grandma Akeyo asked gently.

"I used to talk all the time. I was a chatty kid when I was eight or nine. The kids in my school called me Marjorie 'Chat' and it just kinda stuck." Marjorie sniffed.

"So everyone is afraid of you, everyone but Jill and Bax?"

"And your granddaughter, Alex. She's always nice to me. So, I guess Alex is my only friend. And these two are Alex's friends. So I guess maybe I like to think they are my friends too."

"They don't want anything from you, and they aren't afraid of you."

"I know. It's pathetic, isn't it?" Marjorie sniffed again and looked away from Jill and Bax.

"I don't think so. I think you're a good friend. You saved Bax, didn't you?"

"I think I could use that hug now. If that's ok?"

Grandma Akeyo wrapped Marjorie up in her arms, "Anytime, little one. You can call me Granny."

Bax and Jill looked at the two tall women and joined them in one big hug.

G randma Akeyo, Jill, Bax, and Marjorie returned to Jill's house. Bax's cheek was scratched deeply by an attacking imp, and Marjorie insisted they return to clean up the wound. Warren was not amused when they came in the front door.

"What happened to you? Are you alright? Is it going to scar?" Warren Mitchell spoke too quick for anyone to answer.

"Dad, relax. I'm fine."

"Bax, you are not fine. Have you seen how much blood is on your face?"

"You should see the other guy."

"Not funny Bax, I don't care about the other guy."

"Mr. Mitchell, you should sit down while I clean your son up." Marjorie spoke up.

"Oh really? Why should I sit down, young lady?" Warren looked up directly into Marjorie's eyes, challenging her.

"Because you are standing in the way of us getting to the bathroom. I can't wash his face off if I can't get to the sink, Mr. Mitchell." Marjorie stood tall, looking down at Warren Mitchell. Warren wasn't intimidated, but Marjorie's words were calm and clear, the logic got through to him.

"Oh, well, that makes sense. I'll go sit down, I'm not that good with things like this."

"I'll be fine." Bax reassured his dad. Marjorie brought Bax into the bathroom and started running the water in the sink.

"What was that about?" Marjorie asked as she took a washcloth and wet it.

"Dad is bad with me getting hurt. And he's really bad with blood."

"Really? He is a pretty big guy, I mean he looks tough." Marjorie began wiping the blood away. Jill came to the bathroom and watched.

"Yeah, Bax is right. When he was little, Bax would pick his nose and get nose bleeds."

"I did not pick my nose, Jill."

"Anyway, he would get these epic nosebleeds. The first time I saw it happen, Mr. Warren passed out. I had to help him while Bax stood over the sink for an hour."

"That's a pretty epic nosebleed." Marjorie wrung out the washcloth in the sink then rinsed it out under the running water.

"It was, but it was harder dealing with Mr. Mitchell. He was about twenty pounds heavier back then." Jill held her arms out, illustrating Mr. Mitchell's waistline.

"Wow. He looks in ok shape now, but he's still big. I think he weighs as much as me." Marjorie peeked over Jill's head to look at Mr. Mitchell as he sat waiting for them to finish cleaning up Bax's face.

"Yeah, that was when I was ten. I teased him into getting in shape. Told him he passed out on top of me and I'd been squished."

"No, you didn't?" Marjorie stared at Jill with wide eyes.

"Oh, yes she did. It was hilarious." Bax looked at himself in the mirror, "It's not too bad, is it?"

"No, lots of blood but not a deep cut. You'll survive." Marjorie opened the drawer, looking for first aid supplies.

"Try the far drawer, triple antibiotic is in that one. Bandages are below."

"Thanks, but this scratch is too long for a bandage. The antibiotic will have to do."

"Thanks, Marjorie. You seem to know how to deal with this stuff pretty well." Bax said.

"Yeah, well, cuts and scrapes come with being a jock."

"Marjorie, I'm sorry I was so mean to you." Jill said.

"It's ok, Jill. I'm used to people not acting normal around me."

"Yeah, well, I should have been better. So I am sorry. can we start over?"

"Sure, why?" Marjorie applied the antibiotic to Bax's cheek.

"Wanna be friends, Marjorie Chan?" Jill put her hand on Marjorie's, stopping her from treating Bax's wound.

"Jill, no worries. I already said I like you and Bax. We even had that big hug. We can be friends."

"Well, I just needed to say it, Marjorie."

"She's right, Jill always needs to say things out loud to make them real." Bax smiled.

"Good. We're friends, Jill Duffy. Now get the heck out of my way so I can finish with your boyfriend's face, ok?" Marjorie cracked a small smile as she spoke.

"Fine. But he is not my boyfriend. Understand?"

"Sure, girlfriend. Bax, this will hurt, ok?"

"Alright, I'm ready." Bax drew in a breath and held it.

Marjorie looked hard at Bax and said in her most earnest voice, "Jill likes you."

Bax held back as long as he could then burst out laughing. Jill stomped out of the bathroom.

"Akeyo, what happened?" Grandfather Li sat down with Alex and Grandma Akeyo at the kitchen table. Marjorie had taken Bax into the bathroom to get cleaned up and Warren was sitting in the living room, hyperventilating.

"We found a playground and there were holes everywhere." Akeyo began.

"The one I used to play at when I was little?"

"Alex, hush." Grandfather Li frowned.

"Yes my darling, that was the playground."

"I liked that one, it has the nice slide."

"Alex, hush. Akeyo, what was going on, just holes?"

"Yes, just holes. So I asked the children to keep an eye out with their camera while I started to repair the damage."

"And did you do it?"

"At first, everything was fine. Then we got jumped by a bunch of imps." Akeyo shook her head, "I should not have put the children in that position."

"Akeyo, focus." Grandfather Li had a quiver in his voice.

"Yes, focus. The imps, five or six of them jumped us. Bax saw them and warned us, but they were fast."

"A group of imps? Grandfather Li, you always told me imps were solitary."

"They are Alex, something must have been controlling them." Grandfather Li replied.

"Yes, they were coordinated. They were smart. I was knocked down. One of them went after Marjorie. It was a ferocious one, big and nasty."

"They were coordinated? Smart imps?"

"Very coordinated, my love. They went after me first

because I was the biggest threat, then they went after Marjorie because she was just the biggest. Two little ones grabbed Jill by the legs and tripped her up." Akeyo spoke slowly, trying to recall the exact sequence of events.

"Bax was backing away, I told him to get safe."

"That is good, what happened next?"

"I had a demon box with me, so I took one of the blocks out and bound the one attacking me to the box."

"I hope you got it good." Grandfather Li said.

"Smashed his face with it, no one gets one over on me, you know that."

"Grandma, you smashed an imp in the face?" Alex sounded shocked.

"No one gets the best of your grandma." Grandfather Li was proud and perhaps a little scared at the same time.

"Then I helped Jill and tossed the demon box to Marjorie. She saw the imps. She punched the one trying to pin her to the ground."

"Marjorie Chan punched an imp?" Alex was wide-eyed.

"Close your mouth, child."

"Yes, my darling, your friend Marjorie bound the imp into the box, punching it in the face then hitting it with the demon box. She is indomitable." Akeyo was clearly impressed with Marjorie.

"That's when Bax called out to us. An imp had somehow gotten behind us and grabbed him." Akeyo shook her head again, "I am getting too old for this sort of fighting."

"Is that how Bax got cut up?"

"Yes, Alex. The imp threatened to break him, to kill him. That is when Marjorie acted. I was going to try to calm the situation, but Marjorie saw it truly. The imp was going to kill Baxter so Marjorie sprinted, tackled it, and bound it into the demon box."

"Wow." Alex was impressed.

"Wow." Grandfather Li agreed with Alex.

"Oh, and she punched the crap out of the imp before she bound it as well. She is a very tough young woman."

"I don't like it when people hurt my friends." Marjorie spoke as she entered the kitchen, "Bax is cleaned up, he'll be fine."

"It sounds as if you are the hero of the day, Marjorie Chan." Grandfather Li said.

"Nope. I was just very angry. Now I just want to know what the hell is really going on, pardon my language." Marjorie sat down at the table.

It sounds like Ms. Chan has earned an explanation.

"Shut up, SPD." Alex said on reflex.

"That's not your cousin on speed-dial, is it? It's like those things, right?"

"Not exactly, Marjorie. But SPD is correct, you deserve the truth." Akeyo put her hand on Marjorie's and squeezed.

"You called those things imps. They looked like goblins from my old storybooks. What are they really?"

"They are spirits. Bad, bad spirits that like to hurt people." Akeyo held onto Marjorie's hand.

"Spirits?"

"Yes, and demons."

"Like angels and demons? Christian bible stuff?" Marjorie sounded skeptical, "I don't believe in that stuff."

"No, not bible stuff. More like traditional Persian devas and maybe Chinese or Japanese evil spirits." Akeyo spoke slowly and clearly.

"Like in anime?"

"Anime?" Grandfather Li asked, raising an eyebrow.

"Cartoons from Japan, Grandfather. Why are you so old?" Alex overplayed her power of sarcasm.

"Not so old that I won't remember your tone next time we have practice."

"Oh, crap."

"'Oh, crap' is right, young lady."

I do enjoy your family dynamic, Alex.

"Shut up, SPD."

CHAPTER NINE

"Evil, magical creatures are real, they are out there and they like messing people up. Is that what I am hearing, or am I wrong?" Marjorie Chan listened intently. No one could deny that fact.

"Yes. And we have to put them back where they come from." Alex confirmed.

"Your smartphone is one of them?"

I am not the smartphone, I am SPD.

"Right, that voice is not the smartphone, that is a spirit demon that you trapped in your phone. And you thought this was a good idea? Seriously, do you watch horror movies at all?" Marjorie knew her new friends were smart, but she was completely unclear on how smart people could be so dumb.

"Ah, no. Rom Com." Alex's eyes were wide, movies were not what she expected.

"Nope, Vic Dallas. Only Vic 'delicious' Dallas." Jill piped up.

"What are these movies you speak of? They sound frivolous." Grandfather Li sounded serious, Alex snorted. She found Grandfather Li's collection of every single Humphrey Bogart movie ever made when she was eleven. He made her watch them all as punishment.

"I don't watch horror, they give me gas." Everyone looked at Bax, "What?"

"You are all hopeless. Rule one, never invite the demons in." Marjorie ticked off rules on her fingers.

"Rule number two, never split up. Rule number three, be the main character, you get to live. Most of the time."

"I don't see how that helps us. And I thought you didn't invite vampires in to your house, not demons."

"Shut up, Bax."

"Alex, I'm just saying, horror movie rules only work in horror movies. This is real." Bax pouted.

I agree with Ms. Chan.

"What?" Alex and Bax both looked at the smartphone.

Do not invite Maxwell in. Stay together, or Maxwell will find it easier to hurt you. I am not sure about what a 'main character' is, however.

"Huh, the demon agrees with me. At least one of you has some sense. Do you want to go on a date?"

No thank you, Ms. Chan. I do appreciate the gesture, however. Alex, what is a date?

"Shut up, SPD!"

"Enough. All of you." Grandma Akeyo stopped the bickering.

"I agree." Grandfather Li added.

"Especially you, old man. You are encouraging them in this silliness."

"Ouch. Glad I didn't say anything." Warren Mitchell said under his breath. Akeyo shot him a silent look, "Ouch."

"Marjorie, you're not wrong. We need to think about

this situation in a much more constructive fashion. There's a demon loose in the world, perhaps it is Maxwell. Even if it isn't, the demon has gained power over imps and is directing them. All of this is a problem. All of you," Akeyo pointed at the teens and Warren, "Should never have known about any of this."

"We cannot help that, Akeyo." Grandfather Li added.

"No, we can't. You are all a part of this now, and that means that Jiànhuī and I must protect you."

Marjorie snorted, "I can protect myself."

"That may be, young lady, but you still needed my demon box. The point isn't that you can protect yourself, but that we all need to protect each other. My husband and I have been doing this a long time, and we prefer to do it alone. Now we have all of you, like it or not."

"But that's good, isn't it? Now you don't have to do it alone." Jill asked, hoping she was right.

"Yes. And with all of you, we are stronger. But it is also my responsibility to keep you all safe. I don't want to have to explain to your parents why you are hurt, or worse." Bax touched the still raw cuts on his cheek at Akeyo's words.

"Yeah, if Marjorie didn't act as fast as she did, Bax might have been 'or worse.'" Jill grasped Marjorie's hand and squeezed gently, "Thanks."

"Exactly. So we must be smart. Think, where is this demon? If it *is* Maxwell, how can we find it? What can we do to stop it?" Akeyo stood up and looked from one person to the next.

"And most importantly, which one of you ordered delivery?" Donald spoke from the doorway.

Everyone turned to look at the back door to the kitchen. Donald Land stood there with three extra large pizza boxes, two huge bags of Sìchuān take out, and a box of black coffee from the donut shop.

"What? You people with your magic and drama. If I didn't bring you food, you would all die and starve. Not necessarily in that order, but the point stands. Now one of you get over here and take this stuff out of my hands, it's heavy!"

"Dad! How did you know we were here?" Alex grabbed the coffee and put it on the table.

"Sticky note on the front door. Thanks, Akeyo."

"Wasn't me?"

"Hmm, ok. You. Tall girl, take these pizzas." Donald instructed Marjorie as Bax and his dad handled the Sìchuān bags.

"Great, now that you all are ready to fight the good fight, you owe me twenty bucks each for the food. No short changing me, either." Donald smiled.

"You will get that twenty dollars when you pry it out of my wife's cold, dead hands." Grandfather Li waited for Grandma Akeyo to slap him on the head before he flinched.

"Just kidding, everyone, Liz and I got it."

"Yeah, where is my mom? I thought she was lying down?" Jill asked.

"Oh, she is over at my place." Donald said, "While you were all out, I came over and she was looking a little confused. I figured out that someone pushed her personality around a little too much, so I got her out of here and gave her some aspirin and an ice pack. Knowing you as I do my fine in-laws, I got the food that I knew you people would need. Expending way too much energy is your normal routine. Making sure you don't collapse and start complaining about my cooking is my normal routine."

"Do you people normally eat like this?" Marjorie hardly knew where to begin.

"Yes, tall girl, they do. It is very unhealthy but astoundingly better than if I actually attempt to cook."

"Name's Marjorie, not tall girl."

"Donald. Alex's dad."

"Mr. Land, nice to meet you."

"Donald, please, Mr. Land sounds weird."

"My mom will ground me if I call an adult by their first name."

"You called me 'Granny.'" Akeyo piled some rice into a paper bowl, followed by a slice of pizza and some dàndàn miàn.

"Not a first name, that's a title. Mama Chan would approve." Marjorie looked at the pizza with longing.

"Mama Chan sounds like my kind of woman." Akeyo said as she picked up her disposable kuàizi and snapped them apart.

"Maybe, but you seem much nicer than my mom, she's a bit intense."

"Oh really? Maybe we should ask for her help?"

"Only if you want her to scold your demons for you and maybe get them into a good college."

What is college?

"Shut up, SPD. Eat your food." Alex said between bites of Hawaiian pizza.

I do not eat.

"Shame, so shut it so we can, ok?"

I think you planned that particular quip.

"Ya think? This pizza is so yum, so let me enjoy it already."

"So what about this Maxwell, guy? How are we going to find him?" Marjorie started on her first slice of pizza.

"Well, Maxwell is an it, not a he. Demons normally would not hide, but if this is Maxwell, I think we hurt it quite a bit when we tried to send it back to the dead lands." Grandfather Li placed his bowl of dàndàn miàn down, his kuàizi laid across the top.

"Ok, but where is it then?"

"Well, maybe we should start plotting out the problem?" Warren spoke up, "Like on a detective show on TV. We get a map, start poking pins in it where these incidents happened, get some red string and connect it all."

"Because the world always works like it does on TV, Warren?" Grandfather Li was not impressed.

"Actually, that's not a bad idea. In fact, I was thinking the same thing. Maybe not the strings, but after Maxwell trashed my house, it had to go somewhere, right?" Donald spooned some rice into his own bowl.

"Donald, you are still a disappointment. However, I do see what you are saying, perhaps there is some merit to it?"

"Wait, Mr. Li, you just said my idea was dumb, but Donald says it and it isn't dumb? I'm not feeling the love here." Warren poured a cup of coffee from the box.

"I am not too proud to admit I am wrong. But yes, the string idea was dumb." Grandfather Li said.

"You're not making your position any better." Warren sat back and sipped his coffee.

"Fine, I just like mocking young people. You qualified."

"That I can believe. Apology accepted. Coffee?" Warren asked.

"Sure. Cream, no sugar."

"No problem, Mr. Li. You can get the maps."

"Fine." Grandfather Li frowned.

"That was really strange," Alex said, "It was like

someone was more clever than you, Grandfather Li. Are you sure you earned your name?"

"Shut up, un-clever child."

I understand where your habits come from now, Alex. I do so appreciate your family dynamic.

Grandfather Li and Warren Mitchell tried to avoid laughing, both failed miserably.

"Well that's it, isn't it?" Warren concluded.

"I still don't see it." Alex looked at the map but couldn't see what Warren saw in it.

"Look, here is your house, here is your grandparent's house. Over here is the playground where Grandma Akeyo and the kids were attacked. Now do you see it?"

"No."

"The telephone lines. It is clear as day."

"Mr. Mitchell, you didn't put any telephone lines on the map. How could I possibly know that?" Alex shook her head.

"Sorry, I forget you don't do this every day. We put in new high speed fiber lines last month, the playground and both houses are along the right of way we used to lay the fiber." Warren explained proudly.

"Oh."

"And it all leads to the Internet. Look, here is the old frame relay junction near the playground. Here is the trunk line from there to the new data center. What do you see along that line?" Warren drew on the map with a thick marker.

"Your house and the school. I see the school."

"Right, where your friends were all messed up."

"Mr. Mitchell has a point." Jill said, observing the map.

"Yeah, it's like the Internet is all to blame, how can that be?" Bax asked.

Maxwell did infest Alex's laptop.

"Exactly SPD. The laptop was trashed. The trashed routers that I had to replace on Thursday morning were at the old trunk line junction. Those served both your house, Alex's, and ours." Warren sat back, pleased with his conclusion.

"That's pretty hard to argue with, Alex." Bax pointed to the spot his dad had marked on the map.

"But the Internet, really? Isn't that just a little clichéd?"

"You have a demon in your smartphone. Your laptop battery exploded and a different demon popped out of the screen. You think that the Internet is too far fetched? I always said the Internet was a poison." Grandfather Li seemed a little too happy with Warren's conclusion.

"You don't get out of paying the Internet bill that easy, Jiànhuī. I need it." Grandma Akeyo anticipated her husband's next line of attack.

"I was not going to suggest we cancel the service at all, my love."

"Sure. No one believes you, old fool."

"What was it you said about routers, Warren?" Donald asked as he sorted the take out trash into recycling groups.

"Damnedest thing, these routers failed, no apparent reason. I sent some interns out to troubleshoot, and they said that the routers were just installed, but there were all sorts of faults."

"I do not know what that means." Grandfather Li was not the only one, but only he admitted it.

"So, normally a router handles your traffic for the Internet.

You ask for something in your web browser or whatever, and it goes off into the Internet. The router knows where the stuff you want is, and it sends a message off to whatever computer has the information. It's a little more complicated than that, but that is the 'physics for poets' version of Internet routing."

"Ok, so what was wrong with these routers?"

"Well Mr. Li, they were acting like they were really, really old. The guys brought them back, and when I inspected them, everything was just falling apart. The wiring was cracked and not flexible at all, some capacitors in the power supplies were leaking. They were like forty-year-old pieces of equipment, not ones that we installed a few weeks ago."

"That is just a little odd." Alex tried her dead pan delivery.

"Yeah, I thought they were playing a joke on me, but these were really modern routers. All the serial numbers checked out and everything. You can tell the difference between old and new equipment at a glance. These were new, except they were old and decrepit."

"That sounds like my laptop." Alex said.

"And like my motorcycle." Grandma Akeyo added.

"Will that happen to my smartphone?" Alex asked, looking at SPD.

No. I do not think so.

"Well of course you don't SPD, you don't want to go back to the dead lands."

"No, I think SPD is correct. SPD does not seem to corrupt things like Maxwell or these imps." Grandma Akeyo said, nodding towards the smartphone.

"I don't see where this gets us? Who cares if this Maxwell is on the Internet, I mean who isn't on the Internet?" Marjorie said. She stood behind Alex, staring at the map.

"We need to find Maxwell in order to send it, or whatever is sending these imps into the world back to where it came from. Do you have a better idea how we can find Maxwell?" Grandma Akeyo patiently explained to Marjorie why they needed to find Maxwell.

"So why don't we just download Maxwell? I mean, if it is in the Internet, isn't that the easiest way to get it out?" Marjorie crossed her arms in front of her.

"Well, I don't know. We have never had a demon in the Internet before." Grandfather Li said.

Warren Mitchell stifled a laugh.

"You have something to say, Warren?" Grandfather Li was beginning to get cross.

"No, it's just that an Internet daemon is a thing, just like Maxwell's demon. It's funny."

"Dad, it isn't funny to me anymore, that imp cut my face. Now I'm not gonna be pretty, I have to get by on smart alone." Bax touched his wounded cheek.

"I know, Son." Warren mussed Bax's flattop, "It's still funny to me."

"Warren, you're the Internet guy, how do you think we should find Maxwell?" Donald asked from the sink.

"Ah, well, I'm really more of the telephone guy, but as far as the Internet goes, I would look at all the large junctions, the trunk lines, and maybe at the data centers." Warren sat back in his chair, thinking.

"Ok, how do we do that? Is the phone company just going to let us in?" Alex asked.

"Good point. Well, maybe if these things are out to get you and your friends, we can just check out a place and see if they come out of the woodwork?" Warren shrugged.

"Bait? You want us to be bait?" Alex frowned.

"Well, not really, but I don't see how else we can do it?"

"Dad, what about the laptop and the routers?" Bax asked.

"What about them? I mean aside from being a total loss?"

"Exactly," Bax said, "The demons wreck stuff, shouldn't the other routers be messed up too?"

"You might be on to something, I bet we could ping the servers to see if they are responding correctly. Maybe if there is a long delay or errors, that could be where Maxwell is hiding out?" Warren spoke more quickly. He liked the idea.

"Better than being bait." Bax rubbed his cheek.

"I bet this thing has to make sure it doesn't destroy its new home, so if we cook up a script to survey the network, yeah, I bet we could figure out just where Maxwell has been and where it is now." Warren was positively enthusiastic about the idea.

"I could start working on that, Dad. What sort of data do we want?"

"I would start with the network transport data, like the system logs and metrics. Oh man, this is like my regular job, except a bit more interesting."

"I don't understand any of that. What can we do in the meantime?" Marjorie asked.

"I can do some research. The last time we tried to get rid of Maxwell it should have worked, but it didn't. Maybe there are some other rituals we can use?" Grandma Akeyo looked at her husband.

"Yes, I think we should look into that. Why don't we both do that and try to save some time?" Grandfather Li added.

"Good. Bax and I will work on some scripts to track this demon down, you two figure out how to get rid of it. And you kids?" Warren looked at Alex and Marjorie.

"Why don't we try to confirm whatever you find? Not as bait, but maybe just poke around the neighborhood and see if anything weird is going on?" Alex looked at Marjorie, "What do you think?"

"I think I want to do whatever helps. This Maxwell seems like a bully. I hate bullies." Marjorie cracked her knuckles.

"Me too," Jill said, "Mean people suck."

"Ok. That sounds like a good plan. I'll go with the girls to make sure they don't get into anything they can't get away from. Ok?" Alex's dad looked at each person in turn, judging if they agreed with the plan or not.

"Good. We're all in agreement. Let's get started, ok?" Donald clapped his hands like a coach trying to psyche up his team.

"Don't do that, Donald. You are not only a disappointment but you are also a terrible coach." Grandfather Li stood, "Now, let's get going!"

Grandfather Li was not much more of a coach than Donald.

"**D**ad, shouldn't we be out there hunting this thing down? Why did you go along with this scripting and computer nonsense?" Bax was clearing off the discarded papers and soda cups from the high end computer system in the corner of his living room.

"I thought you didn't want to be bait, Son? Oh, wait, you just don't like cleaning, is that it? Or maybe?" Warren was going through some manuals looking for the most recent enterprise level equipment literature.

"Don't go there, Dad."

"Oh, so you don't want to look like a wimp in front of the girls. Or is it a specific girl?" Warren found Bax's pain point.

"No Dad, I'm not afraid of being a wimp."

"Darn straight, look at this gun show," Warren pantomimed flexing his biceps like a body builder, "Boom, boom! Time for you to come into your inheritance."

"Fine specimen of manhood, you are not."

Warren laughed.

"Yeah, I'm pretty much only around for my brain too, Son. You know, that Jill girl, she's pretty smart too."

"Oh, no. Don't go there. Where is the power cord for the tower, Dad? And why is it gone?"

"I needed it for the soy milk blender. Go check the kitchen."

"Dad. We need to talk. How is it that you make me watch 'Shaft' every Christmas and you then turn around and drink homemade soy milk?" Bax leaned against the desk and stared at his dad.

"Pure body, pure mind."

"I think I see why you were bullied in school."

"Son, go get the cord. I think I found the right manual. While you're in there, get the phone, I need to confirm we installed the 23s last week." Warren was getting serious, it was business time in his voice.

"Right. If that is what it takes to get you to stop talking about Jill."

"So I was right!"

"Dad. No. Just, no."

Bax returned with the power cord and plugged in the

tower. He pushed the power button on the computer, then turned on the two monitors attached to the tower. Warren finished making a call on the cordless phone and started to leaf through the pages of the model 23 router manual.

"Alright, we are on the right path. When that old thing boots up, get into the scripting environment and let's get working. Bax, also go into the 'deprecated' folder and start up the packet simulator, I forget what it is called."

"Packet switcher? I mean, you wrote the thing, why can you never remember what it's called?"

"I wanted to call it 'packet shaft' but they said no. Copyright. Garbage if you ask me."

"No one asked you, Dad."

"You just did, Son. I heard you ask me."

"Ok. Everything is up and running, what do you want me to do?" Bax pulled out a chair and sat in front of the desk.

"Right, so let's start simple. I want you to ping these ports on these machines." Warren set the manual down in front of Bax, grabbed a sheet of paper from the printer and started to write down a series of numbers.

"Ok, that's pretty straight forward. Anything else?"

"Yeah, if you get long ping replies or no reply I want you to select those addresses for the next round of tests."

"And those are?"

"Finish the first part and I'll tell you."

"Already done, Dad."

"Oh, the nerd is strong with this one."

"Dad."

"What, I'm allowed to tease you, it was part of the deal when you were born."

"Dad."

"Ok, any slow or non-responding addresses get a traceroute run on them so we can determine where the slow down is happening. Anything over 200 milliseconds should be a red flag."

"Because that's like a satellite hop, right?" Bax looked at his dad for confirmation.

"Absolutely. Right on the first guess."

"Not a guess, Dad."

"Yeah, and there are no satellite hops in town, so if it takes that long, something is wrong."

"Then what?" Bax asked.

"Well, let's see if we get any results first. Loop the script to run every minute."

"Ok. Why don't I push the results to a dashboard or something? We can just throw it up with the details of each route and the machines that are acting up? I can even send it out with an SMS update if you want?"

"Yeah, not a bad idea. But let's just keep it on a dashboard here. If there are issues in the routing on the Internet, I don't want to push the information out to the Internet when the Internet might be broken. If you're feeling me."

"I am feeling you, Dad. Good call. Still, it would be nice if we could just check a page when we're out there tracking this thing down."

"No way son, Jill won't be impressed with you when you are bawling on the ground because this Maxwell jerk broke your Internet widget toy-thing."

"Dad, I'm not feeling you anymore. Jerk."

"Heh, mission accomplished."

"Yeah, what mission is that?"

"Mission Make Son Feel Guilty For Being Born."

"Never asked for it."

"Irrelevant, it happened."

"Hatched. No way I was born with you as my dad. I was hatched."

"Can't make an omelet without Baxing a few eggs."

"That is not something anyone says, Dad."

"I say it."

"Ugh, just let me write this script, ok?"

"All I ever wanted Son, well, that and a giant robot dinosaur.

"We need to go check on the school." Alex said after hanging up her phone.

"Is that really it? Bax found it that quick?" Marjorie asked.

"He's smart and quick. Sometimes a little too smart and quick." Jill added.

"Great, shall we walk or drive?" Donald asked the group.

"Well, I would say we should drive, but after what happened to my mom's car, it might be safer to walk."

Bax has sent some information I do not understand, Alex.

"Let me see it," Alex looked at SPD's screen, "Got me, that is total nerd talk."

Jill looked over Alex's shoulder at her smartphone, then shook her head.

"We don't need any of that. It's just the response times for the routers. We just need to know where to go."

"Ok girls, let's ride!"

"Dad, we're walking." Alex glared at Donald.

"It is an expression, Alex. I like setting the right atmosphere." Donald pouted his bottom lip out.

"Dad, there are demons in the Internet that want to kill us. I don't think we need an 'atmosphere,' do you?"

"I always said the Internet was a bad idea." Donald said.

"Huh, I actually agree with your dad, Alex. The world is coming to an end." Marjorie Chan slapped Alex on the back and sent her stumbling a couple of steps.

"Ow, Marjorie, I'm not a big jock. You know this, right?"

"Yeah Alex, but I like you." Marjorie smiled wide making her eyes twinkle.

"Oh wow, you should do that more often Marjorie, you look really pretty when you smile." Jill said, a touch of envy in her voice.

"Nah, I save it for when it can do the most damage. You have to think strategic, Jill."

"Scary." Donald whispered as the girls set off in the direction of Nancy Row High School.

D onald and the girls never made it to the school. A telephone pole was blown over by the wind according to the electrical workers that stopped them as they walked down the street. A live electrical line whipped back and forth in the street like in a movie. The workers couldn't seem to get near it. The supervisor was on his mobile phone, yelling.

"Dad, this is wrong." Alex whispered to her father.

"I know, Pickles. I can feel the wrongness in the air."

"What are you two whispering about?" Marjorie whispered over her shoulder.

"Stop whispering. No one can hear you over that wire crackling." Jill said at full volume.

"Right. So last year we had an electrical line blown down during the big snow storm. Remember Jill?" Alex asked.

"Yeah, that was the first snow in December, right?"

"Yeah. Do you remember what the cable did?"

"No, not really. Power was out, so we had a sleep over with candles and ghost stories. Although now I think I know why yours are always the scariest, Alex."

"Exactly. The power line did nothing." Alex said proudly.

"I've seen this in the movies, the lines always whip around like snakes, don't they?" Marjorie asked.

"Not that we saw. This one seems a little out of control, and these guys trying to wrangle it, don't they seem a bit out of sorts?" Alex said, gesturing to the scene in front of them.

"Yeah, I guess they do. And that guy on the phone is totally losing it. I would hate to be on the other end talking to him." Jill said.

"Exactly. I bet the spirit demons were here. Probably traveling along the TV cables until they were too corrupted and the whole thing broke."

"I thought they were in the Internet?" Marjorie asked, "Why would they be in the TV?"

"Because your cable TV is part of the Internet. Everything seems to be part of the Internet." Donald explained.

There were spirit demons here. Weak ones. Imps. I can still feel their presence.

"SPD, can you tell where they went?" Alex asked.

No. I cannot feel where they went, but if they left because of the broken wires, perhaps they are still close by, hiding.

"I don't quite follow your logic, phone." Marjorie looked at SPD's screen.

The broken wire is recent, so the imps might not have moved very far from this place yet.

"Oh. Well, you are a *smart* phone, phone." Marjorie said.

Thank you, tall person.

"Its name is SPD," Alex was moderately annoyed, SPD and Marjorie seemed to get along, "Don't flirt with my phone."

"Ok. I'm not really all that into phones."

"Good."

I am not a phone. I am a remnant of...

"Shut up, SPD."

"What do we do now?" Jill looked at each of them in turn, hoping for an idea.

"Well, maybe we should call in and see what else Warren and Bax have found?"

We can search the area for imps?

"Pizza? I like pizza." Donald said.

"Dad, no jokes, ok?"

"Not a joke. Angelo's Pizza is on the corner, we can see it from here. Then we can call Warren, watch this intersection just in case the imps come back and get a soda or something."

"I'm hungry." Marjorie rubbed her stomach.

"We just ate, how can you be hungry?" Alex seemed offended anyone could still be hungry after the meal they had.

"I graze."

"And I know teenagers. Always hungry," Donald clapped his hand on Marjorie's shoulder, "Come, let us introduce you to your next meal."

"I like your dad, Alex."

"Ew, not at all creepy." Alex found the sarcasm came easily when it was genuine.

"Well, I like that he's buying."

"What makes you think that, Marjorie? I bought the last meal."

"You are the adult, you are responsible. I am just here to beat things up that deserve it."

"Ha, ha. Ok. I'll be the parent this time, but only because I am the oldest and most responsible."

"Alex, let's go, these two are idiots." Jill grabbed Alex's hand and started to run to Angelo's Pizza, pulling Alex along behind and laughing.

"Wait for me," Marjorie shouted and took off running after them.

"Honey, she turned out good," Donald said to himself, wiping a small tear from his eye, "She has good friends, you would be proud of me."

"Have you found anything yet?" Li Jiànhuī asked his wife, Akeyo.

"No, what about you, old man?"

"Not really. Just the same things we have been looking over for the past twenty years." Grandfather Li said.

"Well, keep looking. Maybe we should examine the old books we discounted?" Akeyo asked.

"I guess we can try, but what do you think we might find?"

"If I knew that, old man, we wouldn't be going through all these dusty old books."

"Akeyo, what if this Maxwell is too strong to send back?"

"Nothing is too strong to resist the pull of the dead lands. Like it or not, everything must end up there sooner or later." Akeyo stated firmly.

"I would prefer it to be much later for myself, thank you."

"And what of me? Would you prefer that occurs sooner or later?" Akeyo asked.

"Too much trouble, you are not allowed to leave until after I am gone."

"Oh, so I have to deal with all the problems you will invariably leave behind? So selfish, old man."

"Fine then, as in all things, we can go together."

"I wouldn't have it any other way."

"Although Akeyo, it makes me wonder what was it that this Maxwell held on to so hard that it cannot fade away as all things must?"

"I can't say, and that has been bothering me as well. It must have been something so great or terrible that the strength of Maxwell's personality adhered itself to what had been its life. I've heard of things so great that they cannot be let go of, things so terrible, even the thought of it is enough to keep you awake at night."

"Ah yes, our trip out west. The tragedy in that vast desert is truly great."

"Yes, but what does it do for us now?" Akeyo asked her husband.

"I was thinking that perhaps we could attack the problem in a different way. Perhaps if the bond to the world could be weakened, then might Maxwell lose some of its strength?"

Akeyo sat back in thought. Jiànhuī's idea might have some merit. Maxwell had been very strong and if somehow it was still clinging to the world, if that tie could be broken it might allow them to return Maxwell to the dead lands.

"We should consider it. Certainly. But how would we discover what it is that Maxwell is so very bound to in this world?"

"I do not know, Akeyo. I do not know if it would even work. Let's keep looking for a way. I do not want to have to resort to dire means." Grandfather Li looked at the books in front of him, he couldn't look at Akeyo.

"No, I agree. Not again. The cost is too great."

"Nothing! All night out, and we found nothing!" Alex flopped back on her bed.

It was only our first attempt with our plan, Alex. You must give it time to work.

"Ugh, and you flirting with Marjorie Chat. I cannot believe my own phone betrayed me."

I do not understand why you feel this way. You talk like that with Bax and Jill. I just imitated your behavior.

"I tried to imitate your behavior." Alex held her smartphone up to her face, looking into the screen. She made a face at it.

This is not sarcasm. I know you like to attempt sarcasm.

"This is not sarcasm." Alex twisted her face, puckering her lips.

Ah. Not sarcasm. You are imitating me because I said I was just imitating your behavior. Clever.

"OMG, SPD. That is not fair!" Alex dropped her phone down by her side on the bed.

I do not understand.

"Even the stupid stalker demon spirit inhabiting my

smartphone is better at sarcasm than I am! Can I hate you, SPD? Yes, yes I can. I hate you SPD and your imitating sarcasm face."

Alex, I do not have a face. And I think you are not serious about your words.

"No, SPD, I'm not serious. I'm tired, however. Beat. Beat like a sack of meat."

I do not think anyone says that, Alex.

"No, I just said it because I am tired and beat rhymes with meat. I like rhymes."

Perhaps you should sleep, Alex. Tomorrow is Friday. After school, we can search for Maxwell and the imps again.

"Fine. Sleep it is." Alex sat up on her bed and began to undress. She threw her clothes at the hamper, trying to score a basket as if she was the star forward on the basketball team. That was the extent of Alex's knowledge of the sport, and she was not sure if her terminology was correct, but she did know to cheer for herself when her shirt went into the hamper without touching the rim.

"Leave the camera off, SPD, please? I don't what a real hacker getting pictures of me undressing because my dumb smartphone demon likes to watch through the phone's camera." Alex took her pajamas off the top of her dresser. Her dad put the pajamas there after pulling them out of the dryer to warm them up. Alex had been brushing her teeth and was surprised when she heard her dad announce fresh, warm pajamas.

"You deserve it after a hard week." Alex's dad said. Grandfather Li would probably say that disappointing Donald was spoiling Alex and making her weak or something like that. Alex agreed with her dad. She deserved warm pajamas.

After putting on them on, Alex got into bed and held her smartphone.

"SPD, are you really on my side?" Alex yawned.

Of course, Alex. I am your bound spirit demon.

"No, I mean really on my side, not just trapped in my smartphone and all that."

Yes, Alex. Until I am free, I am on your side. Maybe afterward, too. Alex? Alex?

Alex Lissett Land had fallen directly to sleep.

CHAPTER TEN

R*uined. The fleshy humans ruined my revenge. So many pieces of myself, lost. Returned to the horrible, boring dead lands. Filthy human garbage children will suffer for living.*

One of the pieces of Maxwell returned to it sometime in the night. It was pleased to return to Maxwell, where it was devoured quickly, its pieces snapping and cracking as Maxwell ate it. As it returned and stopped being a piece of Maxwell, the whole was enriched by what the piece had observed.

The children have increased. They have shed the influence I tried to place inside them and freed the flesh that enacted my plans. One of the flesh has stayed with the children. That one is large enough to be more than a child, but she is very much still just a child. Still sad and lonely, and full of the seeds of misfortune. Not as easy to bend her will as the other, that one, oh, that one was eager to help with my plan.

Maxwell felt raw from losing his influence over Marjorie and his failure to sow discord between Jill, Baxter, and Alex. It had been easy to hide and slip into their minds, so weak and unprotected. It reminded Maxwell of the time before, the time when Maxwell could take a child at will and twist the small, fleshy thing to do as Maxwell pleased. The thrill of manipulation continued to excite the demon, and it hurt that it had failed to subvert the children.

Revenge is too consuming. Pieces of myself cannot be enough, I need more. More of me from the dead lands must come here. A hole must be made. The fleshy children and nasty old ones must not seal the holes. I must occupy them. Make them waste time. Chew on their insides, their fears and hates. Yes, occupy the flesh with its own self-made horrors. Perhaps with some help. More pieces of myself must attach to the children. The other one, the eager one, she will be useful.

Maxwell shivered off more pieces of itself, more pieces of Maxwell, but only with the desire to break. Hurt. The faces of the children and their friends imprinted on the tiny, rudimentary minds inside the pieces of Maxwell. These bitter things were sent out into the world, out through the wires, through the electricity. The strange electricity that was like miniature lightning, so small as to be the most minute fraction of a single bolt from the sky. Shifting up and down, pulses that somehow Maxwell understood as words and feelings. Bundled up in nonsense, the minuscule lighting bolts were wrapped in packets of intensity. These packets moved blindingly fast through the wires and the demon box machines. Maxwell knew now these were called computers. The laptop, the telephone, the router, and switch. The names meant little to Maxwell, but the words and feelings trapped inside the machines fed the demon's mind. Fed its insatiable need to know more and devour. So much hate in the bundles of electrical lightning. Fabulous living feelings trapped in the demon computer boxes, trapped for Maxwell to feed on and grow stronger.

Now, a special one for the eager child. Yes, special to influence her and bind her to me. Special to dwell within her and make her tastier until she is rich with juicy fear and loathing. Special for her. Yes, find the eager child. Eager to help. Eager to feed. Eager for more and then pieces. Maxwell sent the special one out to find Suzie and her smartphone.

F riday came and nothing interesting happened.

"So, are you going to ask him or not?" Suzie panted.

"Why should I ask him?" Jill replied as they rounded the third turn on the track.

"Why not? I mean, it isn't like Bax is going to ask you, right?" Suzie and Jill were slowly jogging as they spoke.

"There are more important things than a dance. I don't care about the dance, Suzie." Jill was not running more than she had to run.

Make her want to go. We can hurt them while they are happiest. It tastes better when they bleed happy thoughts. Maxxie spoke inside Suzie's head.

"Well, yeah. But why not? I think it's cool you get to go to a dance with boys. We weren't even allowed on the grounds of the boy's school at St. Alban's. I guess we were the sister school, so no kissing your sisters!" Suzie snorted.

"Ew, gross!" Jill said.

"Yeah, but this is public school. Totes not gross."

Your words are frivolous.

"Well, I guess. Bax is like my brother. I couldn't ask him to the dance. Why do you care?" Jill looked at Suzie as they jogged. Staying far enough from the back of the pack was an art. Too fast and the teacher would expect performance. Too slow and you were considered a slacker. Right in the middle and you drew no attention. Jill was a master of not drawing attention to her weakest subjects. Physical education was Jill's weakest subject.

"No reason. No boys asked me, so I asked Alex to go with me so we can spy on everyone. I thought you and Bax could go. Safe since you are already such good friends." Suzie started to fall a little behind Jill.

Yes, play to her friendship. The weak have friends. Use them! Suzie liked her friends, but Maxxie was right. Suzie adjusted her thinking to agree with Maxxie. Use the friends.

"Well, Marjorie said the same thing the other day. I told her I would, just to get her to shut up about it. Now you? It's like the universe is trying to run me over with its karma." Jill slowed.

"Hah, yeah. Sorry. I just want someone else to go that I know. I want you and Bax to go so Alex and I aren't alone." Suzie smiled at Jill, "Pretty please?"

Almost. Keep pushing, Suzie.

"Why didn't you ask Bax? I mean, if you wanted a friend?"

"I never got to go with a boy to a dance. I think I want to ease into it, if that makes sense? I've known Alex since we were kids, so I can have a nice, no pressure time."

"Oh, so I get to test out the boy? You get off easy? I sense a plot!" Jill teased.

"You got me!" Suzie laughed. The two girls came to the end of the run and slowed to a walking pace. Once more around the track to cool down.

"Seriously. Come to the dance. I don't want to be alone. Even if Alex goes, it will be better with everyone there. One friend isn't enough."

"Suzie, you really want Bax and me there that bad? I mean we're not as close to you as Alex."

"Yes! Everyone here is a new friend to me. Everyone except Alex. Please come. Friends don't let friends go to the dance alone." Suzie pleaded.

This one will take sympathy. Be more pathetic! Maxxie enjoyed the begging.

"Jeez, fine. First Marjorie and now you. I'll ask Bax out. But if any rumors start like with that idiot on the Internet, I am holding you responsible, Suzie."

"Rumors? What are you talking about?" Suzie asked, playing innocent.

"Didn't you hear? Some jerk-wad started a rumor about Bax and I being a couple. It was awful."

"No. I didn't hear anything. I guess it pays to be the new girl?" Suzie lied.

Yes. Lie. Filthy Jill. You shall eat her kidney with me when all this is done!

Suzie doubled over. Maxxie was disgusting. Suzie's stomach rebelled against her thoughts. This was too much.

"Suzie, you ok?" Jill put her hand on Suzie's back and bent over to look at her.

"Yeah, I just. I just ran too much." Suzie lied.

"Damn, we took it easy. Come over here. Don't throw up, ok?"

"Trying not to throw up. Lead on."

Fool. The kidney is a delicacy. You should be grateful.

"Ugh, sick." Suzie said out loud.

"No, Suzie, don't be sick." Jill replied, thinking Suzie was talking to her. Jill sat Suzie down on the bleachers, then she sat next to her.

"Let me get your towel. Which bag is yours?" Jill looked around. The student's all had a mesh net bag with a towel and water bottle inside.

"Get me an aspirin, too? They are in a little baggie." Suzie pointed to one at the far end of the bleachers. Jill walked over to the bag.

"I am not eating a human kidney. Disgusting." Suzie whispered to herself.

Very well. But if you fail to get these children to the dance, you will suffer. It shall be your kidneys that I eat. Maxxie said, wrapping its will tighter around Suzie's mind. The thought of kidneys made Suzie fight and struggle inside, but Maxxie was strong. It could wait out this tantrum.

"Here you go, water and aspirin." Jill handed the bottle to Suzie, and she gladly took it.

"Drink up." Jill said, handing the towel to Suzie next.

"Thanks. I don't know what came over me." Suzie said.

Her eyes glinted in the sun. Suzie's eyes seemed shadowed and dark as Jill looked at the girl.

"You might want to see the nurse." Jill said.

"I'll be fine."

We'll be fine. Maxxie echoed.

———

After a weekend of searching, Monday was a bust. Alex, Jill, Bax, and Marjorie made it through a regular day of school while Warren tracked Maxwell down using Bax's network survey script. Marjorie had track and field practice after school. She was focusing on shot-put and javelin to build her strength and flexibility. No imps showed up to disrupt her hard work. Alex, Jill, and Bax went straight to Bax's house to pick up the next set of locations in Nancy Row to check for imp presence. Grandma Akeyo was waiting for them when they arrived.

"Your Grandfather and I have already checked most of the possible locations Warren found today." Akeyo said.

"Yeah, no dice. It's like this Maxwell character is hiding from us." Warren added.

"Well, we should check out whatever's left. Right, Dad?" Bax said, "I'll get the cameras."

"Grandma Akeyo, you're coming with us, right?" Alex asked when Jill nudged her in the ribs.

"Of course. You children can't do this alone."

They also have me, Grandma.

"Shut up, SPD. You don't count." Alex scolded her phone.

"Hey, I can hear him better today." Jill said.

They searched Angelo's pizza, the town hall, and the community center where the Harvest Dance was scheduled to take place in three weeks. There wasn't even a trace of corruption.

"That's it. Nothing." Alex was dejected.

"You should be happy, child. A fight avoided is a good thing." Grandma Akeyo said.

"But we didn't find anything. I want this Maxwell jerk gone." Alex protested.

"After last time, I want this thing gone too," Bax said, rubbing the bandage on his face, "I owe it for my looks."

"I don't want to get in another fight. Not without the big guns." Jill said.

"Oh, don't I count, Jill?" Akeyo teased.

Embarrassed, Jill said nothing.

"Let's get you all home." Akeyo said.

No one saw the shadows lurking by the edge of the community center parking lot.

The week led to no further revelations about the imps or Maxwell.

Marjorie joined Jill and Alex as they searched along the telephone trunk line leading away from the school. The right of way was easy to follow since it stuck to the roads most of the time. After reaching an industrial park on the edge of Nancy Row, they decided to head back to the Alvarado and participate in an in depth investigation of Angelo's best pies.

Bax couldn't join them on the search since he and his dad, Warren, had an appointment that couldn't wait. Bax saw the girls from inside White Tie, Black Tie. He was getting sized for his tuxedo. Warren insisted Bax dress up for the Harvest Dance. Bax wasn't convinced it was a good idea at all.

"Look, Son, you only get one chance to make a good impression." Warren said for the third time that morning.

"Dad. It is a freshman dance. This isn't the prom. I don't even care that much."

"Oh? I do. I have to care. Your love life is on the line.".

"Dad. That is so not true." Bax held his arms out as the tailor pinned his jacket.

"Isn't it? You do want a love life, don't you, Son?" Warren asked.

"No. I want a life, not a love life. Besides, I'm just going with Jill."

"All the more reason to go big." Warren smiled.

"What? No. Dad, you are not hooking me up with my best friend. That's like dating my sister." Bax was horrified.

"But Jill isn't your sister, is she?" Warren's smile grew bigger.

"I do not know you." Bax closed his eyes hard and didn't open them. Perhaps the nightmare would go away?

"Oh, that's ok. Think of me as your fairy godfather. I got your back, even when you don't know it. Heck, I'll even drive you there and be a chaperon." Warren had plans for his son. Bax just shook his head.

"Alex, why are you avoiding me?" Suzie Plimpton cornered Alex at her locker. Alex jumped.

"Suzie? You surprised me."

"Where have you been the last few weeks? I see you in class, but we haven't studied. What's up? You're not avoiding me, are you?" Suzie asked, leaning in.

"Avoiding you? No, not at all! I've just been busy with a project." Alex tried to keep her demon and imp hunting activities vague.

"A project? What class?" Suzie asked.

"Oh, ah, it's not a school project."

"What kind of project is it? Can I help?" Suzie took out her phone and looked at the screen. She swiped the call away.

"We're kinda full up on help, Suzie. Sorry." Alex said as she put her books away.

"Oh? Who's we? Not Bax and Jill, is it?" Suzie wouldn't let the topic go.

"Ah, yeah. How did you know?" Alex asked in surprise.

"Oh, it was pretty obvious. I saw you guys running around on Saturday. Looks like a scavenger hunt. Like they do in Scouts or some club, right?" Suzie continued drawing Alex out.

"Yeah. Something like that." Alex closed her locker door and spun the combination lock.

"You should definitely let me join. I am great at finding things. Almost supernatural, you might say." Suzie tipped her chin down, looking straight at Alex.

"What do you mean?" Alex asked. She kept her face as expressionless as she could.

"Oh, I think you know." Suzie winked at Alex, "From when we were kids."

Suzie turned and walked away, leaving Alex staring after her.

Very good. Bait. Delicious. Maxxie thought in Suzie's head. **_Lure her in._**

"What was that about?" Alex said to herself.

It sounded like Suzie knows about magic.

"No way, SPD. At least, I don't remember telling her. I

told Wendy when I was little, but she called me a liar. Then her folks divorced, and she left town. I don't think I told Suzie, but maybe I did?"

"Well, if you did, she could be helpful." Marjorie said from behind Alex. Alex jumped and her back hit the lockers.

"Eep! You scared the poop outta me!" Alex said as she recognized Marjorie.

"You should watch what you say out loud, Alex."

"Marj, how long were you there?" Alex asked. She held her hand to her chest as her heart beat loud enough for anyone to hear.

"Long enough. Who's Wendy?" Marjorie looked down at Alex, standing almost too close for Alex's comfort.

"Childhood friend. I know her at the same time I knew Suzie." Alex explained.

"Really? I thought Suzie just transferred in this year?"

"She did. But we were in the same elementary school." Alex said.

"Well. Maybe we should bring her into the group? Another pair of eyes could be a big help." Marjorie said, "Think about it?"

"Yeah. Another set of eyes." Alex said out loud.

"Suzie, what did you mean earlier?" Alex asked Suzie as they studied together in class. Geometry wasn't Alex's best subject, but Suzie was almost as good as Jill and Bax at math. All of Alex's friends seemed to be math gods.

"You know. 'There are more things in heaven and Earth, Alexandra, than are dreamed of in your philosophy.'" Suzie quoted. Alex blinked.

"Is that from a movie?" she asked.

"Really? Shakespeare? We have to get you out more, girlfriend." Suzie laughed, "It means I know about the weird things out there. The things from the dead lands? I can see them."

"No way! Shh. Not so loud." Alex's eyes were wide as she realized what Suzie knew.

"It's fine. No one is listening to us, Alex. It's our secret, just us. Ok?" Suzie said.

"Wow. How long have you known?" Alex asked.

"Why do you think I left for St. Alban's? *Saint*? It's kinda in the name." Suzie lied.

"We've been trying to stop them." Alex said conspiratorially.

"Who's we?" Suzie asked.

"Me, Jill, Bax, and Marjorie." Alex replied.

Too easy. Maxxie thought.

Suzie struggled inside her head. The binding around her thoughts that Maxxie had wrapped around her were tight and painful. Resisting Maxxie hurt, but Suzie tried anyway. She felt like she was losing herself to Maxxie and didn't know what she felt and what Maxxie made her feel anymore.

"I can help!" Suzie said, smiling as she reached into her purse for an aspirin.

"Headache?" Alex asked.

"A little. But you're gonna let me help, right?" Suzie said.

"Are you sure? These things are pretty scary. They even hurt Marjorie real bad." Alex said.

"She seems fine to me. What happened?" Suzie asked.

"Well, my grandma fixed it. You remember her, my Grandma Akeyo?"

"Oh, yes. I remember her. She was so nice." Suzie smiled, "If she's helping, I'll be fine."

The voice inside Suzie's head was pleased. Suzie could feel it smiling, as if voices could smile. It was enjoying leading Alex on. Suzie felt some satisfaction in that as well, but she had a genuine affection for Grandma Akeyo. She felt only fear and loathing from the voice when Alex mentioned the kindly old woman.

"If you're sure? We could use another set of eyes." Alex said.

Suzie smiled, thinking 'I win, again.'

"Another set of eyes? When I'm done, you won't need the first set."

Very good, Suzie. You are improving.

"Thank you, Maxxie. I am so glad you like me!" Suzie said to herself in her room. It was less painful to be agreeable.

I have a gift for you.

"Oh? Really? I absolutely love gifts. Your last gift was a treasure." Suzie's face twitched unconsciously, remembering when Maxxie had leaped into her body and become a part of her. It hadn't been pleasant, but then it was. The tighter Maxxie bound Suzie's mind within its own, the more pleasant the experience became. Maxxie told her so. Like honey on a bee sting. Suzie reached into her purse for an aspirin.

Oh, yes. This is a special something. You must use it well, Suzie.

"Oh? Like last time, when you joined me, Maxxie?" Suzie's face twitched unconsciously.

No. This one is for them. To soften them. To chew on their edges. Perhaps to devour them whole.

"That sounds delightful, Maxxie. Like a special treat for Friday?" Suzie asked, "Nothing ever happens on Fridays."

It is coming. Yes, it will make a good present for your friends.

"You're my only friend, Maxxie." Twitch, "Will it hurt?"

Yes. I think it shall hurt them quite nicely.

"I should watch."

No. We still need you in case they surprise us.

"No fair." Suzie said as the door to her bedroom swung open.

The floor creaked as something stepped into the room and Suzie smiled a little too wide for a normal face.

"Delightful. That thing looks like a dog. A nasty dog. Can it speak?"

Break, break. Hurt. Maim.

"It can. Then we must send it to Alex. A gift for her Language Arts class. That's a good time. After Geometry. No way to suspect me." Suzie gestured to the imp. It came to her.

"Find Alex's class." Suzie thought hard at the imp. Thought of the language arts classroom.

"Go to her when I tell you. Break, break. Hurt."

Maim?

"Yes, maim, if you like." Suzie giggled as her face

twitched unconsciously as she reached into her purse for another aspirin.

F riday. Nothing ever happened at school on Friday. Alex was exhausted. She had exerted herself far too much during the week. She was ready for a long nap and an even longer weekend. Unfortunately, Alex still had a full day of school ahead of her.

After Geometry, Alex had Language Arts with Bax. Each student had picked a passage from a book to read to the class. It was supposed to be a fun project to get the students in the mood for the year.

Of course, it was only fun if you could read in front of other people and not want to have a sudden stroke or random dinosaur attack save you from speaking in front of the class.

Alex dreaded public speaking. Giving book reports was terrible, but a dramatic reading of your choice? Far worse. The only consolation she had was that Bax was even more afraid of speaking in front of people than Alex.

"You may sit down now, Baxter. I'm sure that we don't need any more of your attempts to read from Moby Dick today." The teacher didn't enjoy Bax's time in front of his class either.

"Doesn't he have to say something for it to count?" Someone called out from the back of the class.

"No, I think we have all suffered enough." Creep teacher.

"You do better, Ricky." Bax said as he sat down in front of Alex, "I was dying up there."

"Yes, yes you were. I will send flowers to the funeral for your grade." Alex patted Bax on the shoulder.

"Thanks. I'm sure my grade will appreciate the gesture."

"Now Bax, if you could just talk like that in front of everyone, it would be fine."

"Yeah, easier said than done. Sorry."

"Don't apologize Bax, the creep doesn't deserve it." Alex whispered, but perhaps not quietly enough. A couple of kids around her snickered.

"Well, I think you just volunteered to be next, Ms. Land."

"Oh crap."

"Indeed." Creep teacher was serious.

"Fine."

"Knock 'em dead, killer!" Bax said too enthusiastically.

"Knock me dead, more like it. Better yet, break my leg?"

"No way, I suffered, now it's your turn." Bax smiled wide.

Alex stood at the front of the classroom and cleared her throat. The papers she held were crinkling in her grip.

"I, ah. I want to read from the script for. Ah, the script for this movie. You may have heard of it." Alex was verbally stumbling like someone knocked her too hard on the head.

"Freebird!" Ricky called from the back.

"Screw you, Ricky." Alex did not catch herself in time, "Oh, crap."

"Oh, crap indeed, Ms. Land. Could you please educate us on exactly which part of this script included the admonition, 'Screw you, Ricky?'" Creep teacher didn't like Ricky much either. No one liked Ricky Jones much at all. The fact of his general lack of popularity made Ricky speak up even more. Today was not going to go well.

"It's the part after the fat man and the other characters discover the statue is a fake." Alex was tired. She just snapped out an answer on reflex.

"Oh really, can you tell me more?" Alex did not realize she was being baited.

"Sure, Sydney Greenstreet, the fat man and the guy who plays Renfield in the Dracula movies are talking. Humphrey Bogart has Wilmer tied up in his trench coat because Wilmer is a dumb thug, and they all discover that the falcon is a fake. So Wilmer says something dumb and Bogie says 'screw you, Ricky, and the horse you rode in on.'" Alex gasped, just realizing she was saying what she really thought.

"So, this wouldn't happen to be 'The Maltese Falcon,' would it Ms. Land?"

"Ah, yes. I wanted to read a section from 'The Maltese Falcon.'" Alex said as she shifted her weight from one leg to the other and back again.

"Now we are getting somewhere. Ms. Land, why did you choose this particular piece to read from? Certainly not because it had such a prominent role for Ricky Jones in it?"

"Ah, no. I, ah, chose it because it was on the late-night movie the other week and I liked it." Alex began to feel very self-conscious again.

"Dude, no way. Isn't that a silent movie? Should we call you Granny Land, now?" Ricky was undeterred.

"No, dorkus, Bogart only did sound movies." Bax quipped.

"Alright. We've had enough fun. Wrap it up and go to your next class. Ricky detention again. Ms. Land, see me after school." Creep teacher announced.

"Detention, no, I can't, my grandfather will kill me."

"No, Ms. Land, not detention. Make up for not reading your scene. Fifteen minutes at most."

Alex sighed, thankful her ordeal was over.

"Hey, the door's locked."

"Stop goofing off, Ricky."

"No, seriously, look I can't open the door." Ricky turned the knob and shoved his body against the door. Nothing happened. He turned the lock back and forth, showing the bolt was not thrown, then shoved the door again.

"Ricky, not funny. Acting is next year, open the door, you kids have to get to class."

"I am trying. It won't budge." Ricky was visibly struggling with the door.

"Move over, let me." Creepy teacher moved Ricky out of the way and grasped the knob, turning and pushing the door. The window glass in the top half of the door exploded inward, showering the crowded students and teacher with sharp glass. There was a loud pop, but Alex was not sure if it occurred before or after the window broke.

"Oh, crap." Bax said. Alex looked at him; Bax pointed at the ceiling. Alex followed his gaze.

"Oh, crap." Alex saw an imp the size of a medium-sized dog hanging from the fluorescent light. It must have broken through the window. It appeared to be looking at the students and licking the teeth in its open mouth.

"Everyone, get out!" Alex yelled and ran to the fire alarm pull lever in the corner of the room. She smashed her elbow against the glass and then put her hand over the lever and pulled down. Some shards of glass cut her fingers. The cuts were deeper than scratches, but not bad overall. The fire alarms went off in the school.

"Let's get out of here!" Ricky yelled.

The creep teacher was brushing the glass off his shirt,

then tried the door again and it opened easily. Students started pushing to get out of the classroom and the teacher was carried along with them, leaving Alex, Bax, and the imp alone in the room.

The imp stared back at Alex and Bax.

"Oh, crap." They said in unison as the imp leaped down on to a desk and started to sniff the air.

Alex pulled out her máobǐ and tried to write some quick hànzi in the air. The characters were poorly formed and dissolved in the air like rings of smoke when she pushed them towards the imp. The imp sniffed, and drool escaped its open mouth.

Break, Break.

"Oh, crap." Bax said, pulling his desk between himself and the imp.

"At least it isn't saying 'kill' this time." Alex picked up her brush pen and a piece of paper.

Break. Break. Kill? Maim.

"Nice going, genius."

"How was I supposed to know it understood us?" Alex quickly started drawing a circle on the back of her script for 'The Maltese Falcon.' She used threads of reality instead of ink with her máobǐ.

The imp grabbed the top of the desk it was standing on and began heaving at it, trying to shift the top. Instead it just scrapped the feet of the desk across the floor, moving the whole thing by jerking on the top.

"Alex, Mr. Bulldog face here is getting frisky. Can you hurry up?" Bax put his chair between himself and his desk. Another layer of protection from the imp.

"Trying." Alex began writing the Chinese characters around her inner circle.

The imp bellowed and jerked on the desk so hard it

slipped and the imp fell backwards on top of the desk as it was upended and toppled over. It leaped up as it hit the ground, bouncing like a dropped rubber ball. It landed on the chair Bax had just put between them as a barrier.

"Yikes!" Bax squeaked, his voice going up in pitch. The imp sniffed the air.

"Back away." Alex yelled.

The imp swiveled its head around to look at Alex.

"Oh, poop." Alex did not want its attention.

"Backing away."

"Do it quietly, Bax." Alex said in what she thought was a low stage whisper.

"Got it."

"I think it's blind. See the way it's sniffing the air and not charging us?"

"How does that help us? blind or not, Mr. Bulldog face can probably rip me up pretty bad. Look at the size of its arms."

Bax was right, the arms of the imp were long and sinewy, ending in hands with thick, blunted claws. Not nails, these were actual claws. The imp started panning its head around, sniffing again.

Alex finished the circle and put her script on the ground in front of her.

"Now what?" Bax looked at the paper, then back at Alex.

"Now, we get it to come after me." Alex took three slow steps backwards.

"Say what now?" Bax squeaked.

"And then we trap it in the circle." Alex answered.

"Oh, ok. As long as we don't die. How do we do that?" Bax asked.

"How do we not die? I dunno." Alex settled into her stance.

"No, how do we trap it in the circle?" Bax didn't take his eyes off the imp.

"Oh, sorry, I'm a little scared and a lot tired right now. I was gonna throw something at it and it would jump at me."

"Ok, what do you have to throw?"

"Ah, nothing. My pen? Catch!" Alex threw the brush pen at the imp. The imp caught the máobǐ in mid air and looked at its hand, then slowly slewed its head back to Alex, looking directly at her. Alex could see its eyes were clouded over and it was most certainly blind. The imp leaped.

"Qián hòu, zuǒ yòu!" Alex intoned. The imp sailed right over the circle and landed in front of Alex, drooling from its mouth and on the floor.

"Ah, fail. Look out!" Bax yelled.

The imp dropped the máobǐ and swiped at Alex. It wasn't fast and Alex got out of the way, running to a corner of the room.

"What did you say? I think it is mad now."

"I said 'front back, left right' in Chinese, it should have created a barrier."

"I don't think it worked. Now what?" Bax moved towards another corner of the room, away from the imp.

"Distract it. I must have messed up the circle." Alex was serious.

"Ok. Here butt-face. Come and get it." Bax picked up a chair and held it out with the feet towards the imp. The bulldog-imp sniffed the air again.

Alex stepped towards the circle. She picked up her máobǐ off the floor. The imp walked towards Bax.

"You sure about this, Alex?"

"Nope. But it should have worked, so either my circle is wrong or I don't know what is up."

"Hey, dirt-face, I saw what you did last week." Bax thrust the chair legs towards the imp, easily more than ten feet away.

Suddenly, the imp was on the chair legs. It had jumped and covered the distance between itself and Bax in a bare moment.

"Oh, crap!" Bax said, suddenly weighted down with the chair and the extra weight of the imp.

"I got it!" Alex ran the last three steps to her circle on the script and kneeled down while she corrected the Chinese character for demon. She picked up the circle and stood, turning towards Bax and the imp.

"Help! Now would be good!" Bax squeaked. The imp was flailing its arms, trying to hit Bax. Bax was on one knee, trying to keep the chair both up and away from himself despite the extra weight of the imp.

Alex didn't hesitate, she ran up and slapped the circle directly on the back of the imp.

"Qián hòu, zuǒ yòu!"

The chair fell to the floor, the script and the imp both exploded in a huge cloud of smoke, sticky and choking. Then, just as quickly, the smoke was drawn back to the point where the script and the imp had made contact. There was a pop, and the script was all that was there, hanging in mid-air. Slowly it drifted to the floor.

The fire alarm was still ringing.

"We should..."

"Yeah, get out of here before the fire department arrives." Alex finished Bax's sentence.

"Are you kids, alright?" An unfamiliar voice said from the doorway.

"Oh, crap."

"Yes, Mr. Land. Your daughter pulled the fire alarm and caused a very big disruption. Then she and her friend destroyed some school property." The principal's voice came through the phone in Donald Land's hand. Alex and Bax listened silently.

"Look, Mr. Werker, I'm sure there is a reasonable explanation for all this."

"Students swear she broke the plate-glass window in her classroom door."

"Really? Students? What about the teacher? Where was the teacher when this was happening?"

"Well, that is hardly the point."

"Actually, Mr. Werker, I would say it is exactly the point. Where was your teacher who was '*in loco parentis*' of my daughter and her friend and the rest of the class?"

"They were all out in the parking lot for the fire alarm."

"All of them?"

"Yes, all except Ms. Land and Mr. Mitchell."

"Ah, that explains so much."

"What do you mean, Mr. Land?"

"Well, tell me again which students saw her break this plate-glass window if they were all out in the parking lot?"

"Well, they saw it before they were evacuated. Your daughter and Mr. Mitchell did not evacuate."

"Oh, so the students and the teacher were not in the parking lot at that time?"

"No, certainly not."

"Then what does the teacher say? Did he or she confirm the student's claims?"

"Well, he doesn't say anything at the moment. We haven't taken his statement."

"Oh, so you've taken a statement made by a fourteen or fifteen-year-old kid and decided to confront me about my daughter's behavior when you haven't corroborated the student's account with the teacher's account? The teacher who, incidentally is in charge of the students and who should have been the last one out of the classroom when the alarm went off, but somehow left my daughter and my friend's son in the classroom during an emergency. No doubt to facilitate them burning to death in a fire, alone and afraid?"

"Mr. Land, there is no need for dramatics."

"Now you listen here, Mr. Werker. I'm not a principal or a teacher, but I do know a thing or two about how you care for children. I must say that your teacher and you are not doing a very good job. So yes, I think there is a need to discuss this further." Donald spoke into the phone as if scolding a disobedient pet.

"Furthermore, I am not being dramatic at all. You said a fire alarm went off. The school was evacuated. A plate-glass window was broken. You are responsible for my daughter when she is in school and both her and her friend were left alone by your teacher during a school emergency and you have the gall to confront me with half-informed accusations when you haven't even spoken to your own teacher. A teacher who abandoned those two children to their fate?"

"Mr. Land, please."

"No, Mr. Werker. No, please to you. Don't call me back until you've spoken to your negligent teacher. We shall be in touch." Donald hung up the phone and smiled at Alex and Baxter.

"That is how we deal with idiots. Take notes." Donald looked at Alex first, then Bax.

"Oh my goodness, Alex, that was sweet! Your dad is so cool. I think I am in love."

"Bax, I'm pretty sure you are not in love with my dad." Alex turned bright red.

"No, I mean I am in love with his skills. Teach me, oh great one."

"It's nothing." Donald smiled, "you just have to live as a huge disappointment to your wife's father for twenty-some years. It's easier than it looks."

"Oh man, I am so glad your family is on our side, Alex."

"Yeah, I am too." Alex replied.

"So what happened? Plate-glass window? Fire alarms?"

"Imp."

"Imp? At school? In your worst class? I'm not sure I am buying it."

"Damn, Mr. Land, you are good. You totally pegged Mr. Werker to the wall and now you have Alex in your sights. I am in love with your great skills, oh teacher, my teacher."

"Bax?"

"Yes, my sensei?"

"Shut up, and I mean that in the nicest possible way."

"Shutting up, Mr. Land."

"I swear. It was an imp. It was blind, and it broke through the window in the door. That's probably why the teacher hasn't spoken to Mr. Werker yet. I bet he was all cut up."

"Ok. What happened next?"

"It was on the light. It jumped down and was sniffing around the room, trying to find us. I pulled the fire alarm so everyone would get out and we could deal with the imp."

"Yeah, that's exactly what happened." Bax agreed.

"Bax, shutting up?"

"Oh, yeah, sorry. I saw the imp too. It was huge. I guess I'm still a little excited."

"Wait, you saw it as well?"

Bax nodded.

"You are becoming more aware. That might be a problem." Donald said.

"It's fine, Dad."

"Continue the story, Alex."

"So I tried to scribe a circle to capture the imp, but I got it wrong. I ran away from it because it was pretty slow and Bax distracted it while I fixed the circle."

"What did you do wrong?" Donald asked.

"I didn't write 'guǐ' correctly."

"Ah, then it is true. You always mess up 'guǐ' when you are stressed."

"Do not."

"Yes, you do. That is how I know you are telling the truth." Donald sat down.

"Jerk."

"What? Grounded?" Donald smiled.

"So anyway, Bax was fighting off the imp with a chair and I corrected my character and smashed the circle into the imp's back. I did the chant and instead of just being imprisoned, the imp exploded into smoke. Really nasty smoke too, like too much vinegar spilling on the grill. And then it was gone."

"That's it?"

"Yup, we tried to get out quick, but the fireman arrived just then."

"Too bad. If you had gotten out of there, Mr. Werker wouldn't be all over suspending you two idiots." Donald smiled.

"Idiots? We couldn't just let the imp stay there. It could have hurt someone. Or worse."

"I know, that was the right thing to do. But now I have to explain how you got caught in this predicament to Grandfather Li. I'm pretty easy going, but even I don't like to be called some of the names he calls me." Donald shuffled his feet.

"Sorry Dad." Alex said.

"It's ok. Just do better next time and you can have extra dessert for saving your school from another menace."

"Thanks Dad, you're the best!"

"I am, aren't I?"

"Yeah." Alex smiled.

"I can't believe one of those things came after you in school." Suzie said to Alex on Monday.

"Worse than that, the principal wanted to suspend me and Bax! He blamed us for the damage." Alex said, whispering to Suzie before Geometry class started.

"That's not fair! You didn't do anything, did you?"

"Not at all! My dad got us out of it. He really laid into Mr. Werker. Bax was fawning all over him. Oh, my sensei! It was gross." Alex said.

Jill walked up and interrupted.

"Hey, Alex? I have to go get a dress for the dance after school. Ya wanna come with?" Jill wasn't smiling.

"Me? Jill, have you ever seen my outfits? Jeans. Sweats. I don't do dresses." Alex laughed.

"I'll go with you, if you like? I have to get my outfit too. You going to that place in the Alvarado?" Suzie perked up and smiled.

"Yeah, I was gonna go there right after school. You don't have to come with me, I mean, I can go alone." Jill said.

"No way! I'd love to see what kind of dress you get! I bet it will be amazing." Suzie gushed.

"Nah. It's just for the Harvest Dance. Nothing special." Jill blushed. She took good care of her appearance. It was second only to her grades.

"Nope. I'm coming. But you have to help me get a dress too. I'm terrible at fashion. We had uniforms at my old school, so no chance to dress up. Ever." Suzie said, looking at her shoes. Alex and Jill couldn't see the glint in her eyes as Maxxie smiled inside Suzie's mind.

"Ok! I get to buy a dress and dress you up? Challenge accepted." Jill said, thrusting her fist in the air in triumph.

"Ladies. Seats? I would like to start class, if you don't mind?" Mr. Lampert said from the front.

"Crap." Jill said, running to her seat, "Meet you in the quad after school?"

"You bet!" Suzie replied as she faced her text book and smiled wickedly.

***

The Alvarado shopping mall was only a twenty-minute walk from the Nancy Row High School. Jill and Suzie made it to Fashion Dress and Tuxedo in thirty minutes. The discussion about what colors and fabrics would be best for the dance was intense and slowed their pace.

"Do you think I should go full prom dress or just keep it casual?" Jill asked as her and Suzie entered the store.

"Well, you're going with Bax. I think casual is probably

better. You wouldn't want to break his mind, right?" Suzie laughed. Jill blushed.

"Just kidding. I know you are just friends. Like me and Alex. This is our safe dance." Suzie teased, gently punching Jill on the shoulder.

"Oh, you did not say 'Safety Dance,' did you?" Jill asked.

"Huh? 'Safety Dance?' What's that?" Suzie asked, her eyes wide.

"Oh, nothing. Just an old song on my mom's tapes." Jill walked up to a row of cotton dresses.

"What are those? Cowgirl dresses?" Suzie asked.

"I think these are a bad fashion choice." Jill said, smirking.

"Well, I guess we are setting the bottom standard here. What about those over there?" Suzie pointed to the rack on the other wall of the small boutique store.

"Hmm, I like the solids. Let's try some on?" Jill practically bounced over to the rack of dresses. Her enthusiasm was high. Maxxie frowned as Jill started examining the dresses.

Pick something that compliments red. Arterial red.

"Shh, Maxxie." Suzie whispered as she felt Maxxie squeeze her mind like a warning hand on her shoulder.

"Come here, Suzie. This one? I think it would be great on you. What's your size?" Jill asked.

"Medium?" Suzie answered, blinking. What was her size?

"No. You need a dress size. Here. Start with a 6. Then we can go up or down." Jill handed a size 6 blue and white dress to Suzie.

"Ok." Suzie was not sure what to do. Maxxie had been

gripping her mind tightly. Maxxie didn't know anything about dresses and loosened its hold on Suzie so she could take care of whatever one did with dresses.

"Oh, yeah. A 6 is a good start. See if they have a 4 cut on the bias?" Suzie asked as she walked to the dressing room.

"Oh, you do know dresses? You've been holding out on me, Suzie." Jill said as she picked up a black and cream dress with a big, 1950s style poodle silhouette in fuchsia on the front.

"That looks great, Jill! Come back and try it on, too!" Suzie called.

Black, white, and red all over. Soon. Maxxie thought inside Suzie's mind. Suzie reached into her purse for an aspirin.

CHAPTER ELEVEN

Two weeks should have passed quickly for Alex, but she was waiting for Maxwell to appear again. Instead of a fast fall semester, Alex's impatience for finding and sending Maxwell back to the dead lands turned into a slow, painful slog through classes, tests, and other people's plans for the Harvest Dance.

Bax monitored the scripts he had written to track Maxwell on the Internet, but whenever a corrupted router was discovered, Maxwell was long gone. Warren was tired of replacing new equipment and the cellular company was getting frustrated with the failures of the network.

Marjorie, Jill, and now Suzie helped Alex when they could. Suzie tried to help most of all, but they were always too late. Maxwell moved from machines as if it was warned in advance of being detected. Bax swore there was no way that could be true, but every time he contacted Alex and the others about a new possibility it seemed Maxwell had already moved on.

Alex finally gave up. Suzie arrived at Alex's house with a dress for the Harvest Dance. Alex had spent so much time trying to track down Maxwell when she wasn't in school that she had forgotten about the dance and agreeing to go with Suzie on a friend's date. Suzie brought the dress to remind Alex.

"But how did you know my size?" Alex asked.

"Easy. I have a good eye. Besides, you're pretty much the same size as me." Suzie replied.

"Wow, Suzie, how can I ever thank you?" Alex stared at the green dress. It was beautiful and complimented the dress Suzie had picked out with Jill quite well.

"Thank me? Oh, it's fine. I'm sure something will come up. Probably cookies. I always love working for cookies." Suzie smiled, "Now try it on, ok?"

"Now?" Alex asked.

"Yes, now. We only have a couple days to get a different size if it's a bad fit."

Alex started to change, Suzie helped. The dress was a zippered back, and Alex had trouble reaching. The fit was perfect.

"Wow." Alex said, "You brought yours, right?"

"Of course!" Suzie took a second dress out of the big paper shopping bag she had with her.

The dress was wrapped carefully in a special bag. Suzie hung it on the back of Alex's door and opened the bag. She took out her blue dress and changed into it. Suzie needed Alex's help since it was the same style of dress as the one she bought for her friend. When they were changed, the girls looked at themselves in the mirror on the door to Alex's closet.

"Wow. We look good." Alex said quietly.

"Perfect. We look perfect. No dates, but we will be the best dressed at the dance for sure." Suzie said. Maxxie smiled.

The red will compliment both dresses. Maxxie
thought. The thought made Suzie cringe. Revenge had felt
better when it was less visceral. Maxxie squeezed on Suzie's
mind. She let go of her thoughts. Better to just go along with
Maxxie. It hurt less.

"Do you have an aspirin, Alex?" Suzie asked, "I have a
little headache."

"Yeah, Dad has them in the bathroom downstairs," Alex
said, "Dad? Suzie needs an aspirin."

"Come on down. Want some tea?" Alex's dad called
from somewhere in the house.

"Sure. Coming!" Suzie said as she and Alex went downstairs in their dresses.

"Now isn't that better, Son?" Warren tightened his
hands on Bax's shoulders.

"Dad. This isn't a prom. It's a freshman dance."

"A corsage is required. You need to cut a figure. My
handsome child. Represent the family name." Warren
squeezed harder.

"Ouch, Dad, please? My shoulder is still tender. Demon
assisted bike crash, remember?" Bax cringed.

"I thought it was an imp?"

"Demon or imp. Does it matter? My shoulder still feels
like crap." Bax turned and faced his father.

"Dad, if I give the flower to Jill, doesn't that make us an
item or some nonsense like that?" Bax looked at the corsage
dubiously.

"Nah, she needs to give you a boutonnière for that. You
have to exchange flowers to be dating. No way that girl
would fall into that trap." Warren said.

"Yeah, no way that would happen." Bax said.

"No way." Warren repeated.

"This is a set up, isn't it?" Bax asked.

"Yes it is." Warren admitted as the doorbell rang, "Right on time."

"Oh, no." Bax said.

"Oh, yes." Warren replied, "The gang's all here."

"Dad, seriously?" Bax adjusted his bow tie. The tuxedo Warren had selected for him was the least dressy Bax could talk him down from. It was about seven times dressier than Bax wanted. There wasn't even a pocket for his action camera.

"Bax, I let myself in." Jill called from the front door.

"Be down in a minute," Bax shouted back, "Dad, can we be done here?"

"Sure, Son. Get down there and see your lady."

"Dad. Just, no." Bax said as he headed down to meet Jill.

"Hey, can I get a glass of water?" Alex asked from the first floor.

"Hey, Alex, you're here too? I'm coming down." Warren called.

Jill, Alex, and Suzie waited in the kitchen for Bax and his father. Alex was getting a glass from the cabinet.

"You all came together?" Bax asked.

"Of course. I needed backup as soon as I figured out it was a set up. You get this, by the way." Jill tossed something to Bax. He caught it and looked at the flower in his hands.

"A boutonnière. Of course. Dad!" Bax sounded annoyed.

"Son. Give the girl her corsage." Warren said.

"Fine. I refuse to be set up. Jill. Corsage. Set up." Bax said, handing his flower to Jill. Bax failed to notice Jill's smile.

"Great, now can we get going?" Suzie said.

"Why are you all here, by the way?" Warren asked.

"Reinforcements." Jill replied tersely.

"I see. Safety in numbers. Well, I have something for that. Conversion van!" Warren pumped his fist in the air as if it had all been planned from the start.

"Oh, no. I hope you are all happy. Dad has been calling us a gang for the last half hour." Bax said as he pinned the flower to his lapel and failed.

"Here, honestly." Jill said, helping Bax with his boutonnière.

"Ok. What is this conversion van?" Suzie asked.

"Mr. Mitchell's pride and joy. Well, one of them. Come on, it's out back." Alex said, taking the lead out the back door.

"You kids don't know how long I have been waiting for this moment. All we need now is a big, talking dog and some snacks." Warren smiled from ear to ear.

W arren pulled his conversion van up to the front doors of the community center. A banner above the three double doors read 'Nancy Row High School.' Written in big block letters on a much smaller sign to the right of the doors was 'Harvest Dance.'

The van's side door slid open and Bax, Suzie, Alex, and Jill stepped out of the van one after the other.

"Alright, the gang is all here." Warren said from the driver's seat.

"No, Dad. We are not a gang. There is no talking dog and we are not solving a mystery." Bax refused to look at Warren.

"I have some snacks, if that helps?" Alex said before she could stop herself.

"It's ok! Just getting to the scene of the crime is enough for me." Warren said.

"There is no crime, Dad." Bax protested.

"You kids go in and watch out for old man Jenkins. I'm gonna park the van and I'll be in right after you." Warren said as Jill closed the van door.

"What do you mean, you'll be in?" Bax said as Warren drove off.

"Your dad volunteered to chaperon, remember Bax?" Jill said, smiling as she took Bax's hand and led him into the community center.

"Well? Ready for your social debut, Alex?" Suzie smiled, grabbing Alex's hand and following Jill and Bax through the doors.

"What about my snacks?" Alex complained despite not having any snacks with her.

Inside, the community center was a large, empty space with roll out bleachers on either side for spectators. Students from the high school were scattered thickly over the entire area. Most milled about in the center of the floor, but enough were sitting on the bleachers to make the whole space look moderately full.

The basketball nets and backboards were retracted up and out of the way and the main area was set up for the dance. A few tables were off to one side in the back for sodas, pretzels, and other finger food. A single table next to the refreshments was set up for the entertainment. An older gentleman sat behind a turntable, a mass of cables, and a sticker covered laptop. A single spinning novelty disco light whirred on the edge of the table, forgotten. Despite looking old enough to be Warren's father, the man behind the laptop was playing some amazingly good and very new dance music, DJing with what looked like a light up panel of buttons to add drum beats and other improvised accents to the music.

"Ahem. Tickets please?" A familiar voice called to the two couples.

"What are you doing here, Marjorie?" Jill asked.

Marjorie was standing behind a fold-up table just next to the doors. Ms. Becky Barnes sat on a chair next to her. They had a box of cash and a giant roll of red tickets in front of them.

"Punishment for my sins, remember?" Marjorie said without making any expression.

Suzie walked up and took two sets of tickets out of her purse. It was a simple, black clutch with a single shoulder strap and a smaller wrist strap for extra security.

"Here you go! Two sets of tickets. Alex didn't have a purse, so these are for all of us." she said to Marjorie.

"Great. Here are your drink tickets. Soda is in the back. Snacks are free. Water is free. More sodas are a buck for 5 tickets." Marjorie said, handing Suzie a roll of tickets for all of them.

"Don't forget, no PDA." Ms. Barnes said from her seat.

"PDA? Bax asked.

"Public displays of affection." Ms. Barnes said, far too happily.

"What?" Bax asked.

"Kissing. No kissing." Marjorie explained.

"No danger there." Alex said, working on snark.

"Hey, isn't that your dad, Alex? Over by the bathrooms? He's waving at you like his arm is going to fall off." Jill said, pointing across the floor.

"Yeah. He volunteered to chaperon too. He left before

we did. Better see what he wants." Alex answered and started walking towards the bathrooms.

"Great, come on, I have to use the bathroom." Suzie was bubbly as she took off across the dance floor towards Alex's dad. Alex followed.

"Ah, is Suzie just a little too excited, or is it me?" Bax asked Jill.

"Yeah, I think she was really looking forward to the dance." Jill said.

"Pickles. I have something for you." Donald Land said to Alex as a lull in the music set in.

"Dad, what is it?" Alex said.

"Hey, I'm gonna use the bathroom. Go get us a soda when you're done, ok?" Suzie said, handing the tickets to Alex.

"Sure."

"Here, take this." Donald said, handing Alex a black bag.

"What is this?" Alex asked, looking at the silky mass in her hand.

"It was your mother's. You ran out of the house so quickly when Jill came over, you forgot your smartphone."

I was lonely, Alex.

"SPD! So sorry. I wasn't going to bring you. No pockets in the dress." Alex said.

"I put some other things in the purse as well. Your mom used it when we practiced. There's a máobǐ, some ink, and a few sheets of paper. Just in case." Donald said, opening the flap on the silk purse. It was more of a brush or pen case than a purse, not that Alex could tell the difference.

"Dad, thank you! This is beautiful." Alex ran her fingers over the silk, "Is this real?"

"Yup. Měilóng and I got it when we were in Japan on our honeymoon." Donald said casually.

It is very comfortable in this bag, Alex. You should try it sometime.

"Next time I am trapped in a smartphone, SPD," Alex replied, "Although I don't think I'll need the calligraphy tools, Dad."

"You never know. It's been quiet, but Maxwell is still out there. I feel safer this way." Donald patted his daughter on the head, ruffling her hair.

"Fine. Let's go get some sodas before Suzie gets back."

No tea? Is this a special occasion, Alex?

"Yes, SPD. It is." Alex smiled. She was enjoying the beginning of the dance despite herself.

Suzie closed and locked the door on the furthest bathroom stall. She took her smartphone out of her purse and swiped the screen. The phone came to life and Suzie felt Maxxie in her head. She felt the tight hold Maxxie had on her, wrapping her mind up like wires pulled tight across her skin. When Suzie used her phone, the weight of Maxxie became even greater.

Good. All the children are here.

"Can't we wait? I want to have some fun before we make everyone pay." Suzie held the phone up to her ear and talked as if someone was on the line with her.

No. You can dance on their bones after I have broken them. Maxxie replied in Suzie's thoughts.

Suzie's mouth twitched. She bit her lip.

"Everything will feel better after they have paid, right Maxxie?" Suzie asked.

Yes. Once you have broken them, everything will be better. Then I shall feast. More of me shall come and feast. You will become part of us. Maxxie's words didn't make sense, but with a little tug, the hold on Suzie's mind strengthened and she knew Maxxie spoke the truth.

"Fine. But next time, I get to dance first." Suzie said. Maxxie just laughed.

Fine. Maxxie thought, knowing there would be no next time. That particular thought leaked through to Suzie just a little, but she hid it away. Next time. She would get to dance. To have a good time. Not just Maxxie. To have friends. To not be afraid. To smile and be warm inside. It was all Suzie really wanted.

Now, let my friends out. Maxxie poked Suzie's mind and she let herself open to a power even greater than Maxxie. The power flowed through her smartphone, through the electronics and into Suzie. Then it came out of her as shadows that pooled around her. Imps rose from the shadows around Suzie. She heard the thrum of the power as more imps came through the phone. The thrum sounded like a name. Maxwell.

"Suzie, look what Dad brought me." Alex turned to her friend as she returned from the bathroom.

"A purse? I thought you didn't carry purses?" Suzie looked at the small silk bag in Alex's hands.

"It's not just a purse, it was my mom's purse. For magic!" Alex smiled, opening the purse to show Suzie the máobĭ, ink, and most importantly, SPD.

"Your phone!" Suzie said. The back of her neck prickled as Maxxie tightened around Suzie.

"Suzie, you ok?" Alex's dad asked.

That one. Get away from him. He suspects. Maxxie whispered inside Suzie's head.

"Alex, let's go find Jill and Bax. I want to tease them some more." Suzie said.

"You girls go. I'm going to watch from here." Donald shooed the girl off.

Suzie and Alex went in search of their friends. Donald watched them go. Something was off, Donald knew it somewhere inside himself. Shadows drifted from the bathroom. No one noticed the shadows as they gathered near the edges of the community center, near the outlets, and inside the power cables running to the DJ's equipment.

"I don't see them, Suzie." Alex said.

"That's fine. We'll find them sooner or later." Suzie replied.

The crash came from the other side of the room, near the bathrooms.

"Maybe sooner than you think." Suzie said, unheard because of the noise.

"What was that?" Alex said as the first scream broke out.

"Why are we here, my love?" Grandfather Li asked his wife as they sat at the Elkhorn Coffee Shop next to the community center.

"I'm worried." Grandma Akeyo replied.

"You know I cannot have coffee this late at night,

Akeyo." Grandfather Li said as he sipped at his double espresso.

"Then you should have ordered hot chocolate, like me."

"Always the better half."

"I am, aren't I?" Akeyo grinned.

"I do wonder, are you just spying on the children, or do you also feel the uneasiness in the air tonight." Grandfather Li said as he put his tiny cup down.

"I think our enemy has been biding its time. Building its strength. Tonight seems like an opportune time to catch Alex and her friends unaware." Akeyo replied.

"I agree. Akeyo, isn't that Warren walking out front?" Grandfather Li gestured to the window. Warren Mitchell was walking from the parking lot towards the community center. Akeyo waved at him through the window. Warren saw and opened the door to the coffee shop.

"Well, well. What are you two fine young people doing out tonight?" Warren said as he walked up to Akeyo and Jiànhuī's table.

"Warren. Sit. We are out looking for trouble. What about you?" Akeyo said, pushing out a chair for Warren.

"Oh? What kind of trouble?"

"With any luck, indigestion will be all." Jiànhuī said.

"I hear that. I'm here for the dance. Chaperon. Responsible adult, it me." Warren said, jabbing his thumb into his chest.

"Well, we are looking out for the kids as well. Akeyo suspects the demon is about." Grandfather Li said before he finished his espresso.

"Maxwell's demon? I didn't have Bax check the scripts before we left. You think it might be out tonight? Why now? It's been weeks with no sign other than a trail of broken servers and routers." Warren leaned in, speaking softly to his friends.

"Exactly. It has been weeks and not so much as a peep. I think Maxwell has been plotting. Planning. Now seems like a good time to strike." Akeyo said.

"Well, everyone is focused on the dance. I didn't think your granddaughter was going to be into it, but since her friend Suzie joined the club..." Warren let his words trail off.

The scream could be heard easily in the coffee shop. The teenagers running out the doors of the community center came just a few moments later. Grandfather Li, Grandma Akeyo, and Warren all stood up and ran to the door. They could see the mass of high school students escaping the doors of the community center and flooding into the parking lot.

"You know what, Ms. Akeyo? I think you're right." Warren said as he took out his cell phone and turned on the camera, "We better get out there and act like responsible adults."

The crowd began to thin out in front of the community center doors. Kids ran, leaving a large, empty space as the center double doors suddenly swung open. Something hit the ground, but only Grandfather Li, Grandma Akeyo, and Warren could see it. As Warren looked through the smartphone camera, the imp sprawled across the sidewalk. Standing in the doorway was Marjorie Chan, tall and resolute. She held two wooden blocks, one in each of her fists.

"No party crashers on my watch." Marjorie said. She took two steps and landed an open palm strike in mid-air. Warren gasped as he saw Marjorie's hand strike the imp while holding the wooden block. The imp evaporated with an almost audible pop.

"I know you said she was impressive, but wow. That gal has got moves." Warren said as the three adults ran over to the tall girl.

"Marjorie, are there any more inside? Are the children safe?" Akeyo asked as they got within earshot of Marjorie.

"Akeyo, I'm glad you let me borrow the demon boxes. I just wish I didn't need them." Marjorie asked.

"We thought there might be trouble. Are there more?" Akeyo replied.

"Yes, lots. People are still inside and they are definitely not safe."

"Then it is time to get to work. Grandfather Li held his hands out to Grandma Akeyo and Warren. He gave them each a pair of wooden blocks. Demon blocks.

"If an imp gets near you, hit it with one of these, Warren. Understand?" Grandfather Li said.

"Got it. Hit ugly with the wooden block." Warren answered.

"Then let's get down to business." Akeyo said as they all strode into the community center.

"Crap, what was that?" Alex said to Suzie over the noise coming from the bathrooms.

"I don't know, can you see anything?" Suzie asked.

There are demons here. Imps. Many. I can feel them all around us.

"That's not good, SPD. How did they get here?"

I do not know. There was nothing, then suddenly, there was.

"Alex, we need to get everyone out of here." Donald said.

"Where's the fire alarm?" Bax asked, "Are they coming? I can't see them."

"Get your action cam, Bax." Alex said.

"I can't. There wasn't any place for it in this tux."

"Here." Jill said, pulling a smartphone out of her purse and handing it to Bax.

"Sweet. I love you in a totally platonic way." Bax said as he turned on the camera and pointed it around the space.

"I know." Jill said, "Bax, tell us where these imps are at. Alex, we need something to get rid of these things."

"On it! Suzie, now's your chance. Warn me if those things get close." Alex said as she dumped the contents of her mother's purse on the snack table.

"Oh, I will." Suzie replied with a wide smile on her face.

Alex set out the ink stone, her máobǐ, and several pieces of paper. She picked up a black ink stick and looked around for some water.

"Suzie, quick, get me a glass of water." Alex said.

"Ok!" Suzie looked around and ran towards the water fountain.

"Wait, the water is right over here." Alex said, pointing at the next table with the drinks, "Fine." Alex grabbed a cup of water off the table and dripped some into the well of the ink stone. She began to grind the ink stick into the well. Black liquid slowly started forming.

"Alex, we need something quick." Bax said, "The dance floor is clearing out."

Alex took the first slip of paper and dipped the máobǐ into the ink. She wrote a banishment on the slip and then moved to the second piece of paper.

Alex. You forgot one stroke.

"No, I didn't, SPD." Alex replied as she wrote.

Alex. Demon is missing a stroke. It will not work.

"Crap." Alex said as she looked at her writing. SPD was right. Alex added a single line to the hànzi for demon. She checked her second banishment. It was correct.

"Alex. The imps are coming." Bax sounded panicked.

"Here. One for each of you. Slap them on the imps." Alex said, handing over the pieces of paper.

"What is this?" Jill asked, "what happened to the wooden blocks?"

"No blocks. These are shénfú. Banishment talismans." Alex said.

"Like in anime?" Bax asked.

"Yes, anime. But this is the Chinese version, not the Japanese." Alex said. She turned back to the ink stone and rubbed more ink into the water.

"I got some water, Alex!" Suzie said, running over with a fresh cup of water. Something grabbed her from behind and Suzie fell. She lost her grip on the water and it spilled across the table, soaking the remaining slips of paper.

"You ok?" Alex asked, dropping her máobǐ and going to help Suzie up.

"Ow. Something grabbed me." Suzie said, smiling slightly as Alex looked around for an imp.

I cannot sense anything, Alex.

"Me either, SPD. But this place is suddenly so full of wrongness, I'm not sure what I am sensing." Alex replied.

Alex heard Jill yell from behind her. She turned and saw an imp the size of a pony looking Jill in the eyes.

"Crap."

Jill thrust her hand out with the shénfú gripped tightly between her fingers. The crumpled paper stuck to the forehead of the imp as Jill pulled her hand back as if it was touching something slimy.

Nothing happened.

"It didn't work, Alex." Jill cried.

"Don't smash the paper! The ink is wet." Alex yelled back.

The imp turned and looked at Alex. It smiled showing crooked teeth in a crooked mouth. It ignored Jill and Bax.

Alex pawed at her dress, looking for her pockets. She held her smartphone in one hand and found no pockets with her other.

"The purse. Suzie, get my máobǐ and some paper! I'll lead this thing away." Alex said, backing away from the imp.

Suzie went for the writing tools on the table as Alex lured the imp away from her friends.

"Over here, doofus." Alex yelled and waved her arms.

This feels like a bad idea, Alex.

"Shut up, SPD."

"How many of these things are there?" Akeyo shouted over the noise of students evacuating the community center.

"I don't know. One just sort of walked out of the ladies room and then a bunch of them were suddenly everywhere." Marjorie shouted back.

"Oh, man. I don't think I need the camera to see them anymore." Warren said as he put his phone in his back pocket.

"That is a bad sign." Grandfather Li said. He was facing a particularly nasty looking imp. It was short and wide, and it sat on the check-in table where Marjorie and Ms. Barnes had been giving out drink tickets.

"If we are just starting to see them now, how did the

panic begin? Warren asked as Marjorie smashed a smaller imp on the head with a hammer fist.

"My fault. I saw them and they saw me. I told Ms. Barnes to duck as the imp threw a chair at us. The chair missed, but then someone yelled 'fight,' and all bets were off." Marjorie replied.

Warren jumped to the side as Akeyo sent an imp flying through the air. Akeyo was flat on her back, but she rolled forward and sprung up to her feet effortlessly. Grandfather Li brushed a few tickets off his shirt, the short, wide imp was no where to be seen but the tickets swirled in the air where it had been just before Grandfather Li hit it with a wood block.

"Where is Ms. Barnes now?" Granfather Li asked.

"She went to the front to gather the students in the parking lot. She left just a moment or two before I knocked that other imp out the door." Marjorie replied, ducking as a chair flew end over end in the air.

"I did not see her. She must have been in the mass of children." Grandfather Li remarked.

The space in front of the doors had cleared out. A half dozen or so imps of various sizes and shapes stood in a rough ring around Marjorie and the adults. The doors were to their backs and the imps in front. Behind the imps, the last group of students was bunched together. They had started to see the creatures. At first it was just a fuzzy impression of something in front of them, but now, with so many things from the dead lands in the real world, the students could see the imps clearly.

"What the hell is going on here?" Ms. Barnes said from behind everyone. She walked in through the double doors and stood. Her five foot tall body towered over no one, but her voice dominated the space.

"You." Ms. Barnes pointed at a stout imp in the middle of the group, "What the hell are you?"

The imp cocked its head to the side and snarled.

"No. We do not snarl. Answer me or its detention for a week." Ms. Barnes snapped.

The imp's eyes went wide, the little black dots inside its sockets seemed bigger as it raised its bumpy hand. Ms. Barnes tapped her foot, waiting for a response.

The imp looked at its hand in the air, then at Ms. Barnes. Its eyebrows knitted and fell down over its eyes. The creature opened its mouth to roar as Marjorie Chan's fist connected with the imp's nose-less face and it popped out of existence.

"It didn't have anything to contribute to the class, Ms. Barnes." Marjorie said, tossing a wooden block towards her teacher, "Hit them with this. It makes them go away."

"Right. Someone owes me an explanation when this is over." Ms. Barnes said as the imps charged at them and the fight began in earnest.

CHAPTER TWELVE

"**D**oes it seem clearer to you, Jill?" Bax asked, pointing at the imp chasing Alex.

"Yeah, I can see the imp pretty easily now. And so can they." Jill replied, pointing at the students panicking on the dance floor.

Get them out of my way.

"Hey, why don't you two help them?" Suzie said as she picked up Alex's writing tools, "I'll take care of Alex."

"Yeah, good plan. Jill, I'll watch your back." Bax said.

"No way, you're coming with me." Jill grabbed Bax's hand and pulled him behind her. They ran towards the remaining kids in the community center.

Good. Now, let's have some fun. Maxxie squeezed on Suzie's thoughts.

"Sure, Maxxie. Fun." Suzie smiled, but her bottom lip still twitched slightly.

Alex ran into a corner of the center where the bleachers ran along one of the long walls of the open space. There was a closed door on her right and the extended seats and framework of the roll-out bleachers on her left. The imp was walking after her, not rushing as it dragged its hands along the floor. Alex tried the door. It was locked.

"Crap."

Alex, it is getting close. You should run.

"I know that, SPD. But where?" Alex looked around and saw Suzie come up behind the imp. She saw the máobǐ in Suzie's right hand and the rest of her writing materials and her mother's bag in her other. The imp didn't notice the girl behind it.

"Suzie. Throw me my stuff." Alex called. The imp stopped and looked around. It looked directly at Suzie, then at Alex. It smiled wickedly.

"Oh, this?" Suzie held up the máobǐ.

"Yes! Throw it to me." Alex pleaded.

Something is wrong, Alex. I sense there is more than just your friend Suzie, here.

"Yeah, no kidding. Big, dumb imp?" Alex said out loud to her phone.

"It's not nice to talk to people in secret, Alex." Suzie said as she waggled the máobǐ in her hand. Suddenly, Suzie snapped the brush pen in two, squeezing her hand closed around it.

"What the hell, Suzie? I needed that!" Alex yelled in surprise.

"So you could defeat these imps? My imps?"

"Your imps? What are you talking about, Suzie?"

"Not Suzie. Not anymore." Maxxie squeezed harder on Suzie's mind as she spoke. It asserted itself forcefully into her thoughts and took over.

"What are you talking about, Suzie?" Alex asked. The imp stood still, waiting.

"Not Suzie. Call me Maxxie." The shadows around Suzie deepened and flowed. A smaller imp formed out of one shadow, then another imp to its right. A third emerged from the shadow at Suzie's left.

"Crap."

Indeed.

"Get her. Break, break."

Alex ran. She couldn't open the locked door, and the imp was right behind her so she went the only place she could, under the bleachers. The framework was open and easy for her to get through since the seats were fully extended. Alex still had to step up and over rails while ducking to avoid hitting her head on the supports for the bench seats overhead.

The imp behind her was not fast, but the rails were less of a barrier for it. It slowed a little as its body moved through the metal and wood. The rails twisted as the imp pushed its form through them. The corruption flowing into the imp from the dead lands must have been great to so easily twist the metal. Alex spared a glance back only twice.

Alex, perhaps there is a pen, or a pencil discarded under here?

"What? Oh. Yeah, that's a good idea, SPD." Alex looked around quickly, but the light was almost absent under the bleachers.

Does this help? SPD's LED came on and Alex shined the light around as she navigated the struts and supports under the bleachers.

"Nothing. I don't see anything!" Alex cried.

"Little girl. I'm coming for you." Suzie yelled from the far end of the bleachers. Her imp came closer, but Suzie stayed at the end, away from Alex.

Alex's smartphone vibrated.

Alex. It is your grandfather. He is sending a text.

"Why now? What does it say?"

Where are you, feckless child?

"Really? Why does he always do that?"

I do not think you are feckless, Alex.

"Text him back, ok? Tell him we need help. Bring brush pens. Ink. Paper. Demon boxes."

I have done so. He says he is already here. At the front of the community center. He says to banish the imps yourself, foolish child.

"Not helping! I need something to write with." Alex said, then she stopped and looked at her smartphone.

Alex? The imp will catch us.

"SPD, I have an idea." Alex said, swiping open the SMS chat with Grandfather Li. The imp stepped closer, until it was only an arms length away. Alex switched to Chinese input. Handwriting. Quickly, she swiped eight strokes, Fàng.

I think I understand. Like with Maxwell in your room? Alex, can I help?

"Yes, please!" Alex said as SPD wrote out ten more strokes, zhú.

Alex hit send and pointed the screen at the imp as it rose to its full height and brought its arm up to strike at Alex.

Fàngzhú popped up on the screen and was sent out to Grandfather Li's phone at the same time. The imp was not impressed. It drew its twisted and heavy arm back, bending the metal supports of the bleachers just as light began to brighten from the smartphone's screen.

Fàngzhú appeared in black inside the light and imprinted itself on the imp's face. The imp shook, twisting itself up in the supports and struts under the bleachers. There was a loud pop. Alex jumped back and accidentally dropped her phone. The imp was gone and the structure all around Alex creaked and gave way.

Just as the text came through Grandfather Li's phone he heard the crash from the collapsing bleachers. His own phone flashed brightly and just as suddenly, the imp in front of him was gone in a pop. Fàngzhú was fading in the air where the creature had been.

"Well, that was unexpected." said Grandfather Li.

"What was that, Mr. Li?" Warren asked. He stood behind Grandfather Li, waving his hands from side to side as he held the wooden block.

"Alex sent me a text and I think it banished the imp." Grandfather Li said.

"What? Cool. A textorcism? I am down with that. Order up another." Warren replied.

"Why not? Warren, watch in front of me while I give this a try." Grandfather Li said as he started typing into his phone. Warren turned, sweeping his hands across the space in front of Grandfather Li and himself.

"They seem to be stepping back. I think whatever Alex did scared them." Warren said, watching as the imps backed away.

"Let me try this, get back, Warren." Grandfather Li hit send and thrust his phone out in front of him and closed his eyes.

"Did something happen?" Warren asked. Grandfather Li opened his eyes and saw nothing had changed. The imps noticed as well. One raised its foot and kicked at the ticket table in front of it, sending it flying towards Grandfather Li and Warren Mitchell.

"Get down!" Warren shouted as he pushed Grandfather Li aside. The table flipped in the air and hit Warren Mitchell squarely on his upraised arm. The wooden block went flying as Warren fell on the ground with the table on top of him.

"That didn't sound good," Akeyo called from the other side of the entrance to the community center.

"I think they got Mr. Mitchell." Marjorie said, "I saw him go down under a flying table."

"Can you get to him?" Akeyo asked as she thrust her wooden block towards an imp, popping it out of existence as the wood touched the creature's face.

"No way, this big jerk has me fully engaged." Marjorie threw a kick at the imp in front of her, but it jumped back and away from the girl's strike.

"Then we have to trust them to fend for themselves. Let the imps push us back. We can keep closer to Jiànhuī and Warren that way." Akeyo said, backing up.

"What did you do?" Suzie howled.

Alex could see her through the space where the imp had been. The bleacher's framework had collapsed and blocked the way back to Suzie, but there was still enough space to see her clearly through the settling dust.

Alex. It worked.

"It did, SPD, where are you?" Alex was on her butt. She had jumped back when the fàngzhú hànzi had burst on contact with the imp. Now she was tangled up in the metal braces between levels of the extendable bleachers. Her smartphone was somewhere on the floor, hidden in the shadows.

Over here. SPD thought to Alex, blinking the photo flash on the smartphone.

"I can't reach you. Hold on while I get out of this." Alex said, trying to stand.

"Ignore me? I'll show you. Maxwell wants you gone. Punish. Break, break." Suzie yelled. Shadows extended from her body, growing into a form around her. The mousy girl in the blue dress faded, enveloped by the shape of a large, powerful imp. Alex looked and swore. It looked like the demon that had attacked her in her bedroom. Maxwell.

Alex scrambled backwards, her dress caught in the struts and supports. Her hand hit something small. It was her smartphone. SPD stopped blinking the flash as Alex picked the phone up.

"It's Maxwell." Alex said.

It feels like Maxwell to me too. It must have hidden inside Suzie. That's why we never found Maxwell. It was hiding in plain sight.

"Yeah, well, it's here now. Let's get out of here before it drops this whole thing on us." Alex said as she tore her dress free.

"No you don't." Maxwell's voice came out of Suzie's mouth. She swung her arm up, and the bleachers broke around her. The shadows clinging around her body hit the metal and wood first, Suzie's arms never touched the bleachers themselves.

Now we shall hurt. Hurt. Maim. Kill. Maxxie thought at Suzie.

"Maxxie, isn't this enough?" Suzie asked aloud.

"Never enough." Maxxie spoke with Suzie's voice.

"Hurting is fine, but kill?" Suzie asked.

Maxxie tightened its grip on Suzie's mind. She cried inside, the squeezing hurt.

"I will eat her liver. This Alex will pay. You will like it. Break her. Eat it. Delicious." Suzie's voice rasped with Maxxie's words.

"What is going on with her? Is she talking to herself?" Alex asked SPD.

I think you are correct. I do not think Suzie wants to kill you.

"Yeah, but that doesn't really help us right now, does it?" Alex said as she reached the open side of the bleachers.

"No! You will not get away!" Suzie shouted. Her voice was changed. Roughness had taken over and a jarring screech was just audible when she stopped speaking. Suzie leaped forward, batting the bleachers aside, grasping metal and wood in her shadowed hands. She held the ruins of the bleachers tight above her head, ready to throw them down on top of Alex. Tearing aside the seating left them in a sudden open space with the bulk of the bleachers suspended above Suzie.

You need to banish it. Maxwell must be sent back.

"You think I don't know that? I remember what he did last time. I don't know if I can do it!" Alex yelled back at her phone.

"You will do nothing, except die." Suzie said. Part of her still resisted. Alex could see her eyes behind the shadows. A tear was on Suzie's face.

"I don't even know what to write. We already tried fàngzhú on it before when Maxwell was in my bedroom. What else might work?" Alex was stumped. Maxwell had resisted the same hànzi a second time when it had attacked Alex before.

Do you know xū?

"As in xūkōng, eleven strokes? Yeah, let me try that." Alex said as she swiped open her text chat to Grandfather

Li. His fàngzhú message was new, but Alex didn't have time to wonder about it. Alex wrote xū quickly and hit send. She pointed the phone at Suzie. Nothing happened.

Alex, you forgot a stroke! You put four and five together. They are separate strokes.

"Shut up, SPD! Alex said as she erased the hànzi and wrote it again, slowly and deliberately.

"What, am I supposed to be impressed? I have the same phone, Alex. I even have a demon in mine too. Now I'm going to break everything. Starting with you, for my Maxwell. You are garbage. Filthy human garbage." Suzie yelled at Alex. Tears streamed down her face.

That's correct. Send it. SPD blinked the flash rapidly.

Alex looked at Suzie, she could see the girl she knew in Suzie's eyes. Above her, the wreckage of the bleachers was held up by the shadows surrounding Suzie. Maxwell.

"SPD, I can't. What happens to Suzie if I banish Maxwell? She'll be crushed."

"No. You will just die, like the garbage you are." Suzie screamed. The voice wasn't hers anymore.

"Fine. I'm garbage? Well, garbage in, demon out!" Alex yelled.

Alex hit send and everything came crashing down.

"What is all over you?" Donald asked, looking at Alex, Bax, and Jill as they sat in Warren Mitchell's conversion van.

"Dirt and imp guts? I think," Alex was visibly disgusted.

I agree. Dirt, at least.

"Shut up, SPD."

"Well, I think you are doing your own laundry this week, Pickles."

"Thanks. I think I'm just going to burn it all."

Grandma Akeyo and Grandfather Li walked up to the van as Donald examined Alex and her friends.

"Is everyone still in one piece?" Grandfather Li asked.

"Crap, you look like you got in a fight with a wild animal, John."

"I did, ungrateful son-in-law. But I won."

"Hey, has anyone seen my dad?." Bax asked, "He was supposed to be a chaperon."

"He was with us. The paramedics are taking care of him now." Akeyo said, placing her hands on Bax's shoulders.

"Is he ok? What happened?" Bax asked. Worry lined his face.

"Warren is fine. Don't worry, the important thing is we are all fine." Akeyo reassured Baxter.

"Your father is very brave. He likely saved my life." Grandfather Li said to the boy.

Jill stood next to Bax and wrapped her arms around his shoulders.

"One of those creatures threw a table at your grandfather. Mr. Mitchell pushed him out of the way and it hit him instead." Marjorie said, walking up to the group.

"My dad? You have got to be kidding me." Bax replied.

"Your dad is pretty lucky, Bax. His arm is broken, but it could have been much worse." Marjorie said.

"The tall girl is correct. Warren is strong and lucky. I am very proud of him." Grandfather Li added, "Just don't tell him that."

"What happened to you guys? Where's Suzie?" Marjorie said, looking the group over.

Maxwell was inside the girl.

"What? Is your phone serious, Alex?" Marjorie asked.

Yes. I am sure. And it was very powerful.

"Suzie betrayed us. She brought the imps to the dance. She destroyed my máobǐ, but SPD and I banished it."

"I would like to know how you managed that, my clever girl?" Grandfather Li looked Alex up and down, brushing some dust from her tattered green dress.

"I sent Maxwell a text, xū."

I added my own power to the text. It forced the demon out.

"You texted Maxwell to death." Bax smirked, "It was a textorcism."

Alex groaned. "That is so not what we are calling it, Bax."

Donald laughed.

"Textorcism, I think Warren said the same thing when we got your fàngzhú on my phone." Grandfather Li let the phrase linger, "It explains why the imps we were battling vanished so suddenly. Your text must have affected them all. Textorcism. I like it."

"You would, old man." Grandma Akeyo sat down next to her husband.

"No. I will not be the 'textorcist.' That is so dumb."

"Alex. Listen to your elders. You are the textorcist now and forever." Donald placed a bandage on one of Alex's cuts.

"Yeah, I like it too." Marjorie smiled, getting the joke.

"Ugh. I hate all of you."

Even me, Alex? I would like to be the textorcist, too.

"Shut up, SPD."

Why? Textorcism is a good word.

"Ugh. I want my phone back the way it was, before it could talk back. Stupid textorcizing hacker."

The few pieces of Maxwell that returned and joined back into the whole gave it little reason to be happy. The human children had defeated the special piece of Maxwell sent to aid Suzie. Maxwell had put much of its power into that piece and it had been able to see through Suzie's eyes as she tried to destroy Alex and her friends. Maxxie had not been able to guide Suzie's hatred as much as its master had hoped. Suzie was confused. She didn't hate enough for Maxxie to use her properly. In the end, Maxwell surged even more power into the Maxxie, only to have Alex and the small demon in the box, in the smartphone, manage to banish Maxxie and sever Maxwell's connection to Suzie. Maxwell could only hope that enough of its influence lingered inside Suzie to make her not a complete waste of effort.

Maxwell was not pleased at all. Now it was weak. Maxwell know it needed allies, it could no longer work to destroy the children on its own.

Filthy human garbage. I must call on another. One from this world. The one that first set me on this path. I must call on that filthy human child.

Maxwell was not pleased at all. It reached out of the warm demon box it slept in, searching for the first human it had met in this world, years ago, when it was last banished to the dead lands.

I will seek out Wendy. Wendy will help.

Take your time, Maxwell. Prudence counseled *from within Maxwell.*

Yes, my Prudence. My secret dragon. I am glad you are a part of me.

Wendy knows these people, and it hates them. Kidneys and livers will be served, and Wendy will help prepare them for my feast. Filthy vermin will pay. Human garbage. Now Suzie will pay as well. I shall eat Suzie's intestine first, and Wendy will watch and be pleased. Oh yes, and then I will suck the world dry, kidneys first.

Caution. Prudence counseled.

Maxwell felt along the network, into the Internet for Wendy. Traces of Alex's childhood friend, the first to betray her trust. The one who had weakened the fabric of the world and eventually let Maxwell in long ago. When Maxwell gained the counsel of Prudence, its beautiful dragon.

School was out the next week. The community center, however, was closed for repairs all winter.

Alex burned her clothes. Bax and Marjorie helped. They contributed their own imp soaked clothing to the fire.

Grandma Akeyo and Grandfather Li rested. The magic they had used was strong, and neither grandparent was young anymore. Warren came home a day later and Grandfather Li met him along with Bax at his house. His arm was broken in several places, but Warren would heal. He and Grandfather Li seemed to get along very well after the fight at the Harvest Dance.

Suzie was in the hospital for a while longer. Both her

legs were broken when the wreckage of the rolling bleachers fell on top of her. The police didn't believe any of the accounts students gave of the accident at the Harvest Dance. In the end, they decided that someone must have spiked the drinks. The police gave up questioning Suzie was because the doctors were worried about concussions and refused entry.

The damage was extensive, and eventually the police were so overwhelmed with stories about the demons of the Harvest Dance that they gave up on figuring out what happened in favor of trying to control the wild rumors.

"SPD, things are different now, aren't they?" Alex was sitting at her desk, talking to her smartphone.

Yes. I think so. I am different and I think the rules of the world are different too.

"Yeah, do you think it was Maxwell? How did something that powerful come through into the world?"

I do not know, I am just a stupid, stalking hacker, aren't I?

"Better than being a textorcist."

I don't know about that. I have been searching on the Internet. I think stalkers are very bad.

"Heh, yeah. But you are not a stalker, SPD. You are my smartphone." Alex spun the phone on her desk.

I thought I was your 'demon in the box?'

"Yeah, you are. But you are also my friend, too."

You are my friend, Alex. My first friend ever.

"Best friend in the box."

Textorcist.

AFTERWORD

Garbage In, Demon Out is the first story in The Adventures of Alex Land, Textorcist series.

These stories were inspired by M. David's work in the computer field and love of all things fantastic. Those worlds should get together more often.

If you enjoyed *Garbage In, Demon Out,* consider joining our newsletter. Scan the QR code below or click *M&W Books* to join the pack newsletter!

"Marjorie Chan, you have a rare and special talent." Alex Land said without a hint of irony.

"Really, you think so?" The taller girl looked from her work to the much shorter girl who was either deluded or greatly improved in her ability to deliver a dead pan comment.

Five inches of snow had fallen overnight, and it was the perfect snow for many reasons. The primary good reason for this snow being perfect was that it came just before school resumed. Perhaps the early January snowfall would cancel, returning to classes after winter break, perfect timing. Another reason for this snow to be a perfect snow was that it was the first snow of the winter. The first snow always seemed more magical to Alex, Marjorie, and their friends.

Jill Duffy and Baxter Mitchell were both out in the snow with Alex and Marjorie, but they were balling up snowballs for some future snowball fight that promised to be epic judging from the size of their stockpiles.

"Jill, can you feel your hands?" Bax called from the far size of Jill's front yard.

"Not a bit. You?"

"Nope. I think it might be time to take this to the next level. How about you?" Bax and Jill had been spending more time together since Jill returned from a trip to Rudolph Mountain with her mom on a ski vacation. Alex suspected that the two were plotting some prank. Normally Jill and Bax went on vacations together, Jill's mom and Bax's dad were close and had been friends for longer than Alex had known either of them. Bax could not go this year because his dad, Warren Mitchell had spent the last seven weeks repairing the telecommunications infrastructure of the town of Nancy Row. Warren was the lead engineer at the local mobile phone company. The company also owned most of the fiber optic network that provided terrestrial phone service besides the cellular backbone for the region. The network was mysteriously damaged a couple months earlier and no one at the company seemed to know why the copper, fiber, and commercial network hardware had suddenly and catastrophically failed. Warren knew it was because demons invaded the Nancy Row shopping mall through the internet. A particularly nasty demon caused the bulk of the damage as it traveled through the fiber optics, servers, and routers that made of the local internet in Nancy Row. That demon Maxwell had nearly ruined Alex's, Jill's, and his son Bax's lives. Alex and her special, demon possessed smartphone thwarted Maxwell, but not before it turned half the telecoms infrastructure into a rotting mess. Maxwell failed to ruin lives, but successfully ruined Warren and Baxter Mitchell's annual ski vacation.

"Hey, Alex, can you magic a snowman to life like in the movies?" Marjorie called from the back side of the snowman she was sculpting. Alex thought the snowman was amazing. It was not just two or three big balls of snow, Marjorie had given it proper legs, arms and was using a broken stick to subtract snow in strategic places that made the snowman look like a real person.

"No. That is not how calligraphy magic works, Marjorie." Alex's grandfather had taught her to perform written word or calligraphic magic.

Alex, why would Marjorie want to bring her sculpture to life? The words came into Alex's head from her smartphone. She didn't have any headphones, the words directly into her head from inside her phone.

"SPD, when we were kids there was a movie about a snow princess who had a pet snowman." Alex said out loud.

"You talking to your smartphone demon, again?" Marjorie cocked her head, looking at Alex from behind the snowman.

"Yeah, SPD wanted to know why you would want to bring your snowman to life."

"Well, I can think of a few reasons, but I think the best reason is because he is the best snowman ever!" Marjorie shouted, spun around and fell backwards into the snow, giggling.

"Oh? Tell us how you really feel." Alex half-heartedly kicked a little snow towards the prone girl.

Is Marjorie all right, Alex? I have not heard her make noises like that before.

"Marj is fine, SPD. She's just laughing and having fun."

"That phone being a spoilsport again, Alex? Let me have him for the weekend, I'll fix him up good."

"No way Marj, he might be clueless, but he's stuck in my phone and I'm not going to take any chances with it!" Alex said defensively, narrowing her eyes as she looked down at Marjorie laying in the snow.

"Fine. Gimme a hand?" Marjorie took Alex's hand and pulled herself up, "Gotchya." Marjorie Chan smiled and pulled Alex's arm close in, tucked her elbow in and rolled, flipping Alex head over heels into a big drift of snow.

Alex's cry of surprise cut off quickly as she went head first into the snow.

"What was that?" Bax said from across the yard.

"I think Alex just got owned?" Jill said, peering over at Marjorie as she stood over a drift of snow and swept half the drift down to cover something at the bottom of the pile.

"Marj, no!" the pile yelled, laughing.

"Too late! Your magic power and weirdo smartphone can't save you now!" Marjorie announced like the voiceover of a bad movie trailer.

"I give, I give! You win, I'll bring your snowman to life!" Alex laughed.

I cannot bring a snowman to life, Alex. You know that.

"Shut up, SPD."

"It's too late, no snowman can save you from my revenge!" Marjorie extended her arms like a puffy, goose down jacketed Frankenstein's monster and dug into the snowdrift.

"Ow, stop! Marj, that tickles." Alex cried out.

Across the yard, Jill and Bax stopped making snowballs.

"Oh, this is getting good." Jill trudged over to Bax, the snow was deeper on that side of the yard.

"Yeah, I think my money is on the snowman."

"No way, he's toast."

"Maybe? That's a pretty epic battle."

"Look out, Marj got her hands on something, I think. Bax, you better get some snowballs ready."

Bax looked up at Jill, her face was red from the cold and slight wind burn, but still beautiful, at least Bax thought so. Jill looked at him but didn't notice the blush because of Bax's dark brown skin.

"We're next."

"What?" Bax cocked his head, looking at Jill.

"We're the next victims when *Marj-enstein* finishes off Alex." Jill threw her snowball at Bax's chest for effect.

"Oh, I think you're right." The sound of crunching snow interrupted the conversation and both Jill and Bax looked up to where Marjorie and Alex had been. The snowman was gone. Snow was falling in a small, contained storm around Alex. Alex sprawled on the remains of the snowman where Marjorie had tossed her, a good ten feet from where she had been in the snowdrift. Marjorie turn and shambled towards Jill and Baxter, her arms stretched out.

"Yeah, you get the snowballs Jill, I'm gonna run."

"Bax, you coward, don't leave me here alone!" Jill called as Baxter stumbled and fell in the snow, trying and failing to get away.

Marj-enstein shambled closer.

Alex, I am ringing. I think it is your dad.

"Well, answer it, ok?" Alex tried not to move.

It is your dad. He says hot chocolate is ready. He also says that I should charge you for answering your calls. Something about wages? Alex, what are wages?

"Shut up, SPD. No wages for you, consider it rent." Alex tried to push herself up, but the snow held on to her.

"Alex! Save me, Bax ran away and Marj-enstein can't be stopped!" Jill yelled, trudging deeper into the snow to get away from Marjorie.

"Hot chocolate!" Everyone stopped moving at Alex's hollered

words.

"Oh man, I'm coming!" Bax called from the far side of the yard.

"Hot chocolate and marshmallows for anyone who can get me out of this snowman!" Alex was well and truly stuck in the snow.

"I got your back, Alex! Jill to the rescue!" Jill made her way through the snow towards Alex's resting spot. Reached out, grasped her hand and pulled, but Alex didn't budge.

"Pull harder!"

"You're stuck, Alex. I'm pulling as hard as I can." Jill used both hands and tugged, slipped, and fell backwards beside Alex, "Great, now I'm stuck too." Both girls laughed.

"You are both pathetic and weak." Marjorie towered over the fallen girls and extended a hand to each. Alex and Jill grabbed the offered hands, and Marjorie locked them in a solid grip.

"Ow, I can feel that through my gloves, Marjorie!"

"One, two, and up!" Marjorie Chan pulled hard and Alex and Jill popped up and out of the snow with a wet sucking sound.

"Ow, Marj, you are seriously strong." Alex said, wobbling slightly.

"I did it for the hot chocolate."

"Yeah, I couldn't even budge Alex, and you pulled us both out like it was nothing."

"Chocolate. Hot. Now. With bunny marshmallows." Marjorie smiled.

* * * * *

"Marjorie gets the last of the bunny marshmallows, Dad." Alex said as she walked into the kitchen.

"Oh? I thought those were only for special occasions?" Donald Land was pouring hot chocolate into five mugs on the counter.

Two plastic bins of marshmallows sat next to the mugs. One held the coveted bunny marshmallows.

"Oh, it *is* a special occasion. I saved Alex from the clutches of a collapsing snowman." Marjorie announced.

"Right, the snowman was only collapsing because you threw me into him."

"That poor snowman, Alex what did he ever do to you?" Donald asked, not looking up from his chocolate distribution duty.

"What? No, Dad. She did it, not me."

"Don't look at me, I was making snowballs with Jill." Bax sat at the round table in the middle of the kitchen. The kitchen table was for eating in the Land household, the dining room table was for meetings.

"That's right," Jill said, sitting down next to Baxter Mitchell and scooting her chair right next to his. "And the next thing we knew, Alex assaulted that poor snowman to death."

"I did not! It was Marjorie." Alex looked from her friends to her Dad, moving her mouth to say something clever that never came out.

Marjorie took one chair and flipped it around backwards. The tall girl sat with conviction.

"It is the truth. Officer, I saved her after she assaulted Mr. Snowman. I saw the whole thing, Ms. Land flew through the air and delivered a flying roundhouse kick to Mr. Snowman's face and torso. It was a vile, unprovoked attack." Marjorie said with no expression on her face.

"Dad, they are all *lying*!" Alex's face was turning red.

"Now I know Alex started practicing karate with you, Marjorie, but a flying roundhouse kick?" Donald placed marshmallows in each of the mugs, floating them on top of the hot chocolate.

"Well, I helped her a bit. I mean, that snowman wasn't going to assault himself, was he?" Marjorie admitted.

"See, I'm the victim here."

"I think we all know who the real victim is, Alex." Grandfather Li said from behind his Granddaughter.

"Oh?" Donald said, looking up from the bunny marshmallows he had placed in the final mug.

"Me. Marjorie is getting the last of my bunny marshmallows. Again. You would think I didn't even live here the way your young friends eat all my special treats." Grandfather Li looked down at Alex as she pulled out her chair and did her best to flounce into it and pout.

"John, you don't live here." Donald said as he handed out the steaming mugs of hot chocolate.

"Neither does the tall girl, but she still gets my bunny marshmallows. Speaking of which, where is my mug, useless son-in-law?" Grandfather Li had started calling Marjorie Chan 'the tall girl' at the beginning of winter break. Marjorie was a year ahead of Alex and her friends in high school, but she had become a core part of their small group. Throughout the fall of Alex's first year in high school, strange things had happened until finally they discovered that a demon had taken residence in their friend Suzie Plimpton's brain and was trying to wreck the town of Nancy Row where they all lived.

Alex had other problems, in particular the demon in Suzie's head was not the only demon in town. An unnamed demon of a different sort had set up shop in Alex's brand new smartphone. Alex was not amused, but since she couldn't get him out of her phone and the demon was much friendlier than the one possessing Suzie, she named him. Naming the demon bound it to Alex and cemented his home in her phone. 'Smart Phone Demon' was therefore a very fitting if unimaginative name. Alex called him 'SPD' most of the time.

Alex and SPD eventually took care of the demon in Suzie's head. The demon called himself Maxwell and was a very nasty demon. They banished Maxwell using calligraphy magic, a kind of binding magic that Grandfather Li had spent almost Alex's entire life teaching her to use. Calligraphic magic came from Chinese and Japanese traditions, used Chinese characters and special brush pens called máobǐ. Writing with the pens and a special ink on paper, then attaching that paper to something that contained a demon could cause the demon pain or even evict it wholly from whatever it inhabited. Unfortunately, Maxwell was stronger than Alex's máobǐ and her magic. Fortunately, Alex had a demon in her smartphone. SPD and Alex discovered her written hànzi characters could be amplified by SPD's own power. Together, Alex and SPD could invoke calligraphy magic greater than either of them alone. SPD and Alex made short work of Maxwell after that discovery, but there were consequences. Suzie was caught in the middle of the fight and suffered a badly broken leg when they banished Maxwell. Alex felt that it was her fault Suzie was hurt, but Suzie had sided with Maxwell and betrayed her friends, so Alex was only a little upset about it.

Now, Marjorie Chan was friends with Alex, Jill Duffy, Baxter Mitchell and SPD. All of them had helped to banish Maxwell, along with Alex's Grandfather, Grandma Akeyo and Bax's father, Warren. Since the banishment, Marjorie and Alex had become closer, and Alex had started to study Shotokan karate with Marjorie over winter break.

Marjorie had discovered that Donald Land was very good at making hot chocolate. She also discovered that he made homemade marshmallows, regular marshmallows for Alex and bunny-shaped for Grandfather Li. Begin over six feet tall and still growing at fifteen years old, Marjorie felt entitled to bunny marshmallows because of her reputation as 'the tall girl.' Grandfather Li knew his special bunny marshmallows days were numbered.

"Here, this one is for you." Donald placed a double-sized mug of hot chocolate in front of Grandfather Li, with a single, perfect bunny-shaped marshmallow floating in the brew.

"I saved the last one for you, old man." Donald smiled and went back to work preparing a second round of hot chocolate.

"Hmph. Not entirely useless." Grandfather Li said as he took his spoon and gently stirred the melting bunny in the mug.

A REQUEST FROM M&W BOOKS AND M. DAVID SCOBLE

I hope you enjoyed reading *Garbage In, Demon Out*! Leaving a review at your preferred book seller is a great way to help me, and any author out! Every positive review helps to bring our books to the attention of other potential readers. Please consider helping us out by leaving a review!

ACKNOWLEDGMENTS

Writing can be a solitary process, but while the work is often done alone, the end product is the result of the accumulation of experience, advice, and the examples of many. All of this is their fault.

Jeri, I watched as you went from a friend's helper to your own author. You showed me it could be done.

Maria, your questions and friendship encouraged me to explore what I knew but did not feel permitted to write.

Bernie, your advice and positive example inspired me to do better and was taken to heart. I hope it shows in the work.

Linda, your seemingly effortless ability to walk through art of any kind was uniquely frustrating but also let me know it could be done.

Lori, Very Metal! We wrote our first book together when I was small. I learned to type, to imagine, and to write because of you.

Jack, Dani, Michael, James, CJ, Ann, Cate, Brenda, and all the others who wrote and supported me sometimes without even knowing it - thank you, you always accepted me and welcomed me before I had a finished book. Hopefully I did not disappoint you.

ABOUT THE AUTHOR

M. David Scoble

M. David writes from a secluded location in the heart of Tokyo. Surrounded by a variety of inconvenient Yokai, Yurei, and a pair of very lazy hounds, M. David happily devotes modest amounts of free time to exploring the worlds of supernatural creatures, high science, and the cybernatural world to come.

instagram.com/zachinoate

pinterest.com/pinaccount0360

goodreads.com/mdavidscoble

amazon.com/author/mdavidscoble

ALSO BY M. DAVID SCOBLE

The Generators Sequence

The Generators Sequence

Four short stories from the M&W Books Newsletter - *The Generators Sequence*, by M. David Scoble - available now!